PASSIONATE PATIENT

Taking care of a stubborn man required a great deal of energy, Wynn thought. She decided to grab a nap while she could, but the moment she closed her eyes, strong arms encircled her waist and pulled her against a hard, masculine chest.

"How soft you are," her patient murmured.

"Let go of me!"

"Never." His lips nuzzled her neck while his fingers loosened the ribbon in her hair.

"I'll scream," she threatened, twisting in an effort to loosen his hold.

"And who will hear?"

Warmth seeped into her, and she ceased fighting him. His fingers raked through her hair, combing the long locks in sensual strokes while his lips bade hers to kiss him back. Never had any man kissed her so gently, so skillfully . . . so tenderly. Never had she felt so beguiled, so bewitched.

She shuddered slightly as his mustache brushed the tip of her nose; then his lips reclaimed hers. She was lost in his kisses . . . now and forever.

DANA RANSOM'S RED-HOT HEARTFIRES!

ALEXANDRA'S ECSTASY (2773, $3.75)

Alexandra had known Tucker for all her seventeen years, but all at once she realized her childhood friend was the man capable of tempting her to leave innocence behind!

LIAR'S PROMISE (2881, $4.25)

Kathryn Mallory's sincere questions about her father's ship to the disreputable Captain Brady Rogan were met with mocking indifference. Then he noticed her trim waist, angelic face and Kathryn won the wrong kind of attention!

LOVE'S GLORIOUS GAMBLE (2497, $3.75)

Nothing could match the true thrill that coursed through Gloria Daniels when she first spotted the gambler, Sterling Caulder. Experiencing his embrace, feeling his lips against hers would be a risk, but she was willing to chance it all!

WILD, SAVAGE LOVE (3055, $4.25)

Evangeline, set free from Indians, discovered liberty had its price to pay when her uncle sold her into marriage to Royce Tanner. Dreaming of her return to the people she loved, she vowed never to submit to her husband's caress.

WILD WYOMING LOVE (3427, $4.25)

Lucille Blessing had no time for the new marshal Sam Zachary. His mocking and arrogant manner grated her nerves, yet she longed to ease the tension she knew he held inside. She knew that if he wanted her, she could never say no!

ELIZABETH LEIGH
LOUISIANA PASSION

ZEBRA BOOKS
KENSINGTON PUBLISHING CORP.

Thanks, Mother, for believing in me.
This one's for you.

ZEBRA BOOKS

are published by

Kensington Publishing Corp.
475 Park Avenue South
New York, NY 10016

First printing: September, 1992

Printed in the United States of America

ACKNOWLEDGMENTS

Many thanks to those listed below. Without their help, this book could not have been written.

Dr. John H. Sabatier—internist and lifelong resident of Jennings, Louisiana, who suggested I set a historical novel there

Dr. Deborah Myers—pediatrician and the inspiration for Wynn Spencer

Dr. Greg Brian—general practice

Julia Williams—R.N. and "sounding board"

Norma Franklin—Civil War reenactment nurse who shared not only her personal knowledge but an 1880 medical textbook as well

Ethel Hammon and Annette Womack—general technical assistance

Suzannah Davis and Darlene Taylor—who lent me invaluable research materials

Prologue

The tiny log cabin creaked and groaned under the wind's fierce assault. Its roof sagged from the weight of snow; deep banks buttressed its walls. Moonlight glistened on the expanse of white, illuminating the fields and woods so powerfully it could have been daylight.

Leaning out of the cabin's single window, a boy, only half-grown, hand-shoveled snow into an oaken bucket. When it was full, he dropped the deerskin over the paneless window, secured it at the bottom, and shuffled to the fireplace. He dumped the snow into an iron pot hanging over the fire, then turned to the bed, which had been placed as close to the fireplace as was reasonably safe.

Upon the tick, a woman thrashed about, her pitiful moans echoing in the small space. Her mouth moved but he could not hear her whispered plea over the wail of the wind. He sat upon the bed, sliding his cold hands beneath the warm covers. He found her hand and squeezed it, then leaned his ear close to her face.

"Help," she said. "Go . . . doctor."

"I'm not leaving you here by yourself, Mama! The

7

doctor's coming. He promised me he would come."

He raised his head and turned away; he could not bring himself to look upon her pain-distorted features, nor did he want her to see the gall of defeat on his own face. His gaze ricocheted around the single-pen cabin he and his mother had found abandoned after the accident last summer. At the sight of pristine white flakes drifting through the cracks in the chinking, at the frustration of being unable to hold them back, hot anger roiled inside him, burning a hole in his heart.

Snow shouldn't be white, he thought. *It ought to be black, like the evil thing it is.*

It was so cold. In all of the eight winters he had known, he couldn't remember when it had been so cold. Little piles of snow were beginning to accumulate on the hard-packed earth floor and on the rafters overhead where the wind drove it under the wood shingles.

He watched a flake fall onto his mother's distended belly. Then another and another. He swiped at them, realized the futility, quickly turned away from the makeshift bed and poked at the fire, using the action to conceal the stinging tears coursing down his frosty cheeks. He was all she had left. He had to be strong for her.

And he had to help her. God! He had to help her.

He dumped the meager contents of an old split-oak basket onto the fire: lichened twigs and pieces of half-rotten limbs he had collected earlier, wet from the snow that had clung to them. Acrid smoke billowed from the hissing, crackling heap, choking him, and for a moment he feared he had smothered the fire. Back went the stick he had used as a poker, back into the orange coals, jabbing and stirring until the pathetic flames licked the dampness dry. As he watched the fire consume the last of the fuel, his tears flowed freely, un-

8

checked. Let his mother think the smoke had put them thore. Or let her think the truth. It didn't matter. He couldn't hold them back any longer.

Disgusted, he threw the weathered gray basket onto the flames. It had served its purpose. There were no more twigs to collect. Whatever fodder Nature had once provided she had long since buried in the white fury of snow she had been dumping since daybreak.

That was when he had gone for the doctor. At daybreak, just as the snow started to fall. It was a two-mile trek into town, one way, a trek fraught with hills and gullies and fallen trees and briar patches. Always before, he had delighted in the wildness of the landscape, using it as a fitting backdrop for his playtime adventures as a pirate or explorer. But today the terrain became his enemy, impeding his haste into town, threatening to ensnare him and hold him captive on his way home. The snow, falling fast by then, embraced the brambles in a ghostly white shroud and obscured the landmarks.

The doctor's words echoed in his head. "Just go on back home, son. I have another patient to care for now, another baby to deliver. I'll be out later on."

Where are you? cried the child still trapped inside the boy. *Not coming,* the budding man in him replied. *Not all the way out here. Not in the dark. Not in a snowstorm. He never intended to come. He sent you home to be rid of you.*

The wind charged around the eaves, wailing and moaning through the trees, buffeting an ice-laden branch against a log wall. The boy jumped at the sound, then realized it was the shriek coming from the bed which had startled him.

"I'm here, Mama," he said, taking her hand again and patting it with more assurance than he felt.

9

"Mickey," she whispered, her chest heaving beneath the threadbare quilts and blankets he had piled on top of her. The boy watched the pink tip of her tongue slide out and attempt to soften her cracked lips. "The angel. Give me the angel."

He turned back to the fireplace and removed a tiny porcelain cherub from the mantelpiece. He placed it in his mother's hand.

"I love you, son."

"And I love you, Mama."

"Take care of my baby, Mickey."

She moved his hand to rest upon her protruding stomach. The boy flinched at the force of the movement through the nest of cover. It was the baby, he knew, trying to get out. She had explained that much to him when he had grown concerned about the changes in her body. What she hadn't told him was how the baby had ever gotten in there or how it was supposed to get out. The thought of having to cut his mother open gagged him.

She uttered a low, blood-curdling scream, pressing her son's hand hard against her stomach. Hard ridges rippled beneath his palm, and then, suddenly, he felt the ridges move downward, ever downward, until her stomach felt soft again, like he remembered it before his father died—before the baby had started to grow there. He used to lay his head upon her stomach when he felt bad and she would stroke his hair, and the pillow of her stomach felt so soft and warm and comforting. Like it did now.

The branch scraped lightly against the logs again, then stilled. The wind whispered and sighed, as though it had spent all its energy and must rest for a while.

As his mother must rest.

She looked so peaceful, lying there with her eyes

closed, her features clear of the pain she had suffered for more than a day.

Her hand had gone limp. The boy withdrew his hand from hers and eased under the covers beside his mother. Together they would sleep, and tomorrow the doctor would come and everything would be all right again.

But there was something wrong under the covers. The tick was wet — wet and sticky. The boy eased out of the bed, then gaped in horror at the long red streak on his pant leg. He didn't want to look, but he had to know what was wrong, why his mother was bleeding. Slowly, fearfully, he folded the covers back, then stared dumbly at the mass of flesh and blood between his mother's legs.

He didn't know how long he stood there, staring, before his knees gave way and he crumpled to the cold floor. His stomach heaved with sickening realization. After a while, after he had emptied his stomach upon the hard-packed earth, he eased the covers back over the inert bodies of his mother and his sister, removing the top blanket and taking it with him to the fire.

He curled up on the floor, his lean boy's body wrapped in the thin blanket, his limbs shaking uncontrollably as he sought the same peace his mother had found.

Chapter One

November 18, 1883

Wynn Spencer rested her neck on the low back of the hard wooden seat, let her weary head roll toward the window, and set her gaze on the clear, star-dusted sky. In the three days she had been on the train, she had grown mightily tired of the constant clickety-clack of the great iron wheels and the almost constant influx of ash through the window she left unshuttered. And now, with the last light of day well behind and the night growing colder by the minute, she had the damp chill to contend with as well.

She knew she could lower the shutter, and had done so from time to time in an effort to block out the spray of ashes and the cold air. But Wynn Spencer didn't like being cooped up—abhorred being cooped up, when she was honest enough with herself to admit her phobia. She had to be able to see out, and if that meant contending with cold air and ashes, then so be it.

Wynn drew some comfort from the fact that she no longer had to contend with a horde of disgruntled passengers who didn't understand her irrational fear. Thank goodness, most of them had departed in New

Orleans. The four remaining passengers besides herself had moved well away from her.

Wynn drew more comfort from the realization that the end of her journey was near. She closed her eyes and felt the rush of cool air caress her bare cheeks. The steady rhythm of the clickety-clack, clickety-clack began to soothe rather than irritate. For a while she dozed, until a shrill screech jerked her to alertness, sending her pulse racing.

She felt ridiculous when she realized it was just the train's whistle, signaling their approach to Jennings. She willed her body to relax, yet the dark shadow of trepidation that had followed her all the way from Illinois to the vast prairies of southwest Louisiana prickled her consciousness. Had she made the right decision, she wondered, or would she forever regret the sudden move? Only time would tell, and her sensible side refused to allow the matter further consideration.

She fixed her gaze upon the stars once more. Suddenly, she saw them as constants in an ever-changing world, holding their eons-old positions while the train moved ever westward. She tried to imagine what sort of mood God had been in when He created the stars, and decided He must have felt quite jovial at the time. Perhaps He had tired of precision by then, flinging the stars outward with a carefree hand to land as they would and grasp hold with a grip that must be tenuous at best.

What forces held them there—had held them for ages? Did they ever let go, as she had, and search for another, perhaps safer spot?

As if to prove her theory, a golden arc streaked across her line of vision. *A shooting star—looking for something to hold on to. Just like me. I hope you find your niche, shooting star. Maybe I'll find mine in Jennings.* She smiled and let her eyes fall shut once again.

"What the hell you doin' out here?"

"Sitting."

"I can see that!"

Doc Nolan stumbled into the porch railing, turned around so that he was facing his unusually pensive friend, and scratched his crotch.

"I'd appreciate it if you'd move. You're blocking my view." The words came quietly, without malice.

Doc didn't move. Instead, he squinted at the shadowed bulk of Michael Donovan and perceived even through the haze of his inebriation that the man was a fool if he thought the rear legs of the slender straight chair would continue to support his considerable weight. "I'd be careful if I was you, boy."

"Well, you're not me." The first hint of irritability crept into the deep voice, and a tiny frown pinched dark, shaggy eyebrows together over the bridge of a hawk's nose. "Why should I be careful?"

" 'Cause you're gonna bust that chair leaning back in it like that. It's just a teeny thing, and you're not."

"You're just jealous of my physique, old man."

"Jealous, am I?" Doc's voice rose to the level of a high-pitched whine. "Why, them's fightin' words."

"I don't feel like fighting with you tonight, Doc, but I'm gonna pick you up by your skinny rump and throw you out in the yard if you don't move."

Although Michael Donovan was perfectly capable of doing just that, Doc knew the man didn't mean one word of the softly spoken threat. But Doc respected his brawny companion in a way he had never respected another man before. He moved.

When he had repositioned himself against the porch railing at what he considered to be a safe distance, he watched his friend for a long moment. "What you lookin' at, Donovan? Ain't nothin' out there but a bunch of stars. That full moon got you touched in the head, boy?"

"I told you I don't feel like fighting with you tonight, but I'm gonna fight you for sure tomorrow if you call me *boy* one more time."

"I'll quit callin' you boy when you quit callin' me old man."

"That'll be the day," Michael grunted.

"You just gonna sit out here all night?"

"What if I do?"

"We ain't finished our poker game."

"You're losing again, so what difference does it make?"

"You gotta give me a chance to recoup my losses."

"There's tomorrow night, and the night after that, and the night after that, old man. What else we got to do in this one-horse town?"

From the safety of his shadowed corner, Doc pursed his lips as he considered Michael's bitter words. When he and Michael weren't fighting, they were playing cards. That was enough for Doc, who considered himself long past his prime. What the years hadn't done to ruin him, liquor had. But that wasn't enough—couldn't be enough for Michael Donovan; hell, he was still a boy! If any man ever needed a good lay, he expected Michael did. Doc tried to remember how long it had been since Michael had bedded a woman; it must have been the last time they went to Lake Charles. Why, that was nearly three months gone!

Since he figured he couldn't conjure up a woman, there wasn't anything to be done about it at the moment. In an effort to pacify his friend, Doc said, "They'll come, Michael. You just wait. You was right about this place. You'll see. They won't all be hitched, neither. Some of them's bound to be free."

16

Doc was sure Michael knew he referred to women, but the younger man refused to take the bait. Instead, he said, "I thought you went to school, old man."

"I did!" Doc bellowed.

"Well, I hope you didn't practice medicine with the same disregard for rules that you have for English grammar."

Doc's defunct medical practice was a sore subject; Michael knew it, and Doc knew he knew it. Doc came off the porch railing with the speed of a wounded boar and charged at Michael, holding a shaky fist in his friend's face. "I thought you didn't feel like fightin'."

Michael didn't flinch. "I don't."

Doc dropped his arm but he didn't loosen his fist. "You ain't no fun. I'm goin' to bed," he announced, sounding like a spoiled child even to himself. He waited for a minute to see what Michael had to say about that, but all the boy did was sit and stare at the night sky. After a while, Doc gave up and shuffled inside.

It had been a long time since Michael Donovan had allowed himself to think, really think, about his life. For years he had wandered from one place to another, searching, ever searching for that one spot on Earth that would speak to him, that would say, "This is it, boy. Drop your duds and put down some roots."

Michael thought back more than three years to the time he and Doc had caught the stagecoach out of Morgan City and headed to parts west. What parts they hadn't cared, so long as there was an ample supply of booze and women. But when they stopped for fresh horses at the way station between Opelousas and Lake Charles, Michael Donovan heard that call he had pined to hear. For reasons he couldn't voice, couldn't even understand, the head-high grasses covering the vast prairie beyond the clump of oaks around the station had called to him.

"Who owns this land?" he had asked of no one in particular, but the stationmaster supplied an answer.

"The gov'mint. Southern Pacific's puttin' a line through here. They say the gov'mint's givin' this land away for the askin', narry 'bouts, leastaways. Only costs 'bout twenty dollars to take out a claim."

Michael had heard similar talk in the barrooms and along the docks in Morgan City, but he had considered the sources and passed it off as wishful thinking. This man, though, seemed to know what he was talking about. "You say the Southern Pacific's gonna run through here?"

"You just came over the roadbed, sonny. Why, the SP's already named this place. Called it Jennings, after that pioneer survey engineer, Jennings McComb. The Illinois Central done give his last name to a town in Miss'ssippi. Don't rightly know what to think 'bout a man gettin' two towns named after him. Seems a might much to me."

Michael dismissed the man's ramblings and cut right to the core. "How would a person go about getting some of this land from the government?"

"Land office in Lake Charles'll take care of all the paperwork for you. You're headin' right through there."

Convincing Doc Nolan to settle down had proved far more difficult than securing one hundred and sixty acres of land from the government, but Doc wasn't about to leave Michael behind, even if he did bellow enough about it to make Michael want to hit him. Michael Donovan took out the first homestead patent in that area, selecting the choicest plot. Only a fool would have let what was to become the center of a

18

town go to someone else.

Excited about something for the first time in years, Michael garnered what he thought would be enough capital the best way he knew how — gambling — and headed back to the one clump of trees in existence on the prairie — trees that now belonged to him — to wait for his order of lumber to arrive. He hired the station-master, a jack-of-all-trades, to help him and Doc build a little general store and a hotel beside it near the station.

Almost immediately, Michael was in business. The SP made good its promise and started laying the tracks westward from Morgan City. The railroad men were more than happy to put up at his hotel and purchase tobacco and whiskey from his store. When the line was finished, they said, people would move in there. Hadn't the SP hired a land agent to recruit homestead-ers? Sure as they were going to sling their hammers the next day, Jennings was going to grow. Michael had wondered if maybe he shouldn't build a bigger hotel, but first he had to have a place to live. With the rail-road men staying at his six-room hotel all the time, he and Doc were having to share a room, and that ar-rangement had to come to a halt.

They built a house some distance from the station. It was a small house with only three rooms — Doc would have settled for two, but Michael said he had lis-tened to him snore long enough — and a porch across the front. Michael insisted that the house face south so that when he sat on the porch, he wouldn't be re-minded of what he had willingly left behind from the north and the east nor what he might have missed out on ahead had he continued west. To the south lay marshlands and the Gulf of Mexico, neither of which appealed to Michael Donovan.

The trouble was he didn't spend much time on the

19

porch. Maybe that was why he had gone out there that night — because he needed to rekindle the excitement he had felt three long years ago when he had first come to Jennings. Hell, he didn't know why. But he knew he needed to sit there for a spell yet, even if the false warmth of the whiskey he had consumed earlier was wearing off and the cold dampness was beginning to seep into his bones.

The night was quiet — too quiet. Somewhere, probably from one of the trees around the station, an owl hooted. And then, from way off in the distance, he heard the haunting wail of the train whistle. Michael pulled his watch out of his pocket and squinted at it in the dark, but he had to strike a match to see its face clearly. Ten-thirty. The SP was later than usual. Despite Doc's assurances of settlers coming in, Michael hoped the train didn't have any more passengers getting off at Jennings. He wasn't at all sure he liked having his domain invaded any more than it already had been.

But wasn't that what he wanted? For the town to grow and make him filthy rich? Wasn't money power and power what life was all about?

Hell, he didn't know what he wanted anymore.

Against the velvety darkness that seemed to close in around him, a shooting star blazed a golden trail. For a brief moment, the burning path glistened brightly, then faded to eternal obscurity as abruptly as it had appeared.

"Just like me," Michael whispered to the night. "Full of enthusiasm and hope one minute, burned out the next."

Fate allowed him only that one moment to wallow in self-deprecating reflection. A loud pop rent the stillness and the fragile chair collapsed beneath him.

Wynn's foot struck heavily upon the wooden landing as she completed her descent from the train. She carried her principal luggage—a bulging, almost threadbare carpetbag which held her medical kit and a few basic garments. Shifting the carpetbag to her left hand, she accepted the conductor's proffered hand with her right and stepped away from the portable riser.

The engine belched and hissed, sending a shower of sparks out of its smokestack to rain down upon her. She winced in dismay, certain the sparks had burned tiny pinholes into her only winter wrap, a long, unadorned mantle cut from gray wool. Determined not to let anxiety get the best of her, she focused her attention on what lay ahead. At the moment, that was the depot, which blocked her view of the town proper.

"Need some help, young lady?" The conductor's voice was polite, but, to Wynn's ears, in a cold, uncaring sort of way.

"Could you please direct me to the hotel?" She didn't know much about the town, but according to the newspaper advertisement, it was supposed to have a large, comfortable hotel.

"Just walk around the station house, ma'am. You can't miss it." The conductor raised an arm and flicked his wrist at an indeterminate spot. "Tomorrow you can collect your other baggage here at the depot. Good luck."

The way he said "good luck" bothered Wynn. It was almost as though he mentally added, "You're going to need it." She started to ask him if that was what he meant and why, but he had already turned to the task of lifting the portable step and stowing it away, summarily dismissing her. It was probably just her own disquiet she'd heard.

Wynn lifted her chin in defiance of her own misgivings and tightened her hold on the carpetbag. This was going to work. She was going to make it work. There could be no turning back. She was a shooting star, and this town was her something to hold on to.

Her immediate priority was to get out of the damp chill and into bed. She skirted the depot, wending her way through a stand of oak trees before coming out onto open ground. Moonlight softly illuminated the scene before her. Shocked at what she saw, Wynn let her mouth drop open and stood staring for a moment.

She had conjured her own mental image of the town of Jennings, Louisiana, based on the information in the advertisement—an image that included stately homes with landscaped lawns nestled among giant oaks and a wide main thoroughfare lined with false-fronted stores. Nothing she saw even came close.

Before her lay an open, bare lot, devoid of either grass or shrub. On the far side of the area, two nondescript board-and-batten buildings rose from the dirt, one square and squatty with dark windows and a collection of metal-banded barrels cluttering up its shallow porch, the other a mere two stories and not much larger than her family home in Galena. Neither building boasted sign nor shingle.

Wynn closed her eyes for a moment and tried to call up her fanciful mental image of Jennings, of the town it would surely become. It didn't work. Instead she saw Galena. Galena with its tall church spires and elegant homes. Galena with its gingerbread-trimmed lead-miners' cottages and its steamboat docks. Her Galena made a fairy-tale picture, laid out on the stairstep-like bluffs rising on both sides of the Galena River, just a few miles from its junction with the Mississippi. No noisy trains ran through Galena, for the town council had refused to appropriate land for an Illinois Central Railroad depot.

Her father had been wrong. Nowhere on Earth could there ever be a town as beautiful or as peaceful—certainly not here, where the land was so flat and uninteresting. Not here, where there were no hills, no river, and no trees except those around the depot to break the terrain.

Yet, Wynn Spencer had no desire to go back to the lovely town where she'd grown up. She had made her break, a clean one, and whether she liked it or not, Jennings was where she would have to make her peace.

She lifted her chin again and moved stalwartly toward the two-story building.

"Hit me again!" Doc Nolan bellowed.

"I'd love to hit you, old man," Michael retorted. "Maybe that would knock some peace and quiet into you. I thought you were going to bed."

"I was—till you broke that chair. I told you not to lean back in it." Doc cackled. "Damn, but that was funny!"

"Have you always been so loud?"

"Loud? I'm not loud. You're just too quiet for your own good."

"You ought to listen to yourself sometime. When you're awake, you're screaming at the top of your lungs. And when you're asleep, you're snoring loud enough to wake the dead."

"Aha! So it's my snorin's got you so riled up. Build me a little cabin of my own and you won't have to listen to it anymore."

"That wouldn't do any good and you know it, Doc. You'd just come over here to play poker and drink your whiskey and you'd end up passed out like you always do and then I'd have to put you up for the night anyway." Michael took a deep breath.

"You winded, boy? Hell, that was about the longest speech I ever heard you make."

"If I'd stopped to breathe, you'd have interrupted me, old man."

"You callin' me rude? I don't interrupt!"

"The hell you don't!"

"You sure are in a bad mood, boy, but I know what's wrong with you."

Dark, full eyebrows shot to mid-forehead, revealing wide-open, sparkling green eyes that held more than a hint of mischief. "You do?" Michael asked curiously.

" 'Course, I do. You just need a woman. Something awful! I don't know when I've ever seen a man need a woman so much. You ought to get out of this one-horse town ever' once in a while and take care of that problem, boy. Then you wouldn't be so cranky."

The mischief disappeared. "I'm not cranky."

Doc shrugged. "Have it your way. You gonna hit me again or what?"

Michael glanced across the table at Doc's cards, then made a show of looking at his own downside card again. "You're already at nineteen and I'm at eighteen. You've got me beat this time. Why do you want another one?"

" 'Cause with your luck, you'll pull a four. With your luck, that woman you need so bad will walk in the door any minute now. I've never known anyone with your kind of luck, boy."

Michael ignored Doc's comment about needing a woman. "If you want to beat me, old man, you're going to have to quit hitting that bottle. You're so drunk you can't even cipher right. It would take a three, Doc, not a four. With a four I would go bust," Michael patiently explained.

"Whatever. Just hit me again, boy."

"I told you to quit calling me that."

"And I told you I want another card."

Michael shrugged expansively, but the gesture was lost on Doc. He was watching Michael's long, lean fingers pull the top card from the deck. He had never caught Michael Donovan cheating, but he always watched carefully just in case.

It was the ace of spades.

"Now you have twenty. Are you happy?"

"I'd be happier if I had blackjack."

"Well, you don't. You want another card or you going to stand?"

Between their two hands were three of the four aces in the deck. Doc took the cautious way out and stood.

With obvious disinterest, Michael flipped the next card over. Doc watched again to make sure it didn't get pulled from the bottom of the deck.

"What'd I tell you?" he screamed. "Damn! I knew you'd pull a three! I just knew it!" Doc shot up out of his chair so fast his knees didn't have time to get out of the way. The table, a small, flimsy thing that had seen better days, hit Michael hard at mid-thigh. Cards flew everywhere and Doc's glass of whiskey slid down the tabletop and landed in Michael's lap.

Michael barely had time to right the table before Doc lit into him with both fists flying. Michael's arms were longer than Doc's by several inches. He quickly grasped Doc by the shoulders and held him at bay, but Doc continued to throw punches aimed at Michael's stomach. He just couldn't quite land them.

"Whatever's gotten into you, old man?" Donovan asked with much more patience than the situation warranted. "I know that wasn't rotgut you were drinking. That was good Tennessee sour mash. I brought the bottle home from the store myself."

25

" 'Tain't the whiskey. It's *you* and your damned luck!"

"Hold on, Doc. I don't recall twisting your arm. In fact, best I do recall, this game was your idea."

"It don't make no difference whose idea it was. You cheated!"

"You'd better watch it, old man, or I'm going to have to hit you."

Doc Nolan didn't believe a word of Michael's threat. The two played at fighting, but neither one ever struck the other. The possibility of a real fight between the heavily muscled "boy" and the scrawny "old man" was too ludicrous to consider. But this was one time the boy was asking for it, in Doc's estimation. He pretended to be getting tired. His punches lost their vigor and he began to wheeze. Just as he had expected, Michael loosened his hold on Doc's shoulders.

Doc struck with the swiftness of a tightly coiled spring that had lost its mooring.

When Michael felt the connection of Doc's heavy boot against his shin, he let out a yowl. "Now you've done it, old man!" Michael bellowed.

Doc knew he was in real trouble because Michael seldom raised his voice. Before he could protest, Michael had wrestled him to the floor and was holding his arms over his head. Doc kicked and screamed like a banshee while Michael hollered back at him to shut up.

Neither one of them heard the insistent knock above the din of their shouting match, but the impatient tone in a woman's husky voice did manage to claim their attention.

"Excuse me!"

Doc's feet stopped kicking thin air and Michael let go of Doc's wrists. In unison, they turned toward the front door. Their jaws dropped open and their eyes looked ready to pop out.

Michael was the first to recover. A crimson blush suffused his neck and face. Then, he scrambled to his feet, buttoned up his shirt, and smoothed back his hair. "My apologies, ma'am. We were just wrestling a bit. You see, we'd been playing cards and—wait! Why am I explaining? Don't you know how to knock?"

"Is that the way you greet everyone who comes here?"

"It's not that often anyone comes out here, ma'am, especially a woman, and certainly not in the middle of the night. Folks around here know better."

"Yeah," Doc said from the floor. He was too exhausted to get up right then, but his fatigue didn't keep him from thoroughly enjoying the situation. And he had thought he couldn't conjure up a woman for Michael! He had to test her, though, he decided. He had to see if she had enough spirit to match the boy's. He formed his thin lips into a leering grin. "Most folks know that's as good a way as any of gettin' themselves shot—or worse."

"Shut up, old man. You're liable to scare the little lady off."

The woman lifted her chin slightly and pinned her unflinching gaze on the two men. "Pardon my intrusion and my haste, but I don't have time for idle chatter. I'm looking for Mr. Michael Donovan. Would one of you two yokels please get him for me?"

Michael had been perfectly willing to listen to her until she called him a yokel. Who was this little scrap of a thing, anyway, Michael wondered, with her hat askew and her mousy brown hair falling out of its bun and her ugly gray wrap all covered with cinder burns? Who did she think she was, barging in on him and Doc that way and then calling them yokels? Someone needed to bring her down a peg or two—and he might

27

just be the someone to do it. Then, maybe he'd find out what she wanted . . . if he could just keep Doc Nolan quiet long enough!

It was too late.

"Who you callin' a yokel, young lady?" Doc raised a balled-up fist and shook it at her.

"Hush, old man. Let me handle this."

Doc shut his mouth, but before Michael could say anything more, the woman started snickering and pointed at his crotch.

"Can't you hold your water, sir?" she asked, the corners of her mouth twitching in obvious amusement.

Michael dropped his eyes to see what she thought was so funny. A dark scowl swathed his face when he spied the large, wet circle darkening his trousers. The trickles of whiskey that had run downward made it look even more telling. Calling him names was one thing, but this! She had really gone too far. Michael Donovan was slow to anger, but this woman had managed to push him to the brink of his patience. "Now, just hold on a minute—"

"If you do, I may be able to help you. I'm Wynnifred Spencer. Dr. Wynnifred Spencer." A gloved hand flew up to cover her mouth and she gasped from behind her hand. "Oh! I almost forgot why I came out here."

Michael's wrath had his ears ringing so loud, he didn't hear anything she said. His inattention gave Doc a chance to speak again.

"Why do you want to see Michael Donovan?"

"He owns the hotel, doesn't he? Something needs to be done about the lack of rooms, heat, and blankets. Sick people are lying on the floor in that drafty lobby. They need a warm, decent place to sleep."

Doc let his gaze sweep the cluttered, all-purpose room. The little table now stood aright, but Doc's chair was still turned over. Playing cards littered the floor, lying among tiny puddles of the Tennessee sour mash. The basin on the dry sink was piled high with dirty dishes, most of them chipped and cracked. Above the pot-bellied stove hung two pairs of faded red long-handles on a length of hemp rope that had been strung from the stovepipe to a nail on the wall. One pair was large and neatly patched; the other, smaller pair bore witness of neglect. The windows were bare of curtains and the only covering on the un-varnished pine floor was a tattered braided rug.

When Doc was certain the woman's eyes had fol-lowed the path of his own, he turned to Michael. "This look like a hotel to you, boy?"

Michael responded with a blank stare. "You know this isn't —" he began, then his green eyes began to twinkle and a mischievous grin pierced his cheeks with twin slashes. "No sirree Bob!" he exclaimed. "This sure doesn't look like any hotel I've ever seen."

"Someone needs to shake some sense into the two of you!" Wynn snapped, her pale eyes glaring and her gloved hands on her hips.

What a comical picture she made, standing in the middle of the room with her arms akimbo and her cheeks blazing the color of wild strawberries, Michael thought. When she talked, she gestured with her head. Its bob made the cluster of ostrich feathers on her little black hat sway back and forth.

"I don't know who you two buffoons are, since nei-ther of you bothered to introduce yourself, but I do know where I am. The clerk was very specific with his directions and there's no other house in town any-way — if you can call this isolated location part of town. Now, if you will please tell me where I might find Mr. Donovan, I'll leave you to your . . . cards." Her narrowed eyes surveyed the scattered deck briefly, then lifted to skewer both men with a defiant glare.

"You hear that, boy?" Doc sneered. "The poor lady's all tuckered out from the walk." His gaze took a quick trip down her figure and back up again. "I can't tell much about her from all those clothes she's wearing, but I'll bet there's nothing under there but skin and bones. What do you think?"

Michael dropped to the floor and clamped a hand over Doc's mouth. "I told you to hush, old man! That's no way to talk in front of a lady."

Snorting in disgust, Wynn marched over to Doc's bedroom door and threw it wide. When she had convinced herself the room was empty, she stomped across the common room and threw open the one remaining door. In a moment, she returned to stand by Michael and Doc.

"You men are repulsive. You act like prepubescent boys and you live in a pigsty. Don't you know anything about cleanliness?" she railed.

"I'm trying to help you, ma'am!" Michael said as he struggled to keep Doc from kicking him again. "If you'd just calm down a mite and quit calling us names . . . Youch! Dadburn it, old man, you bit me!"

Wynn paused on her way to the door and glanced back at the two on the floor. "Could be it's because he can't breathe. Look at him. He's turning blue."

Chapter Two

It was a long walk back to the hotel—at least it seemed so to Wynn. She refused to cringe at the rustling sounds in the tall prairie grasses on either side of the trail, assuring herself it was probably too cold for snakes. The chill seemed to be damper and colder, too. The stretch of her stride and the wide, flashing arcs made by the swinging lantern at her side bore witness to her haste.

But more than anything else—more than being cold or knowing her feet were getting wet as the dampness from the slushy ground seeped into her shoes, more than being weary from her long journey—Wynn was mad. She couldn't remember when she had been so angry.

She knew she ought to be accustomed to having men ignore her by now, but she wasn't. She often attributed the problem to her naturally soft, husky voice. Or maybe, she reasoned, her slight weight and short stature accounted for her being overlooked.

Not all men, she had to admit, ignored her. Some, like the "boy" back at Donovan's house, patronized her, while others, like the "old man," practiced their repertoire of verbal put-downs.

But it was not men in general she was so angry at.

31

It was not even those two buffoons back at Donovan's. It was Michael Donovan himself, that slippery, slimy, elusive rascal who was most probably at home and just too cowardly to show himself. Well, she wasn't through with him. Not by a long shot.

"You just wait, Mr. Michael Donovan," she muttered as she marched down the trail. "Just wait until I light into you—you black-hearted rogue! That's what you are, too—a black-hearted rogue, advertising a 'large, commodious hotel,' duping people into believing you have a town! I may be stuck here for awhile, but I'm not about to let those sick people sleep in that drafty lobby without adequate heat or cover. And as for those two vile men . . ."

Wynn's scruples wouldn't let her get away with that last accusation—not completely. *Well, one vile and one not so vile,* Wynn argued with her conscience. *I listened. I saw the patched long johns.*

And you saw that dark curly hair and those broad shoulders and long legs. You saw the way those bushy eyebrows almost meet over the bridge of his nose. That was the first time you've ever seen a mustache on a man and liked it. And you liked his voice, that deep, mellow voice . . .

Wynn's heart joined the fray then, chanting its memory of betrayal, reminding her not to trust a man, any man, no matter how much she might admire his physical attributes.

She refused to listen to the dueling silent voices any longer. She shut them off by resuming her monologue. "And that house you live in! It's a wonder all three of you haven't come down with some dreadful disease from the filth!"

By the time she snatched the planked door open, Wynn had worked herself into a rage. The clerk, who had been dozing, snapped to attention at the sound of her clicking heels and hurried around the counter, but he came up short at the sight of the bright blaze in her pale eyes and the tight line of her lips.

"Please, ma'am, don't raise no more ruckus—"

Wynn ignored him. She raised her lantern high and let her gaze sweep over the blanket-wrapped bodies taking up most of the floor space of the tiny lobby. There were five all together, three of them visibly shaking from the fever raging their bodies. Hacking coughs resounded in the room.

"I am going to raise a ruckus. I'm going to move those three sick people . . . somewhere, and you're going to assist me, or so help me I'll bang on doors until I find someone who will. These people need to be quarantined before they infect everyone else."

"What did Mr. Donovan say?"

She wasn't about to admit she hadn't seen him. "He wasn't . . . concerned."

Wynn cringed inwardly, then mentally shrugged away the fleeting sting of guilt. It wasn't exactly a lie.

"Where you going to move them, ma'am?"

She worried her bottom lip for a moment, then brightened as a possibility struck her. "Does the mercantile have a storeroom?"

The clerk's eyes widened. "Surely, ma'am, you aren't thinking—"

"Yes, I am! Unless you have a better idea."

"Mr. Donovan won't like it, ma'am," he argued.

"I'll deal with Mr. Donovan later. You just help me move these people."

Doc Nolan watched Michael sop up the puddles of sour mash with an old flour sack. The boy was going

33

after it with a vengeance, but Doc figured there was something more important Michael needed to be pursuing. He told him so.

"You better go after that little lady."

"Why?"

"You done made her mad."

"Me?" Michael asked, pausing to look up at Doc. His green eyes widened with incredulity. *"I* made her mad? I suppose you'll say next that I'm the one who called us yokels and buffoons. I don't care if she's mad. You go after her. You were the one leering at her, old man. You were the one suggesting we might take advantage of her. All I did was try to help her, even after she accused me of wetting myself. Now you tell me, Doc. What kind of lady would ask a man—a perfect stranger!—about being able to hold his water? If she's mad, it's her problem and it's your doing, not mine. Besides, I'm tired. I'm going to bed."

"She didn't come all the way out here looking for me, boy."

"All the way out here? Listen to yourself, Doc. It's not that far."

"It's far enough in the dark. Most women would've been scared stiff to make that trip at night."

"Now you're making it sound as though you admire that woman. You didn't act like you admired her when she was here."

"She caught me off guard."

Michael laughed. Actually, it was more of a snort, but Doc took it as a sign that the boy was loosening up. "Yeah, she did, didn't she?"

"I'm not used to brazen women." When Michael lifted his brows at that statement, Doc decided to rephrase it. "Not of her variety, anyway."

34

"Her *variety?* You make her sound like a type of string bean."

"You know what I mean, boy. No matter what you think, that one's a lady, an educated one from the way she talked. None of the ladies I've ever known would have had the guts to walk in on us and then talk to us the way she did. Do you think this place is a pigsty?"

"Don't change the subject, Doc. Pigsty or not, we like this place the way it is."

Michael's narrow-eyed survey of the room belied his words. Damn it all if Doc wasn't right! She did have some guts, even if she wasn't big as a minute. And those eyes of hers. Michael didn't think he'd ever been so intrigued before by something so simple as a pair of eyes. But Doc was probably right about her being nothing but skin and bone under all those clothes.

Michael attempted to refocus his thoughts on something else entirely. Instead, he heard her voice rattling around in his head. It was a gravelly voice, like she had a corn husk caught in her throat, but in a seductive sort of way.

Damn! What was wrong with him? He must need a woman as bad as Doc said if he thought that stiff-spined, self-righteous, nose-in-the-air pipsqueak was desirable! What had she wanted, anyway? He hadn't really listened—and he tried to tell himself he didn't really care. He stood up, flexed his shoulders, and asked, despite himself, "What exactly did she say?"

"She wanted to talk to you. Something about there was some sick people sleepin' in the lobby at the hotel."

"Why would that woman concern herself with a few people coughing this time of year? Hell, this damp cold makes everybody sick."

35

"I don't know. We never gave her a chance to explain."

"You mean *you* never gave her a chance."

Doc knew he hadn't given her much of a chance, but he had obviously heard a lot more than Michael had. If the boy hadn't been paying attention, so much the better. Michael needed to find out on his own that Wynnifred Spencer was a doctor. Doc hoped Fate would allow the boy an opportunity to form a positive opinion of her first.

He grinned behind his hand as he watched Michael cross the room and take his coat down from the nail by the door.

"I'm going for a walk," Michael announced.

"You want me to wait up for you, boy?" Doc teased.

"Let's get one thing straight, old man," Michael said as he slipped his long arms into the coat sleeves. "I'm twice your size and less than half your age. I am not now, nor have I been for some years, a *boy*. I don't need you to tuck me in."

The door had eased shut behind him and Michael was halfway across the porch before Doc muttered, "You're right, boy. You don't need me for companionship. You need a wife. You just don't know it yet. And be damned if Lady Luck didn't send you one!"

Wynn awoke to the soft sounds of a drizzling rain. She didn't know how long she had been asleep, but it couldn't have been for more than an hour or two. Fatigue sat heavily upon her like a full sack of feed, and she snuggled deeper into the bed. Her nose itched and she rubbed it with the back of her hand. She had almost found sleep again when she sneezed.

The sneeze brought her fully alert, and she remembered why she hadn't slept. Partially responsible, she supposed, was the mound of feed sacks beneath her and the scratchy wool blanket covering her. But she suspected that a feather mattress and down-filled quilt would not have made a real difference. It was anger that had kept her awake. Fraud always made her angry.

Renewed anger washed through her then, fueling her bounce to the floor. She paused just long enough to let her eyes adjust to the dim light sifting in through a grimy window set high in the wall before she made her way around a cluster of stacked crates.

The sick people — the clerk had identified them as Orville and Harriet Mason and their daughter, Sarah — were stretched out on a makeshift bed of folded blankets atop a base of wooden crates. The three were sleeping peacefully and did not waken to the gentle touch of Wynn's palm upon their clammy foreheads. She breathed a sigh of relief at their much improved condition, which she attributed to the powdered sassafras and cough syrup she had given them, combined with their removal from the drafty lobby.

I've made my first morning rounds in Jennings, she thought, smiling in satisfaction. Able then to see to her own needs, she located a clean bucket and went outside to find a well.

Jennings' few buildings looked no better by daylight. If anything, they looked worse. Wynn blamed their shabby appearance on the gray skies and misty rain and hurried to collect fresh water.

She found a privy behind the hotel and noted a corral and small barn behind the store, but there was no well. There had to be one — somewhere. Wynn turned slowly around, then walked back to the front of the store and looked toward the depot, which, with its surrounding clump of oaks, obscured her view of Donovan's house. Just realizing it lay somewhere on the other side set her blood to boiling again. Oh, but what she wouldn't tell him given half the chance!

At the present, though, finding water took precedence over talking to Donovan. She marched back toward the privy area and gave the grassy plot acute scrutiny. Here, a trampled path separated the prairie grasses, its three fingers branching off to the barn, the privy—and a pump!

Wynn had grown up in the hills, where there were wells, not pumps rising out of the ground. She honestly didn't trust it, but when she worked the handle, a trickle of clear water dripped out of the spout. If she pumped the handle hard enough, she discovered, the trickle became a steady stream. She filled the bucket and went back inside.

Wynn barely had time to wash her face, comb her hair and secure it into the tight bun she always wore before someone burst in the front door, setting the cowbell ajingle. She gave her hair a final pat, moistened her lips, and assumed her most arrogant pose. Just let Mr. Michael Donovan complain about their using his storeroom for a place to sleep! She was ready for him.

A tall, slender man dressed in a brown tweed suit and holding a beaver hat paced the narrow space in front of the counter. Wynn stood in the doorway for a moment and watched him twirl his hat, watched him pause to flick a piece of lint off his jacket sleeve. What a dandy this Michael Donovan was!

If she had stopped to think about it, she would have realized that this man with the pomaded hair and English riding boots could not possibly belong to the house she had visited the night before. But Wynn didn't stop to think. She was too busy planning her speech. She cleared her throat and moved confidently into the room. Before she could launch her offensive, however, the man pounced on her.

"It's about time!" The words were spoken harshly, the *t*'s precisely enunciated.

"My thoughts exactly," she countered.

"Pardon?"

He seemed at a loss. Wynn gave herself a mental pat on the back for snaring the advantage so quickly. "You owe me and everyone else who has come here an apology and an explanation, sir."

"I do?"

"You most certainly do! You owe us those things and more."

"I do? Why?"

Wynn's eyes sparkled with her ire, and her sharp tone bespoke her anger as well. "You, sir, are guilty of the most cunning deception I have ever seen devised. You have much to repay to those of us who fell victim to your trickery."

"Now wait just one minute, young woman—"

"Oh, no, you're not going to weasel out of this confrontation like you did the one last night."

He held up an open palm, and his face mirrored his total confusion. "Honestly, ma'am, I don't know what you're talking about."

"Perhaps your men didn't bother to tell you about my visit last night. I wouldn't be surprised. They are two of the rudest, most irresponsible people I have ever had occasion to meet. I found their drunken behavior appalling. A man of your station should employ more discretion in his selection of hired hands!"

"I'm quite certain I agree with you, ma'am," the man responded levelly. "I'm just not quite sure which two men you refer to."

Wynn shrugged. "I don't know their names. They neglected to introduce themselves to me, but they call each other Boy and Old Man."

Her remark wiped the confusion from his features and the man smiled broadly. "You must think I'm Michael Donovan."

"Well, aren't you?"

"No. I am," came a third voice.

In unison, the two turned toward the open door.

Wynn thought her eyes must be playing tricks on her. She blinked twice but that didn't help. He was still there, the overgrown boy with the bewitching eyebrows, the man who belonged to the carefully patched long johns hanging over the pot-bellied stove. Was he wearing them under those tight-fitting denim britches? she wondered, then felt her embarrassment at thinking such a thing bloom crimson in her cheeks. She took an involuntary step backwards and placed an open hand over her pounding heart. Her mouth formed the word "you" and her bulging eyes added the question mark.

The man in the tweed suit chuckled. Whoever *he* was, he seemed to be enjoying her sudden lack of composure.

Donovan swept a folded arm across his midsection and bowed deeply. "At your service, ma'am."

He straightened his tall, heavily muscled frame and regarded her with amusement. Wynn wanted to say something truly demeaning, something that would remove that twinkle from his eyes and the near-smirk from beneath his mustache, but all she could do was stare at him open-mouthed. When she did find her voice, she stammered, "Then, who is he?"

A nod of her head indicated the dandy.

"Him? Oh, don't mind him. He's just a *yokel* under the employ of Andrew MacDougall, our local cattle baron. As you can see from what he wears, he can't claim kin to a working man."

Wynn watched the dandy's Adam's apple bob up and down as he nervously adjusted the green ribbon tie at his neck. "Now see here, Donovan—"

"No need to worry, Wilcox," Michael interrupted. "I'm here to load MacDougall's supplies for you. Wouldn't want you straining yourself. They're all crated up and ready to go. Just go on back outside and make sure that frisky mare is tied up good. I'm not chasing her down for you again."

"Ma'am," Wilcox said politely to Wynn, giving her a brief nod in farewell.

How refreshing to meet a real gentleman, Wynn thought as she watched him head for the door.

By the time he reached the exit, Donovan was passing through the doorway into the storeroom. Wilcox shot a scathing look at his back before leaving.

Wynn reconsidered her impression. What a yellow-bellied pantywaist the man was! She might have added another descriptive phrase or two to the list had Michael Donovan's bellow not interrupted her deliberations.

"What the hell is going on here?"

"Sh-h-h!" she admonished on her way into the storeroom. "You're disturbing my patients!"

Patients? Who did she think she was? A doctor?

"I damned well have a right to! They're lying on MacDougall's goods."

"How could I have known you were going to need these crates this morning?" Wynn asked, mentally berating herself for allowing him to put her on the defensive. Then she gasped, "What are you doing?"

41

"Moving them."

In one deft movement, Michael had scooped Orville Mason up and was heading out the door with him. Wynn grabbed her carpetbag and followed close on his heels. The man groaned as his neck lolled against Michael's left elbow.

"This man is sick. He needs rest. Where are you taking him?"

Michael glanced at her over his shoulder without breaking his stride. She was as tenacious as a ferret. "Next door."

"There are no vacant rooms. That's what I was trying to tell you last night. And you—you were there all the time. You knew I wanted to talk to you! Why didn't you tell me you were Mr. Donovan?"

Michael ignored her outburst, addressing the issue of the vacant room instead. "There's at least one vacancy now. Wilcox is going home. The Masons can have that one."

"I thought you said Wilcox was local."

"When we say local around here, ma'am, we mean within a day's ride, not across the street."

"Street?" Wynn huffed from behind him. She was having difficulty keeping up with his long strides. "What street?"

"If you don't like it here, ma'am, you can get back on the train when it comes back through in a couple of days and go back to wherever it is you came from."

"Illinois," she supplied.

"Wherever," he grunted, nodding his head toward the closed front door of the hotel. Wynn hurried around him to open it wide. "Perkins!" Michael barked as he hit the stairs. "Which room was Wilcox in?"

The clerk poked his head out of a door at the end

42

of the second-floor hall. "This one. I'm cleaning it up now."

From all appearances, Perkins had done nothing more than empty the slop jar and straighten the sheets and blanket. Wynn's gaze critically scoured the room and she gasped in horror when Donovan lowered the man to the bed.

"Don't put him there!" she shrieked.

"Look, lady," Michael said as he laid Mason down anyway. "I've just about had it up to here"—he slashed a forefinger across his throat—"with your contrariness. In fact, you're just about the most contrary female I've ever had occasion to meet. Why is it that nothing pleases you?"

"This room isn't clean—"

"And the storeroom was? If this room isn't clean enough for you, you can damned well clean it up yourself. Perkins and I have other work to do."

"And who will care for the Masons?"

"I suppose *you* will, Miss—"

"Spencer. I introduced myself last night, Mr. Donovan, which is more than you bothered to do. Talk about contrary! You have your nerve, sir, to accuse me, a ph—"

"What I have, ma'am, is a busy day ahead of me. Just tell Perkins what you need. He'll bring the other two over here." Without even bidding her good-day, he turned on his heel and stalked out of the room.

Before she could stop herself, Wynn shook her fist at his back, then felt like the yellow-bellied panty-waist Wilcox had demonstrated himself to be. What was it about this Michael Donovan that brought out the worst in people?

What was it about him that brought out the worst

43

in people? Michael wondered.

All his life—at least since he'd been on his own, which was certainly *most* of his life—he'd managed time and again to alienate people. Doc Nolan was the only person Michael had ever met who could tolerate him for more than a few minutes at a time. And even Doc got fed up every so often.

Well, he couldn't be bothered, not now, when there was so much work to be done. He'd set out to build his own empire in this corner of the world, and by dinghies, he was going to do it! He didn't need Miss Hoity-toity Nurse Spencer or Doc Nolan or anyone else to help him do it, either. He didn't need their help or their permission. If they wanted to pack up and leave, let them. He had his land. He owned a town. What else did he need?

I don't know when I've seen a man need a woman as much as you.

No, he argued with the memory of Doc's observation as it intruded in his thoughts, he didn't need a woman. And if by some chance he did, he knew where to find one. He didn't know who but he did know where. It wouldn't be here—and it wouldn't be the Spencer woman.

Wynn spent the remainder of the morning cleaning the hotel room. She cleaned it because it needed it, but the very act of cleaning provided a vent for her outrage as well.

She started by yanking down the square of dusty muslin covering the window, then used vinegar and newspaper to shine the grimy panes. The floor took three scrubbings with lye soap and the walls took two. When the room was clean, she made a disinfectant by mixing some carbolic acid, which she carried

44

in her medical bag, in a pail of fresh water. She sprinkled it on the floor.

Johnny Perkins gave her everything she requested, including clean sheets and an extra tick to put on the floor for the little girl. Before she put the clean linen on the beds, she aired out the straw mattresses.

While she worked, she tried to talk to the Masons, but they were disinclined to say much. At first, she attributed their reticence to a combination of their bad colds and the sedative effect of the medicines she'd given them; but when the little girl, who appeared to be six or seven, tried to talk to Wynn, her parents cut her off. Wynn couldn't help thinking the sharp looks she occasionally intercepted were filled with distrust. No matter. She would earn their trust, just as she had earned the trust and respect of the patients she had served during her residency at St. Luke's Hospital in St. Paul, Minnesota.

By midday, she had worked up quite an appetite.

"I'm going to see if I can find us something to eat," she announced, rolling her sleeves down and then untying the apron Johnny had lent her.

"We aren't hungry," Orville Mason growled.

"I am!" Sarah wailed.

"Hush, child," Harriet admonished, her voice too sharp to Wynn's way of thinking.

"I'll bring you all some broth," she offered, scooting out the door before either of the adults could protest.

Wynn stopped on the bottom step and stared at the empty lobby. Even the young, gangly clerk, Johnny Perkins, was nowhere in sight. A quick inspection of the ground floor failed to reveal a kitchen. No one was on the porch or anywhere around at all, for that matter. There must have been at least a score of people at the hotel the night be-

45

fore. Where had everyone gone? The last thing she wanted to do was see Michael Donovan again, but she could think of no other recourse. She had to find some food, somewhere, and what better place to look than the mercantile?

But there was no one there, either. Wynn stood on the porch and listened to the quiet. The drizzle had given way to pale skies. Only an occasional drip from the porch eave broke the silence. It was downright eerie. Where had everyone gone?

Her gaze swept the landscape. The station house! At least it was worth a try.

She set off across the bare, muddy lot, where countless tramplings had completely worn away the grass. As she neared the open door of the depot, she smelled food and heard the pleasant buzz of friendly conversation.

The stationmaster waved a short, stubby arm at her. "Come in, missy, come in!"

A long trestle table commanded the center of the room. The crude benches flanking it were crowded with people sitting shoulder-to-shoulder. Michael Donovan was seated there, and Johnny Perkins, and the one she knew only as Old Man. At the stationmaster's greeting, everyone stopped talking, laid down their spoons, and turned in unison to pierce her with their stares. She felt like a three-horned cow in a traveling side show.

"We didn't get a chance to meet you last night, missy," the stationmaster continued. "Folks 'round here call me Slim." His laughter at that moniker was as full-bodied as his girth. "They say I'm a purty fair cook, too. Come on in and set with us a spell and get to know everyone while I serve you up a bowl of beef stew. Wilcox was kind enough—bless his cold heart—to bring us some fresh beef when he come to

46

town and this is the end of it, so you'd best enjoy it while you've got the chance."

All the while he talked, he moved, first shooing away from the table a couple of youngsters who had finished their meal and then ladling up some of the steaming stew into a graniteware bowl.

"Is there enough for the Masons?" Wynn asked.

" 'Course, missy. Mr. Donovan told me they was feelin' poorly, so I made 'em a little pot of chicken soup, but if you'd rather take 'em some of this stew, there's aplenty."

"They'd probably rather have the chicken soup. It was so thoughtful of you to make it especially for them, Slim. Thank you!"

Wynn didn't quite know what to think about Michael Donovan. He had seemed so gruff, so uncaring, yet he had given the Masons a room while others still had to sleep in the halls or lobby of the hotel. Then, he had asked Slim to make them the chicken soup. Maybe the man did have a heart after all.

When Wynn had settled herself on the bench, she caught herself seeking his face — and caught him staring at her. No man had ever stared at her quite that way before. It was a stare of assessment and confusion and boldness all wrapped up together. She felt herself blush, then covered her discomfiture by announcing to the room at large, "I'm Wynnifred Spencer."

The buzzing started up again, but this time, many of those seated at the table spoke directly to her, introducing themselves — she learned that the old man's name was Doc — and asking her discreetly impersonal questions. Without really understanding why, Wynn avoided correcting them when they referred to her as a nurse.

47

She hurried her meal so she could take the soup to the Masons. By the time she left, she knew quite a bit about the several families staying at the hotel. By and large they were from the Midwest, children and grandchildren of pioneers who were about to become pioneers themselves. They had come to scout out the territory and had all decided to take out homestead patents. Most of them would be going home soon to sell their farms and pack up their households. Then they would return to start building a new life on the frontier.

She realized that she had misread their stares. These people were not hostile; they were merely curious. It was the near-hostility she received from the Masons that had colored her thinking. Thank God, not all the homesteaders were like her first Jennings patients!

They weren't complainers, either. Not once had she heard a grumble concerning the lack of advertised accommodations. She had thought to air her own grievances with Michael Donovan — and she would, too . . . but privately. She saw no sense in stirring up these good folks and creating hostility where there had been none.

Before Wynn left, she made arrangements with Slim to have her extra baggage stored at the depot until she needed it. She complimented him on his stew — it really was as good as he'd said — and thanked him once more for the chicken soup.

She found the Masons much improved and far hungrier than they wanted to admit. "Renewed appetite is a good sign," she observed. "I'm leaving some garlic ointment for you to apply to your chests, and I'll be checking on you from time to time. Be sure to keep the window open. Proper ventilation is important."

She stood at the door for a moment, her carpet-bag in her hand and her nearly ruined mantle over her arm, watching the Masons eat, hoping one of them would utter some word of gratitude. Wynn had not become a doctor to hear her services praised, but a simple "thank you" from the Masons would indicate the beginning of acceptance, and it was acceptance that she so desperately needed.

As she stalled her departure, she watched Harriet Mason's features soften and waited with bated breath for the woman to speak. But Orville saw the look on his wife's face, too, and he quickly suppressed anything she might have said with a sharp look of disapproval.

Wynn sighed, then added, "If you should need me, just tell Mr. Perkins. He'll know where to find me."

Wherever that is.

Disappointment gave way to apprehension as the full message of her mental postscript drove itself home. Where would she sleep?

In a bed . . . in somebody's bed . . . in Michael Donovan's bed if I have to, she vowed.

And she set off to find him.

Chapter Three

Finding him was a task she couldn't imagine would hold much difficulty, considering the lilliputian size of the village. She started by asking Johnny Perkins, the hotel clerk, who suggested she try the general store. When no one was there, she went to the station house, the last place she had seen him.

"I think he went home, missy," Slim told her. "Said something 'bout wantin' to take a nap."

Slim must have confused Michael's intentions with Doc's, Wynn decided when she found Doc sleeping soundly and Michael nowhere in sight. She shook Doc awake in the middle of a snore.

"I'm looking for Mr. Donovan."

"Out ridin'," Doc snuffled, then rolled over and resumed snoring right where he'd left off.

She hiked back to town, mindless of the damp prairie grasses slapping at her skirts but fully aware of the weight of the carpetbag she carried. Every few minutes she shifted it from one hand to the other, giving her opposite shoulder and upper arm muscles a break. She wished she had left it in Slim's safekeeping.

The damp air bore a hint of chill. It was just cold

enough to vaporize breath but not cold enough to require a wrap. Nonetheless, Wynn's mantle was
thrown over her shoulders, making one less thing to
carry.

She came up behind the small barn, on the corral
side. A big red horse stood in the paddock snorting
steam, a saddle and blanket on his back. He wore his
bridle as well, and his reins were looped over a rail of
the fence. She looked around, and though she didn't
see Michael, she did notice that the barn door was
slightly ajar.

There was no doubt in Wynn's mind that Donovan
was in the barn. She opened her mouth to call out to
him, then thought better of it. Hadn't he been avoiding her all afternoon? His friends had sent her on a
wild goose chase. Now that she had found the elusive rascal, why give him a chance to escape through
the other door? She'd enter via the corral and catch
him unawares.

Wynn set her carpetbag down and sighed. She removed her mantle and laid it on top of the bag, then
cautiously opened the gate. The barn door was a
straight shot ahead, some fifty paces away.

Crossing the paddock should have been easy. it
would have been had the big red horse not moved
when she did. He pranced away from the fence, pulling his reins loose to trail on the ground, then
stopped dead center between her and the door,
blocking her path broadside. When she started to
skirt him on the right, he backed up. When she
moved to the left, he walked forward. Wynn didn't
know much about horses, but anyone could see that
this one was hellbent on contrariness.

"Please, let me pass," she crooned, careful to keep
her voice even and low. He was one big horse—much

51

taller at the shoulder than she, but he seemed gentle enough. Wynn wished she knew his name. She approached him slowly, then reached up on tiptoe and stroked his neck, using the affectionate gesture and her husky voice to calm him.

The horse stood still, nickering softly as she stroked his long neck. "Be still now," she whispered, "and let me by." Convinced that she had gained his cooperation, she backed up one step, then two. Just as she stepped to the left to go around him, the horse bared his teeth, shook his head, and snorted, broadcasting a spray of warm, sticky saliva that hit her full in the face.

She spun away, her weight poised on one foot. The pirouette threw her off balance. Down she went, her backside plopping right into a dung heap.

At that moment, Wynn was aware of only one thing: she had to get away before the horse stepped on her. She gasped for breath, sucking in deep gulps of the damp air and willing the panic away. She wanted to scream but she didn't dare. Lord only knew what such a big horse would do if she spooked him—he was jittery enough already. He pawed the ground at her side and snorted, spraying her again, his nervousness fueling her desire to extricate herself from the muck in all due haste.

She wriggled and squirmed away from him, kneading fresh manure into her lightweight wool skirt. Hauling herself up on her hands, she crawfished backwards, her gaze locked on the horse. His eyelids blinked at her but he stood still. She scrambled away, then stood up. Slowly, she backed toward the gate, her eyes ever on the horse.

The farther she got from the animal, the more her fear subsided—and the stronger she smelled manure.

With the distance, too, came awareness of dampness on her backside. Without conscious thought, she swiped her hand across her derrière, then gagged when she realized what she'd done. Her predicament struck her full force.

"You—you mangy creature!" she hissed. "Look what you made me do!" She couldn't go to the hotel because she didn't have a room, but she had to change clothes and she desperately needed a bath.

Out of the corner of her vision, she saw the trough. She might not be able to bathe in it, not out in the open, but at least she had a ready supply of water. Quickly devising a plan, she eased open the gate and snatched up her carpetbag, letting her coat fall to the ground. From the relative safety of the gate, she assessed the distance to the trough, then edged sideways to it, her ever watchful gaze on the horse. Miraculously, he didn't move. When she got to the trough, she paused long enough to rinse her hand and dampen her handkerchief.

"Lord," she breathed, "please don't let Michael Donovan be in that barn! He'd never let me live this down."

Michael pushed the privy door open with his shoulder, his hands busily adjusting his suspenders. He heard the hoof beats before he saw the horse, but hearing them was enough to send him running.

"Rusty!" he called, tearing around the privy and past the barn. "Come back here!" He put two fingers in his mouth and his whistle rang out loud and shrill.

Rusty stopped short and turned to watch Michael running toward him. When Michael got close, Rusty took off again, his reins flying like a banner beside him. The horse couldn't go far, Michael reasoned, without becoming tangled in his reins.

It never paid to second-guess Rusty. The whistle-halt-run progression continued until Michael had chased after the horse for a quarter of a mile. Finally, he began to see the futility of further pursuit. Hell, he could chase the horse to Texas and Rusty would never tire of the game. Michael decelerated to a slow jog, then stopped moving altogether. He stood his ground for a moment, resting his palms on his thighs and breathing heavily.

"Damned horse," he muttered. "Always did have a mind of your own. I don't care if you never come back, so long as you return that saddle. How in the world did you get out?"

When he had regained his breath and his pulse had slowed to normal, he turned and ambled back toward the corral. His head reeled from the unaccustomed exertion and from trying to figure out how he'd managed to leave the gate unsecured. He stopped and turned back toward Rusty. The horse had stopped, too. Rusty stood looking back at Michael, tossing his mane and arching his tail as though in invitation to resume their game.

Ignoring the horse, Michael headed toward the corral once again. At first, he didn't notice the lump of gray wool next to the fence. The tall prairie grasses growing right up next to the fence had almost swallowed it. But as he reached for the gate, he spied the gray mass. Tiny pinholes pocked the gray wool. He'd seen those holes before.

"I might have known!" he mumbled under his breath. "Damned interfering woman!"

He rescued Wynn's wrap from the damp ground and draped it over the fence. Where had she gone?

54

he wondered. Could she have mounted Rusty and fallen off? His gaze raked the foreground, searching for but not finding a break in the rippling, waist-high grass.

"Miss Spencer!" His voice carried a sharp edge—a combination of concern, frustration, and anger.

Behind him, the barn door creaked. He whirled toward the sound. There was no one in sight, but there was darn sure someone in the barn. Michael snatched open the gate and strode across the corral, his long legs covering the short distance in a matter of seconds.

Wynn saw him coming through a crack in the door. She had thought he was still off chasing the horse until she heard him call her name. If she just hadn't leaned into the door trying to get a better view!

It was too late now; she had spilled the proverbial milk. If she hurried, maybe, just maybe, she could finish dressing before Donovan found her. She yanked her clean skirt off the door where she had hung it and ducked into the stall. She stood facing the wall, her heart pounding, one black-stockinged leg raised and her shoe already through the waist opening when his laughter erupted behind her. Mortified but not defeated, she allowed her foot to complete its mission, then followed it with the other. She jerked the skirt up around her waist and fumbled with the hooks.

"Where is he?"

Wynn jumped as though he had screamed at her, when in reality his voice was flat and cold. She refused to face him until she had secured the waistband of her skirt, which she managed in short order. She took a deep breath and turned around, bestowing upon him a look of sheer disbelief. What kind of idiot was this man? Where was he, indeed!

"Halfway across the prairie, I suppose."

"Who is?"

"Why, the horse — Rusty. Isn't that what you called him?"

"You know damned well I'm not talking about Rusty." His voice was low, his tone accusative.

"I have no idea who or what you're talking about, Mr. Donovan, nor do I appreciate your swearing at me. I *would* appreciate your allowing me to finish dressing in private — oh!" She gasped in astonished comprehension, one hand quickly rising to cover her mouth. "You don't think . . . you *do* think . . . why you — you scoundrel!"

Her chest heaved; her crystal eyes were burning cinders in the shadow of her face. Michael Donovan couldn't decide which he liked looking at more, the half-buttoned shirtwaist exposing the top of her chemise and a tiny bit of cleavage . . . or the startling blue of her hypnotic eyes. His gaze bounced back and forth between the two, then settled on the less dangerous of the tantalizing pair: her eyes.

He took a step closer, his voice still low and accusing but now carrying the merest hint of lasciviousness, his gaze boldly assessing. "I won't have you fooling around in my barn."

Her voice was sharp and riddled with ire, her gaze unflinching. "Fooling around? What did you want me to do, Mr. Donovan? Strip naked out there in the corral?"

And Doc thought she was a lady! A lady of the evening, more likely, or more appropriately, the afternoon—certainly not the virgin he had thought her to be. Michael's thoughts raced pell-mell through the list of men in Jennings. There were the three other bachelors: Slim, Johnny Perkins, and Doc. Which one of them had he almost caught with her? Or had it been one of the Bible-thumping farmers? Or—heaven forbid!—one of their greenhorn adolescent sons?

Suddenly, he didn't want to know. He wanted her for himself. With the speed of a viper, his big hands shot out and grasped her upper arms in a bruising hold, pulling her up against him.

Soft femininity collided with brawny power, knocking the breath, and thus the ability to protest, out of her. Before she could gather her wits, his mouth slammed into hers.

Never had she felt so violated. She attempted to raise her hands, but he held her firmly. She twisted her head, trying to dislodge his mouth, but his lips stayed locked on hers. She writhed and squirmed, to no avail. Her might was no match for his.

No! she thought. She had saved herself from the danger of a nervous horse! She could save herself from this fiend. She was a doctor; she knew what parts made a man a man, knew those parts were vulnerable. Wynn bent her knee and rammed it into his groin.

Michael yelped as pain shot through him. He released her and doubled over, groaning, his eyes wild, his face contorted.

Wynn lost no time putting distance between them, then stopped short when she realized how completely she had debilitated him. He couldn't do anything else to her at the moment, but there was something else she intended to do to him. She picked up the bundle of soiled garments on the dirt floor and threw them at his head. "There, sir, is the evidence you require. It should supply you with sufficient cause for my presence in your barn!"

She retrieved her carpetbag and dashed out the back door, leaving him with a physical pain she knew would be short-lived—and a smear of horse dung on the side of his hawk's nose. The buffoon deserved whatever damage she had done to his pride! And if he thought he had seen the last of her, he was in for the surprise of his life.

If she thought she could get away with clobbering him twice, *she* was in for the surprise of *her* life.

When he could move again, Michael snatched a white garment from the jumble of her clothes and limped outside to the trough. Over and over, he dipped the scrap of cotton in the water. Over and over he scrubbed his face with it. The cool water stung his skin, intensifying the heat of his anger rather than diminishing it. With the fifth or sixth swipe—Donovan lost count, he realized it wasn't the water that stung; it was the lace.

He unfolded the wet wad of white and gaped at the camisole. Row upon row of tiny tucks and narrow white lace decorated the front of the garment, the part he had used as a washcloth. The several dippings had served to suffuse the delicate scent of lilacs that clung to the garment, the repeated scrubbings depositing the fragrance on Michael's face. Every breath reminded him of her, of the icy sparkle in her blue eyes, of the swell of her breasts above such a garment as the one he held. The soft white fabric with its frothy lace brought to mind her other undergarment, the white bloomers with their own lacy frill just above her knees, their fabric stretched tight across firm, rounded buttocks as she lifted one leg and then the other to put on her skirt.

Doc had been wrong. There was a lot more than skin and bones beneath her clothes. A helluva lot more.

He shook his head, trying to dislodge her image. He didn't like being reminded of her. She might be a woman, but she was the dadburnedest woman he'd ever met. Every other woman he had ever touched had melted in his arms, practically swooning over him. But not this one. Not Wynnifred Spencer.

"Why can't you be like other women?" he demanded of the camisole. "Don't you know how women are supposed to act?"

Michael didn't realize how foolish he sounded talking to an article of clothing until Rusty's wet snort sprayed his face. He looked up at the horse and couldn't resist smiling when the animal shook his head vigorously. He wiped his face with the camisole once more, using its smooth back this time, letting the sweet smell of lilacs permeate his senses before slinging the garment into the trough.

The action assumed symbolic meaning. He could rid himself of her just as easily. Anyone who wanted to conduct business in Jennings had to go through him. He could arrange it so she had no choice but to leave town, and that was exactly what he ought to do. But not until he made her pay. Not until she willingly gave herself to him. He might not have wanted her before, but he wanted her now, and, by golly, he would have her!

First, he had to take care of Rusty.

"Come on, you silly horse. Let's get that saddle off."

Wynn had every intention of marching herself right back out to Donovan's house and confiscating his bedroom for the night. She was tired — no, she amended, worn to a frazzle and bleary-headed from lack of sleep. She meant to feel a mattress beneath her that night.

But first she wanted a cup of tea. The only place she figured she could get one was at the depot.

Slim accommodated her in his friendly, good-natured way. "I make tea 'bout this time everyday," he told her. "My usual tea customer ought to be here directly. Be glad to make an extry cup for you. Just take a seat and make yourself comfy."

Wynn's heart slammed into her throat and it was a moment before she could ask, "Your usual customer?"

Lord, don't let it be Michael Donovan. I'd have to be pleasant to him in front of Slim, and I just don't know if that's possible right now.

"Granny Simpson. You met her at lunch. Here she is now. You 'member Miss Spencer, Granny?" Slim waved an arm at Wynn.

"Dr. Spencer," Wynn corrected. It was high time she let people know what she was and why she had come to Jennings. There was no shame in being a physician, she reminded herself, just far too much prejudice against female doctors.

Slim raised his eyebrows and pursed his lips, then shook his head before turning back to the stove and checking the kettle.

Granny ignored him. She seated herself at the table with Wynn and smiled. "You're just the person I wanted to see, young lady. I need your help."

60

"You do?"

Granny nodded, setting the folds of her chin ajiggling. "Rachel and David—that's my daughter and son-in-law—are going back to Indiana on the Wednesday train. My lumbago just won't let me ride that train again."

"There's nothing I can give you for the pain, Granny, except laudanum to help you sleep. Have you tried warm fomentations?"

"Oh, yes. They work wonders. But you misunderstand me, Miss—Dr. Spencer. I don't *want* to ride the train. I want to stay here until Rachel and David come back in the spring."

"But you said you needed my help." Wynn looked and sounded genuinely confused.

"I do. They won't leave me here by myself. They say I need a companion, a *female* companion—"

Wynn thought Granny sounded just the least bit miffed about not being given a choice. She liked this woman already.

"—to stay with me while they're gone. When the hotel clears out some, you can move into a room of your own, if you want to."

Wynn smiled warmly at the elderly woman. Her intuition told her that this was Granny's way of providing her with a room without the stigma of charity. "I'd be delighted to be your companion, Granny. Thanks for asking me."

"Don't be thanking me yet, young lady. You were my only hope. All the other women staying are married. I was thinking I'd get one of the youngsters, but Rachel said no. That girl clucks over me like a mother hen, but if you think I'll let *you* get away with such treatment—"

"I won't cluck, Granny. We'll get along just fine."

And they did.

The more Wynn thought about it, the more she decided she could have lived the remainder of her days without ever seeing Michael Donovan again. Since she had a room, she didn't need to see him, but avoiding him in a place as small as Jennings proved impossible. Besides, she needed her clothes back. The bundle she had hurled at Donovan had contained her only extra set of undergarments.

She had thought he would be gentlemanly enough to return them, but when several days passed and he made no mention of them, she took it upon herself to retrieve them. She expected to find them in the barn, where she had last seen them. Wynn looked everywhere — in the haymows, the stalls, the troughs, among the tack. They weren't there.

Like it or not, she realized, she'd have to ask Michael — privately — what he'd done with them. The events of that afternoon had been embarrassing but certainly not shameful. Still, she didn't want to have to try to explain it to anyone, either — not after the way Michael had misread the situation.

She bided her time until she saw him leave the mercantile and head for home one afternoon. The timing was perfect. She had just left Doc at the depot, playing checkers with Slim, and Granny was taking a nap.

Yet, Wynn debated for some time the wisdom of purposely seeing Michael Donovan alone versus the cost of replacing her undergarments. The undergarments emerged victorious.

She spied him sitting on his porch long before she reached it herself. She half expected him to go inside and lock the door, but he sat perfectly still, his gaze boring into her approaching figure, until she set foot on the step. Then, the front legs of his chair hit the porch floor hard, and he leaned forward, resting his elbows on his knees and his chin in his cupped palms. A grin closely akin to a leer spread across his wide mouth, lifting the corners of his mustache. For a moment, Wynn again doubted the wisdom of her visit. Then the edges of his mustache twitched, transforming the leer into what grew into a friendly smile.

It wasn't. Wynn realized her error in judgment the moment Michael unfolded his long, lean body and stood up. He balanced his weight and rested his right hand on his hip.

Michael faced her with all the poise and confidence of an experienced though reckless gunfighter, like the one she'd watched mow down a less accomplished opponent in the streets of her hometown years before. Though he wore no holster, she caught herself waiting for him to pull out a revolver. A tiny voice urged careful treading. This man, the voice said, could be dangerous.

She'd get right to the point, she decided, collect her clothes, and hightail it back to the hotel.

But it wasn't her gunfight. She just thought it was.

"So," he drawled, "the lady of the afternoon chooses to pay me a visit. Well,"—he waved his arm toward the door—"come on in and make yourself comfortable. If I know Doc, we ought to have at least an hour of total privacy, probably more, and oh, the things we can do for each other in an hour . . ."

As his meaning dawned on her, Wynn took an involuntary step backward and her mouth gaped open. "Lady of the afternoon? How dare you! We've had this conversation before, Mr. Donovan, and—"

"And you won. What're you gonna do? Disable me again with a carefully placed knee? If you were a man, Miss Spencer, I would have decked you for that. You're right about the other, though. You can't possibly be a lady. Ladies don't know about things like that."

"I don't have to defend myself to you, Mr. Donovan. Neither my ladyhood nor my maidenhood is in question. And it's not *Miss* Spencer. It's *Doctor* Spencer."

It was Michael's turn to be caught off guard. She watched his face go blank, just as if she had pulled a shade down over it.

Wynn couldn't fathom why her declaration had shut him up so easily. Granted, most people were surprised to hear she was a physician, but the news had never rendered anyone speechless. She took advantage of his bewilderment before he managed to recover.

"I came for my clothes, Mr. Donovan. You know, the dirty ones I left in the barn the other day. If you'll please tell me where you put them, I'll be on my way."

At first he acted as though he hadn't heard her, but when she started to ask him again, he threw up a restraining hand. "Wait here," he ordered.

Michael stepped inside the front door, then stepped right back out again with a bulging flour sack. The extra length had been pulled tight and tied close to the bulge with a piece of twine, but he held the bag flat in his open palms, like a fragile package.

Wynn accepted it, thanked him as politely as she could manage, and left.

Later, after she had heated water, filled a washtub,

and pulled her scrub board and Octagon soap out of her trunk, she discovered that her garments were all clean, pressed, and neatly folded within the flour sack. She stroked the skirt, which was on top, in amazement; then she shook out each garment— shirtwaist, camisole, petticoat, and bloomers, checking the back of each for manure stains. The garments looked as good—no, better, she decided— than they had before.

And they smelled like lilac water.

The final days of autumn whirled past in a frenzy of activity. There were purchases to make: a plot of land and building materials and furniture for her house. There was a carpenter to hire. And there was a medical practice to establish. Toward that goal, Wynn made a point of meeting every family personally, introducing herself as a doctor and offering her professional services at the present and when they returned in the spring. She had to admit that most folks treated her politely, if with some reservations, but none of them rushed to her door and requested medical attention.

She attributed this attitude to the lack of a proper clinic, which, in turn, fueled her desire to provide one as quickly as she could manage. She couldn't build a house without a lot, and she couldn't buy a lot without talking to Michael Donovan. Wynn didn't want to see him. In fact, she found the very prospect of attempting to conduct business with him most unnerving. But she could think of no other recourse. Besides, she mentally boasted, no man had ever managed to intimidate her before. Why should she let Michael Donovan do so now?

She found him moving crates around in the store-room of the mercantile.

"I'm not in the business of selling residential lots at the moment," he said, not bothering to look at her. "As you can see, I'm busy."

"Then kindly tell me at what time you *will* be in the business, Mr. Donovan."

His answer took the form of a noncommittal shrug.

"I'm quite serious!" she persisted, pushing the edge of frustration from her voice but not able to still the sudden pounding of her heart. The man was—well, he was incorrigible! Surely, she thought, there was a more applicable word, but her supreme irritation prevented her from calling it up at the moment.

He ignored her. She stood her ground, tapping her toe against the planked floor as she watched him deposit what appeared to be a particularly heavy crate.

Wynn could not help wondering if the crate was, indeed, heavy—or if the evidence of strain on Michael's face was a tension of the nerves and not of the muscles. It pleased her to think she might be causing him as much anxiety as he was causing her.

She watched him for awhile, waiting for him to continue, to offer her either a flat refusal or information about residential property in Jennings. As one silent minute bled into another, she felt her muscles grow tense. She wanted some answers—*needed* some answers, and she needed them now.

At long last, Michael stopped moving boxes around and stepped back to assess the effectiveness of his arrangement. Thinking he had, finally, completed his task and would now answer her questions, Wynn breathed a sigh of relief.

Her sigh was short-lived. Michael backed into Wynn, setting his heavy boot heel down hard on her big toe.

"Ouch!" she exclaimed breathlessly.

He took one step forward and whirled on her. "Are you still here?"

She tried to remain calm, but her dogged determination seemed to have no effect on the throbbing in her big toe. Swallowing the harsh words she wanted to fling at him, she hobbled over to a low stack of crates and sat down on the top one.

Michael watched her haul herself up on the stack, noticed how her feet dangled a good twelve inches from the floor. How had he failed to see how short she was? He watched her pull her right foot onto her lap, noticed how shapely her black-stockinged calves swelled above her high, buttoned boots. How had he ever allowed such a tiny person to reduce him to immobility? He watched her rub the toe of the black leather boot between her thumb and forefinger, noticed how the lace-edged ruffles of her petticoat frothed white against her black stockings. And he felt his own big toe begin to throb.

That wasn't the only part of his woman-starved body that responded to her. He felt an unexpected warmth surge through him and his eyelids dropped to half-mast. He took a tentative step toward her, intending to take her boot in his large hands and gently massage away the pain he had caused. But the bristle in her voice stopped him.

"Where did you think I would have gone?"

"Away," he mumbled, frowning suddenly and turning his back to her. "I have work to do. What else do you want from me?"

Her rejoinder came quickly, sharply, her words

like stinging darts hurled at his back. "You don't have to snap at me! I wouldn't be here if you didn't own everything in this town. But if my timing is off, perhaps you could direct me to your personal secretary so I can make an appointment to suit your convenience. Or, better still, you could lighten my load a great deal by giving me the name of your agent."

He felt his jaw clench in reaction to her barbed attack. Personal secretary? Humph! Agent? Humph! He was certain she knew he had neither in his employ. He was also certain of her meaning: she would rather deal with someone else. Well, he would lighten her load, if that was what she wanted. He'd send her to Cary—and good riddance!

He turned on his heel and headed briskly for the door, not breaking his stride as he twisted his head around and called over his shoulder, "All my lots are strictly commercial. The man you need to see is S. L. Cary. He arrived on last night's train. You ought to find him at the hotel. Perkins will introduce you."

She sat on the crate and stared at the empty doorway for some time, thinking about the enigma that was Michael Donovan. Never had anyone intrigued and infuriated her quite so much as he.

Chapter Four

Wynn bought a lot from Cary, the railroad land agent, who had taken out a patent adjoining Michael's on the north. While she was waiting for her house to be built, she organized a clean-up crew at the hotel. Since he had allowed her to clean the Masons' room, it didn't occur to her to ask Michael for permission — not until he stormed into the lobby and pulled her unceremoniously out onto the porch.

"Just what do you think you're doing?" he demanded.

Wynn quelled the shaking in her knees. She wasn't about to let him see that he scared her half to death. Her near-whisper contrasted sharply with his booming voice. "Why did I assume you wanted a private word with me?"

"I do! And why do you answer all my questions with questions? Do you know how frustrating that little habit of yours is?"

"I don't have to defend myself to you, Mr. Donovan."

"This isn't your property, Dr. Spencer."

"Obviously. If it were my property, it would be sanitary. You ought to be pleased that we're cleaning it up for you — free of charge."

"Pleased? Hell, you'll run all my customers off! It smells like a damned hospital in there!"

"Do tell me, Mr. Donovan," Wynn crooned, finding it increasingly easier to combat his hostility with sweetness, "where you think everyone would go. This is the only hotel in town."

"At the present," he conceded, his words losing some of their tartness.

"And in the future, people will know that your hotel is the cleanest one in Jennings. Why wouldn't they want to stay there?"

"No one likes the smell of disinfectant, Dr. Spencer."

"Then you'd better go tell that to all those people who are disinfecting your hotel right now. They must not know they don't like it."

"Hell!" he muttered, lifting his open palms skyward. "Do what you want, Dr. Spencer—but don't you *even think* you're going to clean up my house. I'll pack you up and put you on the next train if you so much as set foot in it. I swear I will!"

Dadburn it! What was wrong with him anyway?

Michael paced the length of his porch. His heavy, booted footfalls struck the boards so hard they jarred his teeth. Something needed to jar him, he silently averred. Something needed to bring him to his senses.

He hadn't known any peace of mind since the night the train had brought that female doctor into town and she had sashayed herself into his house and called him a yokel. No one had ever dared call him, Michael Donovan, any name other than his own. He discounted Doc calling him boy all the

70

time. Doc was just a lonely old coot who didn't give a tinker's damn what happened to him.

But to have a half-pint female call him a yokel — why, that was humiliating! And what she'd done to him in the barn was, well, outrageous. Then, as if those two things weren't bad enough in themselves, her further declaration that she was a doctor was — especially in light of his not only thinking, but actually calling her a strumpet. Well, not in so many words, but they both knew what he meant.

The real rub, though, came from his near admiration of her. Michael found it hard to believe he could hold any admiration — even a potential speck — for a doctor, let alone a female doctor named Spencer. Every time he said her name, he cringed inside. For some reason, the name Spencer bothered him. He wished he understood why.

And every time he cringed, he saw her eyes. Damn those eyes to hell and gone! So crystal clear you could see yourself in them — just like a mirror. He liked them best when she was angry and they flashed icy sparks. Lord, but that woman could get mad! Most days, she burned with righteous indignation. Most times, she had good reason . . . at least her arguments left him thinking she did.

He had to hand it to her. She had guts, standing up to him and telling him and everyone else whatever she had on her mind. She had decided to stay in Jennings, and nothing he did — or refused to do — seemed to daunt her. There was something downright intimidating about Wynnifred Spencer.

Not that he was intimidated. Not Michael Donovan. He just wanted her out from under his skin, out of his town, out of his life forever. Things had been rolling along just fine until she'd shown

71

up. They'd go back to normal if he could just rid himself of her.

There had to be a way to run her off without being too obvious about it. The people who were coming in liked her, and he harbored no great desire to alienate them with a public battle. Michael considered one course of action after another as he paced. He discounted every one until he asked, "What if Doc started practicing medicine again?"

People might like her as a person, but they didn't want her doctoring them. He knew they didn't. What self-respecting man would want a female doctor taking care of him?

He'd have to sober Doc up first, and then he'd make him feel guilty about not practicing when his services were so desperately needed.

Dadburn it! It just might work . . .

There was one important hitch Michael overlooked.

What if something happened to Doc?

Fear gripped Wynn's chest in a tight clinch.

She sat straight up in bed, her right hand splayed at her throat. Her head reeled and her ears rang from the rush of blood while her heart pounded, pounded against her breast.

It was the pounding that had awakened her from a deep sleep. As her head cleared, she realized it was not the pounding of her heart that had disturbed her rest, but rather that of a fist beating upon her door. She sighed in relief and willed the beating of her heart to subside.

The fist continued its abuse upon the portal, but its rhythm changed from constant to intermittent, allowing an insistent male voice to be heard in the time in between.

"I'm coming!" she called out, although she doubted her midnight caller could hear her husky voice above all the noise he was creating. "I might as well get used to this," she mumbled, hastily lighting a lamp and pulling on a dressing gown, "since I'm the only doctor in town."

What Wynn Spencer was having real difficulty adapting to was living alone, sleeping in a house all by herself — a new house, relatively isolated from the business district and with no close neighbors as yet.

Although she had participated in its design and construction, she had yet to fully acquaint herself with its layout and that of her meager furnishings in the mere week since she had moved in. Nor was she yet accustomed to its creaks and moans, or to the way the wind whistled through the caves. Night after night, sleep eluded her, but when she did finally succumb to weariness, she slept soundly, just as she had this night . . . before someone had begun the infernal pounding upon her door.

With lamp held aloft, she made her way down the stairs and unlatched the vibrating door, upon which the fist had never completely stopped pounding. Before she could open it, the pummeling fist struck the door, throwing it wide. Wynn hopped aside just in time to keep from being struck by the swinging panel. She found herself staring into the pale, drawn face of Michael Donovan.

"My God, woman!" he snarled, his voice rife with frustration. "Where have you been? I was about to break the door in." He shouldered his way across the threshold, giving her no opportunity to defend herself. "Where do you want him?"

Had he not carried a writhing Doc Nolan, whose moans resounded in the silent house, Wynn would have ordered him away. She had purposely avoided him—and managed to do so most of the time . . . a tricky feat considering how small Jennings was.

But in the two months she had been in town, she had cultivated a number of friendships, Doc Nolan's among them. The very thought of anything being seriously wrong with Doc momentarily took precedence over her animosity toward Michael. She hastened to close the door against the biting wind and waved an arm toward the back of the house.

"What happened?" she asked.

"The fool shot himself."

"It was an accident!" Doc protested.

Wynn ignored him. "Where?"

"In the leg. He's losing a lot of blood."

Doc was close to hysteria. "I'll lose a lot more if you let her cut on me! Leave me be!"

"Save your breath, old man," Michael muttered gently.

Wynn led him to a room that would, in any other house, have been a back parlor; it was where she had set up an examination room. As she scurried to light another lamp, Michael laid Doc on the sheet-draped table in the center of the room.

"Leave me be, I said!" Doc groaned, trying to fight Michael, who held his arms down on the table. Doc tried to kick him, then bellowed as pain shot down his leg.

"You're going to have to knock him out, Dr. Spencer. He won't be still and he won't shut up."

"I know what to do," Wynn muttered, handing Michael a pair of scissors. "Doc, be still! Now! Mr. Donovan, cut his pants leg off and hold a pad

74

against that wound while I light the overhead fixture and wash my hands."

Michael marveled at the calm authority in her voice and did as she bade. But when he started to leave the room, she stopped him short.

"Just where do you think you're going?"

"To wait in the parlor."

"Oh, no, you're not! You're going to have to help me, Mr. Donovan."

"The hell I am! I don't know *anything* about medicine." *And the sight of blood makes me nauseous,* he mentally added. He wasn't about to let her know that, though. She'd think he was a sissy.

"So much the better."

He shot her a dubious look as he hesitated in the doorway. With all his heart, he wished there were another doctor in town. Why did the old man have to go and shoot himself, anyway?

"I won't have to argue with you about the way I do things if you don't know any different," she explained, her voice tight with a combination of concern for Doc and irritation at Michael's attitude. "Besides, you're going to have to answer some questions about the way this happened. Now, wash your hands and rinse them with the antiseptic . . . and hurry! We need to get the bullet out."

Michael stomped to the basin, his demeanor bespeaking his rebellion against her orders.

"No, we don't," he argued, his voice menacingly soft. Wynn had to strain to hear him over Doc's moaning.

"And why not?" she asked.

"It's not in there. It went straight through."

She removed the pad Michael had left on Doc's leg, then raised his knee to get a better look at the

75

wound. The bullet had entered the top of the fleshy inner side of his left thigh and exited out the back, just as Donovan had said, but Doc had not lost as much blood as Michael thought he had. She pressed two clean cotton pads against each of the wounds to stanch the bleeding. Doc thrashed around on the table so much while she examined his leg, Wynn feared he would roll off.

"We're going to have to sedate him while I clean out this wound."

Michael still hesitated. He wanted no part of doctoring. "If you're going to clean it out yourself, why do you need me?"

What kind of dolt was this man? she wondered, becoming more irritated by the second.

"Just get over here!" she snapped, positioning a cone-shaped mask made of stiffened white cotton over Doc's nose and mouth. With her free hand, she held a can of chloroform a few inches above the mask and let the anesthesia drip one drop at a time onto the point of the cone. Doc began to settle down almost immediately. "We'll need a watch with a second hand," she said to Michael. "Are you wearing one?"

"No."

"Then take one of the lamps and get mine off my bureau upstairs while I put him under."

It seemed to Wynn that he was gone for a long time. Doc appeared to be sleeping peacefully by the time Michael returned to the examination room. In his hand he held the crocheted pouch containing her watch.

"Good job, Doc!" he said.

"Doc didn't do anything. Why are you congratulating him?"

76

"I'm not." He sounded wounded from her rebuff. "I meant you."

"You can't call me 'Doc,' Mr. Donovan. It's too confusing. It's also too early for congratulations. I'm not even convinced he's out yet."

When Wynn had set the can of chloroform on a small stand next to the examination table and slipped the mask to one side, she picked up one of Doc's hands, then let it fall. It seemed limber enough, but Wynn was still not sure, so she pinched the back of his hand. Doc let out a diluted yelp.

Back went the mask and the drops of anesthesia. "Calm down, Doc," Wynn soothed. "I do know what I'm doing. You were smart enough not to hit anything vital. I think you'll live."

After a moment, she slid the mask aside again and checked Doc's pulse against her watch. She pinched his hand again, nodded in satisfaction, and turned to Michael. "You'll have to take over here."

What she was doing seemed simple enough — and he wouldn't be near Doc's bloody leg. He'd do it — for Doc. "What do I do?"

Wynn smiled at his sudden change in attitude. "Repeat what I just did over and over. Position the cone, administer a few drops of the chloroform, ventilate by sliding the mask over, check his pulse against my watch, and tell me if it drops below sixty. Replace the cone and start over. Be sure to ventilate him well. Chloroform is poisonous. Understand?"

Michael picked up the cone and nodded.

As she gave instructions, Wynn cleaned the entry wound with a piece of cotton she had doused with antiseptic. "Tell me how this happened."

"You know Doc, full of bluster but totally harmless. He was waving that blasted pistol he totes, threatening to shoot me if I didn't let him have more whiskey. I've been doling it out to him lately, trying to get him to slow down. Drinking so much is killing him. Anyway, that gun is never loaded; he just uses it as a prop. Why it was loaded tonight is a puzzle to me. I don't even know when he cleaned it last."

"So the barrel was dirty. I needed to know that."

"Why?"

"Residue from the barrel will be in the wound. It will have to be thoroughly cleaned out." Wynn soaked a piece of cotton in an antiseptic solution, then removed a pair of forceps from a flask half-filled with antiseptic and attached the cotton to the end of the instrument. She began to swab out the wound. "So he was waving this gun that wasn't supposed to be loaded, and then what happened?"

Damn her questions anyway! Didn't she know he felt guilty as hell about this? If he just hadn't been so stubborn about the whiskey! Michael let go of the cone mask and slammed the can of chloroform down on the instrument table. "Now hold on, Doc. If you think I was responsible—"

"Please don't fall into the habit of calling me 'Doc,' Mr. Donovan. And there's no reason for you to be so defensive. Of course, I don't think you shot him. I just want to know how this happened."

Why couldn't he, for once, cooperate? she wondered.

"Pardon me, *Dr.* Spencer!"

"You're going to have to pay attention to what you're doing, Mr. Donovan, or you'll asphyxiate him with that chloroform."

"Not when the can's sitting on the table!"

"Then he'll come to."

"I'm not sure which would be worse."

"The point is, Mr. Donovan, that if you will just do what I told you to do, we won't have to deal with either problem. Have you checked his pulse yet?"

"I'm doing that now."

"So what happened?"

Michael sighed. He didn't answer her immediately. How did she think he could count and talk at the same time? Damn, but she was one exasperating female! She'd made him lose count and he had to start over. If anyone else had been lying there except Doc Nolan, Michael would have left right then. But it was Doc, and the old man was depending on him.

Finally, he said, "He was sitting in a chair, waving his pistol and hollering at me. He had cocked it, but he didn't even have his finger on the trigger. Then the pistol slipped out of his hand and when he grabbed at it, it fired. The bullet went clean through his leg and lodged in the chair seat."

Wynn changed the cotton on the forceps and bent back over Doc's thigh, her attention seemingly focused on swabbing out the wound. Michael realized quickly, however, that she was fully aware of what he was doing. "Ventilate," she ordered, "then check his pulse again."

"I remember the routine!"

"What kind of chair?"

"What do you mean?"

"Upholstered or wood?"

"Wood."

"Then I'll have to check for splinters in the exit wound. There were threads from his trousers on this side, but I think I got them all."

She poured antiseptic into the wound from the top side. Doc jerked. "He can feel that. Give him a few extra drops this time before you ventilate. I want him

79

completely under. You're going to have to help me turn him over so I can get to the back of his leg."

"How can I use the cone upside down?"

"You can't. You'll have to switch to a cotton pad. Douse it with chloroform and hold it over his nose for four seconds; ventilate for two seconds. But help me turn him first."

With Doc lying on his stomach, Wynn used a pair of sterilized tweezers to remove myriad tiny splinters from the back of his leg.

"How long before he'll be back on his feet?" Michael asked.

"If he behaves himself, a couple of days—but on crutches. Do you think Slim can make him a pair?"

"I'll ask him first thing tomorrow morning."

"Better ask him first thing *this* morning, Mr. Donovan."

"You know that's what I meant. What time is it, anyway?"

"You've got the watch."

"Almost one."

For a moment silence reigned. Michael looked up from Doc's partially bald head and cast his gaze upon Wynn's glossy brown hair, which hung in twin braids down her back. The rusty burnish of auburn highlights glistened in the golden lamplight. How could he have ever thought the color was mousy? Her concentration provided Michael the opportunity to scrutinize her face without Wynn's seeing him, and for the first time, Michael allowed himself to look at her without the stigmas of lust or scorn blurring his vision.

He noted the pearly essence of her upper teeth, which she held tightly against her lower lip as she focused on bandaging Doc's leg. He noted the fan of her dark eyelashes hovering above the ivory complexion of her face, the perfection of her short, slender nose, the prominence of her cheekbones. He observed the slim column of her neck, saw the pulse beating at the base of her throat, just above the high neckline of a simple cotton nightdress. He let his gaze travel farther to rest upon the proud thrust of small breasts straining against the stricture of a tightly wrapped dressing robe. And the shock of his reaction to her femininity, to his acknowledgment of the existence of Wynn Spencer—woman, jolted him with electrifying intensity.

She finished tying the bandage, but when he thought she would finally look up at him and allow him to gaze into the startling paleness of her eyes, eyes that haunted his every waking moment, she busied herself with cleaning her surgical instruments.

"I don't think it's wise to move him very far just yet. We'll put him to bed in here." She gestured with the forceps toward a narrow bed which had been set against the back wall of the room. Michael scooped Doc up and settled him into the bed. Wynn closed the top of the copper sterilizing pan and sighed wearily. "I don't know about you, but I could use a cup of tea."

"Could you make it coffee instead?"

"Sure. Just make yourself comfortable."

Getting a fire going in the cookstove, grinding the coffee beans, and heating the water took several minutes. It gave Wynn time to think about something besides Doc's injury, and that something was Michael Donovan.

One of the reasons she had so zealously avoided him was the way she felt when she was near him—weak-kneed and not quite in control.

She didn't know exactly when she had stopped being angry with him and started thinking of him as a warm-bodied human being instead of a cold-hearted villain.

More than likely, she reflected, it had begun with the lilac-scented laundry. Later, her opinion of him had risen when she learned from the homesteaders that it was S. L. Cary who had written and distributed the advertisements like the one she had seen in the Galena newspaper. Upon further inquiry, she had learned that neither Donovan nor Cary was actually guilty of fraud. Before the land agent had left Jennings in the fall, Michael had told him he was thinking about building a larger hotel. Cary had, quite naturally, thought Michael would follow through with his plans, but meanwhile Michael had decided to wait and see if Jennings actually needed another hotel. He had recently begun its construction.

Wynn wasn't quite sure why she had held her tongue when she had fully intended to lambast Michael Donovan, but in this instance she was glad she had. When Wynn Spencer was wrong, she said she was wrong. She was just thankful she didn't have to say it and watch Michael gloat.

She should still be angry, she supposed, over his treatment of her in the barn, but the more she thought about that particular afternoon, the more comical the memory became.

Thus, leniency had replaced anger, and with leniency had come that weak-kneed, out-of-control feeling.

But tonight she had maintained some semblance of command over her senses, had felt a sort of kinship with him while they had worked together over Doc. Maybe there was hope for them yet. They

82

might not ever be close friends, but at least they had demonstrated that they could tolerate each other.

While the coffee was dripping, Wynn looked in on Doc. His bandage was clear, his skin felt cool to the touch, and he was sleeping peacefully. Though she had no intention of returning to bed, she knew she should change into a daygown with Michael in the house. But Michael Donovan was nowhere in sight. Not wanting to disturb Doc, she called Michael's name softly as she tiptoed into the front parlor.

Except for the tick-ticking of the pendulum clock in the hall, the house was deathly quiet. She felt an odd combination of relief and disappointment that she was no longer required to entertain Michael Donovan, who had obviously decided to go back home.

For a moment, Wynn stood in the doorway and admired her parlor, then expanded her admiration to include the entire house. It was bigger than she really needed, but she liked its simple, functional floor plan. The front door opened into a wide center hall which housed the staircase. The hall served as an office and waiting room; she had put her new roll-top desk and barrister's cabinet there, and when the medicines she had ordered came in, she would run a small dispensary out of the hall. On the left were the two parlors; on the right were the dining room and the kitchen.

When she had ordered the desk and cabinet, Wynn had also ordered a small camelback sofa and matching chair, upholstered in dark green velvet, and a round cherry lamp table for the parlor. She had yet to furnish the dining room. For the time being, she decided, she could eat her meals at the enamel-topped work table in the kitchen. Upstairs were two dormer bedrooms, but only hers held any furniture.

Since transporting her furniture and then storing it until she could build a house would have cost more than it was worth, Wynn had sold all the large pieces along with the house in Galena. The sale had brought enough money to see her comfortably settled in Jennings, but Wynn felt a bit shaky about her financial future. She could see no point in buying anything she didn't absolutely need and couldn't put to practical use on a daily basis just to fill up a house.

Pale light from the solitary lamp she had left burning in the examination room spilled into the front parlor through the connecting doorway, but it failed to illuminate most of the room. Wynn considered retrieving the lamp, then thought better of it. The cool darkness beckoned to her, offering a moment of respite as Doc slept and the coffee dripped. Taking care of him would demand much of her time and energy for the next couple of days. She would rest while she could.

Wynn stifled a yawn as her slippered feet padded across the bare wooden floor toward the dark bulk of the sofa. Maybe instead of sitting on the plump couch, she would lie down on it for a few minutes. A catnap wouldn't hurt, and she'd be close enough to Doc to hear him if he needed her.

With that purpose in mind, and suddenly much wearier than she had realized, Wynn sank into the plush seat. Her backside hit something hard, but when she tried to move, strong arms encircled her waist and pulled her down against the hardness of a masculine chest.

Wynn gasped and struggled to right herself, but her efforts won her nothing more than a low chuckle from Michael Donovan.

"How soft you are," he murmured, sounding only half-awake, the low baritone of his voice mellow and seductive in her ear. The flat of one hand slid up her back to rest upon the ends of her braids while the other hand held her firmly at her waistline.

"Let go of me!" she hissed, purposely keeping her voice low so as not to disturb Doc. She fought harder, determined to loosen his grasp and win her freedom.

"Never." His lips nuzzled her neck while his fingers loosened the ribbon holding her braids together. Wynn had disturbed a delightful dream, and Michael was not quite ready to let go of its enchantment. He reacted to her nearness, to the accessibility of her woman's body, with his libido—not with conscious thought.

"I'll scream," she threatened, twisting in an effort to loosen his hold, her protests and movements fanning the flames of his ardor rather than dousing them.

"And who will hear?"

His question, spoken with such casual aplomb, gave her pause, gave him the opportunity to claim her lips with his own. Could these lips belong to the same man who had kissed her in the barn? Those lips had been hard and cruel; these were soft and sweet and seemed bent on tutoring her in the art of kissing.

Warmth seeped into her, settling in the nether regions of her abdomen, and she ceased fighting him. His fingers continued their labor upon her braids, releasing the intertwined locks, combing them out in long, sensual strokes while his lips bade hers to kiss him back. When she pulled her mouth away, gasping for air and trying to regain her tenuous hold on sanity, his mouth reached upward to restake his claim.

The act of kissing was not new to Wynn, but the havoc Michael's mouth was wreaking on her senses was. Never had any man kissed her so gently, so skillfully, so tenderly. Never had she felt so beguiled, so bewitched. Never had Wynn responded aggressively to a kiss, but, seemingly of its own volition, her mouth kissed him back. Her jaw relaxed, her lips moved with his. She shuddered slightly, as much from the thought of who she was kissing as from the sensations that kiss was creating.

His mustache brushed the tip of her nose and a deep sigh escaped his parted lips. His fingers completed their work upon her braids. They drove into the burnished cascade just above her ear and held the heavy strands at bay while his lips left hers momentarily to blaze a fiery trail across her cheek. He nibbled her earlobe, and when the tip of his tongue dipped into the cavity of her ear, a flurry of tingles rippled through her.

He felt her shiver, knew the powerful effect of his caresses—an effect he felt as well. He breathed deeply, inhaling the sweet essence of her. Lilacs. She smelled like lilacs. He groaned, assaulted her mouth with his, his tongue probing, plunging, teasing hers into a mating partnership. She tasted as sweet as she smelled.

Her response, timid at first but growing bolder with each stroke of his tongue, quickened his pulse, fed his hunger, demanded more. His hand on her head pulled her mouth harder into his. His other hand left her midsection and slid up her side and over the firm globe of her breast. The hard nib beneath his palm bore testimony to her heightened sexuality. Suddenly, he wanted to touch her all over, to tear away the stricture of her nightwear, to feel her bare flesh beneath his hands, against his own nakedness. Never had Michael Donovan lusted so for a woman.

It was the manifestation of her own lust that brought Wynn to her senses. She groaned, wishing with all her heart she didn't have to tear herself away. He'd treated her once like a common harlot. If she didn't stop him now, she'd prove him right.

She pushed hard against him and he released her. Self-consciously, she sat up and pulled the lapels of her robe across her tingling breasts. Whatever would she say to him now? How could she serve him coffee, face him across her kitchen table?

She sat trembling, uncertain of what to say, what to do next. She fought for composure, for a facade of nonchalance.

Michael lay trembling, desperately wanting to pull her back into his arms, to kiss her senseless, to lose himself again in the sweet softness of her. And she wanted it, too. He knew she did. She had responded to him with far more passion than he had imagined her capable of demonstrating. He had to concede, though, to poor timing.

He raked a hand through his unruly hair and stood up. "I—I'm sorry, Wynn. I don't know what came over me. I'll go on back home now. Tell Doc I'll see him tomorrow."

She sat staring at the front window and didn't move, marginally listening to his boot treads across her floor, to the swish of the front door opening and the click of its closing behind him. Her heart pounded in her chest. A solitary tear rolled out of her eye. He had called her

Wynn. She called herself ten kinds of fool.

Jonathan Matheson was the most charmingly handsome man Wynn had ever met. Never would she forget the day she had opened the door to find him standing on their stoop.

Although three years had passed since that day, its memory dawned as fresh as if it had been the previous week. Wynn had recently returned home from medical school, proud of her new diploma and eager to spend a few months working side-by-side with her father before leaving again, this time for St. Luke's Hospital in St. Paul.

The moment he saw her, he swept his hat from his head and held it against his chest, exposing a shock of silvery blond hair so carefully tended she could not help wondering if he had come straight from the barber's. His mouth had spread in a wide, friendly smile, exposing even white teeth. And his gray eyes shone with a clear, direct intensity.

"Good morning, ma'am," he had said, his voice liquid honey. "Is the doctor in?"

"Yes, I am," she had mechanically replied, her attention centered on the perfection of his chiseled lips.

"Pardon?"

"I'm Dr. Spencer."

"Dr. *Wallace* Spencer?"

She shook herself from his spell. "No, Dr. Wynnifred Spencer, his daughter. My father is also home. I'll call him." Then, remembering her manners, she had opened the door wider and invited him in.

Over and over, she had replayed that scene in her mind. If she had to remember Jonathan — and she couldn't seem to forget him—she'd rather it was from the perspective of her first impression, not from that of the heartache he had later plunged her into.

But the memories of that heartache came flooding back now. Michael's touch—no, she realized, her response to his touch—had revived them. She had vowed never to allow a man to affect her that way again. She wasn't about to recant that vow now. Besides, she argued, she wasn't in love with Michael. She couldn't be . . . now or ever. To be in love required having a heart to give.

She'd left hers in Galena.

Chapter Five

"Does it ever stop raining here?"

Wynn knew Doc heard her softly spoken question but he didn't answer—maybe because he didn't think she honestly expected an answer, maybe because he realized her question didn't have much at all to do with the steady downpour. Which it didn't. The downpour outside and the one flooding her heart bore no resemblance to each other.

Wynn was amazed at the depth of his perception. She found their fast friendship even more amazing. Never would she have believed that she would claim as friend a man who was nothing more than an old drunk—a man whose propensity for impudence increased with the degree of his inebriation. The funny thing about it was that somehow Doc reminded her of her father. She had discovered there was no way to reason that one out, so she just accepted it.

She stood at one of the windows in the front parlor, her gaze almost transfixed on the runnels of water coursing down the glass as she silently questioned the wisdom of her decision to come to Jennings, of planning to stay and live out her father's dream. Wynn didn't know what her own dream was anymore; she wasn't at all sure she'd ever had one.

"It was Papa's idea to come here," she said, only marginally aware that she had verbalized her reflection.

Doc thought he detected a catch in her voice, but it was so naturally husky he couldn't be sure. He wished she would relax just a little bit. Her back was ramrod straight, her shoulders square, her hands closed in tight fists and pressed against her thighs. One hand held a plain, white linen handkerchief, but she had yet to use it.

Doc couldn't figure out what had happened to cause her distress. He could have understood her attitude if he had died; if anyone knew what guilt could do to a person, especially a physician who'd lost a patient, he did. But he hadn't died — probably wouldn't have even if he'd had to rely solely on Michael for medical attention. Of course, he reasoned, he might not be able to get around so well. Wynn was a competent doctor, though; her treatment of him had proved that.

He had never known anyone quite like her, anyone quite so energetic, so full of hope and determination. Before he'd shot himself, he'd watched her closely and come to admire her, though grudgingly. But ever since he had awakened in her examining room the morning after he shot himself, she'd acted strangely aloof. The tension she was feeling was far more obvious than he figured she meant for it to be.

"Tell me about your father," he prompted, hoping to get her talking about her family and her life before she had come to Jennings, hoping it would relieve some of her distress.

She answered him, but in a voice that was flat and dull. "He'd been here before, during the war. That was over twenty years ago, and all that time, Papa wanted to come back here."

Doc waited patiently for her to continue, but after several minutes passed and she said nothing more, he nudged her. "Why did he wait so long?"

"Papa was the only doctor in town. He had left his patients during the war; he refused to leave them again without a replacement. He said he had been unavailable once, before I was born, and two people had died because he wasn't there to care for them. Papa carried that guilt to the grave."

Wynn's voice caught in her throat and it was a moment before she could continue. Her pause stretched out too long, giving Doc's own guilt and grief time to rear their heads. He wriggled uncomfortably on the sofa. More than anything else, he wanted a drink — a long swallow of eighty-proof, straight, with more in the bottle. The constriction in his throat eased a little bit when she resumed her story.

"So, first he waited for another physician to move to Galena, and then he waited for Mama to die." She raised the hanky and blew her nose.

Doc breathed a sigh of relief. *That's it, Wynn. Cry!* If any woman ever needed to cry — really cry, as in deep, heart-cleansing sobs, he thought Wynn Spencer did.

But she didn't cry. She took a deep breath instead. "I know that sounds callous. I didn't mean it that way. Papa loved Mama with all his heart. If he hadn't loved her so much, he would have packed us up and moved here a long time ago, but he knew Mama wouldn't be able to withstand the summers. Papa always said he couldn't explain his need to leave Galena; it was the only home he had ever known. But there was something about this wild prairie that called to him, he said, that haunted him all those years. And then, when he could have come, his own death snatched away the realization of that dream."

She turned away from the window and sat down on the edge of the green velvet chair. "Papa's regiment," she explained, "along with many another from the Midwest, was largely centered in attacks down the Mississippi to cut the Confederate lifeline. While Papa was under General Banks' command during the Red River campaign, he traveled across this vast prairie."

She paused for a moment, her eyes downcast, her hands twisting and turning the handkerchief in her lap, her upper teeth worrying her lower lip. "He never talked about the war, never talked about this prairie until long after Mama died. I was still in nappies when Papa went off to serve in the medical corps, still a small child when the war was over. Although Mama had talked about him and read his letters aloud, he was like a stranger to me when he came home. Maybe more an intruder, I suppose. Mama's sickness struck while he was gone, and I thought of myself as her caretaker, her protector."

"And your father usurped that position. What was wrong with her?" Doc asked quietly.

Wynn had learned that he could speak quite intelligently when he wanted to. It made her wonder how much of the Doc she knew was a facade.

Wynn shrugged. "Papa thought it might have something to do with her thyroid, but he was never sure. She was extremely nervous, perspired profusely, suffered from insomnia, and could not tolerate heat."

"She must have been hell to live with," Doc observed.

"She was, toward the end," Wynn said candidly. "It must have been much worse for her all along than it ever was for us. Mama seldom complained

93

about anything—even when I would ruin supper or Papa would be away all night delivering a baby. Papa was the one who was so hard to live with. He tried so desperately to help her, to discover what had caused her illness. He wrote to doctors all over the country and took her to a surgeon in New York once, a man Papa had met during the war. Everyone told him something different. Papa tried every suggested cure. Nothing helped. Sometimes Papa would catch me studying his medical books and he'd say, 'Find me an answer, daughter.' But I never did."

"Is that why you became a doctor?"

"Partially." Wynn stood up and walked back to the window. "Who am I trying to fool?" She snorted in derision. "Myself, I suppose. Yes, that's why. Medicine was all I ever knew. As a four- or five-year-old child, I was taking care of Mama. She used to call me her 'fierce little guardian' because I was so protective. When I learned to read well enough, I consumed every medical textbook and journal I could find. There had to be an answer somewhere, I thought. Later, I assisted Papa in his practice so long as the patient came to him. I wouldn't leave Mama home by herself. By that time, she was requiring almost constant care. She was ravenously hungry all the time, but no matter how much she ate, her body was unable to sustain any weight. She grew thinner and thinner. And I watched her waste away . . ."

"What happened to your father?"

"I think he must have lost all reason to live after Mama died; I just didn't realize it then. I went away to school, and when I was home, I ran the dispensary and saw patients in town while Papa made his usual rounds in the country. Another doctor finally moved to Galena, a Dr. Matheson." Wynn paused long enough to blow her nose again. "Papa took the new doctor with him on his rounds, to introduce him to all his patients. As soon as I finished school, Papa said, we'd move here and leave the doctoring in Galena to Dr. Matheson."

That hadn't been *her* plan, but she didn't see any reason to expound on that aspect of her story. It was a moot point now anyway.

"But you came by yourself. What happened to your father?"

"A simple case of pneumonia. I wasn't even there when he died. I was at a training hospital in St. Paul. They sent me a telegram."

"That must have been very painful for you."

"The only three people I have ever loved have left me," she whispered hoarsely.

Doc was stone sober. He had been since before the night he had shot himself. He knew he had heard her say *three* people, not two. He wanted to ask her about the third person, but he didn't. When she was ready, she would tell him. She turned her back to him again, her gaze transfixed on the streaming raindrops.

For a long time, silence reigned — the silence of pelting rain and distant thunder, the silence of a ticking clock and the absence of human voice. At long last Wynn turned away from the window and sighed a long, whispery breath.

"I'm ready for a cup of coffee," she said. "How about you?"

Men! What earthly use were they, anyway?

Wynn worked the pump at her sink with every ounce of strength she could muster, then slammed the filled kettle down on top of the cast iron stove.

Oh, she supposed she'd need a man if she ever de-

95

cided to become a mother. That was the one thing she figured she'd never manage by herself. But otherwise? She'd manage without one, thank you very much.

The spring latch on the top of her coffee canister wouldn't pop loose, and she smacked it against the edge of the stove, not caring that she bent the wire clamp in the process or that she broke a fingernail forcing it open. She dumped coffee beans into the grinder, fought with the lid like one attempting to fit a square peg into a round hole, and then turned the crank with a vengeance.

Why couldn't all men be like Doc? Like her father had been? Just companions. That was all she wanted—someone to talk to from time to time, someone to comfort her when she didn't feel well, someone to hear her laughter when she rejoiced. But was that enough? She tried to imagine spending the remainder of her days with Doc or someone else like him, and found the concept lacking.

Lacking what? Love? What was love to men, outside of physical release? Hadn't her relationship with Jonathan taught her that? Hadn't Michael Donovan reminded her with his pawing that he was interested in the sexual act and nothing else? Hadn't she, for a few moments, relished his touch and wanted more?

Unbidden desire seeped into her belly and spread slowly outward, making her breasts ache and her inner thighs tingle, making her so suddenly weak she had to sit down.

Wynn leaned on her elbows and raked shaky fingers through her hair, unconsciously loosening a strand from its plait and twisting its length around her forefinger, her heart filled with a combination of despair and self-loathing.

Coming to Jennings had been a grave mistake. She

should have gone somewhere else—anywhere else. She had fled one heartache and managed to run headlong into what promised to be another.

How dare she think such a thing? she mentally chastised herself. She, Wynnifred Hughes Spencer, was no coward! She'd fought her way through a predominantly male-staffed, male-attended, male-oriented medical school, and graduated with honors. She'd combatted sexual prejudice and overcome obstacles most men would have run from like a rabbit fleeing a prairie fire. She herself had run—once. She wasn't running again.

Michael Donovan would learn that he had a formidable opponent in Wynn Spencer.

Michael Donovan stood on Wynn's front porch, his oilcloth slicker dripping water on the freshly painted boards, his fist poised to strike the portal. He'd avoided her house for three days, manufacturing one excuse after another until he'd run out, except for the rain, which was a damned poor excuse if ever there was one.

By avoiding her house, he was avoiding her, and he knew it. At least a part of him did. He'd thought to allow himself time to forget how she'd affected him, time for her to forget—and maybe forgive—his thoughtless, poorly timed kiss. But he couldn't forget; could Wynn?

No matter how hard he tried, he couldn't forget. A breeze wafting upon his lips bespoke the softness of hers. The raspy song of a brown thrasher perched in one of the depot oaks seemed to mimic her husky voice. A break in the hovering clouds, exposing a clear patch of pale blue winter sky, imitated the crystalline depths of her eyes, eyes as deep and eternal as the sky . . . but far more vibrant.

Whatever would he say to her? He delved into his memory for the apologetic phrases he had so carefully devised, not quite managing to retrieve them.

He had been crazy to think she was attractive in the first place, crazy to kiss her, crazy to let her get under his skin. He'd always stuck by one hard and fast rule where women were concerned: no emotional entanglements. Involving his heart was entirely too risky. All it could bring was pain. Hadn't life taught him that? It wouldn't happen again.

It couldn't happen again if she weren't there. In the face of his failure to sober Doc up, Michael had already launched another plan to rid himself—and the town—of this uppity Illinois woman who claimed to be a doctor. Doctors be damned, anyway. Jennings might have to have one, but he ought to be a man. S. L. Cary had promised him, just this morning, that he would see what he could do about recruiting one.

Michael harbored no doubts that Cary would succeed. Hadn't the Iowan already brought in droves of settlers from the Midwest? The owners of the Southern Pacific had to be pleased with their recruiter. Michael certainly was. Cary's results were making him a rich man.

Not that Cary wasn't benefitting, too. He had secured a 160-acre land grant adjoining Michael's on the north and was selling residential lots out of it almost as fast as the surveyors could mark them off. Wynn had bought her lot from him, and soon other houses would be going up near hers. It was easy to pick out the individual lots by the fruit trees, for Cary had planted one on each parcel. Wynn's was a fig.

The two major landholders should have been ri-

vals, but their different interests served as comple
ments instead: Michael concentrated on developing
the business section; Cary, the residential.

Yes, there was no doubt Cary would come through
for him. The Iowan was as displeased as Michael
that the only doctor in town was a woman. No self-
respecting man would ever let her attend him—unless
he had been forced into it, as Michael had forced
Doc.

Michael felt guilty as hell about leaving Doc with
Wynn Spencer, even if he hadn't had much of a
choice. Slim had given him a report after he delivered the crutches, but Michael had to see Doc himself; he had to know that the old man was all right,
even if that meant having to see Wynn Spencer
again.

He couldn't believe it when Doc answered the
door. The old man stood there on his crutches for a
minute, narrowed eyes assessing his visitor. "Well!"
he snorted. "It took you long enough to show up
here. I was beginning to think you'd deserted me."

"You know better than that, Doc. I've been busy."

"And you haven't missed me at all, have you?"

"Sure, Doc! I've missed your snoring and your
swearing and your disagreeable ways something awful!" Michael meant his words teasingly, but they
came out sounding petulant.

"Then I don't suppose you'd be interested in sharing a pot of coffee with a cantankerous old man."

Michael could think of a whole slew of things he'd
rather do than step foot in Wynn Spencer's house
again, but he couldn't see her anywhere in the hall.
His desperation snagged a possibility: maybe she was
out. Besides, he owed it to Doc. He doffed his hat,
then shrugged the slicker off his shoulders and
draped it over the porch railing.

Doc Nolan hopped out of Michael's way and the younger man followed him to the end of the hall, then turned right into the kitchen.

There stood Wynn, her back to the hall, her glossy brown hair caught in a plaited coil at her nape. Her head was bent forward as she poured cups of steaming coffee, and Michael noted how wisps of soft down swirled on her arched neck below the bun. Her movements strained the seams of a plain, high-necked bodice, pulling it tight across her narrow shoulders. At her tiny waistline, the light gray handkerchief linen met shiny black silk faille, which had been fashioned into a pleated skirt.

Before he'd opened his store, Michael Donovan hadn't known anything about textiles, except that wool felt good in the wintertime and cotton in the summer. At first, he hadn't bothered with yard goods, but with families moving in, he had started stocking them. Thanks to Granny Simpson, whom he had hired to help out in the mercantile, he now could recognize more than a dozen types of fabric. He didn't know if he'd ever be able to look at handkerchief linen and silk faille again without thinking about how delightfully the two met at Wynn Spencer's tiny waistline.

Damn! He'd been a fool to come. He should have known she would be at home. Her being out hadn't been a likely prospect anyway. Only a fool would venture out in such a rainstorm. And that made him a fool twice over, he supposed. He tried to shake off her spell by assuming a nonchalant pose. He formed his mouth into an impervious grin, folded his arms across his ribs, and leaned into the doorjamb.

"Better make that three," Doc said, hobbling over to the enamel-topped table and easing himself into a ladder-back chair.

Wynn turned around and spied Michael standing in the doorway. In reaction, her mouth dropped open, and then she caught herself and snapped it shut. She had known he would come to see Doc eventually, but she had not expected him to come this afternoon, not in the pouring rain. How could he be so casual, she wondered, after what he had done to her just three nights ago? She felt her eyes grow hard and her spine grow stiff as the memories flooded back.

"Doc invited me in for coffee, but if there isn't enough . . ." He pushed himself away from the facing, letting his voice slide off while he cut his eyes toward the front door.

She perceived his game, but she wasn't about to let him weasel out of a visit with Doc, even if she didn't want to see him herself. Almost everyone in town had come by to check on Doc the past two days—everyone except Michael, who was the only one Doc Nolan truly cared about seeing. But she couldn't very well excuse herself; that would make her look like a coward, it would put Doc in an awkward position, and it would probably tickle the pants off Michael Donovan.

Well, she could be just as blasé as he! She indicated her disinterest with a dramatic shrug, then removed another cup and saucer from the cupboard and a spoon from the squatty earthenware crock which held her scanty supply of silverware.

"You can put that spoon back," Michael said as it clattered against the saucer. "I take mine black."

She gave him a swift, disbelieving look. How anyone could drink the vile, bitter beverage without the benefits of cream and sugar was beyond her, but she didn't argue with him. Wynn wondered why anything Michael Donovan did should surprise her anymore.

"I hope this coffee isn't green," Doc said while she transferred the filled cups to the table. "Green coffee gives me the runs."

"Watch your mouth, old man!" Michael admonished.

Wynn hid her smile behind a deliberate yawn and pretended not to have heard either of them as she stirred generous portions of cream and sugar into her coffee.

"You take a little coffee with your sugar and cream, huh?" Michael observed, his voice dry.

Doc knew he had to think of something fast before Michael and Wynn got into a full-blown argument. One way or another, he was going to help these two see that they were meant for each other, but first they had to stop fighting every time they were together. And they weren't together nearly often enough.

Doc had been hoping for something to happen that would bring them together. Though he wouldn't have purposely engineered it, he couldn't have planned a better opportunity than his injury had accidentally provided. Maybe the two of them would carry on a civilized conversation this time. He was there to play referee if he had to.

"How's the new hotel coming?" he asked.

"Thank goodness, we got the roof on yesterday," Michael replied, grimacing as he gulped a too-healthy swallow of the scalding black brew.

"How many rooms in this one?" Wynn asked.

All right, Doc thought. *Keep it rolling.* He wasn't disappointed . . . for a moment.

"Thirty."

"My, my, that big!"

"Won't be nearly enough to hold all those folks Cary says are coming from Iowa."

Wynn found herself wanting to know more. After all, she reasoned, she had a stake in the future of Jennings. At the least, Michael's news assured her she could sell her house if things didn't work out well for her. *But if I leave, I won't be running away from you. It will be because I was unable to establish a successful practice here.* "Then why aren't you building a larger hotel? Where will they all stay?"

"I'm trying to employ some good business sense. Most of them are just looking right now. Those who do decide to stay will have to go back to Iowa, or wherever they're from, and prepare for the move. When they come back, they'll build their own homes and they won't need a hotel anymore. What would I do with a larger one then?"

"Turn it into a hospital."

The words were out of Wynn's mouth before she gave the remark any thought. She was well aware of the prevailing attitude toward hospitals, an attitude female doctors and nurses were trying to combat. But there was something more in Michael's sharply spoken retort than a mere verbalization of society's judgment, something that bespoke a negative personal experience with medical institutions.

"This isn't Chicago, Dr. Spencer. Hospitals aren't for families. They're no better than almshouses or insane asylums—or a place to go when you're dying and no one cares. We have families moving in here. They may not be wealthy people, but they're decent, hardworking folks. They won't be interested in a hospital—just a good country doctor who cares enough about them to make his weekly rounds. One who'll go where he's needed, when he's needed."

Wynn was so outdone by his narrow vision she didn't even note his use of the male pronoun. "A hospital doesn't replace in-home care, Mr.

Donovan!" she spat defensively. "The purpose of a hospital is to provide readily available care in a sanitized environment while isolating contagion."

"All the hospitals I've ever seen were filthy," Michael argued, "and contagion ran rampant."

Doc decided it was time to play referee, and the best way to do that was to change the subject. He gave the new topic brisk deliberation. Who would have thought a question about Michael's new hotel would have evolved into an argument about hospitals? There was simply no way to know where these two would head with a topic—any topic, but it was worth a try.

"But we will need a school," Doc said.

Michael didn't seem to be quite ready to let go of the hospital argument. "Eventually."

"And a church," Doc added, determined to make Michael and Wynn switch tracks.

That recommendation brought a loud guffaw from Donovan. "*You,* of all people! Suggesting we need a church!"

Doc puffed out his chest in genuine offense. "And why not? There'll be babies to be christened and weddings to be performed—"

Thus, quite unintentionally, Doc became Michael's verbal adversary. Wynn sat back and listened to their bickering and, again, wondered what it was about Michael Donovan that seemed to bring out the worst in people. The man carried a chip on his shoulder, and it didn't take much from anyone to knock it off. She wasn't sure when she had seen a person so emotionally miserable.

His behavior brought to mind a lecture she had heard at medical school. According to the professor, a few European doctors were beginning to study the causes and treatment of emotional and mental dis-

104

turbances. It was from this lecture that she had learned the term for her own irrational fear of closed spaces: claustrophobia.

She wished she knew more about mental disturbances, wished one of the European doctors the professor mentioned was available to diagnose Michael Donovan. The more she knew of him, the more convinced she became that he was the victim of a deep-seated anxiety. The physician side of her soon grew weary from the labor of conjecture, however, as her woman's heart counseled her to remember the blow he had dealt her self-esteem.

Suddenly needing to put some space between herself and Michael, Wynn pushed back her chair. "Excuse me, gentlemen," she said, consciously keeping her voice even. "I have a crate of herbs to unpack."

It was a waste of breath. Neither of the men gave any outward sign of hearing her.

Michael Donovan had been far more serious than he let Doc believe when he told him he missed his snoring. He was experiencing true difficulty falling asleep without the accustomed loud snuffles to block out reflection.

He lay upon his solitary bed, the soft patter of raindrops upon the tin roof echoing the husky timbre of Wynn Spencer's voice. Behind the curtain of his eyelids fluttered visions of her face, of her tiny waist and the proud set of her shoulders. For the first time in his adult life, he wanted a woman who didn't seem to want him in return. He wanted her more than he had wanted a woman in a long time, maybe more than he had ever wanted a woman.

Never before had he looked at a woman as anything more than a means to an end. In his estimation, women and whiskey were good for only one thing: slaking a man's thirst. Once that had been accomplished, he could walk away and not look back.

Why would Wynn Spencer be any different, he pondered. He could walk away from her. Couldn't he? He wanted her because she was a woman, not because there was anything special about her. Hell, she was a doctor! And he hated her for being one. All he needed was to bed her once and then everything would go back to normal.

Suddenly, his objective became very clear. In a couple of weeks, he could bring Doc home, and then she would be alone again. He'd woo her like he'd never wooed another woman. It would be a new experience for him, but he could learn. He'd make her want him as much as he wanted her—and then, he'd take her and be done with it. That ought to put his life back in order so he could move forward again.

Despite his resolve, the peace he sought eluded him. He scrunched his pillow, pounding it with his fists; he turned it lengthwise and hugged it close against him. Somewhere, there was solace . . . somewhere . . .

A distant inner voice attempted to add the phrase *there was someone,* but Michael refused to listen.

Chapter Six

Each damp, dull, dreary day blended into another of its kind. And though the sun seldom showed its face, each day held at least one bright spot for Wynn, and that was a visit from Michael Donovan.

At first, she assured herself that she found his company exhilarating only because his visits offered a change of pace, a deviation from the norm. As the days passed, however, she found herself looking forward to his daily calls with a sense of expectancy unlike any she had known before, even with Jonathan.

She searched her mind for some explanation, but the feeling, as feelings often go, couldn't be rationalized. In the inner recesses of her soul, she knew that Michael Donovan had awakened a part of her woman's heart that had lain dormant before, a part that even Jonathan had never touched.

She balked at examining that piece of her heart, however, refusing to pour salt into an open wound that would heal, she hoped, given time. Like a patient who'd agreed once to surgery and sworn off ever going under the knife again, she vowed never to allow another man — including Michael Donovan — access to her heart.

But couldn't she continue to enjoy his company

for companionship's sake? Couldn't they just be friends?

Her question was answered one particularly cold, sunless afternoon, just minutes before the time for Michael's usual arrival. Wynn stood in her bedchamber admiring her new black walnut cheval mirror, trying to convince herself that practicality and not vanity had governed its purchase. She needed a full-length mirror to assure herself about things like bustles being straight and shirtwaists being tightly tucked, didn't she? Besides, the mirror brightened up her bedchamber.

The piece had arrived via train the day before. Slim had brought it to her, and together they had unpacked it and carried it to her room. Later, Wynn had polished the dark wood and the beveled mirror until the entire piece glistened.

Now the lamplight shimmered and sparkled in the glass and lent the burnished wood a golden glow. Wynn ran a forefinger over the arch of the frame and played with the mirror's tilt until she could stand a few feet back from it and see her full reflection.

What she saw amazed her.

Gone was the drab and mousy look that had characterized her in the past. The efficiency was still there, as were the poise and confidence, stronger somehow and yet less abrasive. But there was a softness in her features, a warm glow in her pale blue eyes, a sense of impishness hovering at the corners of her lips. It was a new look, one virtually devoid of the burdensome mold that had shaped her entire being almost from infancy.

Wynn leaned closer to the mirror, scrutinizing her face in an effort to discover whether the lamplight toyed with her reflection. The scrutiny provided further proof that the change to her countenance was, indeed, genuine.

Why, I'm almost pretty!

What had brought such a dramatic change? Unbidden, a vision of Michael Donovan's handsome face wavered in the shimmering glass.

No, she valiantly argued, *it's not possible. I haven't fallen in love with him! Have I?* And yet, she had to admit, the wistfulness shining from her eyes claimed she had.

"It's too soon to worry about wrinkles or gray hair. You're far too young for either."

The deep, mellow voice seemed surrealistic, a vocalization of her own thoughts spoken through the mouth of that one whom she longed to see. It sent a frisson of delight through her and she hugged herself, her lids fluttering closed as she imagined being held again by Michael Donovan — held tenderly, lovingly, as he had held her the night he had brought Doc to her. The memory made her shiver, and her fingers tightened their hold around her upper arms.

"You've neglected the fire," the voice continued. "I brought some coal from the store and refilled your scuttle. It's warming up downstairs and Doc's got the coffee on. I'm ready for a cup. How about you?"

The voice was too casual, the words too practical to belong to her daydream. Her eyes flew open and she whirled around to see Michael standing in the open doorway. He had assumed the pose she was growing accustomed to seeing: his arms crossed over his midsection, his shoulder propped against the jamb. A wicked grin creased his cheeks and wrinkled the skin around his eyes.

Being caught in an act of vanity — a rarity for Wynn Spencer — was embarrassing. Having a man —

especially one whose embrace she had just dreamed of—stand so close to her bed was disquieting. She felt the harsh prickle of her discomfort upon her cheeks, sought to salve the sting with the coolness of her palms while her mind raced with words and bits of phrases that refused to combine themselves into even a semblance of sensible speech.

If he noticed her mortification, he gave no indication. Instead, he pushed away from the jamb and sauntered indifferently toward the stairs.

Wynn made no move to follow him. Holding one palm over her pounding heart while continuing to rest the other against her cheek, she stood in the middle of her room and watched him until he moved out of her line of vision. Still, she didn't budge. Her heart pounded heavily against her hand as she listened to the heavy falls of his boot soles upon the bare treads of the stairs.

After what seemed like an eternity but was actually only a fleeting moment, she felt her heartbeats slow. The very prospect of sitting across from him at the kitchen table, however, lurched her heart into a sprint again. How could she appear normal when the very thought of him made her tingle all over? When he might very well see the look of love in her eyes and know they shined so for him?

Stalwartly, determined to imitate his calm, devil-may-care attitude, determined not to let him see how he affected her, she dropped her hands to her sides, lifted her chin, and followed him. After all, nothing either untoward or unprincipled could happen with Doc there to act as buffer and chaperon.

What am I going to do, she thought later, *when*

Doc decides to go back home and I'm all alone again? The thought was sobering, almost frightening. Wynn had discovered she didn't like living alone.

Once Doc was gone—which was certain to be soon—would Michael ever come back to see her? Certainly not on a daily basis, she was sure, or people would say he was courting her. Heavens above, would that set some tongues wagging!

Wynn tried to imagine how Michael Donovan would handle courting, and though she could not conjure a concrete image of his performance of that act, she smiled at the thought of having him woo her. Would he bring her little gifts and proclaim them tokens of his affection? Would he touch her face and declare it beautiful? Would he profess an undying love and beg for her hand in marriage?

'Tis foolish to allow such mental ramblings, she chastised herself. Courting could bring only one thing, and that was more heartache. Men said women were fickle, but didn't they have to be fickle themselves to recognize the characteristic in someone else? She hadn't understood the meaning of the word until she'd met Jonathan.

If she only had some patients other than Doc, someone else to look after and prescribe for, to go and visit . . . then maybe she wouldn't feel the loss of Michael's company so heavily. If just thinking about it caused so much distress, heaven only knew what the reality of his absence would bring.

Though it would only prove a stopgap measure, she considered asking Granny Simpson to move in with her until Rachel and David returned in the spring. It would buy her some time . . . assure her heart some protection . . .

111

* * *

Doc did move home—the very next day. Michael came for him, insisting Doc lie on a tick in the back of a buckboard instead of walking, which was what he wanted to do. Wynn spent the remainder of the afternoon tidying up the examination room, then walked over to the depot to have supper with Granny Simpson.

"You're sweet, child, to ask me," Granny said, patting Wynn's hand in affection, "but I'd just as soon stay on at the hotel. It's right next door to the mercantile and Mr. Donovan needs me to work there. Besides," she offered in a conspiratorial whisper, "I've discovered I like doing something besides crocheting and knitting and rocking babies. There's a whole lot more life left in me than I've wanted to believe was there. I just need a purpose, a new direction for my energies. I've been thinking of buying myself a plot of land and opening a boardinghouse, come warmer weather. This town's gonna need at least one."

Thus, Wynn began the task of resigning herself to living alone.

The following dawn brought a cold, brisk wind, made stronger by the lack of trees or other natural windbreak on the prairie. The wind whistled around the eaves and penetrated every crack in her house.

Before noon arrived, Wynn put the last of her meager supply of coal into the firebox of the cookstove and set off for town to buy more. She supposed she ought to have Slim build her a coal box and then purchase enough to fill it up, and she would have, given different circumstances. But both Doc and Michael had assured her of the relative mildness of southwestern Louisiana winters. Why tie

112

up her money, what little she had, in something it might take her months to consume? In the meantime, other, far more pressing needs might present themselves.

Wynn had no trouble listing such needs. Food ranked at the top, a cart and horse right below. Then there was a slew of medical supplies she wanted—nay, *needed* should she acquire many patients. Wynn didn't want to consider how she was going to manage financially without those patients.

She shuddered to think how much money she owed the mercantile. Granny always said, "I'll put this on your tab," then adroitly changed the subject if Wynn asked for a total. The last thing she wanted was to be in debt to Michael Donovan. She knew she should insist on paying off the entire balance of her account, even if it bankrupted her, but to do so would prevent her from buying the horse and cart she so desperately needed.

Wynn didn't know what to do. She was so caught up in her mental deliberations she missed seeing the beauty of the day. Instead, she focused on skirting mud puddles as she made her way down the path toward the quickly growing town.

Despite her inattention to its healing powers, the crisp, clean-smelling air, combined with the exercise of her brisk walk, swept clean the cobwebs of indecision, just as the wind was quickly sweeping away the scudding clouds.

"There's no use putting it off any longer," she proclaimed to a fat bullfrog sitting in the middle of a large puddle. "If I am to practice medicine, I must have a cart and horse—and I'm going to buy them . . . today! Besides"—her tinkling laughter was lost on the bullfrog—"today is my birthday. I owe myself

113

a present. I might even bake a cake. Would you like to help me celebrate, Mr. Froggy?"

A song sprang to her throat and her feet fairly skipped the last few yards to the new livery stable.

"I always liked that there tune, specially the part about the frog ridin' up to Miss Mousie's door," Jock Delaney, the livery owner, observed. "Even if the whole idea of a frog marryin' up with a mouse is a bit ridic'lous."

His words brought Wynn up short. Had she been singing "Froggy Went A-Courtin' "? She supposed she had.

Wynn watched him take a bead on a rusty tin can, then shoot a stream of tobacco juice toward it. He missed, backhanded his mouth, and took a bead on her. His narrow-eyed assessment seemed to say, "And what a little mouse you are." But it wasn't Jock Delaney's raspy, uncultured voice she heard say the words; it was the voice of a much younger, far better educated man: Jonathan.

Well, he wouldn't get away with talking to her like that—not again. "I am not a mouse!" she boldly declared.

"Pardon me, ma'am, but I never said you was. I was talkin' about the tune."

Wynn felt her cheeks flame from embarrassment, but she kept her voice even, her tone businesslike. "Of course, you didn't, Mr. Delaney. I—my mind was elsewhere. I've come to ask you to order me a two-wheeled cart. And I'll need a mare to go with it."

"You don't want no two-wheeled cart, Miss Spencer," he replied, pursing his lips and sending another stream of tobacco juice toward the can.

Wynn closed her eyes and counted silently to ten.

If she had been a male doctor, Delaney would never have called her *Mr.* Spencer. Nor would he have argued with her about what she wanted.

"Yes, I do," she averred, digging into her reticule for the advertisement she had torn from a recent copy of *The Medical Index*. This she held out for him to see, pointing to its heading: "DOCTORS, ATTENTION! PERFECTION AT LAST." She tapped an index finger on the illustration. "Look right here, Mr. Delaney. It says, 'A two-wheeled vehicle that will ride as easy as a four.' This says they're especially good for dodging chuckholes, rocks, and other obstacles."

Delaney squinted up his eyes and gave her another long, assessing look. "Jest how many chuckholes, rocks, and other obstacles you seen around here, miss? This here's the prairie. You might find a chuckhole ever' once in awhile, but them carts tip over real bad. You want you a buggy."

Wynn didn't want to argue with him, but she knew what she could afford. The two-wheeled cart cost almost half that of a buggy. "No, I don't, Mr. Delaney. I know what I want, and I know how to handle a rig. If you won't order it for me, I'll do it myself. The address is right here."

After almost an hour of discussion and haggling over prices, the two struck a bargain. The cart would have to be shipped from Yorkville, Illinois, and would take more than a week to arrive. In the meantime, Delaney promised to find her a mare at or below the price she was willing to pay. Since she didn't have a barn and wasn't sure when she could afford to build one, Delaney agreed to quarter her cart and stable the horse for the present.

Wynn tried to haggle with him, too, over his

stabling fee.

"Don't you have a fee bill, ma' am, you bein' a doctor and all?" he asked.

"No . . . I, well, my father and I used one in Galena, but I'm not sure what folks here can afford."

"Same as they can where you come from, miss. You cain't start out cuttin' your fees or lettin' folks get by with not payin' or bringin' you eggs or sech instead of cash. Eatin' nothin' but eggs gits old. 'Sides, eggs won't buy your medical supplies. This here's the voice of 'sperience talkin'. Sit yourself down and make you out a fee bill, and stick by it. That's the only way."

Wynn promised him she would think about it — and she fully intended to, all in good time.

That time arrived sooner than she expected it to.

Late that afternoon, just as she was pouring boiling water into her coffeepot, someone knocked at her kitchen door. "Now, who can that be?" she mumbled. No one ever came to her back door, which was actually on the side and not the back at all. She wiped her hands on her apron, tucked a stray lock of hair behind her ear, and opened the door.

Michael Donovan stood at the base of her steps. Wynn felt her breath leave her at the very sight of him, the wind ruffling his dark hair, his white teeth gleaming against lips red from chapping. Those same lips spread upward in a devilish grin. His cheeks were red, too, from the bite of the wind. He wore work clothes — plain blue denim britches, a heavy sheepskin-lined coat with the collar turned up, knitted gloves, and brown leather boots with scuffed toes and creased insteps — but never had Wynn seen clothes ride so elegantly on any man.

And he had come back to see her—not Doc!

"I brought your coal," he announced matter-of-factly, "and a box to keep it in."

His words shattered her fabrication of his intentions and drew her attention to a handcart parked behind him. The cart was full of coal. *Why, it must be five dollars' worth!*

"But I only ordered enough to fill my scuttle," she argued, her voice rife with a combination of amazement and frustration.

"And how long will that last you? Another day or two?" His questions carried a sharp edge, but his voice softened when he added, "This ought to be enough to take you to spring, maybe into the summer since you'll be using it only in the cookstove once warmer weather arrives."

"But I can't "

"I know." He waved away her protest. "You can't afford it."

"I didn't say that!" It didn't matter that she had planned to say exactly that. The fact that Michael said it instead proved embarrassing. Never had Wynn discussed monetary matters with anyone other than her father—until today. Haggling with Jock Delaney had been bad enough, but now for Michael to throw her sad financial state up to her . . .

"Well, you can afford it now."

Her eyebrows raised slightly, the movement opening her clear blue eyes wider. "Pardon?"

He reached into his pocket and removed a worn leather wallet. "I came to settle Doc's account. How much does he owe you?"

"I—I haven't thought about it."

Wynn watched his nostrils flare in a lightning-

117

quick doublet of sniffs. "Is that fresh coffee I smell?"

"Come on in," she offered, not without hesitation, her better judgment warning her against being alone with him. But it was the least she could do, she argued, the well-mannered thing to do. And it was what her heart wanted her to do. "We can settle this inside."

"Thanks. It's cold out here. Oh, where do you want the coal?" He replaced the wallet, then side-stepped toward the back of the house and took a peek down the back wall. "You don't have a lean-to."

"No, I don't."

"I'll send Slim over here tomorrow to build you one." His gaze raked the clearing skies. "I don't think it'll rain before then, but just in case, I'm going to cover this up. You got a piece of tin left over from your roof?"

She nodded. "Under the house, around at the back—and you'll need something to weigh it down with or this wind will just blow it right off. I think there's some scrap lumber under there, too. Will that work?"

"Ought to." He started pulling the cart toward the back yard.

"Wait!" she called. "Let me fill my scuttle first." Wynn scurried to retrieve the brass bucket, but when she would have followed him, he stopped her.

"Give it to me. This wind's cold and you're not wearing a wrap."

Allowing a man to do things for her was a new experience for Wynn Spencer, but it was one she thought she might learn to relish, just so long as she didn't allow herself to become spoiled by it.

She took paper and pen from her desk in the hall, then settled herself at the enamel-topped table with a cup of steaming coffee as she made out Doc's bill. All the while she worked, she could hear the noises Michael made unloading her coal. Having someone to watch over her suddenly felt good—and right. She smiled without knowing she did.

It was her smile Michael saw when he walked in the door. Damn, but she was pretty when she smiled. And she smelled pretty, too. The heady scent of lilacs wafted in the air, commingling with the sweet smells of butter and vanilla and the sharp though pleasant aroma of coffee.

She looked up at him then, and her smile reached her eyes.

He looked away quickly, coughed, and began to peel his gloves off. "Don't get up. I can get my coffee."

Wynn was only marginally aware of Michael's movements at first—removing his coat and draping it over the back of a chair, the splash of water in the dishpan as he washed his hands, the clatter of china and silverware as he prepared to pour his coffee.

Then, quite abruptly, the mundane, everyday sounds of gurgling coffee and a metal spoon hitting the side of a china cup assumed uncommon proportions. They both felt it, that unexplainable exhilaration that comes from sharing a routine experience with someone special.

Wynn's hand shook, causing a blob of ink to fall and splotch the bill she was writing.

Michael's hand shook, causing him to slosh hot coffee over his fingers.

He mumbled something about being clumsy, catching Wynn's notice. She watched him lick it off and felt a coil of warmth grip her deep inside.

Michael sat down across from her and pulled the inked sheet to his side of the table. He studied it in silence, his face mirroring first amusement, then consternation as he sipped his coffee.

"Is something wrong?"

"Yes, there is." He took her pen and made some notes on the paper, then studied the bill again. Once more, he put pen to paper, marking out some of her figures and replacing them. Finally, when he seemed satisfied, he quickly totaled the bill and pushed it back at her.

For a moment, Wynn could do nothing more than sit and stare at the sheet. She had listed: "Office call, night — $2.00; Dressing — $1.00; Administration of chloroform — $2.00." It was enough to pay for the coal.

Michael had written the number twelve in front of "Dressing" and increased the charge by eleven dollars, then added a room and board charge of fourteen dollars, for a total of thirty dollars. Thirty dollars! Enough to pay off her bill at the mercantile, she was certain, and still have money left over, probably enough to buy the two-wheeled cart.

"But — this is too much," she finally said.

"Why? Didn't you use at least a dozen dressings? And Doc was here for two full weeks. A dollar a day is reasonable for room and board, especially since it came with daily medical care. Thirty dollars is cheap for a man's life. He probably owes you far more than this."

"No, this is quite . . . adequate. And he would have lived, Mr. Donovan. Doc's life was never in danger."

"What if I hadn't cleaned the wound out good

120

enough? It could have become infected. Gangrene could have set in. I don't know how to amputate, Dr. Spencer, nor does anyone else around here, I'd wager. No, you saved his life, whether you want to believe it or not."

Michael wasn't sure he believed it, either, but he wanted her to accept the money, if for no other reason than to ease his conscience. Though he didn't understand why, he'd grown up hating doctors—all doctors—until he'd starting admiring Wynn. Since Doc had retired from medicine long before Michael met him, he'd never counted the old man among the recipients of his hatred.

Michael Donovan considered himself to be as tolerant as the next man. He had, therefore, tried repeatedly to recall the incident that had sparked his prejudice, but the full tapestry of the memory always eluded him. He knew only that it involved something from his childhood, something about somebody dying . . .

Mentally shaking off the melancholy that always accompanied attempted recollection, he removed his wallet again, pulled out a wad of bills, separated the appropriate amount, then returned the other bills to his wallet and his wallet to his pocket.

Wynn's eyes followed the movement of his hand as he picked up the sugar bowl and set it on top of the money. She hadn't noticed before how lean and tan his hands were, nor how long were his fingers. They could have belonged to an aristocrat, but their split cuticles and calluses relegated them to the ranks of a working man. Never, she realized with a start, had she seen hands she liked so well.

They drank their coffee in companionable silence. When Wynn got up to replenish their cups, she re-

121

membered the pound cake she had baked that morning. She had left it cooling in the pie safe, out of sight and, therefore, out of mind.

"Would you like a slice of cake with your coffee?" she asked.

"Maybe after supper. You got something else cooked?"

Wynn's heart flipped at his clearly implied request for an invitation to stay for the evening meal, but her soaring spirits nosedived when she realized she hadn't prepared anything besides the cake. Regretfully, she shook her head. "I was going to eat some soda crackers and hoop cheese, and then stuff myself on cake."

He laughed. "Doesn't sound very healthy."

"It sounds awful, actually, but one should be allowed some indulgence on one's birthday, don't you think?"

"Is this your birthday?"

She nodded. "My twenty-fourth."

"A woman should never tell her age," he teased.

She shrugged indifferently. "What point is there in hiding it? I see no reason for my age to cause me any embarrassment."

"Most unmarried women who have reached your age would be embarrassed."

"Those who would must feel terribly insecure, don't you think?" she countered.

"And you're different? You never feel any insecurities?"

"Of course, I do! I'm human. Ofttimes, I feel inadequate in one way or another."

Michael set his coffee cup down, crossed his arms on the table, and leaned forward, his gaze locked on hers. "Tell me," he whispered, "what makes a woman

122

like you *ever* feel inadequate."

His steady gaze made her feel uncomfortable, but his words warmed her heart. *A woman like you,* he'd said. It made her feel distinguished, important somehow, different in a positive way. She didn't know quite how to answer him for a moment. Wynn had no trouble listing her faults, but she wasn't quite sure she was ready to admit them to this man whom, she realized, she didn't really know at all. When she did respond, it was with generalities.

"There's so much a doctor has to know, and I have so very much yet to learn."

"Whatever made you want to become a doctor in the first place?"

She pondered that for a minute, wondering if she should tell him all the reasons, as she had told Doc, wondering if he truly cared. She opted for the most obvious, most succinct response. "My father was a doctor."

"Was?"

"He died last year. Pneumonia."

"I'm sorry."

They finished their coffee without further conversation, each intimately aware of the other yet neither offering any overt indication of that awareness. Finally, Michael scraped back his chair, unfolded his tall, lean frame, and slipped his arms into his coat.

"No one should spend the evening alone on their birthday," he said. "Why don't you bring your cake over to the depot and have supper with everyone else?"

"I'd rather no one made a fuss over it. Thanks for caring, but I think I'll just stay here."

"Your insecurities are showing, Dr. Spencer," Michael quipped. "Look," he added when she still hesi-

123

tated, "I'll see that no one makes a fuss. Besides, you didn't give us fair warning. There's no time to prepare a proper fuss, and I always say if you can't fuss properly, then don't fuss at all."

His ridiculous-sounding argument won her over. "But I hadn't planned to go anywhere. I'll need a few minutes to change my clothes and comb my hair," she said.

"No problem. I'll have Slim hold supper till you get there."

He slipped out the door as quickly as he could, but still the icy blast of a northwest wind sailed into her kitchen and hovered there. When had the wind picked up, she wondered, folding her arms around her chest and shivering. Suddenly, she wished she had never agreed to walk into town, not in this wind. She dashed to the front door, pulled it open, and hollered at Michael to come back.

But he had set off at a dead run toward town, was almost halfway there. The wind snatched her call, tossing it hither and yon as it buffeted the sides of her house and tore at the strips of tin on her roof.

Seeing the futility of it all, she pushed hard against the portal, fighting the strength of the wind with all she had to give until the latch caught and held. Surely Michael would understand when she didn't show up at the depot. Only a fool would venture forth on a night like this one.

And Wynn didn't count herself among the foolish. Not this time.

Chapter Seven

By the time Michael got back to town, he knew he should never have insisted Wynn leave her house that night. He couldn't remember when he'd seen such wind, certainly not since he'd been in Louisiana. A memory of another night, another wind from long ago niggled at his thoughts, but he cast the shadowy recollection aside and concentrated on what he could give Wynn for her birthday.

He might have promised not to make a fuss, but he didn't see giving her a present on her birthday as making a fuss. It had been a long time since Michael had given anyone a gift to honor a special occasion — so long, in fact, that he couldn't even remember the last time. He and Doc didn't know each other's birth date, nor did they care. But today must be important to Wynn; she had baked herself a cake and made it a point to tell him it was her birthday. He wanted to give her something as a way of saying, "This day is important to me, too."

And it was important to him. The admission drew him up short, and he paused in his flight to town to give the revelation brief consideration. It was important to him, he decided, because Wynn was important to him. He hadn't thought anyone could ever become as important to him as she had, even if she was the contrariest female he'd ever met.

He stopped by the depot, spoke to Slim about holding supper, and hurried to the mercantile.

Granny Simpson had already closed up for the night and gone back to the hotel. Michael lit a kerosene lamp and began to pilfer through the household items Granny had insisted he stock, but he found nothing he thought Wynn could use that she didn't already have. He sorted through the yard goods and bolts of lace, then realized he had no idea whether Wynn could sew or how much fabric was required for a garment.

He turned next to the toiletries, discounted such items as too personal, and went back to the pots and pans and dishes. He considered paying off her account, but a zero balance wasn't something he could actually wrap up and hand to her. Regardless of the lack of packaging, her pride probably wouldn't let her accept such a gift anyway.

No, he had to find something—and fast! But what?

He closed his eyes and called up a vision of her as she'd looked when he'd walked in her back door that afternoon—so tiny and feminine . . . and smelling like lilacs. And damn, if he hadn't taken the only bottle of lilac water home when he'd washed her clothes. It might be inappropriate, but it was the only thing he could think of on such short notice.

Well, he'd just go back home and collect it. He needed to check on Doc anyway.

The old man was snoozing in front of the stove. Michael adjusted the blanket Doc had thrown over himself, added more coal to the firebox, and set a pot of leftover soup on to warm for Doc's supper, all without disturbing the older man. He didn't see any sense in telling him about Wynn's birthday supper. The old coot would want to go, and he had no business leaving the house on a night like this. He probably couldn't make it that far on foot anyway, since Doc was having to use a cane to get around, and Rusty was in the barn in town.

Having the only barn so far from the house proved to be a problem more often than not. Michael had put it there as a convenience for hotel guests like Wilcox who were traveling by buggy or on horseback. He'd intended to build another barn at his house and just never had. Because there was no shelter for Rusty at his place, he and Doc walked back and forth to town.

He eased into his room and retrieved the bottle of lilac water from under some flannel shirts in a bureau drawer where he had stashed it. He set it on top of the bureau, next to the lamp, and gasped when he saw it was half-empty. Hellfire and damnation! What could he do now?

He sat down on the bed and gave the liquid in the bottle a long, hard look. He knew darned well he hadn't used that much when he'd washed Wynn's clothes—just a few drops in the rinse water. Where had it all gone?

He opened the drawer again and the sweet perfume of lilacs hit him full in the face. The bottom of the drawer was damp and so were several of his shirts. He must have knocked the bottle over when he took out the shirt he was wearing, because it didn't smell like lilacs and he couldn't remember having smelled the fragrance so strongly when he'd removed the shirt from the drawer that morning.

Inspiration struck swiftly then, and Michael hastened to find the sewing kit. It was a shame he didn't have time to run back to the mercantile for more appropriate materials, he thought. He'd just have to make do with what he had.

* * *

When she grew weary of trying to keep her toes warm, Wynn called it an early evening and prepared for bed, taking with her some reading material since she really wasn't sleepy.

Her bedchamber was far warmer than any of the downstairs rooms, but the wind still found its way in, depositing its frosty breath on the glass panes and whistling around the window facing. She stripped down to her camisole and bloomers, then donned a flannel nightgown and a pair of heavy wool socks. She added another quilt to the bed, settled herself under the covers, and opened a copy of the *Medical Record* she hadn't finished reading.

A full quarter hour later, Wynn realized she hadn't read a word — hadn't absorbed one, anyway. Despite her best efforts, her thoughts insisted on drifting back to Michael Donovan. Her mind had replayed every word of their earlier conversation, every facial gesture, every nuance of meaning while her eyes had been looking at the printed pages propped on her raised knees.

Was his attitude toward her changing? After all, he hadn't started one argument, hadn't taken the slightest offense at anything she'd said. She could apply the same to herself as well, she supposed. He'd given her several opportunities to display her argumentative side, but she'd kept the peace.

Maybe there was hope for them yet. Lord knows, she needed a friend, one closer to her age and more able-bodied than Doc or Granny. Did she honestly want Michael as just a friend? She pondered all this, feeling herself grow all warm and soft inside just thinking about him. But hadn't Jonathan made her feel that way, at least in the beginning? Hadn't she sworn off all romantic entanglements? Wasn't she still in love with Jonathan? Her better judgment told her to go slowly, to take this change in their relationship one day at a time, at least until she could answer those questions.

She felt the slightest twinge of guilt for not going to the depot as she had promised, but surely Michael would understand. She wasn't a child. She didn't have to celebrate birthdays anymore. It was considerate of him to think she ought to, but getting out in such a fierce wind was unthinkable, perhaps even dangerous.

A loud clatter interrupted her musings. She scurried out of bed, hastened to the window, and pushed back the heavy curtain in time to see moonlight glinting off a piece of tin as it plummeted to the ground. It almost made it before the wind picked it up and tossed it back at the house, hurtling it into a downstairs window. Even over the wind's roar, Wynn heard the glass shatter. The whole house trembled violently, and Wynn feared it would collapse on top of her.

Her heart leapt into her throat, her stomach twisted into tight knots, and her feet refused to budge. She knew she had to get hold of herself, had to go downstairs, where it would be somewhat safer. She forced herself to move, first one foot and then the other, toward the door. On her way by the bed, she took the lamp in one hand, pulled off the top quilt with the other and dragged it with her down the stairs.

All the way to the ground floor she mumbled to herself, "I won't let this bother me. Everything will be all right. I won't let this bother me . . ."

Wynn's failure to appear for supper at the station house both pleased and disappointed Michael Donovan. Although he'd eagerly anticipated spending the evening with her, he was equally thankful she'd had the good sense to remain at home, out of the fierce wind.

129

As the wind began to pull at the tiles on the depot roof, however, Michael grew concerned about her being alone in a house relatively isolated from town. He picked at his food, garnering looks of mild annoyance from Slim. No one else at the table seemed to be paying much attention.

Finally, he shoved back his chair, reached for his coat, and announced, "I'm going out there."

He set off at a dead run, the wind at his back.

Outside of a thin sliver of pale yellow light peeping out from under her front door, Wynn's house was dark. Michael pounded his fist against the portal and called out to her, then pounded again when she failed to answer. He turned the knob, found it locked, and pushed hard against the heavy panel with his shoulder. The door didn't budge.

Perhaps she was in the kitchen and couldn't hear him above the roar of the wind, he thought, heading around the house. No light emanated from the kitchen window, however, and the back door was firmly locked.

"If you're in there, Wynn Spencer, open the door!" he hollered, waiting a moment, and then hollering again. "I'll break a window if I have to!"

The wind, he discovered on his way back to the front of the house, had broken one for him.

He found her huddled up on the hall bench, her back against the wall, her quilt-wrapped body racking with tremors as violent as those shaking the house. The flickering light from a lamp on a table next to the bench illuminated the glassiness of her pale eyes and the furrows of tiny lines on her forehead. Her mouth moved in a continual repetition, but her voice was so low he had to put his ear next to her mouth to hear.

"Trapped," she said. "Trapped."

He knelt on the floor in front of her and took her

cheeks between his gloved hands. "Wynn, I'm here. You aren't trapped. Everything will be all right now."

"I'm sorry," she mumbled, her voice a deep, husky monotone.

He smoothed the hair away from her face. A piece caught at the corner of her mouth and he loosened it with a shaky finger. She seemed so small suddenly, so helpless. It made him feel so strong, so very much in control. It was a heady feeling. "There's nothing to be sorry for," he assured her, his voice soft but firm. "You didn't bring this wind."

"Didn't come . . . trapped."

"You didn't need to go out on a night like this. I should never have asked you to."

"I'm scared, Michael." Her voice shook, stark evidence of her anxiety.

Michael blessed the cursed wind for stealing her composure. Under normal circumstances, she would never have admitted fear—or called him Michael. He was certain of that.

"I'm here now, darling. You have nothing more to fear." He leaned closer to her, intending only to plant a reassuring kiss upon her forehead. But when his lips touched her silky skin, an electrifying shock sluiced through him. While his hands continued to hold her face, his mouth moved downward, over the bridge of her nose, across first one fluttering eyelid and then the other, and back down her nose to the pliable softness of her trembling lips. He felt himself tremble right along with her, and knew in the depths of his soul that the raging wind had nothing to do with the sudden quaking of his own limbs.

Had she responded in kind, he might have taken her right then and there, on the hall floor, with the Oriental runner beneath them, her quilt covering them, and the howling wind orchestrating their lovemaking.

But Wynn appeared unaffected by his kiss. He backed away, his eyes searching her face for an explanation, his heart desperately needing to know why. The glaze had not left her pale orbs nor had the expression of extreme fear lifted from her delicate features. Her teeth chattered and the quilt rippled from the tremors racking her body. He checked her pulse, confirmed its weakness, and noted how shallowly she breathed.

Why, she was in shock! The truth hit him with a force akin to that of the buffeting wind. What do you do for a person in shock? He tried to remember everything he'd ever heard about it, but it kept flying out of his head. He pulled her into his embrace, his long arms going around her slight frame and holding her tightly against him as his mind raced with possibilities.

Out of the corner of his eye, he spied the shelves packed with books in her barrister's cabinet. Medical books!

He resettled her on the bench before standing up and moving quickly to the cabinet, taking the lamp with him. None of the spines read "First Aid." He pulled one after another of the volumes off the shelves, flipping to the index of each and then adding it to the accumulating pile on the floor when he didn't see the word "shock" there.

Finally, he located it, couldn't find the page in his haste, then forced himself to calm down and read the instructions. His mind picked up phrases: *check for injuries . . . apply hot bricks or bottles . . . rub hands and feet until warm . . . cover patient.* Good Lord! He hadn't thought about her being injured.

He left the book open on top of the cabinet and returned to the bench, where he gently coaxed Wynn into lying down. She still had the quilt wrapped around her, and he had to tug at it to get it loose. As he peeled it back, bile rose in his throat and he gagged on the bitter gall. His vision blurred and he shuddered uncontrollably. He glanced at her prone body and saw blood, thick and red, covering her nightgown. "Oh, my God!" he breathed, dropping the quilt and spinning on his heel.

"I'm not going to let her die," he promised himself. "Not like before."

Before? He grasped for the memory but it skittered away, out of reach. Michael closed his eyes, begged the haunting memory to come back and free his soul, but it floated farther and farther away.

He turned back to Wynn, blinked twice to clear his vision, to convince himself that the blood he had seen before was not there, nor had it ever been.

He rubbed her hands and feet hard and, while he had the quilt off, he quickly checked for injuries. Although she seemed incredibly weak, he could see no bruises, could feel no broken bones, could see no blood, real or imagined. He covered her again with the quilt. Then back he went to the cabinet.

"Give shock solution," he read, "made of one teaspoonful table salt and one-half teaspoonful baking soda dissolved in one quart water. Give patient all he will drink."

Michael lit another lamp and carried it with him to the kitchen, where he located the necessary ingredients, mixed the solution, and poured up a cupful. Wynn drank all of it without protest. On his way back to the kitchen for more, he stopped and read the last sentence of instructions: "If available, a cup of strong black coffee is helpful."

Michael worked the hand pump at the sink, filling Wynn's kettle with water. The fire had almost died down in the stove. He added coal to the firebox and checked the reservoir to make sure it hadn't gone dry.

He found her coffee and grinder, worked the crank and measured some into the basket, then reassembled the pot. His racing pulse seemed to beat a tattoo: *Hurry, hurry!*

In spite of his lack of medical knowledge, his instincts told him Wynn's condition could be life threatening. His own inadequacies hit him full force, just as they had the night Doc shot himself. He hadn't known what to do then, but he had Wynn to take him to.

Now Wynn was the patient, and Doc the only other person in town with medical training. Michael gave brief consideration to going after Doc, then quickly dismissed the notion. Wynn's condition could worsen; she could even die while he was gone. And there were no guarantees Doc would know any more than he had learned himself from Wynn's medical book. His only recourse was to stay and do what he could for her.

The wind tore another piece of tin off the roof. Michael felt the force of the gust that pulled it off, heard it clang and bang against the rest of the tin as the wind flipped it across the top of the house. The noise pulled him toward the kitchen window; the shadow of a memory nagged at him as he pushed back the curtain and looked out into the eerie black of night. For an instant, his mind returned to a similar night nearly a quarter century before, and he saw silvery moonlight glistening off banks of white snow and heard a high, blood-curdling scream. He shuddered and dropped the curtain.

He got Wynn to drink some more of the shock solution. Her color had improved somewhat and her breathing seemed to be a bit stronger. By the time the coffee dripped, she was able to sit up and drink a cup.

He knew she was going to be all right when she choked on the first sip and gasped out, "I can't drink this vile stuff!"

"Of course, you can. I drink mine black all the time. Remember? You'll get used to it."

"I don't want to get used to it!"

"You make a most uncooperative patient," he teased.

"I'm fine now. I don't need any coffee."

"Yes, you do. Drink it!"

She did, though she protested with each swallow and sent him looks intended to let him know how very much she detested his treatment of her. Those sharp looks warmed his heart in a way he would never have believed possible, for they told him she was quickly recovering from the shock.

"Are you all right now? You didn't try to go outside, did you? Did you fall down the stairs, or did something hit you? What happened?"

Wynn's eyes clouded over; she dropped her gaze to her lap and began to pluck nervously at the quilt. "No, I didn't try to go outside. Nor did I fall down the stairs or get hit by flying debris."

"Well, something sure scared the hell out of you, then. What was it? A wild animal?"

She shook her head in negation and continued plucking at the quilt. "My mother made this quilt," she said, "out of scraps from my dresses."

"Look at me, dammit! And tell me what happened to you!"

Her head shot up and her eyes blazed with wrath. "You don't have to curse at me! I would have been all right, after awhile."

"How do you know? You were almost in a trance, and you didn't act like you were going to come out of it."

She looked away from him, fixing her gaze on the lamplight, her mouth clamped shut.

Michael gave a low whistle and his eyes narrowed in

135

consternation. "This has happened to you before, hasn't it? You will answer me, Wynn Spencer, if I have to stay here all night to hear it. You scared me half to death and you owe me an explanation."

She sighed deeply and shot him a beseeching look.

"I'm waiting . . ."

"Look, I'm grateful to you for taking care of me, but, really, I'm fine now."

"I'm waiting . . ."

"Oh, all right. I've never told anyone about this before. I never thought I'd have to. You're not going to understand."

"Try me."

Michael could see how hard this was for her, but he had to know. Suddenly, he had to know everything there was to know about Wynn Spencer. He wasn't sure why he felt that way; he just knew he did.

She took a deep breath. "I have this irrational fear. It's called a phobia."

"I've heard of phobias. What is yours?"

"Claustrophobia — an abnormal dread of being in closed-up spaces. I didn't know what to call it until I went to medical school. I, well, I kind of go berserk sometimes."

"Like you did tonight."

"Yes, like tonight. But I always come out of it. It just takes me a while to regain control of myself."

Michael let his gaze roam the wide hall, then looked at her askance.

She answered his unspoken question. "It was the wind. It made me feel . . . trapped inside this house."

"Did you have any supper?"

"No."

"Neither did I. Think we can scrounge up something in your kitchen? I'm starved. I'll even eat soda crackers and hoop cheese with you, if that's all you have."

136

Wynn silently blessed him for changing the subject so adroitly, for not pursuing any further the substance of her weakness. That was what it was, too, in her estimation, a weakness of the mind that robbed her of self-control. She had been fighting it all her life, had pondered the tapestry of her phobia for years, trying to understand what threads of experience had woven its fabric. Never had she arrived at even a probable basis for her fear, let alone a substantial one. How could she explain to Michael what she did not understand herself?

Later, when they finished a light supper, Wynn pulled her pound cake out of the pie safe and served them each a generous slice. When she carried the plates to the table, a small package lay at her place.

A hint of a smile played about her lips as she picked it up. "What's this?"

"Open it, ninny. It's a birthday present."

He'd brought her a gift! Did this mean he was courting her? Trembling fingers pulled the end of the twine and unfolded the square of brown paper. What Wynn saw lying there caught her totally by surprise. She sat, stunned, staring at the puffed red flannel circle.

"It's one of those things you put in your drawer to keep your clothes smelling nice," Michael explained.

"A sachet," she supplied. "And you made it?"

She knew he had—either he or someone else who didn't wield a needle with much expertise.

Michael nodded sheepishly.

Wynn's fingers caressed the worn flannel, from which two not quite equal and somewhat lopsided circles had been unevenly cut, as though he had used a pocket knife instead of scissors. The circles, which she supposed had come from one of his shirts, had been stitched together with black thread in large, irregular overcast stitches, the two ends tied together and their strings left hanging. The sachet had been stuffed with something soft and then doused generously with toilet water; the scent of lilacs emanating from the sachet was so strong it was almost overbearing.

She picked it up and held it as though she expected it to break any minute. "This is . . . one of the most unique and thoughtful gifts anyone ever gave me. I'm, well, I'm overwhelmed." She could see that her speech made Michael a little uncomfortable, so she asked, "What did you use to stuff it with?"

"Cotton."

"Where did you find cotton around here?"

"I took it out of my mattress."

"You did *what?*"

"I took it out of my mattress. I cut a little slit in the side and pulled out some of the cotton. I'll have to go back now and sew the hole up."

He laughed at the absurdity of what he'd done, and Wynn laughed with him. When he had sobered somewhat, he said, "I know it's a little strong with lilac water. Maybe if you let it sit out for awhile, some of the odor will evaporate."

Wynn didn't know when she had felt so special. His gift touched her heart in a way nothing else ever had, for he had put a part of himself into the sachet. She opened her mouth to tell him so, then discovered she couldn't speak for the lump in her throat. Instead, she reached across the table and placed her palm over one of Michael's much larger hands.

Shockwaves of desire shot through her, temporarily stunning her with their intensity. *God help me! I want this man.*

The admission hit her with the impact of a rifle shot. She jerked her hand away and tucked it in her lap, rolling it up in the skirt of her nightdress as though she were wrapping it in a bandage. Indeed, her entire palm felt scorched.

As much as she knew she should, Wynn could not remove her gaze from Michael's face. He felt it, too. She knew he did by the way his lids half-shuttered his eyes and by the deep sigh that escaped his chiseled lips. He stood up a bit shakily and walked around the table to stand beside her chair.

Although Wynn's eyes followed his movements, she felt as though all other bodily functions had suddenly malfunctioned. Her breath came in erratic spurts; her pulse beat a sprinting throb in her ears; her voice deserted her. She could do nothing but sit dumbly while he scooped her into his arms as though she were featherweight and started with her toward the examination room. There, he shifted her weight to his left arm and used his right hand to fold back the covers on the bed Doc had used; then he gently laid her down upon the sheet.

She smiled up at him, hoping he understood the rage of emotion surging through her, emotion she had yet to sort out. Her smile disappeared when he started unbuttoning his shirt.

"What—" she began, moistened her dry lips with her tongue, swallowed hard, and then tried again. "What are you doing?"

"Getting ready for bed."

She couldn't believe she had heard him correctly, couldn't believe the matter-of-fact tone he used, as though they had done this before—and often.

"No . . . not—"

"Shush, my darling," he whispered, bending down close to her face and letting his lips graze hers, then rubbing his mustache on the tip of her nose. Wynn shivered and reached for the covers.

"I'm not going to leave you here alone, not tonight," he explained, "not with that wind still raging and no telling what additional damage it will wreak. If you have to get out of this house in a hurry, I'm going to be here to get you out."

"But this bed—it's too narrow for both of us," she protested, knowing her logic was weak but unable to think of another reason.

"I can't imagine either of us sleeping through this storm, so what difference does it make?"

The difference, she wanted to tell him, lay in which storm he was referring to—the windstorm raging outside or the storm of passion raging within.

Chapter Eight

She would just have to be strong and resist his advances. She would order him from the bed — and from her house, if necessary.

In the dim lamplight sifting in from the hall, she watched him in silhouette take off his flannel shirt and toss it on the examination table. He moved back to the bed, then sat down and took off his boots. She heard them hit the floor, thump . . . thump. He stood up and pushed his blue denim britches down his long legs, sat back down to pull them over his feet, then hurled them toward his shirt. They landed on the table, but not quite solidly enough; both pieces slid down into the dark obscurity of the floor. Michael left them there.

Wynn scooted over as far as she could against the wall and waited, breathless, for him to lie down beside her. Instead, he stood up and padded on sock feet back into the hall. She couldn't imagine what he was doing until the room went completely black. She'd forgotten about the lamp.

He made his way back into the room without the benefit of a light to guide his way, stubbing his toe on the door frame and cursing under his breath as he hobbled over to the bed. The mattress sank under his weight, its shifting pulling her toward the middle. Michael's arms went around her before she could scoot back to the wall, and he pulled her close. She stiffened and tried to pull away from him.

"Come here, sweetheart," he whispered, his breath tickling her cheek. "I just want to hold you close while you go to sleep. That's all, I promise."

Tremors sluiced through her slight frame before she relaxed. She had thought he would be naked, but he still wore both his long johns and his socks. She wondered if the long johns were the patched red ones she had seen hanging over his stove the night she had arrived in Jennings, and she smiled at the recollection. Never had she considered sleeping with those long johns—but much better them than his bare skin. It would have been hard to keep her resolve without the barrier of the union suit.

She breathed deeply, absorbing the essence of him. He smelled like soap and boot leather and the wind—clean but masculine. His body was so long! She knew he was tall, but having his length pressed so close to hers seemed to emphasize the great difference in their heights.

Neither the howling, buffeting wind nor the crashing and banging of its manifestation frightened her anymore—not with Michael there, cuddling her, soothing her, promising to stay but giving no indication he expected anything more from her.

This felt so right . . . so good . . . so perfect . . .

Within minutes, she fell into a deep, restful sleep, her face buried against Michael's shoulder, her heart humming a peaceful tune with a single lyric: "Home."

She was so soft, so sweet, so vulnerable when she slept.

Michael thought of all those times he'd thought she

was too hard, too tough, too strong for a woman. He couldn't help wondering what had happened in her life to make her so fiercely independent. Whatever it was, it had affected her deeply. He didn't know much about phobias, but he suspected that some horrible incident from her childhood had triggered her particular irrational fear, its memory nurturing it through the years. Maybe one day, when she came to fully trust him, she would tell him all about it.

If she even remembered it.

Why did he think she might not? A series of images floated across the veil of his eyelids, images for which he himself had no concrete memory. Images that were no more than shadowy specters from his past. Images of a cold, stormy night. Images of a woman screaming. And always across the images splashed the sanguine red of blood and the pristine white of snow. Why did just thinking about blood and snow always make him slightly nauseous?

An involuntary shudder racked his frame and he held Wynn tighter against him, seeking solace in her warmth, her nearness, her very being. Outside, the wind moaned as though in agony, echoing the torment wailing in his heart.

Morning dawned bright, clear, and bitterly cold. Michael awoke to sunlight glinting off white, lacy patterns covering the windowpanes. The sight sickened him for a moment until he realized he was looking at frost and not snow. Thank goodness, it never snowed in Jennings!

He turned away from the windows, huddling deeper under the covers, pulling Wynn's back against his chest spoon-fashion. They had slept that way through most of the night — at least Wynn had. Michael wasn't

143

sure he'd slept much at all.

Holding her, being so close to her, yet not making love to her had been sheer torture for him. He'd allowed himself the pleasures of burying his face in her fragrant hair, kissing the top of her head, touching her smooth cheeks with his fingertips, cupping her breast in his palm. Despite the harsh bite of the chilling wind, he'd grown overwarm in his long-handles, had more than once thrown back the quilt with the intention of removing them before reason had its sway.

What had been torturous for him in the black of night became pure hell in the blazing light of day. He bent his elbow and rested his head on his open palm, his eyes caressing Wynn as she slept. The morning sun blushed her ivory cheek with the palest peach and set afire the glossy brown strands of her hair, turning them to molten copper. He watched her lips move in a seductive pucker-and-relax exercise, as though she dreamt of kissing. His thoughts became those of a normal, healthy, lusty man, and he felt himself grow hard where he pressed against her soft, round derrière.

Groaning, he tossed back the quilt, shivered as a blast of cold air hit him, and reached for the shirt and pants he had tossed aside the night before. When he had donned them, he tucked the quilt around Wynn, who stirred but did not wake—even when his lips gently brushed hers, then took his boots with him and escaped into the kitchen.

Within a few minutes, he had rebuilt the fire in the stove and started a kettle of water to heat. It was as good a time as any, he supposed, to assess the damage done by the wind. Maybe, at the very least, the task would divert his mind to something less . . . dangerous.

Remaining in sock feet, he eased up the stairs to the bedrooms. Luckily, Wynn's had suffered no damage, but the spare chamber she had yet to furnish was in a shambles. This room had faced the wind, had received the brunt of its mighty force and suffered the consequences. Ragged strips of beaded lumber hung from the ceiling and littered the floor. Golden sunlight streamed in through various sized holes in the roof.

As he stood and gazed at the debris, Michael thought about Doc for the first time since he had walked in and found Wynn ill the night before. Damn! He had gone off and left the old man alone—and asleep—without telling him where he was going. He'd never intended to stay at Wynn's very long—certainly not overnight. Surely, he hoped, either Slim or Johnny had gone out to see about Doc, but Michael knew he'd have to go himself, and soon, just to be certain Doc was all right.

Quickly, he made his way back downstairs, pulled on his boots and his coat, and went outside to refill Wynn's scuttle and check the roof. He walked around the house, counting the strips of tin that had to be replaced and looking for structural damage before he went back inside and made coffee.

Wynn was still sleeping, but he woke her up.

"Coffee's dripping," he said, shaking her shoulder until she yawned and rolled toward him.

"What time is it?" she asked, opening her eyes slowly and blinking at the shafts of light streaming through the windows.

"What difference does it make, silly?" Michael answered, laughter in his voice.

"None, I guess." She came more fully awake then, and gasped. "Oh, my goodness!" She sat up and raked her fingers through her hair, her face stricken with sudden recollection. "You spent the night here, didn't you?"

The mischievous grin she held so dear lit his face, and his bristly eyebrows moved up and down in mocking jest. "Yes," he drawled, his voice low, conspiratorial. "But we won't tell anyone if you don't want to."

"We won't have to tell. Everyone will *know*."

"Don't worry about what anyone thinks. No one should have been alone during that storm, which is why I woke you up. I left Doc by himself and I need to go out to my house and check on him."

Whatever worries she'd had concerning her own reputation dissipated quickly in the face of his announcement. "You don't think —"

"I don't know, Wynn. That's the point." He stood up and headed to the door, stopping and turning back before he stepped into the hall. "I'll be back later. I promise. Your spare room is a disaster, but that's the only real damage I can find, outside of a broken dining room window and the roof. I'll bring some men and materials and we'll do what we can to patch things up today."

He stepped into the hall, then turned back again when she called to him.

She was scrambling out of the bed, her hair a rich brown cloud of wayward strands, her eyes still a bit swollen from sleep. The sunlight streamed through her nightdress, outlining the slender turn of her waistline, the full roundness of her hips. Michael's heart skipped a beat and then pounded, out of control, against the firm wall of his chest.

"Wait. Doc may need me. Let me go with you."

He shook his head, knowing he had to get away from her for awhile before he lost all sense of reason — and propriety. "He's probably fine. I'll send for you if he or anyone else needs you. I have to go now. Are you going to be all right?"

"Splendid. And Michael, thanks."

He passed off her gratitude with a careless shrug and hurried out the door.

Michael didn't come back, either that day or the next.

He sent Johnny Perkins and Joe Corley, the carpenter who had built her house, to repair her roof and board up the dining room window until another unit could be ordered and delivered. When they took a break, they talked nonstop about the storm. Luckily, no one had been seriously injured, although Slim had taken a blow on the shoulder from a flying tile from the depot's roof.

"He's just fine, ma'am," Johnny hastened to assure her. "Got his arm in a sling and taking it easy. Says he's been wanting another chance to give Mr. Donovan orders since they put Mr. Donovan's first buildings up together, and now he's got it. Don't take me wrong, ma'am. Mr. Donovan can work harder'n any man I've ever seen. He just don't know much about carpentering."

"You should see the town, ma'am," Joe put in. "Mr. Donovan's new hotel is nothing more than a pile of rubbish. We hadn't put many of the walls up yet and that wind just whipped right through and pulled it all down. The porch is gone off the mercantile and most of the roofs are gone off the barn and the depot and Mr. Donovan's house. But the old hotel is still standing just as strong as it was before the storm. Nobody can figure that one."

"I can," Johnny said through a mouth stuffed full of Wynn's pound cake. "Granny Simpson says it's because she was on her knees the entire time, begging the Lord to save her so Rachel and David wouldn't find out she was there by herself."

"By herself?" The stark memory of being alone during the first part of the storm came flooding in, almost choking Wynn with its intensity. "Where were you, Johnny? And you, Joe?"

Joe's mouth wasn't quite so full of cake. "I was with Doc, Johnny stayed with Rusty, and Slim was at the depot. Johnny didn't mean she was in the *hotel* by herself; there was other people at the hotel. Granny was in her *room* by herself. She locked her door and refused to come out. Said she'd been through wind before, and there wasn't no sense in panicking. Slim says she was just being ornery."

Johnny grinned broadly. "No ornerier than Rusty. That old ornery horse bucked and snorted and nearly kicked the door out of his stall. I didn't think I was ever going to get him calmed down."

"How *did* you manage it?" Wynn asked, remembering her own experience in dealing with the ornery horse.

"I tried everything. Talking to him and giving him fresh oats and stroking his neck when he'd let me. None of that did any good, though."

When Johnny seemed hesitant to continue, Joe prodded him. "Tell her what you finally did."

The hotel clerk blushed a rich shade of scarlet and looked down at his coffee cup. "I, well, I got in the stall with him and sang to him."

"Tell her what song you sang."

"Oh, I tried a bunch of 'em — 'Blue-Tail Fly' and 'I Ride an Old Paint' — everyone I could think of that had a horse in it. But it took 'The Sow Got the Measles' to really soothe him."

Wynn howled. "You mean the one that goes 'The sow got the measles and she died in the spring'?"

Johnny nodded, smiling at the way she sang slightly

off-key.

"Why would Rusty like a song about a sow dying?"

"Who knows what makes that horse tick? Maybe it was the rhythm."

"More likely the fact that the man made a saddle out of the sow's hide," Joe observed.

The two were good company for Wynn. She silently blessed them for not questioning her about her reaction to the storm, for not mentioning Michael's staying with her through the night.

She worked at cleaning up the spare bedroom while they mended the roof. Because there was a shortage of tin, thanks to the storm, they straightened and tar-patched the pieces that had suffered only minor damage, then filled in with new pieces where they had to. It took them most of the day to finish the job.

"I'll come back in a week or so," Joe promised, "and fix your ceiling. Hope you don't mind, but there's so much other damage, and Mr. Donovan's anxious to clean up that pile of lumber at the new hotel site and get it started all over again. We got you in the dry in case it rains."

Wynn assured him that she didn't mind at all.

What she did mind was Michael not even coming back to tell her he wouldn't be coming back for a day or two. Surely, she thought, if he cared as much as he had acted like he did, he could have found a few minutes to visit her. She had the whole day after Joe and Johnny fixed her roof to sit and brood about Michael's absence, and the more she thought about it, the madder she got.

The next morning she got up and headed to town, but it was mid-afternoon before she got there. The sun was shining brightly and the temperature was much warmer, a combination which put her in the mood to do her laundry. She stripped the bed in the examina-

149

tion room and washed the sheets, along with her spare set of underthings, a basket of dirty towels, several skirts and shirtwaists, and both her flannel nightgowns.

Wynn detested doing laundry, but she detested soiled linen and garments even more. Someone had to do it; unfortunately, she was the only someone *to* do it. Most times, she heated water on the stove and washed out the little bit of laundry she had right in the kitchen, hanging the garments over the stove to dry. But she couldn't do that with bed linens.

She pumped water in the kitchen and hauled it outside to her black iron kettle, which sat in her backyard. Later on when she could afford it, she decided as she hauled bucketful after bucketful, she would get a pump for her backyard.

When the kettle was half-full, she built a fire under it using broken beading from the spare room ceiling for fuel. In went Octagon soap, then the dirty laundry, which she stirred until her shoulders ached, and then she stirred some more. She scrubbed the kitchen linens clean on her scrub board. Finally, everything had to be thoroughly rinsed, wrung out until her hands ached, and then hung on the line to dry.

She was so tired when she got through she almost decided to stay home. But she wanted to look at Slim's shoulder, even if he didn't want her to, and she wanted to see everyone else, too. Even Michael.

Who was she trying to fool? *Especially* Michael.

He saw her coming long before she got there.

"Ain't you glad I didn't pitch these extry tiles?"

When Michael didn't answer immediately—didn't even act like he'd heard the question, Slim tried again. "Good thing I stacked the extry tiles up in the barn, huh? Had to hide 'em from those SP fellers or they would've wanted to take most of 'em back. Think we got enough to fix this here roof?"

Damn, but she was a sight to behold, strutting along the path in her bustled skirt. Michael had to lean over to get a really good view of the way the bustle bounced and swayed with her every stride.

"Watch out, Mr. Donovan, or you'll fall off!"

That got Michael's attention, possibly because he did, suddenly, feel a sensation of falling. Slim grabbed his ankles and pulled as Michael scrambled back onto the red-tiled roof. He couldn't help wondering if Slim understood why he'd almost tumbled off.

"You got to pay attention, Mr. Donovan, on a roof as steep and uneven as this one. If you want to get down now, I think I can manage these last few by myself."

Maybe Slim knew, and maybe he didn't. It didn't really matter one way or the other to Michael, except that he didn't want people thinking something had happened between him and Wynn when it hadn't. If it had, he supposed he'd have to do something about it, like marry her.

The thought was sobering. He wanted her, had planned to have her, too. But that was before he'd come to know her very well, before he'd come to respect her, before he'd realized how fragile she could be. He'd have to watch himself around her, now that he was conscious of how he felt toward her. And that meant he'd have to keep his distance, at least until he had come to grips with those feelings.

He skipped the last rung on the ladder and jumped backwards, his feet coming to ground mere inches from where Wynn stood.

"Whoo!" she breathed, throwing a gloved palm up to her pounding chest. "I thought you were going to land right on top of me!"

"Sorry. Didn't know you were there." He meant he hadn't realized she was so close . . . so close he could hear her short, panting breaths, could smell the fresh scent of lilacs, could touch her and . . .

"I came to see the progress," she said, listening to the words and finding they fell far short of the truth. "And to see about Slim's shoulder," she quickly added.

"We're almost through here." Michael inclined his head toward the depot roof, then realized how unnecessary the gesture was. "And Slim's shoulder's fine now. Huh, Slim? I was just about to grab a bite to eat. Granny's cooking. You hungry?"

Damn! It had just been two days, yet his heart pounded a swift tattoo while his tongue and his brain and his stomach seemed all tied up at once.

Wynn smiled at his rather inept invitation to join him for an early supper. "No, not really," she replied, then felt guilty as she saw his smile fade. "But I would love a cup of tea," she hastily added.

"You'll change your mind when you smell Granny's chicken and dumplings." The grin reappeared, but this time Wynn noted a certain smugness in the tilt of his mouth. It was a look that said, "I know something you don't."

She did change her mind, and without any further coaxing from Michael. Granny's dumplings were big and fluffy, the sauce was thick and creamy, and the whole dish was swimming with big chunks of boiled chicken. Granny served up two bowls full, then turned back to her dishwashing.

"This eats as good as it looks and smells," Michael told her as he blew on a heaping spoonful.

Granny shot him a dubious glance. "It's just plain old country cooking. Nothing special about chicken stew."

Wynn savored the delicate flavors in her first bite. "Michael's right, Granny. This *is* special." Talking about the elderly woman's culinary talents reminded Wynn of the boardinghouse Granny had mentioned building. "You'll fill up that boardinghouse fast, Granny, when word gets around about your cooking."

"Oh, hush, you two!" Granny admonished, her pride showing through her scolding. "Slim might hear you."

"It's too late, Granny," Slim teased as he walked into the depot. "I already heard. And if it'll make you feel any better, I don't care, neither. I'm glad someone else around here can cook 'sides me. Come spring, we're going to have so many people here, both of us together won't be able to feed 'em all."

"God, I hope so!" Michael declared. "Granny, you pray for dry weather — and no more wind like that one the other night, or we'll never get the new hotel finished in time. We're a week into February already."

Michael froze as the date struck him with the force of a well-aimed fist in his stomach, and he almost choked on a mouthful of stew. He seldom thought about the calendar, not in terms of specific dates. To him it was early January or late May or the middle of the month, but never April second or August twentieth. The only dates he bothered to pay any attention to were July fourth and December twenty-fifth.

But he was looking at Slim's calendar, the daily tear-off one the Southern Pacific Railroad had sent him, and there was the date staring him right in the eye: February 7, 1884. It didn't take much figuring to count back three days and know the wind had struck on the fourth — the same day as Wynn Spencer's birthday.

Since he had met her, the fact that her name was Spencer had bothered him. And now the date of her birth did, too. He just couldn't fathom why.

* * *

Whatever had come over Michael? Wynn wondered later as she dressed for bed. One minute he'd been smiling and happy and enjoying his meal, and the next minute he'd turned sullen and seemed totally out-of-sorts with everyone. She replayed the entire conversation in her head but could find no reasonable explanation for his abrupt change in attitude. It must be his worry over the hotel, she finally decided, then promptly put the matter out of her head.

What she couldn't seem to put from her head was the memory of his long body pressed close to hers, his arm circling her waistline as they'd slept together in the narrow bed downstairs. She tossed and turned upon her mattress, yearning for the return of his strong arms around her, his soft breath upon her neck. Finally, she reached in the dark for the red flannel sachet, which she had left upon the small table by her bed. Though it failed miserably as a substitute for Michael Donovan, the sachet was all she had of him at the moment.

Wynn clutched the lilac-scented circle against her breasts and sought rest once again.

"Damned sore muscles!" Michael muttered, twisting and turning in his bed as he sought a comfortable position. In truth, he doubted his inability to rest had anything to do with pain—not of the physical variety, anyway. He was accustomed to hard labor, and he'd rubbed horse liniment into his shoulders and upper arms hours ago. No, he admitted, he was restless because he couldn't get that damned date out of his head.

February fourth. Wynn had said she was twenty-four, which meant she was born in '60. February 4, 1860. Something had happened to him on that date,

154

something that must be blocked out of his mind so completely he couldn't call back the memory now. He had been eight years old in 1860. Michael thought and thought about it, but for the life of him he couldn't remember much of anything from his childhood — not before he had gone to live in the orphanage in Chicago.

God, if he were going to forget something, why not the orphanage? That stinking, filthy, drafty old stone house on the south side with its resident horde of rats and mice and spiders? The people who ran it were no better than vermin themselves, interested only in how much money they could squeeze out of the consciences of wealthy do-gooders and then using it to line their own pockets.

But he couldn't forget the orphanage and he couldn't remember the family he was sure he'd had as a child — the family who had left him all alone to deal with life as best he could.

Alone . . . he'd always been alone. No matter who he'd lived with, who he'd shared his bed with over the years, he'd always felt alone.

Until the night of the windstorm, the night he had held Wynn close and buried his face in her hair as she slept. It was the first time he'd ever slept with a woman and not made love to her.

A part of him desperately wanted to make love to Wynn Spencer, to really make love to her, not just go through the motions. But that meant opening up to his emotions, and that was something he wasn't the least bit sure he wanted to do.

Not yet. Maybe not ever.

Chapter Nine

Granny Simpson must indeed have a channel straight to heaven. Or so everyone in Jennings decided when the weather remained relatively cooperative. An occasional day of rain stalled progress, but by and large, clear, fair skies and mild temperatures prevailed.

By the second week in March, all the wind damage had been repaired, Michael's new hotel was almost complete—only some finishing touches remained—and Joe had started building Granny's boardinghouse. Joe had bought himself a lot from Cary and planned to start building his own house soon. Otherwise, he quipped, he'd never get it done for all the building he was certain to be doing once people started arriving. His own family, a wife and four children, would be among the newcomers, and they would expect to find a house ready to move into.

But he'd promised Granny he'd build her boardinghouse first, before Rachel and David came back from Indiana and pitched the fit Granny assured everyone was coming.

"But if I'm settled and have a business going, they'll just have to learn to live with it. They won't be able to stop me then," she confided to Wynn over tea at the depot. "Are those two ever going to be surprised! They know I don't have much money of my own — but I'm sinking all I have into this venture. It will be the first time I've ever owned any real property." Her aging eyes glistened with unshed tears of pride.

"I'm happy for you, Granny," Wynn said, but her voice fell flat and joyless.

"What's eating at you, child? And don't tell me 'nothing.' I know better."

"I, uh," — Wynn raked her top teeth over her lower lip — "I have a lot on my mind."

Wynn spoke the truth, partially anyway. It was true she had a *lot* on her mind — the lot Michael had sold Granny Simpson, as a matter of fact. As soon as she could politely excuse herself from Granny's company, she hastened over to the new hotel, where Michael was busy staining the lobby wainscoting.

She hadn't seen much of him for the past four or five weeks — not since her birthday, not since the night of the windstorm. At first, she blamed his distance on his desire to allay any suspicion concerning their relationship and had been careful herself not to let her disappointment show when she'd gone into town. Later, she blamed it on the hotel construction. He seemed driven to finish it. Wynn understood determination to complete a project, to reach a goal, and she'd kept silent.

But this! This was too much! She couldn't believe he'd actually sold Granny a lot in town.

He turned around and smiled when he saw her. The smile quickly disappeared, though, at the sight of the snapping gleam in her pale eyes and the hands-on-hips stance she assumed when righteous indignation roiled inside her. He'd seen that combi-

157

nation too many times not to recognize what it meant.

Michael carefully laid his brush down across the top of the open can and sighed. "What have I done now?"

"Sold Granny Simpson a lot."

This constituted the fabric of her anger? This trivial, insignificant act? After he'd spent night after night tossing and turning, fighting the ever-present need to run as hard and fast as he could straight into Wynn's arms? And when he did sleep, he dreamed of holding her, kissing her, making sweet, passionate love to her. God, how he wanted her—wanted to take her right then and there without the benefit of preamble. And he had thought—had even dared to hope—her own need had grown apace with his. But she obviously wasn't interested in him, not as a person. Her interest lay solely in what he could do for her. The realization struck like a dull knife in his stomach.

His voice revealed the edge of his frustration, which he was barely able to hold in check. "And that's a crime? Wynn, I'm in the business of selling lots. You know that."

"Commercial lots," she argued.

"A boardinghouse is a business."

"So is a doctor's office. But you wouldn't sell me a lot. Oh, no. You made me buy one from Cary—way out from town."

"It's not just a doctor's office. It's your home."

"And you think Granny's not going to live in her own boardinghouse? Give me some credit, Michael."

He hadn't actually thought about it from that angle before. Damn if she didn't have a point. But he couldn't tell her he'd hoped she would pack up and

158

leave Jennings at the time she'd asked him to sell her a lot. He couldn't tell her he'd been afraid of her, afraid of how she made him feel inside. She would never understand. She might even laugh at him.

Nor could he tell her he was Granny's silent partner, that he was financing more than ninety percent of her initial costs. Granny had sworn him to secrecy on that matter. There had to be some other argument . . .

"But Cary's lots are cheaper than mine. Didn't he charge you the standard five dollars?"

"Yes."

"I charge seven. See? You saved two dollars." It was a valid argument. Michael picked up his paintbrush, summarily dismissing her.

Wynn refused to let it lie. "But I can't go very far without my cart and horse, and since I have no place to stable a horse, I have to pay Jock Delancy a monthly stabling fee. It's already cost me the piddling amount I saved."

He dipped the brush in the stain, wiped it on the inside lip of the can, and placed a long, smooth stroke on the wainscoting. "You could always build a barn, Wynn. Your lot's plenty large enough."

"Michael Donovan!" she snapped, balling her hands into tight fists at her sides. God, she wanted to hit him! And then, she wanted to take the can of stain and pour it over that knot of a head sitting on his neck. "You are not going to weasel your way out of this. A barn would cost me a small fortune, and taking care of a horse is something I simply don't have the time nor the expertise to do. Thanks to you and your rules—which you bend at will, now I have to walk into town to collect my horse and cart from the livery. On days like today, that's not so bad. But when the weather's nasty or it's the middle of the night, it will be."

"What do you want me to do about it?" His growing anger riddled his voice.

"Nothing, I suppose. What can you do now? The damage is done. I thought you were my friend. Now I know you're not." Her voice caught in her throat and she wheeled away from him.

"Wynn!" he called, but she ignored him. He watched her walk away, her back ramrod straight, her head held high. When she hesitated, he started to go after her, but her sniffle stopped him. Let her go off and lick her wounds, he decided. She'd get over it.

He hoped.

Damn him anyway. Damn him to hell and gone!

As the realization of what she'd thought struck her, Wynn's feet suddenly stopped moving and her mouth dropped open. She, Wynnifred Hughes Spencer, was swearing! Her mother would be turning over in her grave, for surely she had heard, just as God had. She offered a quick prayer for forgiveness and continued on her way.

Soon she had to stop again, this time to sneeze. Her cheekbones were sore and her eyes felt scratchy, too. She diagnosed her illness as a mild case of catarrh and made a mental note to drink some chamomile tea with her supper, then take a hot footbath, bundle up, and go to bed.

As March bled into April, the prairie came alive, waking up from its winter dormancy and embracing spring with a profusion of colorful wild flowers scattered among the fresh, bright green of new grass. The complete metamorphosis amazed Wynn, renewing her hope and thus her vigor. She awoke each day with the sun and set out on a long walk, collecting fresh bouquets to brighten the darker corners of her house and to tie into bundles and hang to dry for potpourri.

People began to scatter across the prairie as well. The Sunday trains from New Orleans brought droves of new settlers. Some Wynn had met in late fall; many were new faces. She met every one of them as they disembarked, introducing herself as a physician and offering her services should they be needed. Most treated her politely enough. She supposed she'd learn how they really felt when they got settled on their land-grant acreage and she started making rounds.

Granny secured a few patients for her through her boardinghouse. Although the building was a far cry from being finished, it did have a roof, panes in the windows, and outside walls, creating some shelter if not much comfort or privacy for the newcomers who were turned away from the hotels. They slept on pallets on the ground floor at night; during the daylight hours, they worked on their own homes while Joe and the crew he'd hired from among the settlers worked on the interior of the boardinghouse.

Both of Michael's hotels were full to overflowing, and still more settlers were arriving. Luckily, many of them brought tents and set up camp on their own property once they had applied for their land-grant patents or purchased lots from either Michael or S. L. Cary.

The lots close to Wynn's—on the south side of

Cary's acreage and, therefore, closest to town—were snapped up first. Her house became an island in a sea of white canvas. All day long, men sawed and jawed and hammered as new-home construction began, creating a pleasant cacophony of background noise for Wynn. The noise meant she wasn't going to be alone anymore—not *as* alone, she corrected. At least she'd have close neighbors.

Word got around about her taking care of Doc's gunshot wound. Everyone who came to see her mentioned it, and one day in the mercantile she overheard a man say, "If that old geezer would allow that female doctor to treat him, she must be all right."

From time to time, people came to see her with minor medical problems. Wynn set broken bones, prescribed remedies for colds, toothaches, and diarrhea, and treated a few fairly severe cuts and burns. A couple of expectant mothers called to ask if she would deliver their babies. These she counseled on the advantages of good nutrition during pregnancy.

One day, in mid-April, Wynn answered a knock at her door to find a pale, thin, sickly-looking young man cradling in his arms a little girl who appeared to be asleep. His face was fraught with concern. Wynn's heart went out to him.

"Ere you the doctor?" he asked, his voice a nasal twang.

"Yes, I am. Come in."

"Granny Simpson sent me," he said as he followed her on wobbly legs to the examination room. "This child has the fever. Can you make her well?"

"I'll certainly try. Put her here on the table." She turned around then, facing him. The man sneezed violently. In dismay, Wynn watched the droplets hover briefly in the air, then fall onto the table, the

162

child, and herself. A shiver slid down her back.

She tried to erase the nervousness from her voice and sound businesslike. "I'll put the kettle on and wash my hands."

Wynn was out of the room for only a few minutes, but when she came back, the man wasn't there. He had left the child on the table. Wynn checked the girl's pulse and found it steady. She laid two fingers and then the flat of her palm on the child's forehead and estimated her fever to be within a controllable level. Satisfying herself that further treatment could wait a few minutes, she took off after the man, whom she assumed to be the father.

Her front door was standing wide open; the man had disappeared. Wynn stood on her front porch and let her gaze roam the countryside. Her view was still basically unobstructed, although several foundations for new housing had been started around her. She couldn't imagine how he'd gone very far so fast, not in his weakened state, but she didn't dare leave the child to go searching for him. He'd be back.

While water heated in the kettle, she pumped more water into her dishpan, removed some clean cloths from a cabinet in the examination room, and dumped some of them into the pan. These she had intended to use to cool down the fever, but when she took another look, a long, hard look this time, she changed her tactics. The child was filthy beyond belief.

She dragged her galvanized hipbath from its corner into the middle of the kitchen floor, in front of the stove, then pumped more water at her sink, transferring it pitcher by pitcher full to the tub. When it was half-filled, she warmed it with hot water from the kettle, using her hands to mix and test

163

the water until she was convinced it was warm enough to clean and yet still tepid enough to aid the reduction of fever. For good measure, she added some carbolic acid. There was no telling what germs the child might be carrying upon her person. No wonder she was sick!

As a precaution, she washed her own face and slipped her bibbed apron on over her clothes. She needed to bathe and change her clothes, she knew, but not until after she cared for the child.

The girl continued to sleep, even when Wynn started to remove her boots and stockings. She started to drop them on the floor, then thought better of such action. They were worn out, simply not worth saving, definitely not worth running the risk of further infecting her house with them. She stuffed them into a crokersack, then followed them with the child's dress, pinafore, and bloomers. She pitched the crokersack out the back door, then picked up the naked child and carried her to the kitchen. Why, the girl didn't seem to weigh any more than a pitcherful of water!

The child stirred when Wynn set her in the tub, her movements weak at first. Within minutes, though, she began thrashing about and her voice came out a pitiful whine.

"Let me out!" she cried. "Daddy, Daddy, help me!"

"Sh-h-h !" Wynn soothed. "Your daddy asked me to take care of you for him. I'm Dr. Spencer. What's your name?"

The little girl ignored the question, and Wynn understood why when she turned brown eyes glazed with fright on Wynn. "I don't like water! Let me out of here!"

164

"Not until you're clean," Wynn said firmly, refusing to allow entrance to the guilt niggling at her conscience. The bath was necessary. "This will go much faster if you'll be still, child. Tell me what your daddy calls you."

She calmed somewhat. "Punkin."

"But that isn't your name, surely. What is your *name?*"

"Punkin."

Wynn didn't believe anyone would name a child Punkin. Perhaps the child didn't know her real name . . . She brightened at an idea. It was certainly worth trying. "What does your mother call you?"

The child dropped her eyes and sniffled. "Nothin'. She went away."

"Where did she go?"

The child lifted a thin shoulder. "I don't know. She was sick and they put her in the ground."

At least she'd learned something, but Wynn refused to give up. "I'm sure your mother loved you very much. What did she call you before she . . . went away?"

The little girl screwed her nose up and gave the question a moment of consideration before she answered, "Prairie."

"Prairie. Prairie. I've never heard anyone called that before, but I like it." Wynn dropped her cloth into the brown water and scrutinized the girl's thin body. "We need to rinse you, Prairie. Do you think you can stand up long enough for me to pour some warm water over you?"

The child nodded, her eyes far more trusting than they had been moments before.

"Just sit still until I check the water in the kettle. I wouldn't want to scald you."

165

Now that she was clean, the child was amazingly beautiful. Her nose was short and stubby with a light sprinkling of freckles across it. Her huge brown eyes were deeply set and fringed with long, dark lashes; above them rode thick, dark eyebrows. Her chin was almost pointed, her cheeks so full Wynn was certain a smile would plop big dimples into the middle of them. Although she was thin, her frame was sturdy with no hint of rickets.

But her hair! Wynn couldn't even be certain what color it was beneath the dusty film that coated every strand.

She wrapped Prairie in a big, thick towel and set her on the enamel top of her table.

"What are you going to do now?" the child asked.

"Wash your hair."

"Oh, no, you're not! No one ever washes my hair."

"Which is exactly why I'm going to wash it now. Don't worry. It won't hurt. And afterwards, we'll have a bite of lunch, if you're hungry."

The child's hair, once clean, proved to be as dark as her eyebrows. Wynn sat Prairie by the stove while she combed out the thick mass, and the heat almost dried it. Its ends curled naturally as they dried.

As she combed, Wynn racked her brain, trying to figure out what she could put on the child until she could get her some more clothes. In the end, she settled for one of her own shirtwaists. Although Wynn was short, its tail hit Prairie at her ankles and the sleeves were almost twice too long. Wynn rolled them up, then shook her head at the way the bodice swallowed Prairie's narrow shoulders and thin chest.

The child fingered the pearl buttons and the rows of lace and tucks marching down the front, her eyes wide with wonder. "Pretty," she said.

Wynn thought about the garments she had stuffed into the crokersack—the stained and torn calico dress, the unadorned pinafore of indeterminate color, the threadbare bloomers. She doubted Prairie had ever had anything really pretty to wear.

They had oatmeal and cinnamon toast for lunch, which was what Prairie requested. Wynn watched in much amazement as the girl opened her linen napkin and spread it in her lap, then touched it primly to her lips and the corners of her mouth as they became soiled. Her refined manners seemed totally incongruous with the degree of filth she had been so determined to keep.

The child ate two large bowls full of oatmeal, adding large dollops of butter and several heaping teaspoonfuls of brown sugar to each serving. Wynn could not help wondering when the child had eaten last.

She tucked the little girl into the bed in the examination room, sitting down on the edge and using her palm to smooth back Prairie's clean hair. "Your fever's almost gone," she said, "but I need to ask you some questions before you go to sleep so that I can take better care of you. Okay?"

Prairie nodded.

"Does your head ache?"

"No, but Daddy's does."

"How do you know?"

"He told me."

Wynn catalogued that bit of information, then continued. "Is your throat sore?"

"No."

"Is your daddy's throat sore?"

"I think so. I'm tired."

"I know you are, darling. I'm almost through, but

167

I need to look at your nose and throat first, even if they don't hurt." Wynn retrieved a spoon from the kitchen and brought the lamp back to the bed with her. "I'm going to use the handle of this spoon to hold your tongue down so I can see into your throat. It won't hurt, Prairie. Now, open your mouth wide and say 'ah-h-h' for me."

Prairie's throat looked pink and healthy enough, and her nose was clear as well. "You're going to be just fine, Prairie," Wynn said, hoping to elicit a smile from the child, smiling herself when twin dimples appeared in Prairie's round cheeks.

"Can I go home with my daddy?"

"Sure thing. Soon as he comes back to get you. If you'll tell me where to look, I'll go and get him while you take a nap."

"I don't know, Doctor—I forgot your name."

"Spencer. You can call me Wynn, though, if you like."

The child rolled her head back and forth on the pillow. "Oh, no. That wouldn't be proper."

Wynn smiled down at Prairie and stood up. "You go to sleep now."

"You—you won't leave me, will you?"

"No, Prairie. I won't leave you. I'll be right here in the house. Just call me if you need me. All right?"

Soothed, the child closed her eyes and snuggled deeper into the bed. Wynn stood there for a long time, looking down at her, wishing she had a child of her own like Prairie.

Finally, she pulled herself away from the bed, then went outside and set fire to the crokersack. When it was nothing more than a pile of smoldering ashes in her burning barrel, she doused it well with the dirty bath water, then prepared a fresh tubful in the hipbath.

Later, Wynn made herself a cup of tea and sat in the kitchen thinking about Prairie. She set her age at about four and wondered when her mother had died. Someone had taught the child well. Wynn could not believe the man who had brought Prairie to him had been that person. If he was, indeed, Prairie's father, he must not care much about the child, else he would have returned to check on her by now.

Unless something had prevented him.

Prairie had said her father had a headache and sore throat. He had looked feverish to Wynn. With those symptoms, the man could have any one of several highly contagious diseases, though Wynn would have to examine him to know which one. If that were the case, though, the town could be in real trouble. Typhoid, diphtheria, cholera, scarlet fever—they could all spread like wildfire—and there were no cures. The man could, at that very moment, be infecting others.

Wynn had to find out, but she didn't dare leave the child alone, not after she'd promised her she'd be there when she woke up. If her house were only closer to town, or if she just had some neighbors . . .

The pounding of a hammer broke into her reverie. She might not have permanent neighbors yet, but she was getting some. She stopped long enough to assure herself Prairie was still asleep, then rushed outside and down the path to a group of men who were busy raising one wall of a new house.

"Pardon me," she called. "I need one of you to help me, please."

"We're busy, ma'am," a large, burly fellow with a full red beard told her, awarding her the most

169

cursory of glances before hollering, "Heave, ho!"

A dozen biceps bulged and half that many necks strained as six men lifted the framework and positioned it on the floor joist. Two held the wall in place; two began hammering it into the joist with long, thick nails; two more set heavy timbers as props between the wall and the ground until it could be tied to perpendicular walls. When one of the latter two moved aside, sat down on an upturned keg, and took out his tobacco pouch, Wynn approached him.

"Please, sir," she began, waiting for him to look up at her before she continued. He squinted at her and shook his head. "Please, hear me out. I wouldn't ask for your help if it weren't important. I need to get a message to someone in town. Couldn't you please take a few minutes to deliver it for me?"

"A message, you say? That's all?"

She gave him an affirmative nod. "I need to speak with Mr. Donovan as quickly as possible."

He still hesitated. "Why don't you go yourself?"

"Because there's a sick little girl at my house I have to take care of. I wouldn't have left her even to come over here if this weren't important. Really important."

He stood up then and dusted the sawdust off the seat of his overalls. "You want me to find Mr. Donovan and tell him you need to see him. Right?"

"Yes. Tell him Dr. Spencer needs to see him immediately. And thanks."

She started to leave, then turned back. "You do know who Mr. Donovan is, don't you?"

"Everybody knows who Mr. Donovan is, ma'am," he said impatiently. "I'll tell him. You go on back home and see about the child. I'm on my way."

170

Wynn thanked him again and hurried back to her house, stopping on the porch and glancing toward town to assure herself the man was, indeed, on his way. He shuffled along, whistling and smoking, seemingly in no hurry to get there. His attitude infuriated her, but he was, after all, doing her a favor. A few minutes one way or the other, she supposed, shouldn't make a difference.

As soon as she opened the door, she heard Prairie's sobs. The child calmed immediately when she saw Wynn, thrusting tight fists into her eye sockets and rubbing hard.

"Where were you, Dr. Wynn? I called and you didn't come."

Wynn sat down on the bed with the child and hugged her close, her open palms rubbing Prairie's head and back. "I just went outside for a minute. I wouldn't have left you."

"Mommy did."

Wynn rocked back and forth on the mattress as she cuddled the child, murmuring soothing words, until Prairie's sniffles subsided. "You didn't take a very long nap," she said. "Do you want to go back to sleep now?"

She felt Prairie's nose rub back and forth across her chest. "Does that mean 'no'?"

"I'm hungry again. Do you have something else to eat?"

Hungry? Again? "I'll have to cook. You want to come with me and keep me company in the kitchen? You do? Good. Now, tell me what you want to eat . . ."

Chapter Ten

It was almost dusk before Michael got Wynn's message. By that time, it had gone through several sets of ears and mouths and suffered considerable alteration in the process, but Michael didn't know that. He had no reason not to believe the message he heard, which was "Go quick. Dr. Spencer's real sick, maybe dying."

Already exhausted from the day's labors, he dropped his hammer and took off running, terrified of what he'd find at Wynn's house. Adrenaline kept him going clean through the pounding he gave her locked front door. He cursed, then backed up to give himself room to kick it in when Wynn, as healthy and hearty as he'd ever seen her, opened the portal.

Relief washed the energy he had mustered right out of him. His head spun out of control, his knees turned to jelly, and he feared he might collapse right there on her porch. In reaction, he bent forward, rested his hands on his thighs, and forced himself to take deep breaths.

"Thank God, you're all right this time," he wheezed.

"Of course I'm all right!" she snapped. "Why wouldn't I be?"

"They said you were sick," he panted, "maybe dying."

"Well," she huffed, "you took your sweet time getting here to save me, didn't you?"

Talking was difficult enough for him; rational thought was almost an impossibility. "Sweet time? Hell, Wynn, I ran as fast as I could!"

"You don't have to sound so miffed about it. I'm the one who has a right to be angry. I sent for you hours ago. Where have you been?"

She was angry? Where had *he* been? He shot her a look of total disbelief and saw, for the first time, the hard flash in her eyes, the tight line of her lips. He didn't have to defend himself to her, and she was crazy if she thought he was going to.

He reached behind his head and ran an open palm down his hair, plucking a strand between his thumb and forefinger and pulling it out for her inspection. In contrast to her bold irritation, his voice was deceptively soft. "Your scissors must have been dull, Delilah."

His remark served its purpose. A look of absolute confusion replaced that of her ire. "Delilah?"

"You're an intelligent woman, Wynn. Figure it out." Michael turned his back on her and started toward the steps, wincing as a cramp grabbed the muscle in his left calf.

"Wait!" she cried, not stopping to close her front door as she dashed after him. He ignored her, but he was moving so painfully slow she had no trouble catching up with him. She clutched his forearm and repeated, though in a

173

much calmer voice, "Wait, Michael. Please."

"Dammit, Wynn!" he moaned without turning around. "Why do we have to fight all the time? I was scared. Do you understand? Scared. I didn't know what I'd find when I got here. I kept seeing you huddled up in that quilt during the storm, shaking like a leaf. Then I get here and there's nothing wrong with you at all, and what do you do? Crawl all over me. Treat me like I was your hired hand. You don't own me, Wynn Spencer. Do you hear me? You don't own me."

She clutched his forearm tighter and stepped around in front of him. Although he couldn't see very well in the pale light of early evening, he was certain the glitter in her crystal blue eyes was that of unshed tears. Despite his best efforts to the contrary, his heart softened a fraction.

Snaring the slight advantage his hesitancy offered, she quickly apologized. "I'm sorry, Michael. I shouldn't have lashed out at you. I'm just . . . distraught is the word, I suppose. It's not your fault."

His head had begun to clear a bit, enough that he heard her say *distraught,* enough to realize she had needed him, perhaps still did. Perhaps another chink in her armor, he mused, smiling at the thought. Obviously, though, she wasn't distressed anymore. Her husky voice rolled like warm honey from her throat.

"Please, Michael. Come inside. I—need to talk to you. It's important. And there's someone I want you to meet. We were about to eat supper. You're welcome to join us."

He continued to hesitate, as much, he supposed,

to needle her as for any other reason. Damn, but she could be one exasperating woman! In truth, Michael wasn't the least bit sure he *could* walk back to town, not with the humdinger of a charley horse that had hold of his calf. And he *was* hungry. "Do you promise to stay calm?"

"I promise."

"The first time—"

"I'll behave, Michael. Just come with me, please. You have to meet her."

Her? Following Wynn's lead, he limped down the hall to the kitchen, shaking his head the whole way.

He'd been dealt a few surprises in his life, but never one quite so startling as seeing the delicate child, clothed in what could only be one of Wynn's shirtwaists, seated at the kitchen table. He was glad he hadn't made a bet on this one.

"Good evening, sir," she piped. "I'm Prairie."

Michael chuckled, sat down across from her, and began to massage his calf. "And I'm Michael."

Prairie wrinkled her stubby nose and gave him stare for stare. "Don't you have another name?"

"Several. Which one do you want to hear?"

"All of them."

"Jason Michael Patrick Donovan, Miss Priss." A broad smile wreathed his face at her round-eyed reaction. Out of the corner of his eye, he caught Wynn's astonished look as well.

"That many names?" Prairie asked. "How did your mommy know which one to call you?"

"She didn't call me any of them. She called me Mickey." Where had that memory come from? His smile vanished and his eyes clouded.

Prairie didn't allow him time for much reflection. "Well, you're grown, so I can't call you Michael or Mickey. I guess I'll call you Mr. Donovan. Is that all right?"

"That's fine." He looked askance at Wynn, who was setting a plate of steaming biscuits on the table.

She mouthed, "I'll explain later," and turned back to the stove. "I hope you like scrambled eggs," she called over her shoulder. "Prairie wanted some sawdust gravy, too, but I didn't have any sausage, so we're having brown gravy instead."

Prairie wrinkled her nose at that announcement. "I don't like toodlum gravy," she pouted.

"Toodlum gravy?" Wynn and Michael asked almost in unison.

Big tears rolled out of the child's eyes; she swiped at them stoically with her tiny hands and sniffled.

"Never mind," Wynn soothed. "You don't have to eat any gravy if you don't want to, Prairie. Would you like me to butter your biscuit?"

Prairie's little pointed chin trembled as she nodded, but she soon regained her inquisitiveness. "What do you do, Mr. Donovan?"

"Do? Why, many different things. I guess you could call me a businessman."

"Do you play poker?"

A loud guffaw erupted from Michael's throat. "Sometimes," he admitted. "Do you?"

Prairie pinned him with an I-know-you-know-better look that was so convincing Michael laughed again. The two kept a steady stream of chatter going throughout the meal. Wynn hung onto every

176

word, hoping to learn more about this enigmatic child who had, for all practical purposes, been left on her doorstep. She honestly didn't believe the man who had brought Prairie would be coming back.

But if she expected Prairie to divulge any new information, she was disappointed. The child exhibited a natural skill at deftly guiding the conversation away from herself.

Michael noted that trait as well, though he spent more of his mental energy watching Wynn, absorbing her essence, thinking about wickedly delightful things. He felt as though he would explode if he didn't touch her soon.

Wynn felt as though she would explode if she didn't get to *talk* to Michael soon. Since privacy was required, she bustled Prairie upstairs and put her to bed as soon as they'd finished supper. "I'll be back up in a little while," she assured the child, "and I'll leave the lamp on if you promise not to touch it."

"Oh, Dr. Wynn, I know better than that! Lamps can cause fires!"

"Promise me," Wynn insisted.

Prairie licked her right index finger and made an *X* over her heart. "Cross my heart, hope to die, stick a needle in my eye."

Wynn shook her head in wonder and frustration and went down to the kitchen, where Michael stood at the sink washing dishes. He had tied her apron, which was much too small for him, around his waist, letting the bib fall over his stomach. She had to hold her hand over her mouth to keep from bursting out in a fit of giggles. Despite her attempt at control, her eyes glistened with mirthful tears and her lips twitched when she dropped her hand to accept the towel Michael handed her.

Before she had time to react, he caught her around the waist and pulled her hard against him. "Come here," he whispered, his lips hovering dangerously close to hers. "I've been wanting to do this for weeks."

She supposed he meant to kiss her—with every fiber of her being, she wanted him to kiss her, but he toyed with her instead, rubbing his bristly chin against the tip of her nose and then laying his cheek against her own. For a long moment, he just stood there, holding her. She felt her heart pound against his chest, felt his heart answer in kind. Her lungs burned from too little oxygen, but she just couldn't seem to breathe properly. Her lips ached for his, trembling in readiness.

At long last he pulled back, his green gaze boring into her blue eyes, asking, begging, for permission. Wynn let go of the dishtowel and slipped her open palms up his chest, up his neck, to his cheeks, then plunged her fingers into the springy hair above his ears. She pulled his face down to meet hers, reaching on tiptoes to plant a kiss upon his lips.

He allowed her to be the aggressor for a moment, until her lips parted beneath his and a long sigh escaped. Then he assumed command, plunging his tongue into the honeyed recesses of her mouth, probing and flicking, eliciting rapturous tremors that racked her small frame. His hold tightened then as his own body shuddered in return.

Michael wanted to do far more than kiss her, but

there was a little girl upstairs in Wynn's bed. His mouth released hers as he remembered Prairie, and his forehead fell into the curve of her shoulder. Her fingers moved through his hair, around his ears, and came to rest on the back of his neck.

When his pulse had slowed, Michael lifted his head and gazed longingly into Wynn's glittering eyes. "Did you get over being angry at me?" he asked, his voice tender and low.

"No. I think I'll always be outdone with you about something."

His bushy eyebrows slowly rose. "But you kissed me."

Wynn blushed and looked away, disentangling herself from his embrace. "I — I need to talk to you about Prairie."

"We need to talk about us."

Oh, dear! Not now, Michael. I'm not ready to talk about us. "We can do that later. This is . . . important."

"And we're not?"

"Please, Michael, let's don't argue about this."

"Why not? We argue about everything else."

"Michael —" she warned.

"We do, you know. You find fault with everything I do. My hotel isn't big enough; then it's not clean enough. I try to help an old lady get started in a business, and you chew me out. One minute, you offer me your kisses, and the next you turn into a shrew. If I didn't like you, Wynn Spencer, if I didn't care about you, I wouldn't be here."

She sighed. "I like you, too, Michael. And we'll talk about us later. I promise."

"All right," he said, his voice resigned. "We'll

179

talk while we finish the dishes. I'll wash; you dry and put away."

She watched him plunge his big hands into the soapy water and drag up a plate, and she tried to remember if she'd ever watched a man wash dishes before. This was a first, she decided.

"I've never been around children much, but that one is delightful. Where did she come from?" he asked.

"A man brought her today. I think he must be her father. He looked sick himself, but he asked me to take care of Prairie. While I was in the kitchen, he disappeared. He never came back."

Michael shrugged away her concern. "He'll probably show up tomorrow. I wouldn't worry about it."

"But, Michael, Prairie said her father had a headache and a sore throat. That might not mean anything, but with those symptoms, it's possible he has one of several highly contagious diseases." Wynn's voice caught in her throat and she had to swallow hard before she could continue. She didn't want to tell Michael or anyone else she was troubled because this man had sneezed all over her. She was thankful Michael didn't think to ask her about it.

He heard her distress, attributed it to female perspective, and countered with, "Don't you think you're overreacting, Wynn? The man probably has nothing more than a cold."

"You didn't see him, Michael."

"Tell me about him."

Wynn took a deep breath. "He was wretched. Thin, pale, dirty. And weak, really weak. I've never

180

seen quite so much pain in anyone's eyes. I've thought about it since, and I don't think it was all physical pain. I've seen enough pain in my life, both emotional and physical, to recognize the difference. This man is definitely suffering from both. I can't treat the emotional, and I may not be able to do much for the physical. But I'm concerned about what he might be transmitting."

Michael had never understood women. Wynn didn't seem to be an exception. If she was so all-fired concerned, why hadn't she done something about it herself instead of sending for him? And then, she'd lambasted him the minute he'd shown up. Well, she wasn't going to put him on the defensive or snare him into another argument. Somehow, he always came out of one of their 'discussions' feeling like the loser.

Even though his concentration on scouring egg film off an iron skillet prevented her from seeing him clearly, he put on his best poker face. Trying to sound nonchalant, he asked, "Why didn't you try to track him down?"

"I wanted to go to town, to see if I could find him, but I didn't dare leave Prairie."

"Why didn't you take her with you?"

"I, uhm, I put her clothes in the burning barrel. They were little more than filthy rags. Besides, if that man is carrying a contagious disease, her clothes were probably contaminated. Do you have anything at the mercantile that would fit her?"

"I don't think I have any ready-made clothes for girls. How about some little boys' overalls?"

Wynn laughed at the very idea, then realized she might have to put Prairie in overalls until she could

181

have some things made for her. The child couldn't continue to wear her shirtwaists. Goodness! She was getting way ahead of herself. Surely Prairie's father would come back tomorrow, just as Michael said. He'd have other clothes for her.

Michael interrupted her reflection. "If I'm to look for Prairie's father, I'll need a better description."

"He's slight of build, in his mid-twenties, I'd guess. Scraggly hair and beard, dirty blond—and I mean dirty, literally. His face was pale and drawn with deep hollows in his cheeks, and he couldn't even walk without wobbling. He was dressed in work boots and overalls and he was wearing a jacket."

"As warm as it was today?"

"Yes. I know he had on a jacket because I remember thinking how uncomfortable I would have been wearing a wrap."

"Did Prairie give you any idea where he might have gone? It would help if I knew where to look, or at least had a name. There're a lot of people in this town now, Wynn."

She sighed. "I know. I couldn't get much out of Prairie. She did tell me that her mother is dead, but I have no idea what her last name might be. Oh!" she gasped. "How could I have forgotten?"

"What?"

"He said Granny Simpson sent him out here. Maybe he's staying at her boardinghouse."

"I'll stop by there on my way home. What do you want me to do if he's there?"

"Tell Granny to make sure no one sleeps anywhere near him. If he's coughing or sneezing, he

182

should be completely isolated. Michael, I really do need to examine him."

"I'll be back early tomorrow morning. If I do find him, I'll stay with Prairie while you go into town. How's that?"

True to his word, Michael showed up shortly after sunrise. His knocking woke Wynn and Prairie.

"It's my daddy," Prairie announced in a voice animated with excitement.

"Maybe," Wynn said, yawning and wondering if she had ever been as chipper so early in the morning. She didn't think so. She got up and pulled on her dressing robe. "More likely, it's Michael — Mr. Donovan. You stay here."

She moved as quickly as her still sleepy body allowed. By the time she reached the foot of the stairs, she knew it was Michael standing behind her door. No one else knocked quite as insistently as he did.

"Where's Prairie?" he whispered, his gaze roaming the hall as he moved on cat feet toward the kitchen.

"Upstairs."

"Good. Fill the kettle, please, and get the pot ready while I get your stove going. I need some coffee. And I'm not talking until we get some dripping."

Wynn did as he bade, marveling over how he made himself at home. The tingly feeling she'd had when they'd shared coffee on her birthday returned, spawning gooseflesh on her arms. He made her feel almost as if they were married.

But there was something about his attitude that alarmed her. His expression bordered on being sour, with the skin around his mouth drawn tight and his eyes dull. On second glance, she noticed he wore the same clothes he'd had on the night before, but now they were wrinkled and dirty, as though he'd never taken them off. His hair fell across his forehead and his eyelids were puffy. From lack of sleep? She knew it was a likely possibility.

She willed him to hurry, to tell her quickly what he had discovered before Prairie came downstairs. Wynn couldn't be the least bit certain the child would obey her and remain in the bed.

Finally, he completed his task and sat down with her at the table. He steepled his hands and rested his chin on his fingers. When he spoke, his words fell bluntly. "The man who brought Prairie to you is dead."

"Oh, no! What . . . where?"

"Down by the river. Your examination should answer your other question."

"The Mermentau is almost four miles from here," Wynn observed. "I'm surprised he made it that far in his weakened condition." She gave that thought brief consideration, then discounted it as immaterial when another, more sobering concern crossed her mind. "Where do you think he was going?"

Michael shrugged. "I'd guess he was leaving here—for good. And he wasn't on foot, Wynn; he was on horseback."

So that was how he'd gotten away from her

house so quickly! Wynn bit her bottom lip as she thought about Michael's supposition. "I can't imagine anyone, especially a parent, abandoning a child like Prairie. Are you sure it's the right man?"

"He fits the description you and Granny gave me."

"Did Granny know his name?"

"Jernigan. That's all he told her. She said he just showed up at her door yesterday and asked where he could find a doctor. She didn't see him again."

"How did you find him, way down by the river? What made you think to look there?"

Michael got up and poured boiling water into the coffee pot. "I didn't know where to look, so I organized a search party. Since a good many of the settlers brought their own livestock, almost everyone had a horse to ride. Otherwise, it might have been days before we found him. One of the groups brought him in less than an hour ago, just before daybreak."

"Where is his body now?"

"In my barn. Slim is whipsawing some cypress lumber together to make a coffin, and some of the men are scouting out a place to bury him. There's not much high ground around here. It took a body dying to make us see that we needed a cemetery."

"Are you going to put my daddy in the ground?"

Wynn and Michael turned in unison toward the pitiful little voice. Prairie stood in the open kitchen doorway, her dark hair a tangled, wispy cloud, her chin trembling as she awaited an answer.

Wynn moved quickly across the room, scooping up Prairie and hugging the child to her breast. "Yes, dear," she said, her heart shattering as Prairie

185

began to whimper. She returned to her chair and settled the girl on her lap, holding Prairie's head against her chest. "I'm sorry, Prairie," she soothed. "I'm so sorry."

Something clicked in Michael's memory, causing his gut to wrench. For a brief moment, he saw his mother holding him, soothing him, just as Wynn held and soothed Prairie. He heard himself cry, *I don't want my daddy put in the ground! Don't let them put him in the ground!*

And then the thread of memory vanished.

They buried Jernigan—that was all they knew to call him—on a knoll east of town where the Mermentau River's winding course almost backtracked, not too far from where they'd found him. The spring rains and high water made traveling there difficult, even with the short funeral procession taking advantage of a low ridge that ran east for most of the way. The body was hauled to the site on a mud boat.

It was a simple ceremony. Since none among them was a man of the cloth, Doc volunteered to read a few scriptures. The group sang a verse of "Shall We Gather at the River," and one of the settlers who attended volunteered to pray for the disposition of the stranger's soul.

As they started back to town, one of the women began to sing "The Wayfaring Stranger," her deep alto flowing through the haunting melody. Doc asked Wynn to walk with him behind the others. When they were out of earshot, he asked quietly, "What did you find when you examined Jernigan?"

186

Both his ignorance and his interest surprised Wynn, as she had given Michael all the pertinent details of her examination. But she saw no reason to keep Doc or anyone else who might want to know in the dark. "Diphtheria."

Doc shook his head sadly. "I was afraid it was something like that. What are you going to do?"

She shrugged resignedly. "What *can* I do? It could have been worse."

Doc pursed his lips and thought about that for a moment. "There's not much worse than diphtheria, Wynn, except maybe smallpox and cholera."

"And yellow fever. I don't think he got close enough to anyone to infect them anyway."

"Except you and Granny. And his little girl could have it. What's her name?"

"Prairie."

"Oh, yes. Unusual name. Where is the child today?"

"I left her with Granny."

"Probably for the best," Doc agreed. "Death is hard on a child." *Hell, it's hard on adults!* "No sense in subjecting her to a funeral, too. Did Jernigan happen to cough or sneeze at your house?"

She hadn't told anyone that Jernigan did; she wasn't sure she wanted to tell anyone, including Doc. Wynn thoroughly understood the increased risk of infection when she became a doctor; quite simply, it came with the territory. She didn't want anyone fawning over her, suffocating her with attention for the next week. The incubation period was short—two to eight days. Two had passed already. She would know soon enough if she had been infected. In the meantime, she decided, she'd

187

just wait it out . . . alone. Still, Doc's observations, questions, and interest piqued her curiosity.

She turned the tables on him by posing her own question. "Why are you called 'Doc'?"

She certainly caught him unaware. He shot her an I-don't-have-to-answer-that look and clamped his mouth shut.

"Is it because you once practiced medicine? Come on, Doc, you can tell me. I can keep a secret."

"I don't want to talk about it" was all he would say, but his failure to deny it convinced Wynn that his nickname was short for "Doctor."

They walked the remainder of the way without further conversation, each of them lost in their own dark ruminations.

Chapter Eleven

While Wynn was tucking the covers around Prairie that night, someone knocked at the door.

"It's my daddy!" Prairie cried, starting to scramble out of the bed.

"No, dear," Wynn soothed. "It can't be your daddy. He's not coming back."

"Yes, he is!" the child protested. "Let me see him!"

Wynn sighed heavily, wondering how to convince her that her daddy was dead, that dead meant gone forever, wondering too if this was going to happen every time somebody knocked. Before she could stop Prairie, the little girl scooted to the opposite side of the bed, leaped to the floor, and tore out of the room. As she envisioned her tripping and tumbling down the steps, Wynn's heart jumped into her throat. She would have to make the child slow down.

Suddenly, the magnitude of the responsibility of taking care of Prairie gripped her with frightening intensity. The few times she'd thought about becoming a mother had brought images of sitting in a rocking chair, cuddling a tiny baby and singing it to sleep. Prairie was certainly not a tiny baby. Nor had her training been consistent. Her antics were a source of almost constant amazement to Wynn; she'd lull Wynn into passivity by playing the role of prim and proper young lady, and then she'd give her full shock treatment by turning into a little hoodlum. If Wynn were to be Prairie's guardian, even on a temporary basis, she'd have to learn how to discipline the child.

"It's Mr. Donovan!" Prairie called out to Wynn, who had walked out of the bedroom onto the landing and could see Michael standing just inside the door, holding Prairie.

He looked devilishly handsome, she thought, in a faded red shirt, its sleeves rolled up to his elbows, and skintight Levi's, their soft, often-washed denim molding to the taut muscles of his trim buttocks and long thighs. The April sun had lent him a portion of its golden glow, tanning his complexion to the color of warm honey while burnishing streaks of molten copper into his dark hair. He looked up at her and flashed her a grin that sent her blood racing.

She looked incredibly beautiful, he thought, standing at the top of the stairs in a dark blue skirt with her stocking feet peeking out of its hem. Her white, highnecked bodice, constructed with numerous seams and darts designed to emphasize the fullness of her breasts and the narrowness of her waist, clung like a second skin. She had dressed her hair uncharacteristically though fashionably high on her head, most probably to accommodate the hat she had worn to the funeral. Some of the strands had come loose, to fall in a soft, wispy fringe across her forehead, over her ears, and down her neck. She glowed with a warm radiance that

190

would put the April sun to shame.

He watched the pink tip of her tongue flicker out to moisten her lips and realized his own had gone suddenly dry as well.

"I can see that, Prairie," she said, her voice huskier, he thought, than usual. "You come back to bed."

"I don't want to go back to bed, Dr. Wynn. I want to see Mr. Donovan. He brought me a present. Hurry up, Dr. Wynn. He brought you one, too."

"Yes, Dr. Wynn. Hurry up!" Michael mimicked, his green eyes bright with mischief.

The mention of a present from Michael brought the faded red flannel sachet to mind, and Wynn smiled. The smile softened the intended sternness of her reprimand. "No more running in the house, Prairie. It's dangerous."

Wynn's smile widened as she watched Michael's expression change from that of imp to taskmaster. He grasped Prairie's chin, turned her face upward, and lowered his forehead so that their noses were inches apart. His voice matched his expression. "You *didn't* run down the stairs."

Unperturbed, Prairie grinned and nodded her head vigorously, setting her curls to dancing. "Yes, I did, Mr. Donovan. I thought you was my daddy."

"Were," Wynn automatically corrected.

"This really is serious, Prairie," Michael continued, resisting the urge to allow his twitching lips to burst into a full-blown smile. "Running down the stairs is dangerous. So is opening the door. Promise me you'll let Dr. Wynn do that from now on."

Her grin disappeared and she dropped her gaze, her attitude appropriately penitent. "Yes, Mr. Donovan. Can I eat my peppermint stick now?"

"You *may* eat your candy tomorrow, Prairie," Wynn answered. "We've already brushed your teeth. I'll put it away for you."

Prairie held the red-striped stick close to her chest. "Where the ants won't get it?"

"I'll put it in a jar. Now, you go back to bed, little lady."

Reluctantly, Prairie handed her candy cane over to Wynn. "Can Mr. Donovan tuck me in this time?"

"Don't correct her!" Michael teased, starting up the stairs. "Make us something to drink, will you?"

"Coffee?"

"No, something cool. Water will be fine."

"Do you like lemonade?"

"I love it."

When he strolled into the kitchen a few minutes later, Wynn was standing at the table rolling a lemon under her palm. She heard him walk up behind her, expected him to sit down. Instead, she felt his arms go around her waist and his chin fall on her shoulder. She waited, breathlessly, to see what he'd do next, but he just stood there, his arms lightly squeezing her under her ribs, his chin becoming increasingly heavier on her shoulder.

"Are you tired?" she asked. The lemon rolled slower and slower beneath her tingling hand.

As he talked, his chin bit into her shoulder. "Worn to a frazzle."

"I missed you at the funeral."

"I don't like funerals."

"Who does?"

"Then why did you go?"

She shrugged. "For Prairie's sake, I suppose."

Her shrug dislodged his chin from its prop. For an instant, she was vexed with herself for causing

TO GET YOUR
4 FREE BOOKS
MAIL THE COUPON BELOW.

Heartfire Romance

FREE BOOK CERTIFICATE

GET 4 FREE BOOKS

Yes! I want to subscribe to Zebra's HEARTFIRE HOME SUBSCRIPTION SERVICE. Please send me my 4 FREE books. Then each month I'll receive the four newest Heartfire Romances as soon as they are published to preview Free for ten days. If I decide to keep them I'll pay the special discounted price of just $3.50 each; a total of $14.00. This is a savings of $3.00 off the regular publishers price. There are no shipping, handling or other hidden charges. There is no minimum number of books to buy and I may cancel this subscription at any time. In any case the 4 FREE Books are mine to keep regardless.

NAME _____

ADDRESS _____

CITY _____ STATE _____ ZIP _____

TELEPHONE _____

SIGNATURE _____

(If under 18 parent or guardian must sign)
Terms and prices subject to change.
Orders subject to acceptance.

HF 105

GET 4 FREE BOOKS

HEARTFIRE HOME SUBSCRIPTION
SERVICE
P.O. BOX 5214
120 BRIGHTON ROAD
CLIFTON, NEW JERSEY 07015

AFFIX
STAMP
HERE

its displacement — until his mouth nuzzled her neck just below her ear. She shivered. His arms unfolded from around her waist, and she silently begged them to return, silently vowed not to move an iota if he would just continue to hold her.

But he wasn't moving away from her as she'd thought. He was merely freeing his hands. His open palms slid lazily up her rib cage, moving ever closer to her straining breasts. She felt her nipples grow hard long before the pads of his thumbs moved across them. His mouth plundered her neck, her lobe, the cavity of her ear. Her hand stopped rolling the lemon altogether. Her eyelids fell shut and her mouth fell open.

Slowly, he turned her around, his hands pausing to cup her breasts on their way to her shoulders, his mouth tracing a hot, wet course across her cheek on its way to hers, his breath as ragged, his pulse as quick, his blood as hot as hers.

"Look at me."

His voice held no more substance than the whispery breeze sailing through the open kitchen window, yet Wynn felt compelled to obey his gentle command. Still, a part of her balked at revealing crystal blue irises that she knew burned hot and bright with the passion he had ignited. Dare she take the risk?

A callused finger tilted her chin up, and the whispery voice came again. "Look at me."

Her eyelids fluttered open then and her gaze locked on his own hungry eyes, eyes that were so very close to hers she could see tiny golden flecks she'd never noticed before in their emerald depths. His mouth was so close to hers she could taste his breath. She longed to devour it.

"I'm going to kiss you, Wynn Spencer. This time, I'm going to kiss you like a man in love kisses his woman."

His left-handed declaration made her heart soar; his kiss sent it into oblivion. His lips were soft and sweet as they molded to hers, his peppermint-freshened breath as delicious as she had imagined, his tongue at once hot and rough as it worked its magic. He held her tightly against his long, lean frame, so tightly she felt his bone and muscle and sinew had fused with her own and melted together into liquid fire. She felt the hard ridge of his manhood rise boldly against her thigh and reveled in the knowledge that he was as affected as she.

His kiss, so very different this time, took her breath, her ability to reason, her power to resist. She knew only that she ached for it to go on forever. She felt alive and whole in a way she'd never felt before.

Michael hadn't meant to kiss her—not like this. But once he'd started, he couldn't get enough of his mouth in hers, or enough of hers in his. There were other parts of her, too, he wanted to touch, to taste, to explore. Slowly, he lowered her spine, vertebra by vertebra, onto the table, one hand under her head, the other sending the lemon thumping to the floor. His free hand sought her then—her breasts, her flat stomach, the curve of her hip, the length of her thigh. The soft fabric of her garments became a fortress he must penetrate in order to gain the prize, and he began his assault by tugging her shirtwaist out of her skirt.

The action sent a frisson of panic through Wynn, restoring a sliver of sanity. She knew she had to stop him, yet she must manage it without causing a rift between them. She took his face in her hands and applied gentle pressure until he pulled his mouth away from hers.

His head hovered mere inches from her own, his green, gold-flecked gaze plunging into the crystal depths of her azure eyes in an attempt to fathom her thoughts.

Wynn couldn't keep him guessing; that wasn't fair. But the words she needed to say caught in her throat as a rush of tears sprang into her eyes.

Michael broke the silence. "I—I guess I went too far."

She moved her head from side to side, her expression begging him for understanding. "No, Michael, it's just that. . . . we need to talk about this."

He gathered her against his chest and dropped his head into the depression of her shoulder. Her torso absorbed the shudder that racked his frame. For a long moment, he didn't move at all, but merely held her until the gradually dwindling tremors dissipated.

As he shifted his weight to his feet, Wynn wrestled with the urge to pull him back against her, to succumb to the desire raging through her, to experience the sweet release his caresses promised. But reason had gained entry and refused to depart.

Michael helped Wynn stand up, then turned his back to her, allowing her time and emotional space to recover. They both knew a moment of painful unfulfillment, both of body and spirit. If she could only see his eyes, Wynn thought, if she could only be certain she hadn't hurt him . . .

She stared at his back, willing him to turn around, to show her either his pain or his understanding, but he was busy tucking in his faded red shirt. Her gaze followed the shirt from its stretch across broad shoulders to its loose tail at his waistline, and she gasped aloud.

When Michael heard the sharp intake of her breath, he spun around, his gaze chasing the lightning-quick changes in her expression as he sought explanation for what he assumed to be alarm. Without warning, she burst into hysterical laughter, sending confusion running rife within him.

"Whatever do you find so comical, Miss Spencer?" he demanded, foregoing the formality of calling her doctor while emphasizing her gender.

Wynn was not offended. On the contrary, his lack of comprehension pushed her closer to the edge of total delirium. She could do no more than wag a finger at a spot near his navel.

This time, there had been no table overturned, no glass of whiskey to slide down and splash in his lap. Yet, Michael's scrutiny focused on the front of his pants. They were clean and dry. Nor was the bulge that had displayed his passion much in evidence anymore.

"Behind!" she chortled, her wagging finger making loops in the air.

He raked his palms across the seat of his pants, but they encountered no moisture. "Quit laughing, Wynnifred Spencer, and tell me what's wrong!"

In an effort to stifle her giggling fit, she gulped air and immediately started hiccuping. "Nothing's *wrong.*" *Hic-up.* "It's, well, it's so *right!*"

"What is?"

Hic-up. "Your shirttail."

Michael turned halfway around and twisted his neck in an effort to see the partially exposed portion of his shirttail, the part Wynn had seen that he couldn't. Growling, he snatched the shirt completely out of his Levi's and pulled the tail around to his side. His fingers slipped right through one of the two large, gaping holes near the bottom of the shirt.

A shade of red deeper than that of the faded fabric suffused his neck and ears. "I, uhm, I should have thrown it away, I suppose, but it's one of my favorites."

Wynn's giggling had subsided somewhat, but her eyes glistened with her continued mirth. "And you never thought about anyone seeing what you'd done to it. You *did* cut my sachet out of that shirt, didn't you?"

He nodded sheepishly.

"I'm not laughing at you or your shirt, Michael. I'm laughing because seeing those two holes makes me happier than anything has in a long time."

He regarded her as one deranged. "Why?"

"The sachet you made me was special in itself. Now, knowing you sacrificed your favorite shirt makes it even more special."

Talking about his birthday gift reminded both of them that he'd brought her another present. Wynn's mind raced with possibilities while he dug into his hip pocket. The crinkle of paper resounded in the sudden quiet. He produced two seed packets bearing Shaker labels and offered them to her a bit sheepishly.

"I don't know much about flowers," he admitted, "but Granny said she thought you'd like these."

"Oh, I do!" she gushed. "I love morning glories and verbena. I just don't have much of a green thumb."

"Granny said these were hearty enough so anyone

197

could grow them, but I have more varieties at the mercantile."

"Vegetables, too?"

"You thinking about planting a garden?"

"I might." Gardening was such a safe topic of conversation! Feeling more at ease in his company, she squatted down and picked up the lemon from the floor. "Having fresh herbs and vegetables right outside the door would prove most convenient. Plus, a garden would be something I could share with Prairie."

She retrieved her juicer from the cupboard and sliced the lemon in half. Michael pulled out a chair, turned it around, and straddled it backwards. For awhile, he observed the economy of her movements as she made the lemonade, and he tried to abolish the lewd thoughts that persisted. If he didn't, he'd take her in his arms again, and neither heaven nor hell could stop him then. He knew they needed to discuss the course of their relationship, but he honestly didn't believe he could talk about it at the moment. Finally, in an effort to banish his lustful thoughts at least temporarily, he asked, "What are you going to do about Prairie?"

"I don't know." She sighed. "I suppose I ought to attempt to locate her nearest living relative."

"Where would you start?"

"I don't have the foggiest notion. All Prairie can tell me is that they came a long way, but how far is a long way to a child who isn't even sure how old she is?"

Any fool could see how good Wynn and Prairie were for each other. He didn't want to be responsible for separating them. Who could say whether Prairie's Aunt Martha would want her, anyway? On the other hand, who was he to say what was best for Prairie?

"You could begin with the letter I found in Jernigan's saddlebags," he said, his voice almost melancholic.

A moment of silence passed before Wynn stopped straining lemon juice and whispered, "What letter?"

He fished a crumpled, water-stained square of paper out of his pocket and handed it to her. She plopped down in the chair across from him and, with trembling fingers, slowly unfolded and smoothed the single sheet. He watched her eyes study the smeared ink, watched her expression change from chagrin to bafflement, watched her turn the sheet over and inspect the blank side, then turn it ink-side up again. He watched the pulse throb in her throat, watched her swallow hard before she spoke. And he hoped he hadn't opened the proverbial can of worms.

"This is all there was?"

He nodded. "No envelope, no address, no date. Only the one sheet."

"But, this doesn't tell us anything, Michael. It doesn't even make sense."

"No, it doesn't," he agreed. "But we do know Prairie has a relative, an aunt named Martha . . . somewhere."

"That isn't much to go on." She bit her lower lip and read the letter again, her expression brightening considerably with the second reading. "We don't know anything of the sort, Michael!"

And he'd thought the *letter* was confusing! "What do you mean?"

"Have you ever worked a jigsaw puzzle, Michael?"

She'd done it again—thrown him off course by answering a question with a question, but this time he grinned instead of growling. "I've never liked puzzles of any sort. Why?"

"We're trying to make this letter a piece of Prairie's puzzle when it may belong to Jernigan's. We're *assuming* Jernigan was Prairie's father, right?"

"It's a logical assumption, Wynn."

"We're also assuming this letter belonged to Jernigan."

He nodded slowly, beginning to see the track her mind was taking.

"The writer didn't call him by name; she just wrote 'My dearest brother.' "

"But why would he carry around someone else's letter?"

"What else was in Jernigan's saddlebags?"

He did another double-take. "A few strips of jerky, a pipe and a pouch of tobacco, a tarnished brooch, and less than a dollar in change. Not much for a man who came a long way."

"Humph! Not much for a man traveling with a child. What did he expect her to eat? No wonder she was so hungry!"

"He didn't have much, that's the truth."

"But we can't be sure the saddlebags even belonged to Jernigan."

"They were on his horse." He held up a restraining hand. "I know what you're thinking. We can't be sure the horse was his, either. Is there anything we *can* be sure of, Wynn?"

In reply, a tender smile touched her lips as she carefully refolded the letter, handed it back to Michael, and went back to making the lemonade again.

"What do you want me to do with it?"

"Put it back where you found it, and then put the saddlebags in a safe place. One day, we'll give them to Prairie."

"*We* will?"

"Well, one of us will."

"And in the meantime?"

Wynn stirred the lemonade vigorously with a wooden spoon. "She'll stay here, of course."

"She needs to belong to a family, Wynn."

She answered him with an enigmatic smile and said simply, "She will."

"You aren't thinking of sending her to an orphanage . . ."

"No! Of course, not. Why?"

"I grew up in an orphanage, Wynn. I'll take the child myself before I see her sent to one of those 'venerable' institutions."

Finally, she thought, he'd given her a peek into the boy behind the man. As she poured up the lemonade, she watched him shift uncomfortably in his chair, watched him pull on his mustache. Wynn sought to ease his discomfort by entertaining him with anecdotes reflecting Prairie's precocious nature and her own often amusing attempts at disciplining the child.

He laughed with her, his green eyes twinkling, until he caught himself staring at the bottom of the empty glass. Although Michael had never been concerned with propriety, he knew Wynn was. Out of respect for that concern — and knowing if he stayed much longer he couldn't be held responsible for his actions, he thanked her for the lemonade and made some flimsy excuse about needing to get home to Doc.

Wynn walked him to the front door—the exit propriety demanded he use, and surprised him by rising on her tiptoes and brushing a chaste kiss across his lips. "Thanks for the seeds," she murmured against his mouth.

"God, Wynn!" he groaned, grasping her upper arms and pulling her into his embrace. "You shouldna done that."

His kiss was long and slow and languid. Wynn savored every second of it, every lazy flicker of his tongue, every tender movement of his lips against hers. His fingers bit into the flesh of her arms as he struggled to keep them there.

She understood that struggle well, for she had her own to contend with. She slipped her hands between them and placed them flat upon the hard wall of his chest, which was covered only by the thin, soft flannel of his shirt. Her fingers itched to slide the buttons loose and bury themselves in the dark, springy hair on his chest, to discover how much more of it existed than the bit that peeked out over the V of his shirt.

She had loosened two buttons before Michael tore his mouth from hers and set her gently away from him. "I have to go now, Wynn." His voice was raspy. "Good night."

Long after he left, she stood in the hall, staring at the closed door through the tears streaming down her face.

Jonathan Matheson strolled into her life with *savoir-faire*. Eighteen months later, he strolled out of it without losing one ounce of his self-possession. As much as Wynn hated him for it, she

202

hated herself more.

She hated herself for offering him her heart, and she hated him for taking it. She hated herself for giving him her love and her trust. She hated him for betraying them. She hated herself for allowing him to break her spirit. She hated him for not caring what he did to her.

For almost a year, that dual hatred had simmered inside her like a pot of dried pinto beans left to cook on a warm stove. One facet of her hatred had seasoned the other until the two blended together like fatback into the pintos. She had thought she could run away. She discovered there was nowhere to hide from one's own emotions.

Somewhere along the line, though, she'd failed to tend the hatred, and it had scorched and burned. The only cure for charred beans was to throw them out, scour the pan, and start over.

As she stared at the door, her vision cleared and she knew that at some point she'd not only tossed out the hatred but purged its stench from her soul as well. She was ready to start over. Never again would she shed a tear for Jonathan Matheson.

She might always despise him. She might never forgive him for marrying someone else while he was engaged to marry her. But she knew, in the depths of her heart, that the memory of his duplicity no longer ruled her life.

At last, those bonds were broken. She felt whole and well and deliriously happy. She was free.

And it was Michael Donovan who had freed her.

Wynn was more content over the next few days than she'd ever been in her life. She had Prairie's company to fill her days, Michael's to fill her evenings, and peaceful sleep to fill her nights.

The three sat at the depot on Sunday afternoon, first visiting with the townsfolk who had congregated there, and then purchasing fresh milk and butter and a basketful of fresh fruits and vegetables straight out of a boxcar when the train arrived in the evening.

Prairie laughed at the peddler's ninety-mile-a-minute speech as he hawked his produce, but she proved herself to be the better salesman when she talked Wynn into buying at least one of everything.

The two planted Michael's flower seeds along the front of the house. Wynn showed Prairie how to make a tiny knife slit in the morning glory seeds, then how to put them just under the earth close to the porch railing so the vines would have something to cling to. They dug a bed for the verbena, marked off a small rectangle in the back yard for a vegetable and herb garden, and hauled in plenty of Rusty's manure using Michael's handcart.

While they worked the warm earth with April's golden sun beating down upon them, Granny worked at making Prairie some clothes. Wynn couldn't wait to get the child out of overalls and into something feminine. On the fourth day following the funeral, while Wynn and Prairie were in town selecting seeds for their garden, they stopped by Granny's boardinghouse for a fitting.

"Aren't you worried just a mite about coming down with the dip-theria?" Granny asked Wynn over tea.

"No. Are you?"

"I wasn't ever closer than six or eight feet to

Jernigan," Granny insisted. "He stood on my porch, right at the top of the steps, and I stayed inside the doorway. I didn't like the looks of him, not at all, but I felt for the child. I hated to send him to you, but I didn't know what else to do. Later, I felt awful when I learned he died from the dip-theria. I hope you'll forgive me."

"There's nothing to forgive, Granny. I wouldn't have had it any other way. I'm a doctor. Taking care of sick people is my job. Besides, I don't think I've ever felt better in my life. But do promise me, Granny, that you'll send for me immediately if you have a headache or sore throat or fever — or even just a little cold."

"Don't worry, child. I'll send for you." Granny shook out the dress she'd been hemming, dismissing the subject. "Bring Prairie in here and let's see if this fits."

Wynn awoke the next morning with a slight headache and blamed it on too much sun. By noon, the headache had worsened and she felt feverish. Fatigue, she assured herself. That's all it was. Too much physical labor and too much sun. By the time she put Prairie down for her nap, Wynn was so tired she could barely keep her eyes open.

She'd just lie down in the examination room and take a little nap while Prairie slept, she decided. That was all she needed . . . a little nap. Rest was such an excellent curative. She'd wake up feeling herself again, and she and Prairie would make some oatmeal cookies. They'd eat them warm with tall glasses of milk to dunk them in. Prairie would tell her all over again how much she loved her new dresses and pinafores and how much she loved Granny . . . and how happy she was to be staying with Wynn until her father came back for her . . .

Chapter Twelve

Wynn did wake up feeling better, but not good enough to make oatmeal cookies. Her head still hurt just a bit, but more than anything, she felt incredibly tired.

Well, she had a right to be tired! Didn't she?

She mentally shrugged away the foreboding that seemed determined to badger her and set about preparing a simple meal. But while she worked in the kitchen, that nagging little voice kept pestering her. *I'm not getting sick!* she answered it. *I merely haven't taken good care of myself lately. That's all.*

After supper, she read aloud to Prairie from *Tales of Mother Goose.*

"Which story do you want to hear?" Wynn asked.

" 'Sleeping Beauty'!"

Wynn groaned melodramatically. "But, we've read that one every day for a week. Wouldn't you rather hear another one, maybe one you haven't heard before?"

As she was wont to do while making a decision, Prairie screwed up her stubby nose. Wynn almost burst out laughing. If she felt like laughing, she thought, she was going to be all right.

"Mommy used to read 'Sleeping Beauty' to me

207

every night. It's my favorite. Please, read it to me again, Dr. Wynn."

Little by little, Prairie was revealing bits and pieces of her life. From what she had told her, Wynn gathered that Prairie's mother must have been a well-educated, cultured woman. The fact that she'd married a man like Jernigan didn't make sense. Wynn couldn't help wondering if the man they had buried was, indeed, Prairie's father, although the child insisted he was.

By the time Wynn finished reading Prairie's favorite story, they were both yawning. Normally, Wynn put Prairie to bed several hours before she herself was ready to retire, then she went downstairs to wait for Michael. But this night she climbed into bed with the child fully dressed, thinking to rest until she heard Michael's knock.

Several minutes after Wynn turned out the lamp, Prairie said in a pouting voice, "Dr. Wynn, aren't you going to kiss me goodnight?"

Wynn always planted a kiss on the child's forehead when she tucked her in. Something—that nagging voice!—stopped her. "I—well, it's not that I don't want to kiss you, Prairie. I'm just not sure it's a good idea right now. Not until we're sure we aren't sick."

"Like my mommy and daddy?"

"Yes, dear."

"When will we know, Dr. Wynn?"

"In just a few days—definitely by the time your new furniture arrives." Wynn yawned again. "Let's go to sleep now, Prairie. I'm . . . incredibly . . . tired . . ."

If Michael ever came, Wynn didn't know it. She fell almost immediately into a deep, sound sleep.

Sometime during the night, a severe attack of nausea awoke her. To avoid disturbing Prairie, she quietly hurried downstairs—barely making it to the kitchen and grabbing a dishpan before she vomited. Assuring herself that, for some reason, supper hadn't agreed with her, she rinsed her mouth and cleaned the pan. She was halfway up the stairs when she had to rush back to the kitchen.

Determined to end her bout of illness as quickly as possible, she drank a tall glass of tepid water to induce further vomiting and, thus, completely empty her stomach while lessening the painful retching.

She was still awake—and still nauseated—at daybreak. She was sitting in the kitchen, holding warm towels on her abdomen and around her neck, when Prairie came downstairs.

"What you doing that for, Dr. Wynn?" the child asked, her brown eyes wide.

"To help my stomach and my throat feel better," Wynn rasped.

Prairie burst into tears. Wynn threw the towels aside and quickly gathered the child to her breast, murmuring soothing platitudes until she calmed somewhat.

"You're sick like Mommy and Daddy!" Prairie explained through her tears.

"No, sweetheart. Not like your mommy and daddy. It's only an upset stomach. I'm much better now."

Although her assurances seemed to placate the child, they didn't convince Wynn. *Dear Lord,* she prayed, *spare me, spare all of us from this dreadful disease.*

All morning long, the thought of a diphtheria epidemic raging through Jennings nagged at her. And if she came down with it, who would care for her and any other victims? She wished Doc had confided in her, wished she knew if he was capable of waging a one-man battle against an epidemic, wished she felt up to going to talk to him about it.

Within minutes of putting Prairie down for her nap that afternoon, Wynn stretched out again on the bed in the examination room. *I'm just tired,* she told herself. *I was up half the night. No wonder I'm sleepy.*

"Dr. Wynn, wake up! Wake up, Dr. Wynn!"

The childish voice sounded tinny to Wynn, as though it were coming from afar. Small hands pushed at her shoulder, then tugged at a lock of her hair. Wynn had thought she was dreaming, but one didn't feel pain in a dream and her scalp hurt where the hair had been pulled. She forced her eyelids open halfway, enough to see a tiny, glowing angel dressed in white standing by the bed. Her lids fell shut. It must be a dream.

The voice gained volume and became more strident. "Dr. Wynn, wake up!"

The angel pinched Wynn's arm.

What a nuisance this angel was!

"Go 'way," Wynn rasped, the sound tearing at her throat as it passed through. She rolled onto her side, thus turning her back to the nuisance. It didn't help. The nuisance climbed onto the bed and placed a cool palm against her cheek.

"Does your head hurt, Dr. Wynn?" the angel asked, her voice much softer, much kinder now.

"Yes."

"Is your throat sore, Dr. Wynn?"

"Yes!"

"Don't go away, Dr. Wynn! Please, don't go away

210

where my mommy and daddy went!"

Drops of water, so cool, so soothing, fell onto Wynn's exposed cheek. What a blessed little angel this one was after all! But then the drops turned to ice, burning, searing ice. Wynn rubbed her cheek against her shoulder and snuggled deeper into the bed, pulling the covers over her head, willing the nuisance to go away.

Something was wrong with Dr. Wynn. She was acting just like Mommy and Daddy did before they . . . went away.

Slowly, Prairie walked back down the hall to the staircase, sat down on the bottom step, and stuck her thumb in her mouth. Big tears rolled out of her huge brown eyes and fell, plop, plop, onto the skirt of her white petticoat. With her free hand, she pushed herself up one step and then another, scaling them backwards on her behind until she reached the second-floor landing.

For awhile, she sat there, looking down the stairwell. It was a long way to the bottom. She thought about how big Dr. Wynn's house was, bigger than any house she'd ever been in before. And Dr. Wynn had asked her to stay there with her; she'd ordered some furniture for the empty room upstairs and Prairie could have it all to herself.

She couldn't imagine what it would be like to have a room all her own. Dr. Wynn said she would have to keep it clean, but it would be worth it. She'd learned to live with a clean body and clean clothes. It wasn't so bad, once you got used to it. Besides, Dr. Wynn let her use some of her sweet-smelling soap when she bathed, and sometimes she allowed her to wear some of her jewelry.

Dr. Wynn had so many pretty things. Just thinking about them made Prairie want to look at them again. She took her thumb out of her mouth and crawled on all fours toward Wynn's bedroom until her knee caught on the bottom of her petticoat and threw her flat on the floor. Her top teeth came down hard on her bottom lip, tearing it open and making it bleed. Prairie's silent sobs turned into loud wails.

She knew Dr. Wynn could hear her. Any minute now, she'd come to see what had happened to her. She cried louder, just in case. Dr. Wynn didn't come.

Prairie touched her swollen lip. It was awfully sore, and she screamed in protest. What was wrong with Dr. Wynn? Why didn't she come? Prairie wanted somebody to look at her lip, to hold her close and make the pain go away. She beat her fists on the floor and screamed again and again.

Michael was unpacking a crate of syrup and stacking the jars on a shelf in the mercantile when he felt a tug on one leg of his pants. He glanced down to see Prairie standing beside him and he grinned at her. He'd been thinking about Wynn all day, thinking he'd get caught up eventually and go out to see her, to explain how he'd gotten tied up last night and to tell her how much he'd missed her.

Since she and Prairie had come to town, maybe they'd stay and have supper with him over at Granny Simpson's. It was Thursday. Granny served fried chicken, mashed potatoes, and big, flaky buttermilk biscuits on Thursday. Just thinking about the meal made his mouth water. Lord, but Granny could cook. It would be good for Wynn, too. In his estimation, she worked too hard and stayed by herself too much.

Where was Wynn, anyway? Just thinking about

her made him hungry, too, but in a different way — a much different way. His gaze lifted then and searched beyond the child for sight of Wynn. He didn't see her.

"Where's Dr. Spencer?" he asked.

"Home."

Although its meaning didn't register, the single word drew his attention back to Prairie, who had turned her face up to him. He noticed her swollen lip and a spot of dried blood on her pointed chin.

"What happened to you?"

"I fell."

"Are you all right?"

She sniffed loudly. "It hurts."

Certain Wynn was somewhere in the store, Michael looked up again and took a step toward the front. Prairie's grasp on his pant leg stopped him. He bent over, scooped her up, and settled her on his hip. Michael strode purposefully up and down the aisles, out onto the front porch, back into the store, and finally into the storeroom.

Baffled, he asked again, "Where did you say Wynn was?"

"At home."

He heard Prairie that time, but it still didn't make any sense to him. "But you're here."

"I came by myself."

Wynn allowed this child, who couldn't possibly be more than five, to walk into town by herself? Michael looked at Prairie then — really looked at her. For the first time, he noted the wild, tangled mass of her hair. Her dress was unbuttoned all the way down the back and the foot resting on his stomach was wearing the shoe intended for the one riding his hip.

"Who helped you dress?"

Her face beamed with pride. "No one. I did it all

by myself."

A dull pain settled itself deep in his gut. "Why didn't Dr. Spencer help you?"

"She's asleep. I couldn't wake her up."

Wynn asleep at four o'clock in the afternoon? The pain sharpened. Michael ignored it for the moment, refusing to panic. "You must have worn her out this morning. What did the two of you do? Dig up the garden patch?"

"We didn't do anything, Mr. Donovan. Dr. Wynn didn't feel like working. And now she won't wake up."

The pain twisted and knotted and spread upward to his chest and throat. "Let's go see about her," he said when he could talk, already carrying Prairie out of the store and toward the barn. Saddling Rusty might take a minute, but riding the horse would save far more time, especially with Prairie along.

"Have you ever ridden a horse?" he asked.

"Yep. Me and Daddy came here on one. He let me ride up front, but I had to hold on to the horn."

Ten minutes later, Michael rode up to Wynn's front porch on Rusty. He took Prairie with him as he dismounted, flipped the reins over the porch railing, and hurried inside. When he started up the stairs, the child stopped him.

"She's back there." Prairie led the way to the examination room.

When Michael saw Wynn huddled up under the covers, her knees pulled into her chest, a pain shot through his gut. He grasped Wynn's shoulder and turned her over onto her back, but he couldn't rouse her, either. When he touched her forehead, his hand snapped back in reaction to its heat. Hastily, he found a cloth and dampened it with cool water, using it to bathe Wynn's face. When she stirred, he folded the cloth and laid it on her brow.

"Hello, sleepyhead."

His voice was low and tender and brimming with concern, but his face was hazy when Wynn tried to focus on it.

"Can you tell me where you hurt? Can you tell me what to do?" Michael asked, his callused palm gliding over her hot cheek as he talked.

Wynn rolled her head from side to side. "Diph-diphtheria," she whispered. "Go 'way."

"I'm not leaving your side, Wynnifred. Tell me what to do."

"You'll . . . get it . . ."

"Then you'll just have to get well so you can take care of me, doctor."

She clutched her throat. "Hurts."

Michael knew it must. He couldn't believe how raspy her voice was, how painful her expression when she tried to talk. "I'll try to ask you 'yes and no' questions, Wynn. A nod for 'yes,' a shake for 'no.' Try not to talk at all. All right?"

She nodded.

"Are you thirsty?"

She nodded again.

"Come on, Prairie. Let's get Dr. Wynn a glass of water." Once he got the child into the kitchen, he sat her down at the table and handed her some soda crackers. "I'm going to try to help Dr. Wynn get well," he explained to Prairie. "We don't want you to get sick, and you might if you get too close to Dr. Wynn, so you stay in here for now."

Amazingly, the child didn't argue with him.

He helped Wynn sit up enough to drink out of the glass, his right arm supporting her shoulders. She took a few sips, then feebly pushed at his hand holding the glass.

215

"Drink some more," he ordered, gently but firmly. She shook her head. "Hurts."

Michael didn't know whether she needed to drink more or not—or whether she should have drunk any at all. He did know that liquid had always soothed his throat when it was sore. Maybe something hot would feel better to her.

"Would you rather have coffee or tea? I can make you some."

Her head moved from side to side. "Try to swallow just another sip or two," he said.

She did, then balked again.

"All right," Michael sighed. He eased her shoulders back to the mattress and tucked the quilt around her. "I'll be right back."

Never would he have thought he'd ever play the role of doctor, but this made the third time since Wynn had come to Jennings. The night Doc had shot himself, he'd had Wynn to tell him what to do. The night of the windstorm, his own intuition and her medical books had been his guide, and those were all he had to go on this time, too—unless he could talk Doc into helping.

He set the glass of water on a table in the examination room before hurrying to the barrister's cabinet and beginning a search through her medical books again. Because he wasn't sure how to spell diphtheria, he overlooked it in several indexes. When he did find it listed, it was in a surgical manual. The text explained how to slit a hole in the patient's neck directly into the windpipe, should the diphtheria membrane obstruct the patient's breathing. This procedure, the book said, was necessary to save the patient's life in such instances.

So far, Wynn's throat didn't seem to be obstructed, but knowing it might become that way scared the hell out of him. He wasn't about to take a scalpel and cut her throat. He'd probably kill her while he was trying to save her. No, he'd have to talk Doc into coming. He had no other choice.

When he checked on Wynn, she was sleeping again. Michael couldn't decide whether to take Prairie with him or not. He hated for Wynn to wake up and find herself alone, but what could the child do to help? Prairie wouldn't be able to work the pump or help Wynn sit up—or keep her from getting up if she decided she wanted to. Besides, Prairie had no business being so close to Wynn, not when he considered the very real possibility of her becoming infected with the disease.

Why Prairie didn't already have it buffaloed him. But, no, he wouldn't allow additional risk to the child. He'd take her and leave her with Granny—and he'd make Doc come back with him if he had to tie the old coot to the saddle.

Michael snatched a piece of paper off Wynn's desk and penned her a hasty note: "Gone for Doc." This he slipped into her hand, folding her fingers around it and hoping she continued to clutch it.

Prairie kicked and screamed when he told her he was taking her to Granny's. "No!" she wailed. "I'm staying with Dr. Wynn!"

"You're going with me, and you're going quietly." He made his voice low and menacing. This was not the time to placate a child—or to allow that child to manipulate him.

Prairie calmed immediately.

"Do you know how to pray?" he asked her.

"Yes, sir, Mr. Donovan."

"Then pray for Dr. Wynn. That will be the best way you can help her."

He tried the low, menacing voice approach on Doc. It didn't work, so he switched to bullishness.

"Damn you, old man! You're going to drink this coffee if I have to prop your mouth open with a stick and pour it down your throat!"

Doc swatted a hand at Michael and staggered from the doorway of his room over to the table, where he promptly knocked over the chair he'd planned to sit in. Michael stood the chair back up and held onto the top slat to keep it steady until Doc settled into it.

"Whas got you so riled up, anyways?"

Michael winced at the slurred words. The old man was really soused this time. Anger, born of supreme frustration at his own inadequacies, sliced through him. Life had dealt him what appeared to be a losing hand, challenging him to turn the game around. He had thought Doc was his ace in the hole—until he'd come home to find him drunker than a boar stuffing himself on sour watermelon rinds. The bare truth was he had to have Doc . . . *Wynn* had to have Doc—sober. There wasn't another doctor for miles. He'd have to go all the way to Lake Charles or Opelousas to find one, and there simply wasn't enough time. The old man would just have to sober up—and fast.

Michael set a tin cup of strong, black coffee in front of Doc. "Drink it!" he ordered, reminding himself of a similar directive he'd given to Wynn barely a half hour ago. "I'll tell you what's got me so riled up. Wynn Spencer is sick with the diphtheria, and I don't know what to do for her. You have to help her."

Doc shook his head, making his gray hair fly. "*No,* I don't. I don't do *no* doctoring *no* more." He swiped his hand at the cup, slinging it off the table. It hit the wall before it clattered to the floor, splattering coffee everywhere. He stood up a bit unsteadily and staggered back toward his room. "My head hurts. I'm goin' back to bed."

"Oh, no, you're not!" Michael dove at Doc, catching him around his trunk in a bear hug. "I've threatened to throw you by your skinny rump more than once, but I've never made good that threat — until now."

Michael hauled Doc up so his feet didn't quite reach the floor and started out the door with him, never feeling Doc's bare feet kicking him in the shins. When he got him outside, he did throw him, right into the rain barrel.

Doc sputtered and coughed and tried to claw his way out of the water, but Michael's open palm on top of his head prevented him from going very far. "Let go! You're going to drown me!" Doc wailed.

"I just might do that, unless you promise to drink some of that coffee and then go out to Wynn's with me. She's on the verge of death, Doc. I can feel it in my gut. You owe it to her, you owe it to me, and you owe it to yourself to help her. Are you going to or not?"

"Oh, all right! Just let me out of here. This water is *cold!*"

Dusk had fallen by the time Doc and Michael mounted Rusty and rode up to Wynn's. Riding double had slowed them down a mite, but Michael didn't dare let Doc go by himself and they didn't have another horse.

Michael had made Doc take a bath, which the old man insisted he didn't need, and put on clean clothes, which he was hard put to find in the wreck that was Doc's room. After the dunking in the rain barrel, Doc dutifully drank the strong coffee, but Michael wasn't convinced the man was thinking clearly at all. He kept mumbling something about somebody named Emma dying. Michael had never heard Doc mention Emma before, so he had no earthly idea what Doc was talking about.

"Come on, Doc!" he fussed when the old man lagged behind on Wynn's porch. Concerned that Doc might remount Rusty and flee, he stepped aside and made Doc walk in front of him.

Gray shadows swathed the hall and an eerie stillness pervaded the house. Michael's pulse raced and his mouth suddenly felt cottony dry. His fingers fumbled when he lifted the globe off a lamp and he almost dropped it. Nervously, he struck a match, adjusted the wick, and reset the chimney. Seldom did Michael Donovan pray, but he did then. *Please, God, let her be alive.*

All the while Doc examined Wynn, Michael prayed. He didn't know if God heard him or not, but he dared not stop trying. He kept remembering what he had told Prairie: "Pray for Dr. Wynn. That will be the best way you can help her." And, he supposed, it was the best way he could help her, too.

"Go make some coffee," Doc said.

"For Wynn?"

"No, for me. I expect you could use some, too. And don't make it so strong this time."

Doc shook his head after Michael left the room. There was no doubt in his mind now that Wynn had diagnosed herself correctly. Not only did she have diphtheria; she had it bad. It was going to be touch and go for awhile. He'd seen the disease before, treated it often during the war. He hadn't had much success with it then, nor was he the least bit certain he could remember everything that needed to be

220

done. It had been a long time since he'd practiced medicine.

He and Michael would have to take turns sitting up with her, bathing her face with a cool, wet cloth and making sure she could breathe. There was nothing else to be done.

While Michael was busy in the kitchen, Doc pulled the upholstered chair from the front parlor into the examination room. If he was going to sit there for awhile, he might as well get comfortable.

He'd never forget the day he'd sworn off medicine. As long as he lived, he knew he would never forget that day. Its memory came as clearly to him now as though it had happened just that morning.

He'd been out all night, attempting to save the life of a six-year-old girl suffering from dysentery. Doc knew the little girl's name then, and if he searched his memory hard enough now, he'd know it again. But he didn't want to remember. It was easier to take if she remained nameless.

He had failed—failed miserably, in his estimation. There should have been something more he could have done, should have done. It just wasn't fair, watching the child grow weaker and weaker, watching her parents wring their hands from a kneeling position, their eyes gazing heavenward, their lips moving in silent prayers.

Close to dawn, that darkest of all hours, the child breathed her last breath. She died in her sleep, blissfully unaware of the pain her passing had caused her family, of the guilt it had created in the doctor who had tended her.

No one blamed him but himself. The father had followed Doc out to the barn and helped him hitch his horse to his buggy. "Thanks, Doc," the man had said. "We know you did all that could have been done. She's in heaven now, God rest her soul."

It was not the first time he'd lost a patient, Doc told himself on the ride home, and it wouldn't be the last.

But it was.

When he'd left home early the day before, Emma had kissed him good-bye. He'd touched her swollen belly, felt his child—their child—kick against his palm, reveled in life's renewal, in the knowledge that soon he would become a father. The memory of Emma's kiss and their baby's kick had sustained him through the long hours he was away. That same memory called him back home.

At times like these, he wished he'd never gone into medicine—or wished, rather, that his profession didn't require extended absences from home. Sometimes, he was gone three or four days, maybe as long as a week, depending upon the distance he traveled and the needs of the patient. He'd never minded too much before he'd married Emma.

Now it seemed as though he'd always been married to her. They'd met at a cornhusking at a neighbor's barn, not long after he'd returned from the war. Emma was only sixteen and he a mature man of thirty-one, but he'd known when he'd seen her that she was special. He'd known he wanted her the moment he took her in his arms and whirled her around the dance floor. Less than two months later, she was his wife. Now, almost four years later, she was carrying their first child.

Doc's heart sang with the sweetness of the thought of her as his ever-faithful Dobbin clop-clopped toward home. She'd be in the kitchen, checking a pie in the oven or stirring up a batch of biscuits, a smear of flour on her cheek, a lock of her honey-gold hair falling across her forehead. She'd wipe her hands on her apron and open her arms to him, and he'd hold her close, their child between them, reminding them with its kicks that it was strong and healthy and raring to be born.

By Doc's figuring, Emma had three weeks left in her term. She had fared remarkably well, and he anticipated a normal delivery when the time came. They'd spent hours talking about it. Emma knew what to expect, and he would be there with her to make sure everything went all right.

The noon hour had come and gone before Doc reined Dobbin in at the barn. Doc's stomach rumbled, as much from the thought of one of Emma's meals as from a general need to fill it. More than anything, he wanted to leave the horse right there and dash into the house to see her, but he owed Dobbin much better treatment than that. The horse, seeming to have human sense, had saved a preoccupied Doc from more than one serious accident.

He thought she would at least come to the door, though, and wave at him. He kept watching out of the corner of his eye, waiting for her to acknowledge his return. As the silent minutes passed, Doc grew concerned.

The minute he had Dobbin free from the harness, he put him in his stall, refilled his feeding bin, drew up a fresh bucket of water, and hurried to the house. The rubdown would just have to wait.

Emma wasn't in the kitchen, nor did she answer when he called. Doc's heart skipped a beat. Maybe she was out visiting. Or maybe she was at the church. Or maybe . . .

Doc rushed from one room to another, creating places she might be, trying to convince himself she was safe and sound . . . somewhere.

They'd bought a big old house with too many rooms, but it was what Emma wanted. "You need plenty of space for your practice," she'd said, "and I want to fill it up with the laughter of your children."

There were too many rooms . . .

Where was she? Where was his darling Emma?

The door of the nursery stood slightly ajar. Relieved, Doc pushed at it hard with the flat of a palm, then stood almost frozen as the door defied his directive and creaked slowly open. And then he spied her, lying on the daybed, a pair of pillows under her head, one leg hanging off the side, a look of complete repose on her face.

He flew to the daybed, calling, "Emma, I'm home." When she didn't respond, he cried her name, his voice tearing from his throat. "Emma!"

Her golden brown eyes were open wide, her gaze fixed on the white iron crib with its frothy white bedskirt and the blanket she'd embroidered draped over its side. He fell to one knee and took her cheeks between his open palms, turning her gaze up to meet his, his mind refusing to acknowledge the cold that seeped into his hands. He struck one of her cheeks in rapid succession, shouting, "Emma! Emma! Wake up!"

Slowly, reluctantly, he tore his gaze from her frozen features and turned his head toward the crib, seeing for the first time the tiny feet that the draped blanket failed to hide. He felt as though he watched himself rise stiffly and take the two steps necessary to reach the crib. Upon the mattress lay their baby, a boy, his body stiff and blue.

"Oh, God, Emma!" he wailed, the truth only partially penetrating. He hurried back to the daybed, fell on his knees by her side, and pulled her limp frame against his chest. "I'm sorry, God. I'm so sorry! I should have been here, Emma. . . . I should have been here when you needed me."

Her head lolled from side to side, then fell forward and hit his shoulder.

And he sat there on the floor, all that day and most of the night, holding his Emma, begging her to wake up, begging her to come back to him.

Toward dawn, he laid her stiff frame on the daybed and moved lethargically downstairs to find a shovel.

Chapter Thirteen

She was a cloud in a black, black sky, floating high above the earth, sometimes drifting, sometimes soaring, but never motionless. Being a cloud made her feel loose, unencumbered, and deliriously clever for her ability to defy gravity. It was a heady feeling.

Until the blistering sun came out and chased away the cool darkness. Its unrelenting heat pressed upon her then, scorching her skin, shoving the dry, cottony substance of the cloud into her mouth, parching her lips, until she thrashed about upon the cloud and begged the heavens for rain.

God always answered her plea, bathing her face with dew and calming her thrashing with His deep, mellow voice.

And she would rest then for awhile, sometimes drifting, sometimes soaring, but never motionless — until the sun came out again.

Michael Donovan was not accustomed to sitting still for any length of time. Indeed, never could he recall ever having sat in one place for hours on end. Sitting still allowed time for introspection, and Michael had never liked examining himself too closely. Had he not cared—really cared what happened to Wynn Spencer, he would not have put himself through such torture now.

But he did care. The longer he sat by her bed and watched her fight the disease, the more he realized how very much he cared. Her illness forced him to reassess his priorities; the very real possibility of her death forced him to sort out his feelings for her.

Suddenly, Michael did not want to imagine his life without Wynn Spencer. That didn't mean he wanted to marry her, he quickly added to his deliberations. He just liked having her around. She could infuriate him more than any woman ever had, or probably ever could, but for the first time in a long, long time, she had made him *feel* something. Feeling wasn't quite as agonizing as he remembered its being, so long as Wynn lived.

Doc gave her a fifty-fifty chance of survival. If she died . . .

Her mumbling and thrashing forestalled further reflection, creating a mixed blessing for Michael. He placed a palm on her brow and felt its heat. Wynn vacillated between chills and fever. When she was cold, he wrapped her well in one of the warm blankets that were draped on a rope he and Doc had strung beside her cookstove. When the fever hit her again, he removed the blanket, opened the window, and bathed her with cool water.

Michael went through the latter motions then, placing a cool compress on her brow, another around her throat, and using a third cloth to sponge her arms and legs, talking to her all the while. When she calmed, he slid his arm under her shoulders and pulled her into a half-sitting position.

"Can you drink some water?" he asked.

227

She didn't answer, but she didn't fight him, either. Not at first. Michael could never get her to take more than a few sips at a time.

"It's time to gargle again, Wynn. Do you understand?"

Wild, pale eyes darted about, focusing on nothing. Though the movement of her chin was almost imperceptible, Michael was certain she nodded.

Doc had mixed up a solution of permanganate of potash and water and insisted she use it to rinse her mouth and throat twice an hour. Hopefully, Doc said, the disinfectant would destroy the diphtheria germs. As a safety precaution, both he and Doc gargled several times a day with the solution, too.

Michael poured some of the iridescent purple liquid into a glass and held it to Wynn's lips. She swished the liquid around in her mouth, then leaned her head back to allow it access to her throat. He winced at the pain evident on her face as she made gurgling noises.

When she had spit the disinfectant into a pan Michael held for her, he checked it for red streaks. Thankfully, there were none. Evidence of blood would mean the false membrane was shredding, which, according to Doc, would cause Wynn extreme pain. And then it would simply reform itself over the mucous membrane.

Shortly after they'd arrived — had it been three days ago? — Michael had demanded to know all Doc could tell him about diphtheria. The two had left Wynn resting and were sitting in the kitchen drinking coffee. To Michael's way of thinking, Doc still needed some sobering up.

Doc scratched his nearly bald head with a fingernail. "I suppose I saw it for the first time back in '56, 'fore I ever started practicing on my own." He thought about that for a moment, then nodded hard. "Yep, that's when it was. I was in my early twenties and was studying under Doc Hatcher. He didn't have any more formal training than I'd had — which was none, but he'd been around for a long time. Knew his stuff, Doc Hatcher did. A severe epidemic swept the country that year, and I guess we lost close to half, maybe more, of the diphtheria patients we treated. Pour me another cup, will you?"

Michael shook his head, forever amazed at Doc's propensity to change the subject without transition. Doc waited for his refill before continuing. "Funny thing about diphtheria. A body can have it and hardly know he's sick. Minor sore throat is all. Then, it'll kill the next person. Children are more inclined to have dire cases, though."

"How does it spread?" Michael asked.

"It's certainly contagious — highly contagious, but I've known folks to have it when no one else around them did."

"How do you know when it's diphtheria and not something else?"

Doc explained about the false membrane. "You get one when you have croup, too, but it's different. The diphtheria membrane is grayish-white at first and tough and leathery. With croup, the membrane grows over the mucous membrane in the throat; with diphtheria, it grows *into* it. That's why you can't go in there and tear it out. You just damage the tissues, and then the false membrane grows right back. The membrane can also occur in the nose, on the lips, inside the cheeks, on the gums — anywhere in the mouth."

Michael thought about that for a minute — thought about how painful diphtheria must be. "And Wynn — Dr. Spencer has one of these membranes?"

229

Doc nodded, smiling inside. So, the boy was calling her by her first name. *Progress!*

Doc didn't want to be there, didn't want to have anything to do with medicine ever again, but he couldn't just let Wynn Spencer die. He supposed he liked her too well for that, but he had to save her for Michael's sake as well. The boy needed Wynn Spencer. He needed her bad. "In her throat."

"If you can't remove it, how do you get rid of it?"

"Let it finish growing. It'll get big and turn a yellowish-gray. Then we'll change tactics. I'll tell you when the time comes."

"But—" Michael was remembering the surgical procedure he'd read about in one of Wynn's books.

"You don't need to know now, boy. You'd just get confused about what you're supposed to be doing. You're going to have to help me with her, whether you want to or not."

Michael knew better than to argue with him. Instead, he asked, "What's going to happen now?"

"Now?" Doc shrugged. "She's going to be one sick little lady for awhile. Continued chills, fever, nausea—possibly with diarrhea or vomiting, general malaise, severe sore throat with offensive breath, muscular pain, husky voice—or maybe no voice, perhaps difficulty in breathing. Depends on how bad her case is."

Well, it was damn sure one bad case, Michael thought as he lowered her shoulders back down to the mattress, used a cloth to clean the brown stains the permanganate of potash left on her teeth, and began to sponge her fevered skin again.

To facilitate matters, he and Doc had stripped her down to her camisole and bloomers, thus leaving her arms and lower legs bare. As he bathed her legs, he pushed the ruffled bottoms of the bloomers up to the top of her thighs. At any other time, he would have relished caressing the creamy color and silky feel of her limbs with both his eyes and his hands, but not now. Not when she was so very ill, possibly so close to death.

Michael promised himself, though, that after she had fully recuperated, he'd bathe her again—when they could both enjoy it. And she would live to enjoy it. If he had to go without sleep for days and nights on end, he'd make sure she lived.

When her skin felt cooler, he pulled the sheet over her, leaving the compresses on her forehead and throat. While she was plagued with fever, he rinsed these regularly in an effort to keep them as cool as possible. He wished with all his heart that he could get his hands on some ice. At least the fresh water he pumped in the kitchen was fairly cool, but it warmed quickly in the heat of the day.

Michael watched the darkness outside the window fade into soft, pinkish-gray light. Since Wynn was resting again, he moved into the kitchen, put more coal into the stove's firebox, and pumped a kettle of water for coffee. Doc would be down soon to relieve him, and then he could take a bath with disinfectant in the water. Afterwards, he'd ride into town, just as he had each of the other two mornings he'd been at Wynn's, and pick up whatever Slim had cooked for Wynn, Doc, and himself. He'd go to see Granny and Prairie, to assure himself they were both well, to assure himself no one else in Jennings had come down with diphtheria.

The last thing Jennings needed was a full-blown diphtheria epidemic.

But that's what the town got.

231

Amazingly, neither Granny nor Prairie was affected. Even more amazingly, Doc started making rounds.

"This is just temporary," he insisted to Michael. "Just till Dr. Spencer gets well. But someone has to help these folks try to get over it, and I guess that someone's got to be me right now."

Whether or not Wynn was ever going to get well was still a matter of grave concern. As the diphtheria progressed, she became prostrate, her pulse weakened and slowed, and her face took on a sodden appearance. Her neck swelled and turned shiny as well. Doc finally proclaimed the false membrane, which had become extensive, fully grown.

"Now we change from cold to hot," he told Michael. "Hot fomentations on the throat instead of cold compresses. And she'll need to breathe warm vapor fifteen minutes of every half hour, twenty-four hours a day. You're gonna need some help, boy."

"No, I'm not," Michael said emphatically.

"But you have to rest sometime. You'll wear yourself out. What good will you be to Dr. Spencer then?"

Michael pinned a mean bull look on Doc. "There's no use arguing about it, old man. I don't trust anyone besides the two of us to look after her properly — except maybe Granny, and then who would watch after Prairie? Besides, I don't want either one of them over here until Wynn is convalescing and we've thoroughly disinfected this house."

Doc grinned at that. "I thought you didn't like the smell of carbolic acid."

"I don't, but it's not my house."

For a minute, Doc sat pensively, sipping his coffee. "You know," he said, eyeing Michael over the rim of his cup, "if we had a central place we could put these sick folk, it'd make everything a helluva lot easier on all of us."

He might as well have been a toreador waving a red cape at a wounded bull.

"You're treading on thin ice, Doc."

Doc threw up an open palm, conceding defeat. Before he left, he explained in detail how much vinegar to put in the kettle of water and how to use a towel or blanket to confine the vapor so Wynn could benefit best from it. Michael made him promise he'd come back to Wynn's house to sleep. "That way," Michael said, "you'll be right here if — if I need you."

He couldn't bring himself to say, "if she collapses."

Minutes bled into hours, hours bled into a day; the day bled into night and night into another day, but Michael never left Wynn's side. So he could watch her constantly, he'd pulled her bed into the kitchen. All the while he pumped water or tended the stove, he watched her. Though he forgot to eat himself, he never failed to feed Wynn. A few spoonfuls of thin barley gruel or a few swallows of milk was all she could manage at a time, but he offered her something every couple of hours. Fifteen minutes of every thirty, he propped pillows at her back and held the kettle and towel while she inhaled the vinegar vapor.

When none of his efforts seemed to make a difference; when Wynn's condition seemed to be worsening instead of improving, he railed at Doc.

The physician lowered his head and pressed a palm over his pate. "I don't know what else to do, boy."

Michael heard the defeat in Doc's voice, remembered then how the old man's feet had dragged when he'd come in moments before, and he noted the lines of fatigue around Doc's eyes and mouth. "I — I'm sorry," Michael mumbled, turning to the stove and shaking the coffee pot, pouring up the last cup and handing it to Doc. "This is just so damned frustrating!"

"Epidemics always are."

Michael pumped water for another pot of coffee with much more vigor than was necessary, trying to work out his anger. "Any new cases?"

Doc nodded slowly. "Three."

"Anyone I know?"

"No one you know well. All newcomers. One of 'em's that Mason fellow Wynn nursed when she first come to town."

Michael put some beans in the grinder and cranked it hard. "We're almost out of coffee," he announced. "You bring any groceries home?"

"Slim brought 'em in the cart. They're on the stoop."

"I'll bring them in while you're looking at Wynn."

Later, Doc confirmed what Michael knew in his heart but hadn't wanted to believe. Wynn was dying.

"If the membrane would just loosen up, we could induce vomiting."

"Why?"

"To finish dislodging the membrane. If she can cough it up, she might live."

"*Might* live? I thought it was the membrane that made her sick."

Doc's eyes, red-streaked and watery from exhaustion rather than inebriation, begged Michael for forgiveness. "At the outset, that was true. But the diphtheria poison could have very well entered her bloodstream by now. Even if she expectorates the membrane, the poison can kill her."

Doc knew he ought to tell Michael, too, how devastating the aftereffects could be, should Wynn pull

234

"You aren't going to die, dammit! I'm not going to let you!"

Wynn heard Michael's husky oath, though its sound was weak, coming to her ears as from a great distance.

A tiny part of her knew she hovered at the brink of death. Though needle-sharp, this realization prompted no emotion, for it could not gain entrance to her soul. From time to time, she was marginally aware of Michael's presence by her bed. More often than not, she slipped into peaceful oblivion, where she was blessedly free from the incredible soreness in her muscles, free from the incessant pounding of hammers against her brain, free from the excruciating pain in her throat.

Now that pain strangled her with its size and intensity. She needed to tell Michael that her throat was closing up, but she couldn't get any sound through. She tried to swallow and gagged on the modicum of saliva she had managed to gather in her mouth. She lifted her hand, grimaced at the stinging sensation knifing through her arm but forebearing the pain as she brought her palm to her swollen neck.

Michael watched her, watched her eyes widen, watched the tiny, pulsing movement of her neck muscles as she attempted to draw breath. A slowly dawning horror gorged his own throat as her meaning began to penetrate. He'd learned this could happen from Wynn's medical textbook. Oh, God! Where was Doc?

There had to be another way. He couldn't cut into her neck with a scalpel. He wouldn't know how, or what to do once he had, anyway. There had to be another way . . .

Think, dammit, think!

Lightning quick, he pulled her up, piling pillows and blankets at her back to hold her torso upright. Wynn continued to choke. "Hold on, baby," he breathed. "Hold on."

He closed his eyes briefly, swallowed hard, then jerked her forward and rapped sharply on her back with the side of his hand. Miraculously, to Michael anyway, she stopped gagging. He laid her back against the pillows and snatched up the spoon from Wynn's gruel.

"Open your mouth," he coaxed, using the spoon handle to hold her tongue down so he could see into her throat. The odor from the disease was so foul he had to hold his own breath while he looked. He found himself staring at the huge, ugly, yellow-gray membrane, its leathery mass pulsating as spasms tore at her throat, a portion of its edge fluttering weakly.

"It's loose, Wynn! Dammit, it's loose!" He didn't know whether she fully understood, but the almost imperceptible yet unmistakable curve of her parched lips let him know that at least she caught his enthusiasm.

What had Doc told him to do when the vapor finally loosened the membrane?

His mind whirled with bits and pieces of his recent conversations with Doc, but his counsel on this point remained buried. Out of utter frustration, Michael held the spoon high, intending to hurl it across the room. A split second before it left his fingers, he thought better of the rash action and set it back in the bowl instead. He knew he had to calm down to think clearly. He took a deep breath, closed his eyes, and silently willed the recollection.

Induce vomiting. He could hear Doc's voice saying

the words. But how? Why hadn't he asked him how to do it? It had to be gentle but effective. If he wanted to vomit, he thought, he'd just ram a finger down his throat. He couldn't do that to Wynn, though. It wasn't gentle. More importantly, if he tore the membrane, it would grow back.

The only other way involved swallowing some sort of emetic, and Michael wasn't the least bit certain Wynn could manage it. Just thinking about her choking again made him shudder. He'd try the vapor one more time. Maybe that would help to loosen more of the membrane—and it would give him time to figure out what to do.

Long, lean fingers ransacked dark hair that hadn't seen a comb in days, then traversed the back of his neck and came to rest on his shoulder. Mechanically, he massaged the aching muscle for a moment before scraping the same hand across the two-day stubble on his chin. Dark, bristly brows perked downward in a point over his hawk's nose and his tongue raked at the coating on his front teeth. All the while he fussed without conscious thought over his general need for grooming, his mind raced with possibilities and his gaze darted about the room, chasing after something . . . something he could use to induce vomiting.

Like an arrow spinning toward a target, his probing gaze hit the bull's-eye. There it was, on Wynn's pantry shelf. Alum. If his own mouth recoiled at the very idea of having bitter alum poured into it, surely Wynn's stomach would insist on regurgitating it.

He took a step toward the pantry, his hand going up, reaching for the can long before he was close enough to touch it. The bite of steam on the back of his raised hand stopped him. The vapor! He'd forgotten.

The minutes crawled by as he assisted Wynn with

the vapor, her ragged inhalations pulling at his heart-strings. When the prescribed duration had passed, though, she seemed a bit stronger, her breathing a bit easier. She would need whatever strength she could gather for the reaction to the dose of alum.

Michael decided to let her rest for a few minutes. Deep down, he was hoping Doc would show up. The triangular piece of sky, framed by the white curtains at Wynn's kitchen window, flamed with striations of pink, magenta, and peach, signaling the end of daylight. Doc should be home soon.

He fixed his eyes on the triangle, watched it change from a glorious pastel palette to a screen of shadowy fuchsia smeared with lavender to the deep purple sheet of dusk. He struck a match and lit a lamp against the encroaching darkness, wishing something could put a light in his soul as easily.

If he had a single regret, it was that he had never told her he loved her, for he knew now that what he felt for her could be called nothing else. He wished, too, that he had demonstrated the depth of his emotion by making love to her. He couldn't stand the thought of Wynn Spencer dying without ever knowing, fully and completely, how very much he loved her. The fact that he'd already demonstrated his love with his constant, devoted care never crossed his mind.

He listened to the swing of the hall clock's pendulum. He breathed deeply, exhaled slowly, and breathed deeply again, letting the sickroom smells of disinfectant and vinegar penetrate his senses. He reached out and touched Wynn's clammy brow, her sodden cheek, her swollen neck. He pulled his palm down over the light blanket that covered her and grasped her hand in his own. He felt her fingers fold over the back of his hand, felt a rush of warmth fill the cavity of his chest, felt a congregation of tears fill his eyes.

For a long moment he sat very still, holding her hand, using his free hand to smooth hair stiff with dried perspiration away from her face. "When you're stronger," he whispered, his throat thick, "I'll wash it for you."

Her eyelids flickered over pain-dulled irises and one corner of her lips stretched the tiniest bit upwards. A sound gurgled in her throat.

His fingers moved from her hair to her lips and hovered there. "Shush, my sweet. Don't try to talk. I understand." He hesitated then, wishing with all his heart he didn't have to cause her further pain but knowing he had no choice. Finally, he asked, "Can you swallow?"

She dipped her chin forward.

"Good. I think that membrane is about ready to let go, but you're going to have to help it out. I'm going to give you some alum water to drink."

She dipped her chin forward again, but this time he thought he saw a flash of anticipated torment on her face.

Quickly, he mixed the alum water, not sure how much of the white powder to stir in, hoping he'd done it right. She choked repeatedly on the bitter concoction before she got it all down. Michael winced with every gag, then felt his own stomach churn as he knew Wynn's must be churning.

And then he waited. He held her hand again as the minutes ticked by, their passage marked by the swinging pendulum and the steady beating of Michael's heart. It hadn't been enough. God! He hadn't put enough alum in the water, and now he'd have to put her through that torture all over again.

He felt a tightening in her fingers seconds before

he heard the strangling sound in her throat. Without stopping to think about what he was doing, he reached for the pan with one hand and pulled her forward with the other.

Her pitiful retching tore at his gut, but he persevered, holding both Wynn and the pan firmly until she had finished. He laid her back on the pillows, watched her eyelids flutter closed, and shuddered at the extreme paleness of her face, the dark lavender pallor around her eyes, the whiteness of her lips. She looked like death, and it scared the hell out of him.

He didn't know what to do with the pan, so he slid it under the bed without inspecting its contents. If she hadn't vomited up the membrane, she was certainly too weak to try again now. Doc could check it when he came in. He'd need to examine her throat, anyway.

Michael checked her pulse, found it weak but steady, and expelled a long breath he hadn't realized he'd been holding. Suddenly, a wave of weakness washed over him. He couldn't remember when he'd slept last, for he hadn't allowed himself the luxury of even a catnap while he'd been responsible for Wynn's care. But Doc would be back soon. He'd just rest until he got there.

He lay down across the foot of the bed, leaving his knees on the chair seat, letting his feet hang over the side.

He'd just rest for a minute . . . God, he was so tired!

Chapter Fourteen

It was almost midnight when Doc came in, his eyes bleary, his mind dull, his spirits sagging. He had just diagnosed the thirty-seventh case of diphtheria in Jennings. This last one was a two-year-old boy whose chances of survival were extremely slim.

This is why I quit, he reminded himself. He knew doctors should be able to detach themselves from their patients, but he'd never learned how. Though fifteen years had passed since he'd last practiced medicine, nothing had changed. But with Wynn sick, there was no one else to do what had to be done. He couldn't sit by and watch people suffer, not if he could alleviate their pain—even if he couldn't save their lives.

Doc refused to consider what he might have to do if Wynn didn't survive.

He wanted to head straight upstairs and collapse on her bed, but his determination to make sure she survived propelled him down the hall and into her kitchen. What he saw there dropped his heart to the pit of his stomach. Wynn was too pale, too still, too lifeless.

He rushed to her side, lifting her limp wrist from

where it lay by her hip. Fear and sadness and defeat almost overwhelmed him when he couldn't find a pulse. Then he realized that, in his haste, he hadn't held her wrist properly. Granted, it was no more than a thin thread, but it was steady. And, by God, she was sleeping like a babe! She hadn't slept that soundly since the day Michael had brought him here . . .

Doc had paid no heed to Michael's prostrate form at the foot of the bed until then. The boy hadn't slept either, not for days. He looked incredibly uncomfortable, lying on his side with his torso on the mattress, his hip on the chair, his feet dangling, but he was sleeping soundly. Doc wasn't about to disturb him.

As he moved away from Wynn's side, his toe struck the dishpan Michael had shoved under the bed. Doc hunkered down, pulled it out, and shook his head in wonder. For someone who viewed the practice of medicine as negatively as did Michael Donovan, the boy had performed well. Extremely well.

Wynn's recuperation was slow and painful, but steady.

Michael and Doc continued to stay with her. Michael took care of her during the day while Doc was out making rounds. Doc's staying there at night helped keep up appearances. Though neither Michael nor Doc cared one whit what anyone thought, they both knew Wynn cared.

For the first few days, Michael was far too exhausted to do anything that wasn't absolutely necessary for survival. But as soon as he caught up on his sleep and Wynn was resting better, he gave Wynn the bath he'd promised her, lathering her entire body with lilac-scented soap and washing her hair. She was still far too weak to claim impropriety—or to be unduly embarrassed by her nakedness. Bathing her became a daily ritual, one Michael simultaneously savored and abhorred.

One day, he promised himself, he'd bathe her as her lover, not her nurse. In the meantime, he had to wax content with feasting his eyes upon the delicate pink tips of her breasts, the ivory softness of her limbs, the nest of dark brown hair between her thighs. Not being able to do anything about his own physical response to her beauty made him ache all the more for the day he could.

During the day, while she was resting, Michael cleaned and disinfected her house, one square foot at the time, for he was determined to rid every surface of any diphtheria germs that might be lurking there. He took down all the curtains and washed them, along with all the linens, including the ones in her cupboard, and all Wynn's clothes, using disinfectant in the wash water. Michael didn't like the smell of carbolic acid any better than he had before, but circumstances had taught him the importance of its use.

Although Prairie's furniture had arrived days earlier, he'd had Slim hold it at the depot. When he determined Wynn's house to be clean enough, he sent for it, then spent most of a day setting it up and decorating the spare bedroom.

Doc laughed out loud when he saw it. "Hell, boy! I never would have believed you could be domestic," he teased.

Michael wasn't offended. On the contrary, he beamed with warranted pride at his efforts. "I never would have believed it either," he easily admitted. "Now, we can bring Prairie home."

He sounded, even to himself, like a father. But to be a father, he had to become a husband first. He'd had ample time to consider that notion, and the more he thought about it, the better he liked the idea. Wynn's scrape with death had brought his priorities clearly into focus. As soon as she was strong enough, he planned to ask her to marry him. And once they were married, they'd see about adopting Prairie.

Before the epidemic played itself out, a score of graves had been added to the plot of ground next to the river where they'd buried Jernigan, making it a real cemetery, albeit an inconvenient one. The disease had taken the lives of both children and adults. Many more—at least one member of almost every family who lived within the confines of the quickly growing town—had been afflicted. It would be a long time, folks said, before the early residents of Jennings forgot the spring of 1884.

While no one else blamed Doc for a single death, he himself did. The first day Wynn Spencer was able to be up and about, he vowed, he was moving back home and resuming his old lifestyle. He missed being a cantankerous old drunk. He'd done what he could, even if he didn't think it was enough, but he'd be happy to turn the responsibility of health care back over to Wynn.

Fate conceived a different plan.

"Morning, sleepyhead."

Wynn sat up in bed and stretched luxuriously, then lowered her arms and smiled at Michael, who was opening the curtains in the examination room. Once she'd started convalescing, he'd moved the bed back. Knowing he'd hardly left her side for days on end

244

warmed her far more than the early May sun stream
ing through the glass. And even now, almost two
weeks since he'd made her drink the alum water, he
was still there, taking care of her.

"Good morning to you. Is it late?"

"Nine o'clock. Prairie's been up for hours!" He
groaned melodramatically, sat down on the side of
the bed, and took one of her hands in his. "How are
you feeling?"

"Wonderful! Never again will I take well-being for
granted."

His long, lean fingers stroked the back of her
hand, and his voice was scratchy. "Nor I. When I
thought you were dying . . ."

She watched his Adam's apple bob up and down a
couple of times and silently begged him to finish the
sentence. When he looked away, she sought to ease
his obvious discomfort with the subject of her illness
by asking, "Where is the little angel this morning?"

"Little imp, you mean," he corrected, an easy grin
lighting his eyes as he turned back to her.

Wynn laughed. "What did she do this time?"

"Wanted to play house. You should see the
kitchen—pots and pans everywhere."

"I'd love to see it. If you'll help me, I think I can
walk that far."

His dark eyebrows shot to mid-forehead. "Do you
mean it? I mean, are you sure you should try?"

"I'm the doctor, remember? Just don't let me step
on the rolling pin."

With her left arm circling Michael's waist and his
right arm around her shoulder, they slowly made
their way into the kitchen. When Wynn tried to put
her weight on her left foot, it didn't want to cooperate. That was only because she hadn't used it for
such a long time, she assured herself. The feeling

245

would come back as she continued to improve. She knew it would.

"Good morning, Dr. Wynn!" Prairie piped, giving Wynn only a cursory glance as she stirred a pot of water littered with pieces of torn fig leaves. "I'm making you some breakfast."

"She just took a few, Wynn," Michael quickly explained.

"That's fine, Prairie, but don't pick the new little figs or we won't have any to eat later."

The child looked up from her stirring and wrinkled her nose at the sight of Wynn's faltering steps. "What's wrong with you, Dr. Wynn? You can't walk good any more?"

"It's been a long time, Prairie," Wynn said on a whispery breath. "I have to get my strength back, and then I'll be able to walk just fine again."

At the moment, Wynn believed that to be true, but as the days passed and her left foot and leg remained numb, her prospects of ever being completely whole again grew dimmer. She allowed her muscles a full week to decide to cooperate, not sharing her growing fear with anyone in the interim.

Then one morning when Michael started to help her out of the bed, she stalled him. It was high time, she decided, to find out once and for all. "Please bring me a needle first, Michael," she said. "You'll find one in the sewing kit in my bedroom."

"What color thread do you want?" he asked.

"I don't need to mend anything, Michael. Just, please, get a needle."

When he returned a few minutes later, she instructed him to poke her left leg and foot with the sharp point of the needle.

"Why?" he questioned, his face dark with a combination of concern and confusion. "Won't that hurt?"

246

"I certainly hope so!" When he seemed reluctant to proceed, she insisted, her voice brooking no argument. "Don't squabble about this, Michael. Just do it."

Following her guidance, he pushed the point of the needle into the bottom of her foot, then the top, working his way up her left leg all the way to its junction with her hip. With each gentle stab, he watched her expression. Although he carefully avoided drawing blood, he expected Wynn to feel some pain. Not once did she so much as wince, but by the time he had finished, her eyes were awash with unshed tears.

He stuck the needle in the end of her pillow and gathered her against his chest. "God, Wynn! I'm so sorry," he moaned. "I didn't mean to hurt you."

Her voice was thick. "That's the problem, Michael. You didn't."

He pulled back, suddenly needing to see her eyes. "What do you mean?"

"I didn't feel anything."

"So?"

"So my leg is paralyzed."

It took a moment for that to sink in. When Michael could speak past the lump in his throat, he uttered one word. "Why?"

Wynn blinked away her tears and took a deep breath. "It happens sometimes, after diphtheria. The paralysis is usually of the soft palate and pharynx, but it can occur in any of the muscles."

"Is there a cure?"

"Fresh air and exercise are supposed to help. I—" she gulped—"I treated a few paralysis victims at St. Luke's, but their problems resulted from either accidents or strokes, not diphtheria. I honestly don't know what to expect from this. But, Michael"—she laid a hand on his forearm and kept her steady gaze

247

trained on his face—"this could be permanent."

"Don't even think such a thing!" he declared, hugging her close for a moment and then scooping her into his arms.

"Michael! What are you doing?" A tinkle of laughter erupted from her throat.

"Carrying you to the table. Don't you want some coffee?"

"Exercise, Michael. I need exercise. Put me down!"

"You'll get a dose of both fresh air and exercise today and every day. I'll see to it."

"But, Michael," she argued, "you've neglected your own work for weeks now. We'll get Slim to cut off Doc's crutches and I'll be able to get around on them just fine."

He pursed his lips and set her down in a chair by the table. "This topic is not open for discussion, Wynn Spencer. I got you through the diphtheria, and I'm going to get you through this paralysis thing as well."

For the next two weeks, Michael massaged Wynn's leg from ankle to hip several times a day. He helped her dress every morning after breakfast, walked her through the house until she grew tired, then took her outside to watch him work her garden. If the ground was dry enough, she sat on a quilt close to the house, using one of the foundation pillars for support, a cushion at her back. But more often than not, it rained during the night, leaving the earth far too damp for such an arrangement. Then, she sat in one of the ladder-back chairs and used a nail keg as a hassock. Even with cushions on the keg and in the chair, she was uncomfortable.

One day, despite her giddy protests, Michael tied

his bandanna around her eyes after breakfast, carried her outside, and sat her down in what could only be a new chair. With the blindfold gone, Wynn gasped in amazement.

The chair was made like a chaise, its slatted seat and back set on a curved frame that hugged her knees and supported her spine. A folded quilt provided a comfortable cushion and a man's oversized umbrella had been attached at the back to provide shade.

"How do you like it, Dr. Wynn?" Prairie asked, climbing onto Wynn's lap, her brown eyes wide with anticipation.

"It's — well, it's wonderful! How . . . where . . . who . . . ?"

"So many questions!" Michael teased, clucking his tongue at her. "I told Slim what you needed and he made it."

"But — it fits me!"

"I measured you while you slept."

Wynn ran her hands over the wide arms, leaned her head back against the neck rest, and sighed in pleasure. "I don't know what to say."

"Your glowing face says it all. I'm glad you like it, sweetheart."

"I thought I was your sweetheart," Prairie pouted.

"And so you are," Michael quickly assured her. "Can't a man have two sweethearts?"

As long as one of them is a little girl, Wynn caught herself thinking and realized how possessive of Michael she had become. She was a woman in love, and he must — judging from his actions — love her, too.

But she had grown too dependent on him. Her mother had taught her how destructive to oneself and unhealthy to a relationship dependence could be.

Somewhere along the line, she had lost every shred

of both modesty and independence. She allowed Michael to do everything for her—from bathing her and helping her dress to washing and combing her hair. At the outset, she hadn't the strength or the will to feel anything more than gratitude. But as her body grew stronger, it began to respond to his every touch as though it were a lover's caress. Well, she wouldn't—couldn't allow that to continue. If there were to be any future for them, she first had to regain sovereignty over her body and her life.

If Michael took note of her sudden pensiveness, he gave no indication. He set Prairie to work using a hand rake to dig up weeds on one side of the garden patch while he took the hoe to the other side.

Through half closed eyes, she watched him work, noting the power in his arms and shoulders as he slung the hoe. She almost gasped aloud a few minutes later when he removed his shirt, revealing to her hungry eyes rippling muscles and a tan line where his brown neck met pale bronze skin that would grow darker, she was sure, as summer progressed. For a long time, she could see only his back, could only imagine the sculpted beauty of his chest, as she had so often.

Finally, he turned around, seemingly oblivious to her scrutiny as he started working toward her. His nipples were brown, browner than she had imagined. And they peeked out of a thick dusting of dark, almost black, curly hair that spread wide over his chest and narrowed to a point where it entered his denim britches. When he paused for a moment, resting his left forearm on the handle of the hoe and raising his right arm to wipe at the sweat on his brow, her breath caught in her throat.

Michael Donovan was, without doubt, the most virile, the most handsome, and the most considerate man she'd ever known. What had she ever done to deserve him, even for a short time? Trying to hold on to him wasn't fair, not when he could have any woman he wanted, not when she was only part of a woman.

Her heart yearned for him then, and she fought her physical need, fought the urge to cry out to him, to beg him to take her back inside and make love to her, to teach her what being a woman was all about before it was too late.

But she stilled her tongue, even if she couldn't quite manage to still the throbbing ache in her loins.

After lunch, when Michael left to collect her cart and horse from the livery for their daily ride, Wynn asked him to take Prairie and leave her with Granny for the afternoon. She felt a stab of remorse at the wicked gleam that appeared in his eyes. But, she argued with her conscience, this thing must be done, the bond must be broken, and the sooner she got it over with, the better for both of them.

He came back with a buckboard, claiming her cart unsafe for the route he had planned. They headed due north on land squishy from the spring rains. It seemed to Wynn the lighter-weight cart would have been far safer than the heavy buckboard. "We're going to bog down out here," she claimed.

"No, we won't. Honest."

At first, the going was slow, but as the ground became firmer, Michael clicked his tongue at the team of draft horses, and they picked up speed. An hour or so out of town, the prairie began to change dramatically, the monotonously brown, head-high Indian grass giving way to a marvelous palette. Dozens of kinds of grasses rose around them, their variegated shades of green and bronze and wine and gold rippling, swirling, shining in the sunlight.

"Oh, Michael," Wynn whispered, unabashed reverence in her voice. "This is breathtaking!"

He hauled on the reins, calling "Whoa, there!" and then setting the brake. His gaze roamed the sea of shimmering grasses, gently swaying in a light breeze, before settling on Wynn's awestruck countenance. "Not nearly so breathtaking as you are, my sweet," he murmured, his mouth close to her ear.

A shiver snaked down her spine and she folded her arms beneath her breasts. "Michael, please," she begged, "don't make this harder."

Her plea set off a warning bell in his head, but he ignored it. His need to express his feelings for her, to show her and tell her how much he loved her eclipsed all other instincts. He grasped her shoulders in a gentle caress and turned her toward him, then slid his hands down her arms to her elbows, tugged her hands loose, and guided them around his rib cage.

"Michael, please, don't do this," she begged again. "I—we need to talk."

He silenced her protests with his lips, first plucking teasingly and then running his tongue along the seam of her mouth, until she finally moaned and gave in to his tender assault. His tongue plundered hers, its tip flicking and taunting hers into a willing partnership. When his hands moved upon her breasts, hers moved up his back.

While his mouth worked its magic on hers, his fingers slowly released the buttons down the front of her shirtwaist. A part of her, the independent part she was trying so desperately to regain, knew she should stop him. But another part, the part that had reveled in the sight of his bronzed, hair-dusted chest that morning, the part that yearned to be taught the carnal secrets of life, won the battle.

Her own fingers worked the buttons on his shirt,

which were larger and fewer in number and easier to release than her own. Thus, she finished her pleasurable task before he did. She slipped her hands inside his shirt, burying her fingertips in the curly hair as she had longed to do. His hair was crisp and cool and felt wonderful between her fingers.

Michael groaned into her mouth and tugged her shirtwaist free from the waistband of her skirt. His fingers worked at untying the ribbons that held her camisole closed until he, too, could explore the wondrous flesh of her chest. Where his was firm and muscular, hers was soft and pliable. His palms cupped her bare breasts. He felt them mold to the shape of his hands, then pressed the pads of his thumbs across her quickly hardening nipples.

She followed suit.

He groaned again.

She made mewling sounds in her throat.

His mouth left hers and forged a hot trail down the side of her neck, stopping to suckle gently where her neck curved into her shoulder, then continued its wet path downward until it reached a straining crest, which he swept for a moment with a side-to-side motion of his mustache. He replaced the mustache with his tongue, laving the areola and teasing the bud into throbbing hardness before he took it into his mouth.

Wynn thought she had surely died and gone to heaven.

"Oh, Michael," she whimpered. "Please, don't do that."

His lids opened to half-mast and he looked up at her face without releasing her nipple. "Why?" he asked against her breast, drawing out the *wh* so that his breath tickled her.

"Because." It was all the speech she could manage.

He raised up then, using his thumbs again to taunt

her while he spoke. "Because when I do this, you lose control. Let go, Wynn."

"I can't . . ."

"Yes, you can. You want this as much as I do. Admit it."

"No."

He pushed the firm mounds of her breasts upward, pursed his lips, and blew first on one nipple and then the other. His eyes devoured their proud, upward thrust. "Do you know what most women would give for breasts like yours?" he asked in a voice thick with passion.

"No."

"I've looked at them for weeks now, Wynn. Every day I've looked at them and yearned to hold them, to touch them, to caress them as your lover. I've looked at all of you, Wynn Spencer. Looking isn't enough anymore."

He lowered his mouth to her other breast and lavished upon it the same attention he had bestowed on its mate. While one hand held her breast, the other unfastened the hooks on her skirt, then pulled the ends of the ribbon drawstring ties that held her petticoat and bloomers at her waistline. When these were loose, his palm slipped over her abdomen and downward until his fingers plunged into the nest of soft hair that sheltered her most intimate place.

"Tell me you want me," he whispered.

"No."

He flicked his tongue across her nipple and moved his hand deeper, his fingers seeking, finding the moist, throbbing heart of her femininity.

"Tell me you want me."

"No."

His other hand left her breast and moved behind her head. Slowly, ever so gently, he lowered her spine onto the quilt-covered seat of the buckboard. His mouth claimed hers then, his tongue thrusting deep into the moist cavern of her mouth even as his finger thrust deep into the moist cavern at the juncture of her thighs.

Never had she felt so light, so airy, so completely feminine. A part of her knew his seduction had been methodically precise, the product of much experience, but she didn't care.

"Tell me you want me."

"Yes. God, Michael. Yes!"

They lay in the back of the buckboard, the quilt that had been folded over its seat under their dew-kissed bodies, the warm May sun beaming down upon them, their eyes drinking in the essence of each other. A soft breeze ruffled over them, its breath carrying the sweet scent of the prairie grasses. A meadowlark swooped down from the crystal blue sky and perched on the side of the wagon, then opened its throat and honored them with a solo performance.

Michael's knuckles grazed Wynn's cheekbone. "You are so beautiful."

Wynn felt a gathering of moisture in her eyes and she lowered her lids. "Please, Michael, don't say things like that."

"Why shouldn't I, when they're true?"

She sighed, then shivered when his fingers left her cheek and replanted themselves on her breast. "We have to talk about this."

His arms slipped around her bare back then, and he pulled her against the length of him. "Yes, I suppose we do. I intended to ask you before, not after."

Wynn stiffened. "Ask me what?"

He blew on her temple, smoothed back her hair

with his callused fingers, then took her face in his open palms. "Look at me, Wynn," he said, his voice ragged. "I can't do this if you're not looking at me."

She opened her eyes, revealing their dampness to his steady gaze. Her heart thudded out of control.

"I love you, Wynnifred Hughes Spencer. I never thought I'd say that to a woman, but it's the truth. I do love you. And I want to marry you, if you'll have me."

"Oh, Michael!" she cried in a voice wrought with sorrow. "I love you, too, and I never thought I'd say that to another man, not after the last one jilted me."

Michael's eyebrows met in a deep *V* on his forehead. "Jilted you?"

She nodded.

He'd heard her sorrow and attributed it to remembered heartache. "I won't do that to you, Wynn. We can leave tomorrow, on the Sunday train, and be married in Lake Charles on Monday."

"No, we can't." There was a note of finality in her voice he didn't like, but he tried to ignore it.

"No problem. I'll send for a preacher and we'll be married here. Then you can invite Granny and Doc and whoever else you want. Prairie can be your flower girl and—"

"You don't understand, Michael."

"What is there to understand?"

"I can't marry you."

Chapter Fifteen

She'd hurt him. She'd hurt this wonderful, tender, compassionate man. She could see the confusion, the pain, the anguish in his eyes, and for the rest of her life, she'd have to live with that memory, she'd have to live with her own anguish, she'd have to live without Michael.

But she had to try to explain. "Michael, I'm sorry. I didn't mean to hurt you—"

The pain disappeared, lightning quick, as though he'd pulled a shade over his feelings, shutting himself off from her. His voice was cold, unfeeling. "Don't flatter yourself, Wynn. It's unbecoming."

He scrambled up, snatching up his pants and turning his back to her as he jerked them on.

"Michael, please, come back here," she pleaded. "Let me explain."

His voice was sharp, his words daggers piercing her heart. "There's nothing left to be said, Dr. Spencer. Either you'll have me or you won't. I've never begged for anything in my life. I'm not about to start begging now."

Anxiety ripped through her. "That's not it, Michael. That's not it at all!"

"Isn't it? Does it please you to have fooled me so well?"

"Michael—" She choked on a sob.

He stalked around on the quilt in his bare feet, gathering up her clothes and then hurling them at her. "Get dressed," he snapped.

His callousness finished her off. The pain consumed her and she burst into tears.

Wynn hadn't dressed herself without his assistance since she'd come down with diphtheria, but he offered her no help this time. She leaned as far forward as she could, stretching her arms until she thought she would dislocate her shoulders, hot tears plopping unchecked onto her knees as she struggled to slip the leg opening of her bloomers over her left foot.

"That would be much more easily accomplished," he noted dryly, "if you bent your left knee. It will bend, you know. You just have to manipulate it yourself."

He jumped off the wagon and strode off through the waist-high grass, leaving Wynn to work out the problem of getting dressed by herself, leaving her to deal with a heartache far worse than any she'd ever known.

They drove back to town in complete silence. He sat stiffly beside her, and when the buckboard bounced over a rut and their thighs touched, he jerked away from her as though burned.

She fought back the tears that threatened to erupt again and wondered if Jonathan had felt even a shred of this pain when he'd rejected her. She didn't think so. She didn't think he'd hurt at all. He'd never loved her, not really, not the way she loved Michael Donovan. Nor was it Michael she was rejecting. No, not him nor his love for her, which she knew in the depths of her soul was genuine.

It was her own inadequacy. Didn't he see that? Didn't he know he deserved a whole woman, one who could pleasure him in every way, one who could walk and run and dance? One who could take care of him, clean his house and prepare his meals? One who could be everything a wife was supposed to be? Not a cripple. That's all she was, all she might ever be. She'd tell him those things, make him understand, if he would just listen.

But he wouldn't. His mind was clamped as tight as the seal on her coffee canister, and it would take more than a bash against the stove top to open it.

Damn the sneaking, conniving bitch to hell and gone!

He'd thought she was different. He should have known better. He should have known she didn't think he was good enough, smart enough, well-bred enough for her. She'd wanted him only for what he could give her. Hadn't she made that perfectly clear? She'd told him he lived in a pigsty. She'd called him a yokel.

And he guessed that's what he was.

He didn't have her background, her education, her manners. But he loved her. Didn't that count for something?

He should have run her off when he had the chance. Now he was stuck living in the same small town with her, seeing her at the mercantile and running into her at the train station on Sunday afternoons. He'd know her from a mile away with that gimp leg of hers. And every time he saw her, his body would remember how sweetly she'd given herself to him one warm Saturday afternoon in May. Then he'd remember what she'd said to him afterwards and his heart would twist up like a knot in his chest.

They stopped off at the boardinghouse long enough for Michael to go in and collect Prairie. The child sensed something was wrong between her two favorite people, but when she tried to find out what it was, they both told her to be quiet.

When they got back to Wynn's house, Michael helped Wynn down from the buckboard and into the house. But the second he had her deposited on the parlor sofa, he bounded up the stairs so hard it made the house shake.

Wynn winced with every vibration, feeling as though he were physically striking her. She heard little metallic noises overhead as he slung clothes around, the tinny sounds of snaps and buttons and buckles striking the wood floor and then being scraped across it as the garments were picked up. She jumped with each clink as though it were a piercing signal of alarm.

Wynn could see into the hall through the open parlor door. She watched Michael leap off the bottom step, snatch open her front door, and leave without looking back.

When Doc came in shortly thereafter, he found her sitting on the sofa, trembling violently, a dazed look on her face. Prairie sat next to her, as close as she could get, her tiny hand stroking the length of

Wynn's arm. "It's all right, Dr. Wynn," he heard her say. "My daddy's coming back and so is Mr. Donovan."

Damn the boy, anyway! Doc thought, understanding immediately what had happened to distress Wynn. Well, it was nothing a cup of strong coffee and some friendly conversation wouldn't cure. All lovers had spats at one time or another. He'd just have to find out what was wrong between the two of them and then try to fix it.

An hour later, he was still certain of the diagnosis, but not nearly so confident of the prescription. At least Wynn wasn't trembling anymore. If he could just get her to make sense . . .

"You're telling me that Michael Donovan—the Michael Donovan *I* know—asked you to marry him and you refused?"

"Yes."

Her voice was so low, Doc had to strain to hear her, but her feeble nod convinced him he'd gotten that much straight. He didn't need to ask her if she loved Michael; Doc knew she did. What he wanted to ask her was why she'd refused to marry the boy, but he didn't dare at the moment or she'd probably go all sobby feminine on him again. Funny, he'd never thought of her in terms of blatant femininity before, not the frail side of femininity, anyway. The best way to combat this weakness, he decided, was to make her mad.

"You know what, Wynn Spencer? The first time I laid eyes on you—the night you came to town and called me and the boy yokels, I thought to myself, 'Doc, this woman's got spunk. She's just what Michael needs.' I'm disappointed in you. Real disappointed."

Though he was careful to keep his features molded into near meanness, he grinned inside when he thought he detected a spark in her eyes. He drove ahead, adding shame to his repertoire of persuasive tactics. "Do you have any idea how hard it was for that boy to ask you to marry him? I've known him for a long time, and I've never known him to be smitten before. Not like this. He must be hurtin' something awful."

Wynn sniffed. "I know he's hurting, Doc. That's why I'm crying."

Though she gave little sign of outward tears, Doc knew what she meant. His heart had shed its own tears — once.

It was time for some shock treatment. He needed it as much as Wynn did. "If you're so all-fired sorry you hurt him, then why in blazes don't you do something about it?"

She blinked. "Like what?"

"Like tell him you *will* marry him."

She hung her head and stared at her lap. "I can't."

"Did you tell Michael why you couldn't marry him?"

"No."

"Why didn't you?"

"He wouldn't listen."

"I'll listen. Tell me."

He refilled their coffee cups, sat back down, and waited for her answer. Prairie came in and wanted to know what they were having for supper and when they'd be eating. Doc gave her some soda crackers and shooed her away.

"It — it's hard to explain," Wynn finally said.

"Try." *And if you tell me he's not good enough*

for you, I'll pack up and leave myself.

Her response floored him. "I, well, it's just that Michael deserves someone better."

"Better than you?" Doc guffawed. "Wynn Spencer, you're the best thing that ever happened to that boy!"

"But I'm not . . . a whole person."

"Why not? Because you've got a bum leg?"

She nodded.

"Hell, that's just about the most ridiculous thing I ever heard!"

"Am I always going to be crippled?"

She was hurting, too. Doc knew she was hurting, knew he probably ought to be more gentle with her, but there was no easy way to deal with her, not that he could see. "I don't know, Wynn. I honestly don't know. You're the one with the formal training. What do you think?"

Defeat colored her voice, but she seemed somewhat calmer. "I don't know either." She lifted her coffee spoon and twirled it, focusing her attention on its spinning bowl. "Do you believe in premonitions, Doc?"

His eyes slid shut for a second, long enough for Doc to see himself rushing through a big house, calling to his Emma, fear and dread gripping him. Yes, he believed in premonitions. But he wouldn't tell her that. She might ask for a reason. "I've never given the subject much thought. Why?"

"Because the night I came here, I felt this terrible foreboding, like I was making a huge mistake. I couldn't imagine where the feeling came from at the time, but maybe this was why I felt that way. Though I wouldn't have believed it then, now I know that nothing that happened to me in Illinois was as bad as this."

"What are you going to do about it?"

"Continue the fresh air and exercise routine, I suppose. It'll be harder by myself, but I'll learn to cope."

"I mean, what are you going to do about Michael?"

She dropped the spoon and it clattered against the enameled top of the table. "Nothing."

Doc ignored the note of finality in her voice. "Don't you think you ought to try to talk this over with him in another day or two, when you've both calmed down?"

"No. Even if he listened, it wouldn't change anything. I see no point in causing both of us additional heartache, and that's all that would happen, Doc. I'm going to focus on learning to live with the paralysis and taking care of Prairie."

He considered the sadness in her eyes and the dullness in her voice and made a hasty decision, one he hoped he didn't live to regret. "You won't have to go it alone, Wynn. I'll stay on and help you—with the paralysis and Prairie . . . and your practice."

She seemed to brighten a bit. "You will? Are you sure?"

Doc knew he'd dug himself a nice, deep hole, but he wouldn't go back on his word.

Michael sought solace the only way he knew how: hard physical labor that left him bodily, if not mentally, exhausted at the end of each day. Finding something to do required little effort. He'd let his

264

business interests slide during the six weeks he'd been otherwise occupied, and there were a score of other projects he was ready to start—several of them, like a church and a school, important to the growth and development of Jennings, but he snatched at anything that offered to take his mind off Wynn Spencer.

Obstinately, he tried to avoid thinking of her at all, especially by name. Spencer . . . why did that name bother him? Who had he known named Spencer? Was this mystery person male or female? Was Spencer the Christian name or the surname? Though he dredged through every clear recollection from his past, he couldn't find a single answer.

But, he reminded himself, there was so much of his past he didn't recall anyway. What had happened to him before he was eight years old, before he went to live at the orphanage in Chicago? That portion of his life had lain buried, like a broken Oriental vase covered by the sands of time. It was odd how he'd known it was there, but he'd never had a clue to its design until he'd met Wynn Spencer. Since she'd arrived in Jennings, however, his memory had unearthed several shards of the puzzle's pottery. Yet, he had no firm notion of how to put them together to form the whole.

Wind . . . snow . . . a sick woman . . . a quilt-covered bed . . . blood . . . a date: February 4, 1860. And painted on each piece was the name Spencer. He was convinced, too, that his lifelong abhorrence of doctors was somehow related to the puzzle.

He thought of Prairie often. What a dear little urchin she was! And an orphan with no apparent recollection of her early years, just like him. Would she spend the rest of her life wondering about her beginnings? He wished he could be there for her, really be there, as a father—not just a friend across town. He missed her already.

And he missed Wynn, too. God in heaven above, how he missed Wynn Spencer! No amount of effort at pushing her from his thoughts could push her from his heart.

Sometimes at night, he lay awake for hours on end, his body and soul yearning for a reconciliation with her. When he slept, he dreamed of her, dreamed of their bodies entwined upon an old patchwork quilt in the back of a buckboard while prairie grasses swayed in the breeze and a meadowlark piped a lover's tune.

Negotiating the stairs proved too much for Wynn. For awhile, she slept on the bed in the examination room and Doc continued to use her bedchamber upstairs. She wasn't happy with the arrangement, but she didn't complain, telling herself that one day soon she'd be able to return to her room, have her things around her again, and regain her privacy.

Doc thought more pragmatically, more objectively than Wynn. He solicited some local muscle, namely Johnny and Slim, and the three of them moved everything from Wynn's room downstairs to the empty dining room. Then they collected Doc's furniture from Michael's house and put it upstairs in Wynn's old room.

When the work had been completed, Wynn sat down in her chair and surveyed her new bedchamber. Tears sprang into her eyes.

"This is just temporary," Doc explained at the

sight of her tears, "just till you can walk again, then we'll switch your furniture back and I'll move home."

"You don't understand, Doc," she said. "This is—well, this is one of the nicest things anyone ever did for me. Thank you."

But with regained privacy came regained desires. The summer brought long, hot days fraught with the heat of her frustration, and hot nights fraught with hotter dreams.

The days of summer dragged by in a slow and tedious column. The residents of Jennings spent them swatting at mosquitoes and wiping at sweat. The sounds of hammers striking metal and saws chewing wood rang out during the long, sweltering hours of daylight as one after another building rose from the prairie floor.

Michael sold lumber and other building supplies hand over fist. He sold almost every lot out of his original 160-acre parcel; a few buyers took entire blocks at a time. His hotels stayed full of guests, and his general store stayed empty of merchandise. Although he had more money than he'd ever dreamed he would accumulate, he was unhappy. Money brought power, as he knew it would. But it didn't bring happiness. Not without Wynn.

He donated a plot of land for a church, another for a school, and held still another in reserve for a public library. His philanthropy earned him abundant praise from the townsfolk, but he took no succor from their gratitude.

His extensive business dealings took him to New Orleans more often. Or, perhaps, he used business as an excuse to make the trip. He wasn't sure which way it fell, nor did he care. He'd always found solace in New Orleans; he'd find it again.

Some nights in the Crescent City, he played poker until dawn, amassing a small fortune without effort, not caring if he lost every penny he'd ever had. But when the last man folded and Michael raked in his winnings, he felt no satisfaction.

Other nights, he wandered into brothels along the river front, searching the menu of available strumpets for one with crystal blue eyes and a cloud of rich brown hair, encountering instead eyes dull with disenchantment and hair dyed fiery red or bleached mustard yellow. The very prospect of touching their pasty skin or kissing their rouged lips turned his stomach inside out. He remembered a time when he had allowed such women to pleasure him and wondered how he'd ever thought a mere slaking of physical thirst was enough.

He strolled the streets in the French Quarter for hours on end, blessing the sweltering heat for stealing his vitality and then cursing the ever-present image of pale blue eyes and soft, pliable lips that his sapped energy failed to erase.

His life became a vicious cycle of meaningless activity with unyielding pride as its hub, but never would Michael Donovan have admitted it was so. Still, he felt like a loose marble on a runaway roulette wheel.

Wynn had never seen a roulette wheel. She felt like a coffee bean caught between two blades in a grinder, waiting for her heart to release her so she could be free again, but fearing if that happened, the blades of indifference would chew her up, destroying her ability to feel. And she needed to feel the pain. It was a form of penance for the pain she'd caused Michael.

There was, quite simply, no way to win.

Maybe some of the guilt she was carrying would be released if Michael would only listen to her explanation. But every time she thought about confronting him, she chickened out. One day she realized there was nothing wrong with her right hand; she could write it down for him and hope he'd read it.

Thus resolved, Wynn sat down at her desk and penned him a rather long missive, leaving nothing to his imagination. Wanting to assure herself she hadn't left anything out or used a word or phrase that might be misconstrued, she read through it — and felt her heart sink. The tone was all wrong. It made her sound like a martyr and Michael, like a heel. Another day, she decided, she'd try writing to him again, using this letter as an example of the wrong approach so she wouldn't make the same mistakes again.

She folded the pages, took them to her room, and deposited them in the little drawer of the table that stood by her chair. Despite her intention, she didn't take them out again.

Doc Nolan thrust a hand in his pocket and jingled his change. Wynn had offered him an old pigskin coin purse to keep it in, but if he did that, he couldn't jingle it. No, thank you, he'd told her; he'd leave it loose. He liked listening to the tinkly sound, even though it usually brought Prairie running and begging for a nickel. He always gave her one, then walked her to the new, much larger general store "before it burned a hole in her pocket" so she could buy herself some peppermint or licorice.

In truth, having an excuse to go to town was part of the reason Doc jingled the change so often. The exercise was good for him; even more, he enjoyed visiting with the newcomers, seeing the old-timers, and staying caught up on both the current gossip and the new construction. Jennings was growing faster than he'd ever imagined it could. Michael must be pleased.

Since he seldom saw him anymore, Doc wasn't too sure how the boy felt about things, especially about Wynn. But there was no doubt Michael was miserable, with the clearly evident tenseness in his jaw and the faraway look in his eyes. If Michael was in town, Doc fully intended to corner him that morning and tell him a thing or two.

The hand that wasn't in a pocket clutched Prairie's tighter, and she giggled.

"Does money burn a hole in your pocket, Uncle Doc?" she asked, taking the expression literally.

"Yes, child, it does," he answered, smiling at her calling him 'uncle.' "I'm just glad to have some fuel to start the fire with."

Prairie wrinkled her nose in confusion, and Doc knew he'd never make the child understand how long it had been since he'd had any money to call his own—any he'd earned, anyway. He'd known for years that Michael purposely lost an occasional bet so he could give Doc money without its looking like a hand-out, and when Doc lost, Michael would say, "I'll put it on your tab." The boy was always careful to preserve Doc's pride. Why, then, couldn't he see how fiercely Wynn clung to hers?

What a destructive thing pride could be, Doc thought, when it ceased representing self-esteem and became folly. He knew he was feeling a bit too proud of himself that day, but regaining his self-esteem was a wondrous feeling. And he had Fate and Wynn Spencer, he supposed, to thank for returning it to him. Otherwise, he might never have resumed his medical practice. Gradually, he was learning to cope with death; in the meantime, he was rediscovering the joys in treating common, everyday accidents and illnesses.

Out of one eye, Doc watched Prairie's wide-eyed awe at the selection of candies stored in clear glass canisters arranged on the register counter. Out of the other, he looked for Michael Donovan, finally spying him as the boy stalked into the storeroom.

"Hurry up, Prairie," he gently urged, his head suddenly pounding with indecision. But this thing had to be done. He'd allowed Wynn and Michael ample time to settle their differences between them, and they just hadn't cooperated. Wynn would be mad as a wet hen when she found out he'd interfered, but she'd get over it.

Doc kept an eye trained on the storeroom doorway as Prairie made her selection and paid for her candy stick, then he bustled her over to a display of lick salt and sat her down on one of the blocks. "Stay right here and eat your candy," he instructed. "I'll be back in a few minutes. All right?"

Prairie's pointed chin bobbed. "You going to talk to Mr. Donovan?" she asked.

Doc had learned that this child didn't miss much. "Yes."

She beamed. "I'll stay here."

The August sun streamed through the open back door, momentarily blinding Doc with its intensity. When his eyes adjusted, he saw that Pete, a strapping youth Michael had hired to help out with the stock, was unloading crates from a buckboard and handing them to his boss. Doc made his way toward them, then cleared his throat to gain Michael's attention.

That one whirled on him, a dark frown marring his brow. "What do you want?" he snapped.

Don't blame me for your misery, boy. Doc forced a smile and a voice to match it. "Well, I'm fine, thank you. How are you?"

The unexpected rejoinder caught Michael off guard, as Doc had hoped it would. The frown disappeared—almost. "Sorry, old man, but I'm busy. Maybe we can talk later."

Doc nodded toward the buckboard. "The unloading can wait, and you know it. We've been friends for too long, Michael, to let something come between us now."

Michael's shoulders lifted nonchalantly. "Pete," he called, "run over to the hotel and ask Johnny for the list of supplies he needs. We might as well fill his order now."

Doc stepped into the sunlight and sat down on a crate; Michael followed suit.

Before Doc could form an appropriate opening remark, Michael said, "I don't care what we discuss, so long as it isn't that female doctor you've taken up with."

That got Doc's dander up. He wagged a crooked finger in Michael's face. "Now you listen to me, boy—"

Michael's neck suffused a deep red and he shot to

his feet. "I'm thirty-two years old, Doc, and I'm not going to sit here and let you lecture me as though I were ten. I've worked too hard to get where I am, and if I'm not good enough for that stuck-up pipsqueak—"

Doc blinked in confusion. *"You're* not good enough? Whatever gave you that idea?"

"Well, if that isn't . . . then why?"

"Her leg, boy. She thinks *she's* not good enough for *you.*"

Slowly, Michael sat back down, his full, dark eyebrows pulled low over his eyes. "Now why would she think something that stupid?"

Doc thought he could ask the same of Michael; instead he said, "Why don't you ask her yourself?"

Wynn took full advantage of the privacy Doc and Prairie's trips to town afforded her. At times, she read; at others, she napped; but mostly she filled the hour-long or so stretch soaking in the hipbath, which she'd get Doc to pull out and fill before he left. She had learned to manage fairly well, but there were still some things she found difficulty in accomplishing. Preparing her bath was one of them.

She leaned back, letting the warm, scented water work its wonder on her leg, a conspiratorial smile lifting her lips as she closed her eyes. At last, the paralysis had begun to dissipate, but Wynn was keeping that bit of information to herself. A complete recovery depended on too many factors; some of them Wynn figured she wasn't even aware of. She didn't want anyone, including Doc, pestering her about her progress. Wynn realized, too, that her silence on the matter was a form of self-protection, insulating her from anyone's disappointment, other than her own, should her leg never get any better.

"But, Lord," she prayed aloud, "for Michael's sake, please make me whole again."

Michael found Wynn's front door not only unlocked, but not even tightly latched. He started to knock, but when his hand touched the portal, it swung open on silent hinges. Had Doc left the door that way on purpose, Michael wondered, knowing if Wynn were given the opportunity to slam it in his face, she probably would? And he wouldn't blame her if she did.

So he sneaked in like a thief, thinking to catch her unaware but never expecting to find her taking a bath. God, how he'd missed seeing her! Suddenly, standing there in the hall, he wanted nothing better than to strip off his clothes and join her. But he didn't dare. Not yet. Not until they'd talked.

Michael strolled into the kitchen and pulled out a chair.

Wynn's eyes popped open when she heard him. She gasped and slid back down under the cover of a froth of soap bubbles.

He ignored her obvious discomfort, turning the ladder-back chair around and straddling it, as she'd seen him do so many times before. Her breath caught in her throat at the heart-stopping sight of his long, denim-clad legs and dark, sun-burnished complexion. Lord, how she'd missed seeing him!

A long, low whistle escaped his pursed lips, which then spread into a wide, devilish grin.

Wynn found her voice, but her protest came

out sounding reedy. "Michael, I'm taking a bath!"

"So?"

"So, you shouldn't be here."

He chortled. "It's not like I've never seen you in the buff before."

"But that was different."

He cocked a dark eyebrow and let his gaze roam from the top of her piled hair to the tip of her big toe sticking up at the opposite end of the galvanized tub. "Not really."

"Yes, really. Take yourself off into the parlor until I can get dressed. Please!"

He shook his head. "I'm not going anywhere, Wynn Spencer, until we've got a few things straight. Besides, how are you planning to get out of that tub by yourself?"

In answer, she snatched up one of the crutches she'd left leaning against the hipbath and pointed its tip at his chest. "If you don't leave, I'll—I'll—"

"You'll what?" he teased, wrapping his fingers around the crossbar of the crutch and pulling gently.

Wynn pulled back, starting a tug-of-war with the crutch.

Michael's grin immediately diminished as his lips formed themselves into a circle and his eyebrows moved up and down in rapid succession. His eyes darted about like stray bullets, his gaze hitting first one part of her anatomy and then another, finally settling on her chest.

Wynn was so preoccupied with regaining possession of the crutch, she didn't pay any attention to his silly facial expression at first. But when he burst out laughing, she glanced down and realized that each of his tugs pulled her torso straight up out of

275

the water, thus exposing her breasts. She let go of the crutch so fast, Michael tumbled over backwards out of the chair.

It was Wynn's turn to laugh, and she did, loudly, raucously, delightfully. The healing power of her mirth amazed her. When her laughter subsided, she said, "Getting out of here by myself is a chore. And I never manage to rinse off very well. If you'll agree to help me as though I were still your patient, I'll listen to you."

The chore, Michael decided, lay in keeping his hands off her. Once, he slipped up and laid a caressing hand on the side of her breast. He felt Wynn's sharp intake of breath beneath his palm, saw a look of excruciating pain slice across her face, and quickly moved it. *Good heavens!* he thought. *Does she hate me so?*

If it had not been for his promise to assist her, he would have left right then. Yet, he couldn't remove the image of her shimmering, naked flesh from his mind. His desire seemed to grow apace with her resistance to his nearness.

Finally, she sat before him at the kitchen table, looking as prim and proper as a schoolmarm in her high-necked shirtwaist and gored black skirt. Their eyes met and held for a long moment. He saw tenderness there, not hatred. He took a deep breath and asked, "Have you changed your mind?"

"About what?"

"About marrying me."

He watched her lick her lips before answering. "No."

She watched his Adam's apple bob up and down. "Will you tell me why?"

Wynn reached across the span of the enamel-

276

topped table and placed her hand over his. "Jason Michael Patrick Donovan—did I remember them all correctly?"

His grin bespoke more remorse than amusement. "Yes."

"Jason Michael Patrick Donovan," she began again, "you are the most wonderful man I have ever known. I never thought to meet anyone who could match my father in my eyes, but you, I think, may be a better man than he."

A shadow fell across her face, and she worked her throat for a moment before continuing. "I watched my father sacrifice his dreams to care for my mother, who was an invalid for many years. Don't you see? I can't allow the same thing to happen to you."

"But I can help you get over this paralysis thing, I know I can!" he protested.

Supreme sadness swept through her. "My father thought he could make my mother well, Michael, and he was a doctor."

"Then, I'll wait for you to get over it."

She pivoted her hand, forcing him to clasp it, weaving her fingers between his and squeezing hard. "Harboring false hopes wouldn't be fair, Michael, to either one of us. We must be realistic."

"But, I love you! Doesn't that count for anything?"

"It counts for more than you'll ever know. I love you, too. That's why I can't do this to you."

"But this is what I want—"

"Michael, believe me, you may think you want it now, but you'd grow weary of a wife who couldn't walk without the aid of a pair of crutches, who'd never be able to run or dance." Tears welled in her eyes. "This is not easy for me, either. Please, try to understand."

"Will you promise me one thing?"

"That depends on the promise."

"Promise me you'll tell me the minute your leg begins to heal."

"That could be false hope, Michael. But if it should heal completely, you'll be the first to know. I promise you that."

"Will you let me make love to you one more time?"

She shook her head sorrowfully. "It would only make things more difficult."

She watched Michael rise from the chair, watched his knees lock and then flex again as he came around the table and bent down in front of her.

"Well, it's like this," he said. "I *am* going to kiss you again—and this won't be the last time. You can bet on it."

Chapter Sixteen

Wynn carried the memory of his kiss and the surety of his promise in her heart. If she couldn't have Michael, she thought, at least she could have the memories.

But memories, she discovered, quickly emptied themselves of any residue of substance. Gazing at the stark blue morning glories and the delicate purple verbena wasn't enough. Holding to her breast the faded red sachet he'd made for her wasn't enough. Sitting in her chaise and admiring the bountiful garden he'd started wasn't enough. She longed for the fulfillment of a lasting relationship with him, one that would continuously generate such sweet memories. Yet, she refused to succumb to that longing. It was better this way, she kept trying to convince herself.

Throughout the sweltering days of August, Wynn concentrated on putting her life back together without Michael. With Doc's assistance, she exercised her leg and absorbed as much fresh air as the heat allowed. Her business became that of staying busy — at anything and everything she could manage. The phenomenal growth of the town provided some distraction, though not nearly enough.

More and more people poured into Jennings. On Sunday afternoons, it seemed the entire population turned out to wait for the train to come in and meet the new arrivals. Among the newcomers were the new school teacher, Ruth Williams; the new minister, Reverend Geoffrey Vanderhoeven; and two new doctors, Jesse White and Abel Atwood.

Wynn and Doc met each of these four in turn as they arrived, then were honored later by individual visits from each of them. The doctors' motives stemmed from professional courtesy; the minister's, from an effort to build a congregation; and though Doc viewed the teacher's motives as possibly circumspect, Wynn had no doubt why the tall, raw-boned woman chose to visit them—and it wasn't to determine whether or not Prairie would be attending school that fall.

The bare truth was, at least the way Wynn saw it, that Ruth Williams was smitten with Doc. She didn't think she'd ever seen a woman go after a man quite as aggressively as Ruth went after Doc.

It wasn't that Ruth didn't try to be subtle; she just didn't seem to know how.

"That woman's got more imaginary illnesses than Bloody Mary had," Doc observed after one of Ruth's visits.

Wynn hid a smile behind her hand. "I'm not sure all of Mary's were imaginary, Doc. She had a tumor, you know."

Doc was unperturbed. "Maybe I don't recall my history too good, and maybe you don't, either. It doesn't matter. The point is that woman makes up reasons to pester me. You're a woman. Why isn't she one of your patients? Maybe you could tell her how to keep that flaming red hair of hers from being so frizzy."

Wynn laughed. "She asked you that?"

"Yep."

"I think you like her frizzy hair, Doc, and those buck teeth, too."

Doc put his hand over his heart and faked a near swoon. "Lord, deliver me from female logic!"

"What does logic have to do with it, Doc?"

"Well—anyone can see I'm too old . . ."

"Just how old are you, Doc?"

He shrugged. "Near 'bout fifty."

"That's not old, Doc."

"The hell it's not!"

He could debate the subject all he wanted to, Wynn thought, but he was as smitten with Ruth Williams as she was with him. He just didn't know it yet.

Wynn had her own minor problem to contend with.

In his own way, Geoffrey Vanderhoeven was as guilelessly aggressive as Ruth Williams. Although he had taken a room at Granny Simpson's boarding-house—and everyone knew what a wonderful cook Granny was—he invited himself to supper at Wynn's several times a week. Since he was paying for his meals anyway at Granny's, the only possible explanation, in her estimation, was that he wanted an excuse to spend time with her.

Yet, he was careful never to single her out, directing as much conversation to Doc and Prairie as he did to Wynn, never complimenting her nor bringing her a gift, although he did contribute occasionally to the pantry. As he rightfully should, Wynn thought, as much of her food as he ate!

Despite his lack of personal attention to her, Wynn counted herself lucky to have both Doc and Prairie in constant attendance when Geoffrey was around, and more often than not—to assure herself of additional company, she invited Ruth for supper when she knew Geoffrey was coming.

For reasons she couldn't fathom, the man gave her the creepy crawlies. He was pleasant enough to look at, she supposed, and certainly young enough, and though he was a bit on the brassy side, his personality was congenial.

At first she thought, *I don't like him because he isn't Michael*. Knowing that, she made appropriate allowances. But the better she knew Geoffrey, the less she liked him—and the more something about him she couldn't quite put a finger on truly bothered her. It was as though what he said with his mouth was totally incompatible with what he said with his eyes.

With Doc's encouragement, Wynn hired Joe to build her a barn.

"If you're going to be an effective doctor," Doc said, "you need your horse and cart handy—not way off in town where you can't get to 'em in the middle of the night. Babies and accidents and illnesses don't know a thing about daylight being a proper time to happen. And you don't want to get stuck way off somewhere without your own cart and horse to get you home."

He didn't mention the fact that she couldn't walk to town anymore, which constituted the major reason she needed the barn, and she blessed him for that. Still, she debated the need.

Doc countered all her objections with sound logic, promising to teach her how to care for Carmen. "As for the cost, you'll make it up in no time with what you'll save in stabling fees. Delaney's high as a cat's back."

"That's because he doesn't have any competition," Wynn suggested.

"That's because he's a no-good crook," Doc alleged.

With Carmen and the cart so conveniently housed, Wynn and Doc began taking long rides across the prairie a couple of days each week, stopping by every tent or house they came to. Most of these were surrounded by saplings, since the government would grant an additional 160 acres to those who agreed to plant ten acres in trees, thus increasing the homestead patents to 320 acres.

Occasionally, they were asked for advice, but seldom for treatment. The homesteaders would look hard at Wynn leaning on her crutches and shake their heads, as if to say, "What good can you do for us when you can't fix your own problem?"

She wished she knew what to do for herself. Lord, how she wished she knew. Wynn had begun to think she'd imagined ever feeling the slight tingles in her left leg. She'd begun to think, too, that she never would again. False hopes, she'd told Michael, and false hopes they seemed to be.

At times she wondered, too, if she'd only imagined Michael's love for her. She longed to see him, to hear his voice say "I love you," to feel his lips upon hers and his arms around her. She couldn't fault him, she supposed, for staying away, for following her own directive, but that didn't keep her from wishing he'd ignore what she'd said.

Jennings might be growing, but it was still a small town, with a small town mentality. Everybody knew everybody else's business.

Michael and Wynn were the talk of the town. No other residents were quite as well liked or as well respected as these two. In the estimation of the townsfolk, Michael was the backbone of Jennings and Wynn, its heart. They all prayed for Wynn's complete recovery—and hoped eventually to see her and Michael married.

Anyone who'd been there for any length of time knew Michael Donovan was sweet on Wynn Spencer. Those who hadn't been there during the diphtheria epidemic had heard how Michael had seen Wynn through it. Anyone with a lick of perception could see how miserable the man was now that she was lame, could see that they were both wound as tight as watch springs. And though no one dared broach the subject with either of them, everyone watched and waited, knowing something would eventually happen to release the springs.

Shortly after dusk one Friday evening in mid-September, Wynn was sitting alone in her room, reading an article on paralysis that had been published in a recent edition of the *Medical Record,* when someone knocked at the door. Her heart skipped a beat at the insistent pounding; her head reeled with lightheaded anticipation; her lips moved to form a name: Michael. No one else knocked quite the way he did.

She called, "I'm coming!" and hoped he heard her—hoped, too, he'd give her enough time to get to the door before he gave up and left, for no one else was at home.

One of the settlers had come by earlier and said a doctor was needed out on the prairie to help deliver a baby. Wynn wanted to go, but Doc insisted she stay home and let him handle it.

"A little solitude will do you good," he'd said. "Those folks have a passel of kids. I'll take Prairie along—it'll give her someone to play with. You just relax and enjoy yourself for a change."

He was so good about not pointing out her handicap, but they both knew that it prevented Wynn from performing most tasks well. The best she could do during a delivery was supervise.

Just getting up out of a chair was a monumental task. As the insistent pounding continued, she set aside the journal and moved the shawl she had draped over her legs to the arm of her chair. She had to manually lift her bum leg off the hassock and set her left foot down on the floor; then she reached for the crutches. At times like this, she seriously considered ordering the chair on wheels she'd seen in a medical supply catalog. But using such a chair would mean she'd given in to the paralysis, and Wynn wasn't ready to give in—not yet.

She hobbled from the converted dining room into the hall, reveling in the exhilaration rushing through her, knowing her feelings were treading dangerously at the moment and not caring. She wanted to see his devilish grin, feel his arms surround her, hear him reaffirm his love and affection. She wanted him to make love to her again. If there were hell to pay later, so be it.

Her heart plummeted to her knees when she opened the door.

There stood Geoffrey Vanderhoeven where Michael should have been, the light from the hall lamp Doc had left burning showing his face clearly.

"Good evening, Dr. Spencer," he intoned in his best Sunday-morning-in-the-pulpit voice.

Wynn swallowed hard and forced back tears of disappointment. "Good evening, Reverend Vanderhoeven. What brings you out tonight?"

"Why, the luscious feel of autumn in the air, and the moon shining so brightly, and the stars just beginning to twinkle. There isn't a single cloud in the sky. No one should spend such an evening alone, don't you agree?"

How did he know she was alone? A warning bell resounded in Wynn's head and a shiver of alarm sluiced through her.

"Don't you agree?" he repeated when she failed to respond.

No, she didn't agree. She would have, had he been Michael Donovan, but the prospect of spending an unchaperoned evening with Geoffrey Vanderhoeven didn't set so well. Yet, she couldn't tell him that. Instead, she said a bit inanely, "I, uh, I was reading."

He clucked his tongue and cast a gimlet eye upon her. "Not a proper activity at all for such a lovely night, my dear." He paused, craning his neck to see around her into the hall before asking, "May I come in?"

"Well," she hesitated, "I was . . . about to leave."

The minister crooked a blond eyebrow at her and centered his skeptical gaze on the crutches. "Perhaps I could accompany you," he offered, turning slightly and waving a hand toward the steps. "I rented a rig from Delaney."

"Perhaps," she hedged.

"Where were you going?"

Lord, she should have known that question was coming. Where was she going indeed? She snatched at the first thought that entered her mind. "To Granny Simpson's for supper."

"Oh, you were going with Doc, I suppose." He seemed genuinely disappointed.

"No, actually, Doc and Prairie aren't here at the moment."

His lips twitched, but not in amusement as Michael's so often did. The way Geoffrey's twitched unnerved Wynn. "You were going that far—on foot?"

"I . . . I'm hungry." What a lame excuse, she thought, with food aplenty in her own kitchen.

"Then, please allow me to take you there. Do you need to leave Doc a message?"

This is called painting yourself into a corner, Wynn thought, knowing she had no choice now but to go with him. At least there would be other people at Granny's—lots of other people. A combination of defeat and disgust riddled her voice, and she answered without giving her response proper consideration. "No, that won't be necessary. I'm sure I'll be back before he will. Just let me get my shawl."

"Permit me," he said, shouldering the door open and stepping past her into the hall, then turning a questioning glance her way. "Where?"

Wynn inclined her head toward her bedchamber door. "In there, on the arm of the chair."

A simple collecting of her shawl should not take so long, she thought as she waited for Geoffrey to return. Her chair sat close to the front window, its position hidden from her limited view. "Can't you find it?" she finally called.

"Oh, yes, here it is on the foot of the bed. You must have forgotten where you left it."

She hadn't forgotten. She might not be able to see the chair, but she could clearly see the foot of her bed from where she stood in the hall. He had not taken her shawl from the bed—he hadn't even gone near her bed. Why would he lie? What had he been doing all that time? A sense of foreboding stabbed at her.

The feeling stayed with her throughout the ride

into town. Geoffrey was pleasant enough, she supposed, but in a self-important sort of way. Once he'd helped her alight from the buggy and assisted her up the steps and into Granny's foyer, he disappeared. Wynn breathed a sigh of relief, hoping he wouldn't come back. She'd find someone to take her home—or she'd stay the night at the boardinghouse if Granny had the space.

Since many of her boarders took full advantage of the daylight hours to work on their own homes, Granny was accustomed to serving stragglers. She welcomed Wynn with open arms, planting a warm kiss on Wynn's cheek and hugging her against her ample breasts.

"I've missed sharing tea with you," Granny said, walking Wynn into the dining room and ignoring the minister completely. "And I've been meaning to come see you, but I can't ever seem to get very far away from here. There's so much work to do keeping this boardinghouse going. But I'm fine," she hastened to assure Wynn. "Never felt better in my life!"

"How's the lumbago?"

"Pshaw! Hardly know it's there anymore."

"And Rachel and David?"

"Couldn't be better. We're getting along just fine. I don't know why I worried so over their reaction to this boardinghouse. Rachel said to tell you to come see her when you get time. I'm going to be a grandmother, come winter."

"I'm happy for you, Granny." And she was. She wished she could be as happy for herself.

She'd told the truth when she said she was hungry. Granny served her big, flaky buttermilk biscuits, a thick slice of baked ham, red-eye gravy, and black-eyed peas. Wynn cleaned her plate, sopping up the last of the gravy with the heel of a biscuit.

"There's sweet potato pie for dessert," Granny announced, "and a fresh pot of coffee brewing. Since everyone else is finished, why don't you have yours in the kitchen? You can keep me company while I wash dishes."

A half hour later, thoroughly sated and feeling more relaxed than she had in months, Wynn sighed contentedly. "Thanks, Granny. That was a delicious meal."

"My pleasure," the older woman replied, her face beaming as she joined Wynn at the table. "I've been dying to talk to you," she confided.

Wynn caught the conspiratorial gleam in Granny's eyes. "Why?"

"Doc came by here with Prairie the other day, and she talked to me about her mother."

Wynn's mouth gaped open and her heart thudded in her chest. A part of her didn't want to know anything about Prairie's roots, but she found herself asking, "Really? What did she say?"

"Her name was Anna and she was from a place called Big Spring. Prairie said they never lived in Big Spring, but her mother talked about it."

Wynn waited with bated breath for Granny to continue, but she sipped her coffee in silence. "That's all?"

Granny nodded.

"But, that's not—"

"I know, Wynn. There's still nothing to go on. But at least the child's remembering."

"She didn't tell you where she and her parents lived?"

"No."

"Do you think she knows and she's not telling us?"

Granny shrugged. "I don't know. I think they moved around a lot, lived like gypsies. Prairie doesn't seem to have a real sense of home. Haven't you noticed how she runs her hands over such common things as window sills and banisters, as though she's fascinated with them?"

"Yes, you're right. I have noticed. I've just never stopped to think about why she would do that. Have you watched her eat?"

Granny cackled so hard she had to hold onto her jiggling sides for a minute, then wipe her moist eyes with the skirt of her apron before she could respond. "That child sure is a pleasure to feed. Why, she'll eat anything that doesn't eat her first—except brown gravy."

Wynn nodded pensively. "I know. I wonder why . . ."

"She calls it 'toodlum' gravy. Says that's what her mama called it to make it sound special. They must've had it with every meal."

"Her mother—Anna—must have been a really special person."

Granny patted Wynn's hand affectionately. "So are you, my dear. You're a fine mother to Prairie yourself, and don't you never think you're not."

Wynn had no idea how long she and Granny had been talking when Geoffrey strolled into the kitchen.

"Are you ready to go home now?" he asked. "I need to take the rig back to Delaney before too long."

Wynn and Granny hugged each other again, and Granny said, "Why don't you and Doc and Prairie plan to have dinner here after church on Sunday? Then we can all go down to the depot together."

"You can count on it. Thanks, Granny."

She'd needed the time with Granny, Wynn realized after she left. The older woman had a knack for shedding a different light on matters, especially those of the heart. Granny had fussed at her about letting her one bid to happiness slip by her. "You ought to know better than most of us how uncertain life is, Wynn," she'd said. "God gives us one day at a time. What we do with each of those days is entirely up to us. If you want my opinion, you're wasting yours."

Maybe Granny was right. Maybe she was being unreasonable. Maybe she was sacrificing the only real happiness she'd ever have. Maybe she had made a decision for Michael she ought to let him make for himself.

The night sky was as lovely as Wynn had ever seen it. She breathed deeply, relishing the slight burning sensation of the crisp air in her lungs, thankful the long days and nights of oppressive heat were finally gone.

"It is rather invigorating, isn't it?"

So caught up was she in her own reflections, Wynn had momentarily forgotten Geoffrey. "Yes, it is." Her voice carried a dreamy quality.

Soon, they pulled up in front of Wynn's house. When he had helped her out of the buggy and up the steps, she said, "I appreciate your taking me into town tonight, Reverend Vanderhoeven."

"My pleasure. And, please, call me Geoffrey."

"Geoffrey." The name sat distastefully on her lips. "Good night, then."

"Oh, but let me help you with the lamps," he insisted. "Wouldn't want you tripping over something in the dark."

She supposed he had a point. But as she watched him move around, lighting lamps, that strange sense of foreboding visited her again. Had he actually paid such careful attention to the placement of lamps when he'd come calling?

"Do you want me to light a fire?"

Wynn shook her head. "No, thank you. Suddenly,

I'm quite fatigued. I think I'll go straight to bed."

"I'd hoped you would agree to sit with me a spell, my dear."

Unaccountable fear rippled down her spine. *Good Lord, Wynn,* she fussed to herself. *The man's a preacher!*

"Honestly, Rev—Geoffrey." Her mouth went dry. She gathered saliva and swallowed. "I really am tired."

He advanced on her with long, purposeful strides, reaching her before she could maneuver out of his way but not before she had time to fully grasp the danger she was in. His hands clutched her upper arms and his face hovered mere inches above hers. It was as though she were staring into the eyes of a rattlesnake. She could feel his breath on her face, could hear her heart beating wildly out of control.

"You are so beautiful," he whispered. "I've dreamed of little else besides possessing you."

His lips descended on hers, his mouth slanting across hers, his tongue pressing against her clamped lips, seeking entry. Revulsion rose bitterly in her throat, galling her. Feebly, she struggled against him, trying to remove her mouth from his. She didn't dare remove her hands from the supporting crutches or her right foot from the floor, lest she fall and damage her paralyzed leg. Without the benefit of pain, she might never know what she'd done to it.

Lord, help me! she prayed.

Her struggles communicated her repugnance effectively enough. Geoffrey's head snapped back and his snake eyes pierced her gaze. Terrified of what he might do to her, she looked away, not wanting him to see her loathing, fearing he already had.

His voice was sickly sweet. "Is it because I'm not Michael Donovan?"

Her eyes widened in surprise.

"Oh, yes, I know all about the two of you."

He pushed her from him. Had she not had the wall at her back, Wynn would have fallen. She struggled with her balance, reestablishing her weight upon the crutches.

He surveyed her with something akin to pity in his gaze. "You needn't fear me, my dear. Not in the physical sense."

His words carried no true reassurance. Instead, she felt a threat in them. Although he jerked the door open then and strode briskly across the porch, Wynn's fright intensified.

As quickly as she could manage it, Wynn closed and locked the door. For a long time, she leaned against the heavy portal, sweat streaming off her brow, her heart thumping, thumping in her chest, her breath coming in short gasps. She'd heard the clatter of the buggy wheels, the clop-clopping of the horse's hooves, and she knew he'd left. But she didn't trust him not to return. With her own horse and cart gone, she had no method of escape, and there was no way on earth Doc would be back before daylight.

Wynn considered seeking shelter with one of her new neighbors, but quickly discounted that idea. They'd think she was crazy, being afraid of the minister!

Michael! her heart wailed. *I need you.*

She sat up all night, Doc's pistol in her lap. She'd had one doozy of a time making it up the stairs, finding both the pistol and a box of bullets in his room, and then coming back down again, but she'd found the strength. Wynn wasn't the least bit certain she could hit anything with it. She'd empty the chamber if she had to.

Sometime close to dawn, she nodded off. The morning sun, streaming though the parlor windows, jerked her out of a troubled sleep. Her disoriented gaze darted about the room. Why had she stayed on the sofa all night?

Her fingers clutched something cold and hard in her lap. Doc's gun. Memories came flooding in. She sat there for awhile, staring at the long barrel of the pistol and shivering. In the bright light of day, her fear seemed unfounded, unrealistic, but she trembled nonetheless.

At long last, she reached for the crutches, determined to put the memory of Geoffrey's piercing eyes and mocking voice behind her and seek solace in a cup of hot coffee. And that was all it was, she thought. His eyes and his voice frightened her. Nothing else. He wouldn't harm her. He'd said he wouldn't.

She stood up and, without thinking, set her weight on her left foot. Needles of pain shot up her leg and she collapsed back onto the sofa.

"Oh!" she gasped aloud, tears of happiness spilling down her cheeks. "This is wonderful!"

Eager hands pulled her skirt and petticoat out of the way, folded her leg at the knee, and rubbed her stockinged calf hard. She shouted, "I can feel it!" at the top of her lungs, realized how ridiculous she sounded with no one to hear, then shouted again. Let the neighbors come running. She wanted them to. She wanted to share this news with someone.

But no one came.

Wynn waited a moment for both the pain and the joy to subside, then stood up again, exercising a bit more caution this time. As she made her way to the kitchen, she put the smallest amount of pressure on her left foot and delighted in the barbed sensations.

While the water was heating, she collected the pistol from the parlor, took it to her room, emptied the chamber, and put the gun and the bullets away in the top drawer of her bureau, out of Prairie's reach. She was closing the drawer when she noticed how mussed were her underthings, not neatly folded and precisely stacked, but undone and disheveled, as though someone had dumped them out and then thrown them back in.

She slammed the drawer shut and pulled open the one beneath it. One after another, she opened and closed the drawers. Each one bore evidence that someone had gone through its contents.

Almost in a daze, she hobbled to the bed and fell across it. Her exuberance evaporated as an all-consuming weakness overcame her. Anger, frustration, and fear roiled together in the pit of her stomach.

Who had done this thing? What did he think to find? Money? Jewels?

With nothing more than will, she got up and moved stiffly into the hall, working the crutches with a vengeance. Stopping in front of her desk, she propped her weight on her good leg, took the key from one of its drawers, and unlocked the roll top. It creaked as she pushed it up, caught when she pushed one side harder than the other, and refused to budge. She slid her hand into the opening, groped for the metal box she and Doc kept their cash in, found it, and pulled it out. Her hand trembled and her heart beat erratically as she pushed on the latch.

The top popped open, revealing a stack of greenbacks. Shaking fingers rifled the bills. As best she could recall, all of their hard-earned, carefully saved money was there.

It didn't make sense. What kind of thief ignored a desk? When had he come? She'd stayed awake most of the night . . .

Suddenly, she knew — who and when and what he'd hoped to find.

"Oh, God," she breathed, "let me be wrong."

But when she stood in her room again and realized nothing was exactly where she'd left it, when she opened the tiny drawer in the table that sat by her chair, she knew she was right.

The letter she'd written to Michael but never given him was gone.

And Geoffrey Vanderhoeven had taken it. Knowing Doc was gone, he'd come back to her house while she'd visited with Granny.

Oh, what a cunning man he was, this minister. He'd known she was alone before she told him Doc was gone. She'd been like putty in his hands, telling him she didn't expect Doc back until this morning, letting him woo her away from her house.

Yes, she knew who her thief was. She knew when he'd come and what he'd taken. But she didn't know why.

Chapter Seventeen

Wynn didn't have to wait long to discover the reason Geoffrey Vanderhoeven wanted proof of her intimacy with Michael.

Most of Saturday, she debated telling Doc what had happened while he was gone. She didn't want him worrying about her every time he left her alone or to think he couldn't move back home at some point. In the meantime, her house *was* his home, and she had to acknowledge the possibility that something of his might be missing as well.

Besides, she owed him some explanation for her behavior. She'd never felt so violated, so abused, so helpless. And she knew it showed. Putting on a false front had never been her forte.

While she waited for Doc and Prairie to return, she exercised her leg, hoping to work out some of her frustration as well. Round and round the house she went, using the crutches for support but relying on them less and less as the feeling began to return to her leg. It would be some time yet, she knew, before she could permanently retire the crutches, but the marked improvement tempered her anger and frustration.

Doc and Prairie drove in around mid-afternoon.

While Doc took care of Carmen, Wynn started the kettle for coffee and bathed Prairie's face and hands.

"Oh, Dr. Wynn!" Prairie exclaimed. "The Millers have a new baby. She's so tiny and pink, just like Susie."

"Susie?" Wynn questioned. "You've never mentioned Susie before."

Prairie's pointed chin trembled and a tear trickled out of a brown eye. "I lost her."

Lost her? When Prairie referred to death, it was in terms of burying, not losing. "Where did you lose her?" Wynn prompted.

"When I was on the horse with Daddy. I went to sleep and she fell off."

"Didn't she cry?"

Prairie's hair flew as she shook her head. "No, Dr. Wynn. Dolls don't cry."

Wynn resolved to replace Susie at the first opportunity. "What did the Millers name their baby?"

The child's cherubic features brightened considerably. "Suzannah."

"For your doll?"

"Yep."

Doc came in about that time. "Yes, *ma'am*," he corrected, scooping Prairie into his arms. "I know a little girl who needs a nap," he declared. To Wynn he said, "She wouldn't go to sleep last night for fear she'd miss something." He tweaked Prairie's stubby nose. "Come on, Miss Priss. I'll tuck you in."

"Prairie isn't the only one who didn't go to sleep last night," Wynn told Doc a few minutes later, biting her bottom lip, suddenly not wanting to talk about Geoffrey's aberrant behavior and the theft of her letter, but putting it off was the

She took a fortifying sip of coffee and proceeded to tell him everything that had happened in the past twenty-four hours.

As she talked, she watched Doc's expression change from disbelief to indignation to barely suppressed anger. By the time she'd finished, his round face and bald head were so red, she almost expected to see steam coming out of his nostrils. He didn't say a word, just scraped back his chair and headed for the hall.

"Where are you going?" she asked.

"To get my pistol."

"No, Doc," she pleaded. "Please, just let it lie. Nothing happened—not really, and I have no proof Geoffrey was the one who took my letter. I can't even figure out what his motivation could be. Can you imagine how this story would be received in a court of law? The jury would laugh me out of there, and you'd hang for murder."

Doc dragged his feet back to the table and sat down again. "I suppose you have a point, Wynn," he grudgingly admitted. "But if that son-of-a-bitch masquerading as a preacher tries anything else, he'll have to answer to me. I can assure you of that."

As little as Doc and Wynn wanted to set eyes on Geoffrey Vanderhoeven again, they didn't want to miss church, either. Ever since the church building had been completed, Sundays had become special occasions in Jennings, a time for everyone to congregate and enjoy mixing and mingling for the entire day. Following the service, the townsfolk went home to eat, while those who'd taken grants on the outlying prairie ate the dinners they'd brought with them off the tailgates of buckboards. Then everyone gathered at the train station for the afternoon.

Wynn and Doc weighed their options over coffee. "If we skip the service, we'll have to skip Granny's, too," Wynn observed. "The preacher will eat his dinner there." She couldn't quite bring herself to say his name.

"And if we skip both the service and Granny's, and then go to the station, everyone will want to know where we've been," Doc put in.

"And if we skip everything, we'll have Prairie's disappointment to contend with. Besides, I'll have to face him again sometime. I'd just as well get it over with."

Concern filled Doc's countenance. "Are you sure?"

She nodded. "I'm not running from this."

But that strange sense of foreboding returned the moment she walked into the vestibule of the church.

Wynn took comfort in having Doc and Prairie flank her during the service, but when Ruth sat down next to Doc, Wynn found herself wishing she could draw strength from Michael's presence as well. Although he had donated the property, he refused to attend church. Even if he were there, they probably wouldn't sit together—but if she could just see his face in the crowd, she'd feel better.

Her mind seized upon the word "if." If she'd only let Doc go over to Michael's yesterday and tell him what had happened! If Vanderhoeven did have the letter, Michael deserved to know about it. And if he did have it, what did he plan to do with it?

300

Possibilities raced through her thoughts all during the song service and the offertory. But when Vanderhoeven started his sermon, she knew. *Oh, God, she prayed, not this!*

He read from the sixth chapter of First Corinthians. She'd read the passage many times before, but never thought about having it used against her. Bits and pieces of the passage seemed to hang in the air, long after Vanderhoeven had uttered them.

" 'Now the body is not for fornication, but for the Lord. . . . Know ye not that your bodies are the members of Christ? Shall I then take the members of Christ, and make them the members of a harlot? God forbid. . . . Flee fornication. Every sin that a man doeth is without the body; but he that committeth fornication sinneth against his own body. . . . to avoid fornication, let every man have his own wife, and let every woman have her own husband . . .' "

This—because she'd spurned him?

I'm not a harlot, she silently argued, *nor a fornicator. Michael's the only sexual partner I've ever had—ever will have. I would be his wife and he my husband were it not for my affliction.*

Throughout the next several minutes, Wynn waited breathlessly for Vanderhoeven to accuse her, but instead he elaborated on the meaning of the passage. Doc reached over and squeezed her hand. She felt some of her tension evaporate.

And then the ax fell. Doc's grip tightened and she watched his temples pulse with anger. Her own anger and embarrassment flooded through her, blinding her with warranted intensity but failing, unfortunately, to render her deaf as well.

"There is a harlot among you," Vanderhoeven

301

shouted, "a woman who disguises herself as a healer. This fraud uses her position in the community as a front. Unbeknownst to many of you, she flaunts her body before unsuspecting, innocent men, luring them to her bed and then lying with them, defiling their virtuous bodies with her evil. There is not one among you who can deny that this is true. God demands that you good people of Jennings take a stand against such wickedness. God demands that you put this harlot on the train this afternoon and run the witch out of town!"

A hush settled over the entire congregation. From her position near the front of the sanctuary, Wynn felt as though every eye were trained upon her. Suddenly, she wanted to hang her head in shame. Her inner voice stopped her cold. *You have nothing to be ashamed of,* the voice harshly admonished. *Don't act as though you do.*

Wynn listened to the voice and obeyed its command, though with some difficulty. She pretended someone had put a brace on her neck which prevented movement. She managed to keep a steady gaze on the florid face of Geoffrey Vanderhoeven and wondered how she'd ever thought the man's features to be pleasing. Even when he asked everyone to bow in prayer, Wynn watched him.

But Doc didn't. Instead, he whispered something in Ruth's ear. Without success, Wynn strained to hear what he said to the school teacher.

The prayer was blessedly short. The second Vanderhoeven said, "Amen," Doc jumped to his feet and turned around.

"Listen to me!" he hollered over the sudden buzz of conversation.

"Doc, please, don't!" Wynn hissed at his side.

302

He lifted the front corner of his black suit jacket, showing her the whip he'd stuck in the band of his trousers, and spoke to her *sotto voce*. "Shush. I know what I'm doing."

To the crowd, he called, "We men should discuss this problem further with the good reverend. Stay for a few minutes, please. You women and children can wait outside. This won't take long."

Wynn, Ruth, and Prairie filed out at the end of the line of women and children. Ruth put her arm around Wynn's shoulders, ostensibly to lend her physical support. The teacher leaned close to Wynn's ear and whispered, "Don't worry about a thing. Enoch knows what to do."

Enoch? Was that Doc's real name?

Musing on Ruth's words provided a modicum of distraction while they stood outside, waiting for the men to emerge. *Don't worry about a thing,* the buck-toothed teacher had said, but how could Ruth be so sure, when that very afternoon Wynn was liable to lose what little she had left to her. She'd already lost Michael, her health, and now her reputation. Within hours, she'd more than likely lose Doc and Prairie as well.

Her heart wrenched in pain. *Oh, Lord, what will happen to Prairie?*

More than the few minutes Doc had promised passed. Whatever was going on inside? She remembered the whip. Doc must have suspected something like this would happen, but what had he planned to do with the whip?

A cry of terror from within the church provided an answer.

Three of the women started for the door, but Ruth beat them there. The tall, raw-boned woman stood pressed against the portal, her arms outflung, her eyes blazing. "No," she said firmly. "Trust your menfolk to take care of this."

Wynn's gaze darted among the throng of women then, searching their faces. What she saw surprised her. Instead of being accusative, their looks bore evidence of either anger or sympathy. She hoped the anger was directed at the minister, the sympathy at her—but she'd rather deal with their anger than with their accusations if the reverse were true.

When the women had moved back, Ruth turned to Wynn. "Let's go. Enoch has some unfinished business to attend to. He'll meet us at Granny's."

As usual, by the time the train rolled in, everyone had gathered at the depot. But the atmosphere that Sunday afternoon was not one of jocularity, but of tightly-strung tension.

Wynn was there with Doc, Prairie, Ruth, Granny—and Michael, who stood with his arm wrapped possessively around Wynn's waist. Doc had gone straight from the church to tell him what had happened, and Michael had come back with him to Granny's.

With Doc's encouragement, Wynn had decided it was time to tell Michael how her leg was improving. Now that he stood by her side, she itched to be alone with him.

"I have something to tell you," she murmured, the smile she turned up to him showing her nervousness.

"Later," he said, squeezing her rib cage. "I don't want to miss a minute of this. I've never seen the actual administration of poetic justice before."

The brake's loud hiss filled the air as the big iron wheels rolled to a stop on the tracks. Buckboards moved into place next to the boxcars and some passengers began to disembark.

"Make way!" a male voice called over the din, pulling everyone's attention away from the train and toward the depot.

The crowd parted like the Red Sea, leaving an open path for the several men who came out of the depot hauling Geoffrey Vanderhoeven by the scruff of the neck—or by the scruff of the collar, as it were. His shirt hung in blood-soaked shreds and his chin touched his chest. At first, Wynn feared Doc had killed him. But when the crowd started booing and hissing, the preacher's head popped up and he muttered, "You don't understand. I have proof."

Wynn was standing close enough to hear him. Her heart skipped a beat and her head swam. Had it not been for Michael's hold on her, she would have collapsed. It wasn't over! He was going to show them the letter . . .

"If you know what's good for you, you'll shut your mouth," one of the men said. With a start, Wynn recognized him as Orville Mason, a man she'd never expected to count on her side.

"Yeah," another chimed in. "We bought you a ticket that'll take you as far as Beaumont. And if you ever set foot in this town again, you won't live long enough to get back on this train."

Wynn's heart swelled with gratitude toward these men. Not one of them nor any of their womenfolk had even remotely suggested, either in word or deed, that she was the "harlot" Vanderhoeven had censured in his sermon.

Although she was certain Doc had instigated the

305

whipping—and probably suggested the method of final punishment, which was surely as poetic a justice as she'd ever imagined, she was glad both he and Michael stood at her side. Their detachment from the proceedings minimized her own involvement.

A familiar female voice interrupted her reverie. "Why, if it isn't Wynn Spencer!"

Although Wynn immediately recognized the young, blonde-haired woman standing before her, she blinked twice, thinking this wasn't possible. "Mabel! What are you doing here?"

"I could ask the same of you. We didn't know where you'd run off to after—" The woman paused, decided she'd almost said too much, and changed course. "John and I decided to take advantage of the free land the government's giving away. Can you see me as a farmer's wife?" The woman laughed, twisted around, and called out, "John! Come see who's here!"

A short, balding man with a paunch as round as his pregnant wife's ambled towards them. "You remember John Bradshaw, Wynn. He and I were married last winter."

Wynn did, indeed, remember John, though not well, since he was several years older than she and Mabel. Trying to imagine the former bank clerk as a farmer was far more difficult than trying to imagine Mabel as his wife. Wynn made the requisite round of introductions, explaining that she and Mabel had grown up together.

"We're so happy to meet all of you," Mabel gushed. "There's so much we don't know about all this, having come from a little mining town like Galena. Perhaps you good folks could advise us. Is

306

there some place we could all sit down, maybe have a cup of tea? Wynn, you've just got to catch me up on everything, tell me about those crutches and that darling child and that handsome man there by your side. You didn't introduce him as your husband, but I can see . . ."

Mabel never had known when to hush, Wynn thought as they made their way toward Granny's boardinghouse. She remembered how Mabel's mouth had kept her in perpetual trouble at school. At least the Bradshaws weren't planning to live in town. Wynn didn't think she could stand a constant dose of Mabel Bradshaw.

Running into the couple at the train station served to ruin the quiet evening Wynn had thought to spend with Michael. Following a noisy tea, Michael and Doc left with John to collect their baggage from the depot and deposit it at the hotel, where the Bradshaws would stay since Granny had a waiting list.

Although Mabel had asked for advice, she seldom hushed long enough to hear any. Wynn breathed a sigh of relief when Doc and John returned. Surely, now, she could be alone with Michael for a few minutes.

Doc's words shattered that prospect. "Michael said to tell you something urgent had come up over at his new house. Are you and Prairie ready to go home?"

New house? No one had told Wynn that Michael was building a new house. Something urgent had come up on Sunday? No one in Jennings worked on Sunday, not anymore. It didn't make sense.

But Wynn was more than happy to escape Mabel's constant chatter.

She tried to pry some information out of Doc on the way home, but all he talked about was Michael's house. It was to be a grand painted lady, three stories high with a turret and porches all around and enough gingerbread trim to make even Queen Victoria jealous. Why, she wondered, did Michael want to build such a house? And why hadn't someone told her about it before now?

And why hadn't he come back to Granny's? She'd told him she needed to talk to him.

"Doc," she said just before they reached her house, "will you please take me to see Michael?"

"Now?"

"Yes, now."

Doc cleared his throat and fixed his eyes on Carmen's flowing mane. "I don't think that would be a good idea, Wynn. Just give it some time. He'll come around."

Whatever that meant, she didn't know, nor would Doc elaborate. But it frightened her. Maybe she'd lost Michael after all.

Michael sat with his back propped against the tiled fireplace in the unfinished parlor and stared at the beaded wainscoting on the opposite wall. From time to time, he scrunched up his right shoulder and pressed his nose against his shirt so he could get another deep breath of the lilac fragrance that hovered there. For the moment, the fragrance sustained him, but what would he do tomorrow and the next day and the day after that, he wondered, when the scent was gone and there was no hope of its ever returning?

Until today, there had been hope—hope that

308

Wynn's leg would heal, hope that she would put aside her martyrdom even if it didn't, hope that he and Wynn and Prairie would become a family, hope that the three of them would live together in this new house.

Now that hope was gone.

Mabel Bradshaw's mouth had destroyed it when she'd unwittingly supplied the missing piece of the puzzle: the name of the mining town where he'd grown up—Galena, Illinois.

Tears streamed down Michael's face, blurring the vertical lines of the beading, and he let them fall, barely conscious of their wetness on the tucks of his Sunday shirt. He was a little boy again, a little boy in Galena, Illinois, standing barefooted in the sandy road, waving good-bye to his father in the pale light of early morn.

"I love you, Papa," he called.

"And I love you, son," the tall man called back, his long strides taking him quickly away from the blue miner's cottage where they lived. "Take care of your mama while I'm gone."

"I will, Papa."

A syrup bucket with a lunch packed inside swung by the man's side. The boy watched its arcs, watched the rising sun glint off the gray metal, and pictured himself as a grown man, going off to work in the morning and telling his own little boy to watch out after his mama until he returned.

About mid-afternoon that day, a man the boy had never seen before came riding up on a spirited mare. The boy watched the man tug on the reins, watched the mare prance about before the man got her under control, and he thought about having a horse of his own one day. The man dismounted, tipped his hat at the boy, and asked to see his mama.

"She's scrubbing the floor," the boy said, "and my papa's at work."

"I know where your papa is, son. I'm his boss. I need to see your mama. Will you please go tell her I'm here?"

There was an urgency in the man's voice that frightened the boy. He scurried inside. The look on his mother's face when he told her about the man waiting on the porch frightened him even more.

"You stay in here," his mama said. "I mean it, Mickey. Don't come outside right now."

She wiped her hands on her apron and smoothed back the scraggly strands of almost black hair that had escaped from her bun.

The boy did as he was told. He always did as he was told. Almost always. When he didn't, she switched his legs hard with a hickory stick until he wished he had.

She was gone a long time. The boy sat down in a kitchen chair and watched the water dry up on the floor until only a few damp patches were left, and still she didn't come back inside. After awhile, when he couldn't stand it anymore, he tiptoed into the front room and peered out the window.

The man and his prancing mare were gone. His mama was sitting on the top step of the porch, her head bent over and buried in her apron and her shoulders shaking. He'd never seen his mama cry, but he supposed that was what she was doing.

The boy stayed at the window for a few more minutes, watching his mother and wondering what the man had told her that had upset her so much she would cry about it. Finally, she wiped her eyes on her apron, stood up, and started toward the door. The boy darted back to the kitchen and sat down again. If his mama had wanted him to see her cry, she would have come back inside earlier, he reckoned.

He thought she'd tell him right off, but she went back to scrubbing the floor instead. She must have forgotten he was there, he decided, when she didn't send him back outside. She always sent him outside while she scrubbed the floor.

In and out of the bucket she dipped the scrub brush; back and forth across the wooden planks she pushed it. He didn't know his mama was so strong, that she could push a brush so hard. She moved from room to room, scrubbing the planks with a vengeance. Not once did she say a word, though she lifted her apron skirt occasionally and wiped her face with it. She didn't act like she knew he was in the world, much less in the house, until she'd pitched the dirty water out the back door and set a kettle of water on the top of the iron cookstove.

"Go draw me some water, Mickey," she said then, her voice cold and detached. "I'm going to take a bath."

While she bathed, he sat on the front porch and watched the miners drag home from work. Their feet kicked up a lot of dust, and the early evening breeze tossed it around a bit before letting it go. Some of the men glanced his way and nodded at him, just as they did every day, except this time they seemed a little sad—or maybe just more tired than usual.

His papa would be home soon, the boy realized, and Mama hadn't even started cooking yet.

He heard her voice behind him. "Mickey, come

back inside now and get cleaned up. I've fixed your bath water."

A bath on Tuesday? Why did she want him to take a bath on a Tuesday?

"Scrub your head and comb your hair real pretty and put on your Sunday-go-to-meeting suit."

He picked himself up off the steps and followed her inside, his head swimming crazily. Something was wrong. Why didn't she tell him what was wrong?

"Where's Papa?" he asked, feeling a constriction in his throat and not understanding why.

"They're bringing him, Mickey. Now hurry up and get yourself cleaned up so I can have the kitchen free. I'll have to wash your papa good before I put his suit on him."

"Wash Papa? Why can't he do it himself?"

He watched her chest swell out with a deep breath, watched her fix her gaze on a tiny porcelain cherub his papa had given her for her birthday last year. She'd set it on the kitchen window sill, next to the blue Mason jar where she kept a vining sweet potato. He wished she'd look at him and not the cherub.

"There was an accident at the mine today, Mickey. Your papa's dead."

"Papa's dead," Michael said through blubbery lips. "Papa's dead." He pulled his shirt out of his britches and wiped at his tears with its tail. "I remember. Papa's dead."

And he did remember. For the first time in twenty-five years, he remembered—everything.

His papa had been an Irish immigrant who

worked in the lead mines of Galena, Illinois, and they'd lived in one of the gingerbread-trimmed miner's cottages there. His mother kept the cottage as clean and neat as a pin, and she cooked the best pot of beef stew he'd ever eaten, bar none. She'd serve it with a big, round loaf of soda bread slavered with creamery butter, and he'd eat until his tummy hurt.

And then his father had died and the foreman who rode the prissy mare had told his mama they had to move. The cottages were for the miners only; she'd have to move out so they could have it for his father's replacement. He'd heard her ask the man to hire her, but the foreman had laughed in her face. They didn't hire no women, he'd said, and if they did, they wouldn't hire one who was expecting a baby.

That was the first time Michael had known he was going to have a brother or sister soon.

His mama had cried again after the foreman left. His papa hadn't saved any money nor did they have any relatives in Illinois. They had no place to go.

Michael tried to get a job at the mine, but they wouldn't hire him, either. He roamed the countryside then, looking for a deserted house or a barn or a cave or anything else that would give them shelter. He found the ramshackle log cabin, a couple of miles out of town, up in the hills, with plenty of wood around for fires and plenty of game for the cookpot. He went home to collect his mother.

Little by little, they dragged what furniture they could manage to the cabin, using his wagon and a small handcart for the smaller items. They sold the cookstove and the parlor furniture and used the money to buy flour and lard and some fatback. In

313

the spring, he'd get a job somewhere, he promised his mother, make enough money to buy more staples. But they had enough to see them through winter.

And they had fared fairly well on rabbits and squirrels and their love for each other—until the day his mama had started having pains and told him to go for the doctor, the baby was coming.

That was February 4, 1860. The day Wynn Spencer was born.

And her father was the doctor who'd let Michael's mother and sister die so his own wife and child could live.

Michael had sworn that day to hate Wallace Spencer and his spawn for the rest of his life.

Now that he knew Wynn, he couldn't imagine ever hating her. But could he love her still? Could he look at her every day of his life and not remember? If his sister had lived, she'd be Wynn's age—exactly. And every time he looked at Wynn now, he'd wonder how his sister would have looked all grown up.

But he wouldn't see her all grown up. He'd see her again as a bloody mass lying on a white sheet. He'd hear the pitiful cries of an eight-year-old boy curled up in front of a meager fire. And the guilt and anger and remorse he'd felt then would flood in and wash away any positive emotion.

Chapter Eighteen

Wynn spent the next several days soaking up sunshine and fresh air, exercising her leg—and waiting for Michael to come out to see her. Not being able to share her joy with him was the only thing that put a damper on her happiness.

Early in the week, she worried about what people would think of her after the incident with Vanderhoeven, but talkative Mabel Bradshaw laid that fear to rest. If anyone was spreading gossip, Mabel would have heard—and she would have considered it her Christian duty to inform Wynn. No one knew more about that aspect of Mabel's personality than Wynn Spencer, for Mabel had been the person in Galena who had kept Wynn abreast of everything Jonathan Matheson was up to, whether Wynn wanted to know about him or not.

Doc severed another of Wynn's concerns when he handed her the letter Vanderhoeven had taken.

"How did you get this back?" Wynn asked.

Doc grinned. "Took it off him right there in the pulpit, while had his shirt in one fist and was giving him what-for. He was so scared, he never knew I took it!" Doc hooted at the brilliance of his craftiness, then sobered somewhat. "Wynn, I hope you learned a lesson from this."

"I hope I learned several. Which one did you have in mind?"

"*Never* put anything in writing you don't want someone else to read. It'll get you in trouble every time. I don't know what you wrote in there, but just be thankful that son-of-a-bitch didn't read it out loud to the congregation last Sunday."

Wynn waved the folded sheets at him as she headed for the cookstove. "This is nothing but a declaration of my love for Michael."

Doc crooked a gray eyebrow at her. "Then why didn't you ever send it to him? I would have taken it anytime."

She opened the door to the firebox and shoved the paper inside. "I know you would have, Doc, but I didn't want Michael to read it. When I wrote it, all I meant to do was try to make him understand why I couldn't marry him. Instead, I heaped sainthood upon my own head and made Michael look like an insensitive lout. I should have destroyed it then."

"Don't be too hard on yourself, Wynn. Everyone knows Michael lived here for weeks; course, I was here then, too. And most folks know he stayed the night of the windstorm. Vanderhoeven drew his own conclusions. But you know what I think?"

"What?"

"I think that no-good Vanderhoeven would have pulled his stunt, anyway, with or without the letter. He never did like you 'cause you're smart. There are some men who can't—and won't—tolerate an intelligent woman. If you had given in to him that night, he would have used that against you. When

316

you didn't, he thought he had to find some evidence of a weakness in you, just to satisfy his warped sense of justice."

Wynn breathed an audible sigh of relief. "I'm so thankful he's gone! What do you think will happen to him now?"

Doc shrugged. "Who cares? The man will get what he deserves. People like him always do — eventually. My Emma used to say, 'What goes around, comes around.' "

He'd never mentioned Emma before, and his closed-off expression prevented Wynn from asking who she was. Doc would tell her, in his own good time.

Michael was taking his own sweet time!

Although Wynn's leg seemed stronger every day, it wouldn't hold her weight by itself. Otherwise, she would have taken the cart into town and tracked Michael down. By Friday morning, she was beside herself with longing to share her joy with Michael.

"I'm going to see him, Doc," she said emphatically over coffee.

"Wynn, give him some time."

"Time for what?"

Doc shook his head. "I'm not sure. He wouldn't tell me. He just said he needed some time to work things out in his head."

"This isn't over Vanderhoeven? He doesn't think — "

"No! At least, I don't think so."

"Well, I have to know, Doc. Don't you understand? I have to *know*."

Doc tried to reason with her. "He's really in a bad

way, Wynn, and he won't tell me why. Even your refusing his marriage proposal didn't affect him this bad. If you try to talk to him prematurely . . ."

"But don't you see? I need to tell him I *will* marry him now. He needs to hear it. *I* need to say it! If you won't take me into town, I'll go by myself."

"Well," Doc hedged, "if you're so all-fired determined. But don't say I didn't warn you."

Finding Michael Donovan took some looking.

He wasn't at either of his hotels, either of his stores, or at his new house. Slim hadn't seen him at the depot, Granny hadn't seen him at the boardinghouse, and Rusty so much as told them, with his prancing and pawing to get out of the corral, that he hadn't seen him either.

It all put Wynn in mind of the way she'd spent her first afternoon in Jennings looking for Michael and his finding her half-dressed in the barn. That memory had mellowed so much since then that it wasn't even accurate anymore.

"Maybe he's out at the house," Doc said wearily.

"Why don't you and Prairie stay in town and I'll go out there by myself?" Wynn suggested. Seeing Doc's raised eyebrows, she added, "If he's there, he can help me out of the cart. If he's not, I'll come right back to town anyway. My leg won't keep me from driving, Doc."

So much change in such a short time! Wynn was amazed as she passed building after building that had sprung up in the past few months. There were

318

no streets as such, and the phenomenal growth had swallowed up the old path leading out to Michael's house, making it far more difficult to find than Wynn had imagined.

And then, there it was, sitting off by itself, looking a bit old and ragged and forlorn among the shiny newness. And there was Michael, her Michael, sitting on the front porch, staring right through her as if she weren't there. She shivered in the warmth of the September sun.

Wynn drove up close to the porch, hauled in on the reins and sat, waiting for him to rise, to speak to her, but he sat perfectly still, staring, almost trancelike.

Finally giving up on him, she said, "Hello, Michael."

He shook his head and looked at her, really seeing her now, she thought.

"Go away," he muttered, locking his jaw. "Please, just go away and let me be."

Wynn stiffened her back and gave him stare for stare. Her voice was even and low. "I'm not leaving, Jason Michael Patrick Donovan, until we've had ourselves a little talk."

He stood up stiffly, favoring his knees like an arthritic old man. "You might as well turn that cart around, Dr. Spencer—"

Dr. Spencer? Did he actually call her Dr. Spencer—and flinch when he said it, or did she merely imagine he did?

"—and head right back to town. We have nothing to say to each other."

"Oh, but we do, my dear Mr. Donovan. Actually, I have something to show you. If you would kindly help me out of this cart—"

319

"No!" he bellowed, then closed his eyes for a moment. Wynn watched his hands clench into tight fists on his thighs and then open again, but this time they clutched his denim britches instead of hanging loose.

"Don't you understand?" he pleaded. "When I look at you, I see my dead sister. Go away. Please, go away."

The last words tore from his throat. He blinked, turned on his heel, and walked inside the house. The door closed with a soft click.

"Michael!" Wynn called. "Michael, please come back! Please!"

He stood with his back to the door, trembling all over, tears streaming down his cheeks, listening to her call his name.

Why did she have to come out here? his heart cried. Why couldn't she just leave him alone, pretend he never existed? Why did he have to remember now, after all this time? Why did the woman he loved have to be the one he'd vowed to hate almost twenty-five years ago?

"Get out of my heart, Wynn Spencer," he whispered. "Please, go away . . ."

Wynn sat for a long time, staring through damp eyes at the closed door, knowing that even if her leg were strong enough, she wouldn't go after him.

Doc was right. Michael was hurting. And fighting hurt was pointless. She'd only make it worse. But she wasn't through with Michael yet. No, not by a long shot. He'd have to do a lot more than tell her to go away if he wanted to get rid of her.

What had he meant—"When I look at you, I see my dead sister"? He'd told her he grew up in an orphanage; never had he mentioned a sister. Why had it taken him so long to see the resemblance? And why did a mere resemblance tear so at his heartstrings?

Maybe Doc would know.

But he didn't. Doc couldn't answer any of her questions. She felt bewildered and powerless, and the longer she let those two emotions mingle, the madder she got. As soon as she put Prairie down for her nap, she returned to the kitchen and vented her frustration on Doc.

"I don't know how men can ever say women reason without benefit of logic!"

"Calm down, Wynnifred," he soothed in a parent's voice. "Anxiety never cured anything—including asininity."

"Michael isn't asinine!" she staunchly defended.

Doc smiled at her loyalty. "Maybe not, but his thinking is—or so it seems to us. Come and sit down. Pacing never cured anything, either. Drink your tea before it gets cold, and let me tell you a story."

She shot him a mulish look but did as he bade.

Doc gave her a minute to relax before he began. "As you know, years ago I practiced the art of healing. And as you are well aware, medicine is never an exact science. We do what we can, when we can, the best we can, and leave the rest to God. I forgot the part about leaving the rest to God once, and He and I had a bad falling out about fifteen years ago. At least, I had a bad falling out with Him, and that's when I quit doctoring.

"I guess God was always there, protecting me from myself. He sent Michael when I was at my lowest point, living in a drunken stupor on the streets of Memphis, trying my best to commit suicide the slow, painful way. Michael rescued me from that part of myself. You've helped me restore my self-esteem, and you did it without ever setting out to do it. You did it just by being you."

"What does all this have to do with Michael?" Wynn asked.

"I've come through without having you or Michael ever pry into my personal misery. We know something has his feelings in an uproar. We don't know what, and we're not going to ask. Give Michael the space he needs to work it out. In the meantime, all you need to do is be here for him when he comes through and realizes he needs you. And he does need you, Wynn."

"I hope you're right, Doc," she said on a long sigh. "And I hope it doesn't take him fifteen years. I don't think my patience will last that long."

In truth, her patience lasted a grand total of fifteen days.

For two weeks, Wynn concentrated all her physical energy on strengthening her leg and all her mental energy on strengthening her patience.

By the end of that period, she had retired the crutches and replaced them with a cane. With the aid of a wooden step stool Slim made, she could get into and out of her cart by herself. A sturdy iron handle attached to the side of the stool allowed her to lift it with the crook of her cane once she was seated in the cart. Regaining her physical independence provided a natural boon to her spirits. But at the same time, the newfound freedom served to erode the patience she had so carefully nurtured.

Staying away from Michael hadn't been so difficult, so long as she couldn't go very far by herself nor ask Doc to take her when she'd promised to stay away. She didn't like going back on her word, but she vowed nevertheless to seize the first opportunity to confront Michael with, as Doc had so aptly called it, his asininity. They'd wasted enough time already.

That opportunity came on a bright, sunny Saturday afternoon in mid-October.

Since the incident with Vanderhoeven, Doc never left Wynn by herself. His attention was understandable—but stifling. He wouldn't have left her that day had Mabel Bradshaw not dropped by. Doc didn't like Mabel, not even a little bit. And though the chatterbox certainly didn't fit into Wynn's list of favorite people, she silently blessed Mabel that day.

"Why don't you take Prairie into town while I visit with Mabel?" Wynn suggested to Doc, hoping she could rid herself of Mabel's company before he and Prairie came back.

Doc snatched the bait.

A quarter hour later, Wynn claimed a sudden cramp and rushed outside to the privy as quickly as her game leg would allow. "I ought to warn you this might be contagious," she told Mabel upon her return to the kitchen. "I treated a man with acute dysentery the other day. I don't know if this town could take another epidemic."

The woman's face paled and her voice shook. "But will Doc be back in time?"

"Don't worry yourself about me, Mabel. I know

what to do. Besides, Doc's never gone very long."

Mabel was already headed to the back door. "Well, then, if you're sure—"

"Your buggy's out front," Wynn reminded her.

As soon as Mabel was out of sight, Wynn proceeded to the barn and hitched Carmen up to the cart. She'd never done anything really sneaky before, and a pang of guilt stabbed at her chest. Her hands trembled and her heart pounded, but she held to her resolve. At the last minute, she went back in the house and collected her medical bag, which would serve as cover.

She wished she'd had time to fancy herself up a bit, put on something not quite so serviceable as her cream-colored shirtwaist and dark brown pleated skirt, and maybe pile her hair up on her head. But she'd never put on airs before and she supposed there was no reason to start now.

Wynn drove north and then east before turning back south, giving the town a wide berth. She knew there was a good possibility Michael wouldn't be at his old house, but it was worth a try.

The place had a deserted, unkempt air about it. Weeds grew in the yard and the uncurtained windows gaped darkly. Wynn stopped Carmen out front, dropped her stool, and got out of the cart. The tapping of her cane punctuated each step up to the porch and across its wooden planks. She listened to its echoes in the stillness of the afternoon and thought the noise would surely bring Michael to the door.

It didn't.

She took a deep breath, folded her right hand into a fist, and rapped sharply with her knuckles, to no avail. Not yet convinced he wasn't there, she

324

peeked in each of the two front windows, making a canopy with her hands to shield the glare. He was not in either room.

Determined to find him if he was there, she tried the front door and found it unlocked. A quick but thorough search of the house indicated an absence of several days' duration, evidenced by the cold stove and a thick gray mold growing on a dirty plate.

A tear born of utter frustration escaped her eye and she swiped at it irritably. All her careful planning had come to naught! Well, she told herself, she'd managed it once; she'd manage it another time. She might even be able to make it back home and unhitch Carmen before Doc got back—if she hurried.

She skirted the town again and was more than halfway home when a pair of riders approached, one of whom she recognized as the dandy she'd met in the general store that first morning she was in Jennings, the man she'd erroneously thought to be Michael Donovan.

"Whoa, there, Dr. Spencer!" he called.

As she pulled back on the reins, she searched her memory for his name. What had Michael called him? Wilcox.

"We need you out at the ranch," he wheezed, taking a linen handkerchief from the inside pocket of his suit coat and wiping his brow with it. He looked totally incongruous next to the other rider, who was sensibly dressed in denim britches, chaps, and a plaid flannel shirt. "Jamie—Mr. MacDougall's son, has been shot."

"Where?"

Wilcox dismounted and hastened to tie his horse's

reins to the back of the cart. "In the chest. We must hurry. He's bleeding to death!"

She recalled Michael saying that MacDougall's ranch was a whole day's ride from Jennings. Chances were they wouldn't make it in time, anyway. Deep down, Wynn didn't want to go. She grasped at a valid argument. "But there are other doctors here now—two men. Why not get one of them?"

"Because we already have you." Wilcox climbed into the cart and sat down next to her. "Let me have the reins. I know the way."

"But I don't have anything with me except my medical bag. And I'll need to tell someone where I'm going."

"George'll take care of that. Just tell him who."

Wynn bit her bottom lip, wishing there was some way to get out of having to go with Wilcox. But there wasn't, at least none that she could see. She couldn't claim her handicap anymore; Doc and Granny would take care of Prairie between them; and she was a doctor. This was part of her job.

"Doc Nolan, I suppose. Or Granny Simpson at the boardinghouse if you can't find Doc. And, please, bring me some clothes."

"Will do, ma'am," the one called George said, tipping his Stetson and spurring his horse toward town.

Wilcox flicked the reins and they started across the prairie.

Wynn had done a lot of wishing that day. Right then, she wished more than anything else that Michael had been at home. If he had, she'd have missed Wilcox completely.

While she was thinking about Michael on her way out to MacDougall's ranch, he was sitting in a bar in New Orleans thinking about her.

He'd hoped leaving Jennings for a few days would give him a different perspective. It hadn't. A generous consumption of Kentucky bourbon hadn't helped, either. He should have known it wouldn't. It hadn't worked before.

What a vicious cycle is life, he silently moaned. And he knew better than most people; he'd come full circle.

A raspy voice interrupted his dark musings. "Hi ya, honey. Why d'ya look so sad?"

Michael dragged his gaze from the rich, dark brown glow of his whiskey to the dull, lifeless brown eyes of the woman at his side, the woman who was rubbing his denim-clad thigh with an open palm and shoving her ample breasts almost into his face. The powdered breasts threatened to spill right out of the tight-fitting bodice of a glaring red gown. If he stuck out his tongue, it would touch the mole she'd painted just above one crest.

"I can solve all your problems, honey," she drawled. "The name's Wanda, and I got me a nice private room upstairs. Won't nobody bother us."

Her hand moved from his thigh to his crotch, and Michael jerked as violently as if someone had poked him with a hot branding iron.

"Eew! Does it feel that good?"

"No!" he barked. "It feels that wrong." None too gently, he removed her hand, then stood up and threw a coin down on the counter.

"You didn't finish your drink," Wanda pouted.

"It turned sour," he said through clenched teeth,

then wheeled and walked out into the blinding, purifying sunlight.

"Give this horse a good rubdown," MacDougall's ranch hand, George, told Jock Delaney at the livery. "He's been ridden hard. Don't give him too much water yet, and be sure you give him some sweet oats. I'm goin' to find me a bite to eat, and then I'll be back to collect him."

"I know how to tek care of horses," Jock muttered at George's retreating back, "an' I don't need no cowpoke talkin' to me like I don't." He bent down to loosen the girth straps. "I don't know who folks think they are, walkin' in here and talkin' to me like I ain't got no sense. It all started with that female doctor and her frickin' cart. Nobody's given me no respect since."

He heaved the saddle off and set it on a block nearby. "I thought I'd got her good when I told that preacher 'bout her and Donovan. Then he had to go botch it. I'll git me another chance, though. She's gonna pay. Yep. She's gonna pay."

Wynn rolled her shoulders back and stifled a yawn. It was going to be a long night. At least they had arrived at the ranch before it started raining.

"What do you think, Dr. Spencer?"

Andrew MacDougall had stood quietly by the bedside throughout the entire examination, holding his breathless question until Wynn pulled the sheet up over his son's shoulders.

Jamie MacDougall tossed about restlessly, and with good cause. Although he'd never been in real danger of bleeding to death, as Wilson had said, the youth's life hung in a delicate balance. Reduction of his fever was the first priority.

"Continue bathing his face, Mr. Wilcox," Wynn instructed. "I'll speak to Mr. MacDougall privately."

The cattleman nodded his understanding. Wynn followed him down the hall and into a study paneled in gleaming mahogany. MacDougall sat down behind a massive leather-topped desk upon which burned a single lamp; Wynn sat in front of it. His clear blue eyes bored into hers, begging honesty, fortifying his spoken request. "Please, speak candidly."

Wynn nodded, hoping he meant it. Incurring his wrath held no appeal. "Luckily, the bullet didn't hit anything vital, although it barely missed his lung. He must have had his left shoulder thrown back when he was struck, which probably saved his life—thus far. The simple cleaning I gave the entry wound in his chest and the exit wound under his arm should prove sufficient to hold off infection there. But the arm itself—that's another matter entirely, I'm afraid. Cleaning out the re-entry wound will not be enough."

MacDougall's bushy gray eyebrows narrowed over the bridge of his long nose. "The bullet is in the arm. You'll take it out. Where's the problem?"

Wynn shook her head. "I can't take it out, Mr. MacDougall. It's no longer in one piece. It shattered the bone and then broke up into shrapnel, which is more than likely scattered from his shoulder socket to his elbow."

"How do you know?"

"Because I removed some of the shrapnel while I was probing the wound. Infection from shrapnel can be very dangerous. I would suggest that we amputate immediately."

The blue eyes blazed in anger. He slapped the flat of one hand upon the leather top of the desk and rose halfway out of his chair. "No!" he bellowed.

"Mr. MacDougall, please! Lower your voice. Do you want Jamie to hear you?"

He shook his head and slowly lowered his backside to the seat of the chair.

"We must discuss this calmly," she continued, working at keeping her husky voice from fluttering with her own ambivalent feelings. "Amputation is never pretty—and quite often, unsuccessful. But if we treat Jamie's arm in the normal way, gangrene might very well set in without our knowing it."

"Explain, Dr. Spencer. What is the 'normal way'?"

"For an upper arm fracture, the arm is bandaged from fingers to shoulder, flexible splints padded with wool are secured with rollers to the upper arm, and a covering made of leather is stitched over the splints to hold everything in place. The arm is then hung in a sling until the bone mends itself."

"So? Where's the problem?"

Wynn sighed. "The bone isn't fractured, Mr. MacDougall. It's shattered. Either way, the pain must be excruciating. A fracture is set—the two pieces are put back together. There's nothing to set in Jamie's arm. If we proceed with bandaging and splinting, we will minimize his discomfort, but we can only hope the bone will grow back together. With the arm completely covered in the interim, we won't be able to see what's happening with infection. It's extremely risky."

MacDougall frowned and scratched his jaw

through his heavy gray beard. "We could remove the bandage daily."

"Then the bone would never mend. And the pain would be unbearable." Wynn reached a hand across the top of the desk and laid it on top of Mac-Dougall's. "I know this is difficult for you—"

He snatched his hand away. "Difficult?" he hissed. "Difficult, Dr. Spencer? There is nothing difficult about it. There will be no amputation."

"Perhaps you should send for one of the other doctors. I'll be happy to stay until your men can return with a replacement."

"No. The other doctors are all men. Men enjoy sawing off limbs. That's why I wanted you, Dr. Spencer. You'll stay and care for my son. You'll make him well. Whatever you need, I'll send for. But you will not take off his arm."

Chapter Nineteen

Never had Wynn felt so frightened, so defense-less.

Not during the windstorm. Not when she'd sat in church and listened to Vanderhoeven's accusations. Not even when she'd thought she was dying. She'd had Michael's loving support to sustain her through two of those trials, Doc's loyal friendship as a buttress through the other.

But she couldn't count on them this time. Not when neither they nor anyone else knew where she was. Almost a week had passed since Wilcox had driven her to MacDougall's ranch. Surely if anyone in town knew of her whereabouts, someone would have come by now.

Wynn had only herself—her own skills and inge-nuity—to rely on. She hoped they were enough.

A multitude of threads wove the fabric of her terror. In reality, she supposed, she was the victim of a rather cunning abduction, for George, presumably on instructions from MacDougall, had not given Doc her message nor brought back any of her clothes. The ransom was high: the preservation of Jamie MacDougall's life, a task complicated by his father's stubbornness, which Wynn termed beyond unreasonable.

Logic had proved an unsuccessful ploy. As she bathed her patient's fevered skin, her most recent argument with Andrew MacDougall filtered through her consciousness.

"You can't hold me prisoner here!" she'd railed.

"Oh, but I can, Dr. Spencer," he'd said, smiling.

"But that's illegal!"

He shrugged his massive shoulders. "Says who? There's no law hereabouts, except me."

"I'll file charges."

He seemed unperturbed by her threat. "And it will be my word against yours. Who do you think the judge will believe—a law-abiding landowner who's lived here for several decades, or a young upstart female doctor who's been publicly accused of harlotry?"

"How do you know about that?" she gasped.

"People do talk, Dr. Spencer."

"But this is all so unnecessary. I'm dedicated to medicine and to the well-being of my patients. I'll stay as long as your son needs me. There's no reason to lock me in, or to deny me my clothes, or to keep my presence here a secret."

His lips twisted into a sneer. "You're unhappy with the garments I've provided? That gown was one of my wife's favorites. Cost me a tidy bundle."

Her eyes focused on the dress she wore. Other than being a bit too large and overlong, she could find no fault with the daygown. "You've missed the point completely, Mr. MacDougall. Intentionally, I think. It's not a matter of mere dissatisfaction with a garment and you know it."

"Ah, but you contradict yourself, Dr. Spencer. You just said you stay willingly. I'm only insuring that you continue to do so. Please, do not tempt my patience with your ramblings again." His subtle threat effectively closed that particular topic of discussion. "I sent for you so I could hear a report on my son's progress."

He wasn't going to like what she had to say, but he needed to hear it. Wynn took a deep breath and looked him squarely in the eyes. "Your son is going to die, Mr. MacDougall, unless you allow me to amputate."

She flinched involuntarily when he raised a hand to strike her, and she breathed no easier when he slowly let it fall. Angry blue fire danced in his eyes and fury pulsed in his temples, belying the composure in his voice.

"If he were your son, Dr. Spencer, would you take off his arm?"

"To save his life? Most assuredly."

"But you aren't his parent. You don't even have a child of your own. So you don't really know what you'd do, do you, Dr. Spencer?" He gave her a moment to digest his question, time to think about Prairie. Would she take off one of Prairie's arms? "You yourself said that amputations were often unsuccessful. Can you guarantee he will live if you amputate?"

"No, of course not. There are no guarantees in medicine. But I *can* guarantee a better chance of survival."

MacDougall held out his left arm and looked at it hard. Wynn watched him closely, hoping he would change his mind, but his expression remained inscrutable. "I fought in the war, Dr. Spencer. I watched butcher after butcher chop off arms and legs, and then I watched man after man die anyway. If Jamie is going to die, he will die with both of his armo intact."

This is not the war, she wanted to scream. *That was twenty years ago, and we've made great strides in medicine since then.* Certain the outrage she felt would anger him further should she put voice to it, Wynn counted slowly to ten and mustered all the sympathy she could manage for this irrational man. "Please, Mr. MacDougall," she implored, "send for one of the other doctors in Jennings. Get another opinion."

His answer had been simple and direct—and utterly predictable. "No."

MacDougall had then called to Wilcox, who stood just outside the study door. His "insurance" included an around-the-clock guard on her person and the removal of all her surgical instruments from the sick room. "Dr. Spencer is ready to return."

Now, as she rinsed the cloth and applied it to Jamie's hot forehead again, questions for which she had no answers chased each other around in her head. Why didn't MacDougall want one of the male doctors in town to treat his son? She didn't believe her "mothering instinct" had anything to do with it. What was going to happen to her when Jamie Mac-Dougall died? And he was surely going to die. The fever that raged through his body indicated severe infection. She had to do something . . .

"Mr. Wilcox, I need a pair of scissors," Wynn announced.

"Pardon?"

"Scissors, Mr. Wilcox. Now."

"But, Mr. MacDougall said—"

"This leather casing must come off. If necessary, I'll break the stitches with my teeth. Such action will, of course, cause needless pain to this patient from the pressure I shall be forced to place on his injured arm in order to hold it stationary while I bite out the stitches. Do you want to be held responsible for such pain?"

Wilcox stood and moved hesitantly toward the bed. "You wouldn't—"

"Oh, but I will."

"Stand aside," he barked, then removed a slender pocketknife from his trousers.

Wynn watched him slice through the stitches over Jamie's left shoulder. When he backed away, she said, "You'll have to cut the ones down the side as well, Mr. Wilcox. The casing is too tight to slide it off his arm."

"Are you certain this is necessary?"

"Absolutely."

With the casing off, Wynn unwound the muslin strips that held the splints in place, then removed the bandage covering the young man's arm. The odor of the diseased tissue filled her nostrils and she choked on the bile that rose in her throat.

"Open the door!"

"But, ma'am," Wilcox argued, "the windows are already open."

"Just do it!"

He did.

With the air flowing freely, the odor dissipated somewhat. Nevertheless, Wynn moved to the window, hung her head out, and took great gulps of fresh air into her lungs.

Two hands clapped themselves on either side of her rib cage and hauled her roughly back into the room.

"I'm certain if I wanted to escape, I could devise a better plan," she scoffed, pushing his hands away. "I'll need some fresh charcoal, stale bread—preferably molded—with the crusts removed, milk and a pot to heat it in, more clean cloths, and plenty of hot water."

Wilcox blinked at her.

"Must I write it all in a list, sir?"

He shook his head and strode into the hall. "Matt!" he called down the passageway to one of the ranch hands. The echo of shuffled boot steps followed, then low murmurings, with Wilcox keeping an eye pinned on her all the while.

Wynn sat back down and forced herself to look more closely at Jamie's red-streaked, swollen arm. When she tentatively pressed against it with the pad of her thumb, the youth jerked and moaned.

"I'm sorry, Jamie," she soothed, passing a palm gently over his forehead and smoothing back a stiff strand of his golden blond hair. "I didn't want to cause you this pain, but it's all I know to do now. I'm putting some laudanum in your water. Here, take a few sips."

A few minutes later, he stilled somewhat, although his face remained drawn up in a tight grimace. Wynn had set his age at seventeen, or thereabouts, a youth on the threshold of manhood. Should he survive, Wynn doubted he'd ever regain use of his left arm. But living with a shriveled limb was better than not living at all. She'd debate that with Andrew MacDougall to the death, if she had to.

While she waited for the supplies, she pondered for the umpteenth time why Jamie had been shot— and by whom. Although she'd asked MacDougall and each of her guards in turn, no one would tell her. Something was terribly wrong about all of this . . .

A loud, blustering voice intruded upon her

thoughts.

"Just what in hell's name do you think you're doing?"

She twisted her torso to face Andrew MacDougall. "Attempting to save your son's life."

"But you told me his bone wouldn't heal properly if you removed the splints!"

"Please calm yourself, Mr. MacDougall. You're disturbing your son."

"I demand an explanation," he seethed, his voice much lower but his anger still much in evidence.

"His arm is infected. Surely you can see it and smell it, even from across the room. What good will a perfectly healed bone make if the infection kills him? Face it, Mr. MacDougall. Your son will never be perfectly whole again. It may be too late for any measure to prove effective, but I am going to try to draw out the infection with a poultice. You possess the undeniable ability to stop me, if you wish. It's your conscience at stake, not mine."

MacDougall shook his gray head and whirled on Wilcox. "Give her whatever she asks for, within reason," he snarled, "and keep me informed."

Wynn worked at saving Jamie MacDougall's life with a vengeance, driven by both the physician in her and the woman wanting desperately to survive. She shuddered to think what the elder MacDougall would prescribe as punishment should her efforts prove unsuccessful. He'd started mumbling things like "an eye for an eye" when he visited the sickroom. Did he mean to punish her, she wondered, or the person who had shot Jamie?

He had, as yet, provided no information concerning the shooting. Although Wynn could see no

338

practicality in knowing the details herself, the fact that MacDougall refused to reveal anything about it furnished cause for uneasiness.

As she worked with the poultices, Wynn lost count of the hours and days that passed. Her father had proclaimed a bread and milk application to be the most effective of all poultices. It was certainly the most conveniently prepared. She began by finely crumbling the stale bread into a basin, then pouring in boiling milk and stirring until the mixture was perfectly smooth. This she spread thickly on a piece of tightly woven cotton fabric, which she had cut large enough to extend beyond the youth's elbow and shoulder and to wrap completely around his arm. Over the mixture she sprinkled a thin layer of powdered charcoal. The addition of a piece of muslin between the mixture and Jamie's skin allowed her to apply a much hotter poultice without burning him.

"How is that going to do him any good?" George asked skeptically during his sickroom guard duty.

"The heat opens the pores, the milk draws, and the charcoal absorbs," Wynn explained.

"I don't understand."

"Then go to medical school!" She was surprised to hear the irritable tone of her voice, and she felt the sudden tenseness hovering between them. "Forgive me for snapping at you, George."

"That's all right, ma' am. You've earned the privilege."

Was he alluding to his own part in the duplicity? For awhile, he watched her in silence, then surprised her.

"I'm sorry, ma'am. I, well, I didn't know what they'd planned, you see. All they told me was to make sure no one followed so's you could give

Jamie here your undivided attention for a few days. It's been nigh on to two weeks. I reckon there's some folks back in town wonderin' what's happened to you."

"I reckon so," Wynn agreed, worrying her bottom lip as she pondered the depth of the ranch hand's loyalty to his boss. Soliciting his assistance was worth a try, she supposed. "George, are you going back to town anytime soon?"

"Oh, no, ma'am. Sometimes I go with Wilcox, but mostly he goes by himself. I couldn't do it for you no way, ma'am. I'm sorry."

His words indicated to Wynn that he'd understood her perfectly. Despite his declaration, however, he sounded truly sympathetic. Wynn could not help thinking he might prove a valuable ally.

"Where in hell can she be?"

Michael raked long fingers through his dark, limp hair and turned away from Doc, but not before the older man saw the agonized expression in Michael's eyes.

"Walkin' the floor won't bring her back."

"And sitting there drinking coffee will?"

"If it hadn't rained the night after she left, we might have found some tracks," Doc offered in defense.

"Yeah, but none of us are professional trackers, Doc. With so many homesteaders coming and going all the time, it would have been tough. But someone had to see something. She didn't just vanish into thin air."

"Everyone in this town knows she's missing, boy. Most of 'em have joined the search, at one time or another—"

Michael whirled around. "Who doesn't like her, Doc?"

"Why, nobody. You saw how they all backed her against Vanderhoeven. By the way, I heard he was tending bar in Beaumont." Doc cackled.

"Serves him right. But think about it, Doc. Everyone has at least one enemy, whether they know it or not. And so does Wynn. But who?"

Doc shook his head. "Beats me."

Michael strode purposefully toward the door. "Where you going, boy?" Doc called.

"To ask Granny—and Slim and Joe and Johnny and Mabel and anybody else who might have an idea."

"It's a shame you can't ask Rusty."

"What?"

Doc snickered. "That old horse sees and hears more'n anybody else in this town, I'd swear."

Michael's face broke into a grin and his long strides brought him swiftly to Doc's side. Before Doc could react to Michael's impetuous change in attitude, he found himself caught up in a bear hug.

"You touched in the head, boy? You ain't never hugged me before, and I sure don't see any cause for it now."

"Oh, but there *is* cause, old man. I think you've pinned the tail on the right donkey."

Doc pulled away from Michael with a long, hard stare. "That horse can't talk."

"No, but Delaney can. If there's anyone in this town who doesn't like Wynn, it's Jock Delaney."

Doc began to understand Michael's logic. "You might have something there, boy. But what makes you think Delaney will have any information about

Wynn?"

"Because he owns the livery. He sees more of the homesteaders than any of the rest of us. No matter why they come to town, they leave their horses with him."

"What are you going to do when you find her?"

"Do? Bring her home, I suppose."

"And what if she doesn't want to come? What if she left here of her own free will?"

"I don't believe that, Doc, and I don't think you do, either. Some of the neighbors saw her take the cart out by herself. We don't know why. Perhaps only to go for a ride on the prairie, maybe to see a patient, but she couldn't have planned to be gone overnight or she would have packed a bag. We don't know what happened to her after that, but she's alive and well, Doc. I'd feel it in my gut if she weren't."

"So you're going to find her and bring her home. Then what?"

Michael frowned in confusion. "Then we'll all stop worrying about her, I suppose."

"Come back and sit down, boy, while I make us some more coffee. We need to have a chat before you go off looking for her again. You just might find her this time, and I'd hate to see you ruin your life 'cause you went off half-cocked."

"I don't need any coffee, old man," Michael argued, heading for the door again, "and I'm not going off half-cocked."

The click of a thumb on a pistol hammer stopped him cold. Slowly, he pivoted around to see Doc's gun pointed straight at his torso. "What are you doing, Doc?"

"Forcing you to sit down. If I have to, I'll shoot you in the leg. Then we can have this conversation

342

while I'm removing the bullet." He waved his pistol toward an empty chair. "You're going to talk and I'm going to listen."

Michael remembered the last time he'd seen Doc wave his pistol, the night he'd accidentally shot himself. He pulled out the chair and sat down. "You really are serious, aren't you?"

"Yep."

"What am I going to talk about?"

"Wynn refused to marry you because she didn't think she was whole. Her affliction was physical and she conquered it—as much for you as for herself. Now you have an affliction, a mental one or emotional, whichever you want to call it. If you'd conquered it already, you'd be telling me you were going to bring Wynn back to marry her—not to ease our worries. So you're going to tell me what's been eating at you since the day we put Vanderhoeven on the train."

Michael's face paled and his hands shook. "I can't, Doc."

"Yes, you can! You can and you will. Don't you see? You have to tell somebody. You can't conquer whatever's eating at you if you keep it inside. It'll just fester until it eats you up, like a slow-growing cancer. I know, son. I wandered that road for fifteen long years, and it damn near ruined my life. You can start by telling me about your dead sister."

Michael shook his head. "No, Doc, that's the end of the story, not the beginning."

Afternoon bled into dusk while Michael talked. He started with his father's death and ended with his mother's. Doc put his pistol away and made another pot of coffee, but Michael never noticed.

"And that's why I've always hated doctors," Michael said in conclusion.

"Because a father chose to deliver his own child?"

"Because my mother needed him. He promised to come. She died, Doc! She and my sister died because Wallace Spencer broke his promise."

"You said it was snowing. Don't you think he might have tried to come and couldn't make it in the blizzard?"

"I don't know. I don't remember what he said the next day, when he finally came, when he found me half-frozen on the cabin floor. Whatever he said, it was too late. I'd already vowed to hate him, to hate the child who'd been born when my sister had died. All those years I spent in that filthy orphanage were his fault. Don't you see, Doc?" he pleaded. "Now that I know who Wynn Spencer is, I won't ever be able to look at her without remembering. I can't marry her. It wouldn't be fair to either of us."

"Do you still love her?"

Michael's response was low, his voice scratchy. "Yes."

Doc refreshed their coffee cups. "Have you ever thought you wouldn't be alive yourself if her father hadn't come when he did? Have you ever thought Wallace Spencer might have felt guilty about your mother and the baby later?"

"No, well, I—" Michael clamped his mouth shut and glared at Doc.

"You've never asked me why I quit practicing medicine and I've never told anyone, but I'm going to tell you now. My own wife and child—a son— died because I wasn't at home to take care of them when they needed me. I was miles away, treating a little girl who died despite my best efforts to save her. We all have to make decisions, boy. A doctor doesn't choose one life over another. And he isn't God. He can't be two places at one time. If I'd

344

been here that Saturday afternoon, Wynn wouldn't have disappeared. You weren't even in town. But I don't hear either one of us taking the blame."

"This is different," Michael argued.

"Not really," Doc countered. "It's the flip side of the same coin. Guilt is guilt. It's excess baggage in any form. Your hatred is a form of guilt, whether you want to see it that way or not. You blamed yourself when your mother and sister died, didn't you? You thought there must have been something you could have done. But thinking that way hurt too bad, so you laid the blame on Wallace Spencer. It's time to put the hatred and the blame and the guilt away, Michael. Nothing will ever change what happened. Don't let it continue to control your life."

"Is that what I've done, Doc?"

"Isn't it, Michael?"

"Please, hold the lamp a bit closer, George," Wynn whispered in deference to her patient's restful state. Jamie MacDougall had fought the infection right along with her, remaining stoically silent when Wynn knew he had to be wanting to scream his lungs out from the pain, when Wynn herself desperately wished for more laudanum to give him. But the meager supply she kept in her medical bag had run out days before. MacDougall had reneged on his promise to send someone into town for medical supplies.

With the infection apparently cleared, Wynn had replaced the bandage and splints and was in the process of stitching up the leather casing. Now that his arm was stationary once again, Jamie had drifted off into much-needed sleep.

The ranch hand shifted his position and that of the oil lamp until Wynn nodded affirmatively. "You've worked a miracle here, Dr. Spencer. I hope Mr. MacDougall appreciates it."

Her shoulders rose in a slight shrug as her fingers continued to place the stitches. "My motives haven't been the most honorable, I'm afraid. I did this for me — for my own preservation. I've learned what a powerful incentive greed can be, when that greed is the continuation of one's own life. In this case, saving my life meant saving Jamie's as well."

"You don't think Mr. MacDougall would have actually harmed you had Jamie died, do you?"

"You know him better than I, George. What do you think?"

"I don't know, Dr. Spencer. He can be a hard man."

"Unyielding, uncompromising, unwavering, you mean. I find his indifference toward seeking out and punishing the man who shot Jamie totally out of character." Wynn tied off the last stitch over Jamie's shoulder and cut the heavy thread.

"That's because I shot myself."

The youth's declaration momentarily stunned Wynn. Even when he was conscious, he'd spoken few words these past two weeks, and then only to communicate his discomfort. And now he'd told her something she found difficult to believe. Her uncertain scrutiny darted between Jamie and George, whose faces wavered in the flickering light the one lamp provided, and then settled on Jamie's beseeching gaze.

"Be careful what you say, Jamie," George warned.

"She deserves to be told. Anyone else, including my father, would have given up on me a long time ago."

"But — why?" Wynn managed.

Jamie turned eyes as blue as his father's away from her steady gaze, fixing them on the flashes of lightning mirrored in the window glass. "Nothing I do pleases him. I've lived with that all my life. But he, uh, he accused me of liking men better than women, and, well, I just couldn't take it anymore." Jamie swallowed hard, and pale light glistened off the dampness in his eyes. "I just wanted to die, but I was no better at that than I am at anything else. My hands were shaking so bad, the rifle slipped when I pulled the trigger. I guess I should have used a pistol."

"Thank goodness you didn't!" Wynn cried. "Promise me you won't try this again."

"That depends on my father, Dr. Spencer."

"No, Jamie," she argued gently, adjusting his sling, "it depends on you. You have more inner strength than you give yourself credit for. I know. I've seen it." She waited patiently for him to acknowledge her counsel. When he nodded, she said, "You know you aren't over this yet. You may never be able to use your left arm again."

"I know," he murmured.

Thunder rolled ominously close by and a brilliant flash illuminated the room for an instant. The scene almost instantly replayed itself, but this time, the clap came from directly overhead, shaking the house so hard the windows rattled. Wynn's heart jumped into her throat and a shudder racked her body. She busied herself with putting away her supplies, then tidying up the bed.

"Try to go back to sleep now, Jamie," she murmured as she tucked the covers around him. "You need your rest."

The young man smiled weakly. "I'll try, but I don't think this thunder will let me." He pulled his right hand from under the blanket and laid it tenderly on her shoulder. "Thank you, Dr. Spencer."

She smiled down at him. "You're quite welcome, Jamie."

The door burst open and Wilcox rushed in. "Take them to the bunkhouse!" he yelled at George. "And hurry! The house is on fire!"

Rusty raced as swiftly as the wind whipping down the prairie grasses and threatening to capture his rider's worn Stetson.

"You feel it, too, don't you, boy?" Michael said, referring to the sudden sense of urgency that gripped him. The threat of danger was so strong, he could taste it — vile and bitter in his throat.

He should have done this a week ago . . . two weeks ago . . . the day he'd come back from New Orleans. He should have thought of Delaney then, he muttered, castigating himself. But he'd been so wrapped up in his own misery at the time — and Doc was right. It had all been for nothing. A part of him had hated Wynn for something she'd had no control over. And thank God, he thought, she had been born! Thank God, Wallace Spencer had been there to deliver her, to see that she survived. It had all happened the way it had for his benefit, for he was meant for Wynn Spencer and she for him.

Michael knew that now — knew it from the depths of his soul, could see the preordination of the events in his life more clearly than he'd ever seen anything. They were two halves of a whole, he and Wynn. The very thought of her being in some kind of grave danger now scared the hell out of him —

and drove him onward through the black of night.

In the distance, a flash of lightning shot down from the black heavens like the forked tongue of a snake. Rusty whinnied nervously and balked.

"Come on, Rusty," Michael pressed, fighting to control the recalcitrant horse. "This is no time to show me your ornery side."

They moved ahead again, toward the lightning, toward MacDougall's ranch. Although Michael had no hard evidence Wynn was there, it was the only lead he had. MacDougall never sent George Harrell—or any of his other hands except Wilcox—into town by himself. And Delaney had insisted George had come into the livery alone and with only one horse the very afternoon Wynn had disappeared.

"God!" Michael breathed from his hunkered position over Rusty's neck. "Let her be there!"

Chapter Twenty

Wynn snatched up her cane and medical bag while George scooped up Jamie. As quickly as their burdens permitted, they made their way down the dark hallway and outside into a wall of smoke and ashes borne on the breath of a fierce wind and a night turned unnaturally bright by fire and lightning. Without looking back, the two hurried toward the gray hulk of the bunkhouse, some hundred yards away.

When they reached its shallow porch, however, they turned in unison to stare openmouthed at the flames leaping along the wood-shingled roof of the low-slung ranch house. Men rushed around like ants whose hill has been disturbed, seemingly without direction as they pumped water into buckets and ran back to hurl the liquid at the roof. Wynn's heart pounded erratically, yet she felt a thrill of unexpected exhilaration at the sight of such chaos. Perhaps—

"They'll never put it out," Jamie observed, his tone bland, uncaring. "You can set me down now, George. I can walk."

When the ranch hand looked to Wynn for advice, she nodded. "Be careful, Jamie. Use the wall for support. You're still weak." To George, she said, "Go. Help them fight the fire. I'll see to Jamie."

George hesitated, watching Jamie as he placed his right hand on the wall, moved toward a straight chair on the porch, and sat down. "You'll do what has to be done?" he said to Wynn.

The obvious double-meaning took Wynn by surprise. "Yes, George."

He took her right hand in his and squeezed it tightly. "You're a special person, Dr. Spencer. Real special. Please, be careful."

"Thank you, George. I will."

For a moment she stood perfectly still, her vision following the ranch hand's quick gait toward the main house, her head swimming with the sudden prospect of escape. Dare she leave Jamie, though, she asked herself, realizing his safety was far more important to her at the moment than her own.

A hand closed over her forearm. "Go, Dr. Spencer, now, before it's too late."

She turned to stare at Jamie, who'd left his chair to stand beside her. "But surely he'll allow me to go home tomorrow," she insisted.

"I wouldn't make bet on it. He'll find some excuse. And if he thinks I might have told you I tried to kill myself—and why, he'll never let you go."

"Why?"

Jamie sighed. "You don't know him, Dr. Spencer. His pride . . . he's ruthless."

"But what of the storm? The weather can become ruthless, too, you know."

"There's a line shack five miles or so due east. It's a little out of your way, but you can seek shelter there until the storm passes."

Still, she hesitated. "What about you? What if you need me?"

"I'll be fine here on the porch. Do you need some help saddling a horse? I do have one good arm."

A lump formed in her throat. Wynn shook her head and adjusted his sling, then pulled his lithe frame briefly against her. "Take care of yourself, Jamie. Don't try to use that arm. I'll be back in a week or two to check on you."

"And I'll look forward to seeing you again, Dr. Spencer. But please, don't come alone."

Wynn shivered. "I won't."

"Go now," he pleaded, "before it's too late."

She left him then, skirting the bunkhouse and walking toward the barn at a pace as fast as her gimpy leg and the buffeting wind would allow. Occasionally, she glanced toward the big house to assure herself that MacDougall and his men remained occupied with the business of fighting the fire. She struggled to maintain her spirits, knowing her hold on freedom was tenuous at best. If someone should see her . . . if anyone was in the barn . . . if Carmen and the cart weren't there . . .

As she neared the barn door, the shrill, prolonged neighs of terrified horses assailed her ears. Wynn hesitated, setting her medical bag on the ground and placing her free hand over her suddenly constricted throat. She took a deep breath. Warily, she slipped the crossbar loose from its moorings, grasped the edge of the door and eased it open, waiting breathlessly for the charge of horseflesh.

The wind snatched at the portal, threatening to pull it from her grasp. Wynn stumbled, almost tripping over the extra length of her borrowed skirt. In the process, she dropped her cane and clutched the door with both hands for support. Attempting to ignore the pain shooting through her leg, she gritted her teeth and pushed on the door. When it hit the barn wall, she leaned against it, let her eyelids fall shut and breathed deeply, regathering her strength.

The horses continued to neigh, but since they remained in the barn, Wynn assumed they were all trapped in their stalls. The compassionate side of her wanted to free them, but logic assured her that neither she nor they were in any real danger . . . yet.

Bracing her shoulder against the door, she bent down and felt along the ground until her hand touched the large, heavy block that was used as a doorstop. She worked it over, an inch at a time, until it was in position.

"So far, so good," she whispered, standing up and locating her cane.

The unnatural light illuminated the immediate interior of the structure, leaving most of the building in shadow. There must be a lantern, somewhere . . .

For a long time, the prevailing elements of the storm waged a dry battle, but every humid gust of wind, every deep rumble of thunder, every blinding flash of lightning teemed with the promise of rain. Michael smelled it coming.

So did Rusty.

The big red horse whinnied nervously and gamboled sideways.

"Easy, boy," Michael soothed, patting the side of Rusty's neck and coaxing the mount onward. With each burst of lightning, his gaze scanned the horizon, searching for shelter though not expecting to find it. Yet, he reasoned, some new homesteader had, perhaps, taken out a grant in that area. He couldn't be sure because he didn't know where he was anymore. Between his occasional inability to control Rusty and the storm's obliteration of the stars, Michael had become hopelessly lost.

When the elements chose to fulfill their promise, all hell broke loose. Torrents of blinding rain pummelled the earth, quickly turning the prairie into a bog, slashing into man and beast with cutting vengeance.

Rusty bucked and reared. Michael held on for dear life. The big horse leapt forward, hurtling his forelegs into unknown territory, kicking up clods of earth and prairie grass as he sped along. Michael let the horse have his head, praying the creature saw something, sensed something he himself didn't see — couldn't see through the wall of water.

They were almost upon the line shack before Michael saw it. He hauled back on the reins, stopping Rusty on a dime with change to spare.

"Good boy, Rusty!" he praised, bouncing out of the saddle and leading the horse around to the door and into the dark interior of the shack.

She had to be near the line shack, Wynn thought, her gaze searching the landscape for some sign of the building. Carmen plodded faithfully forward, her snorts and whinnies begging Wynn to remove her from this madness.

And it *was* madness. But she couldn't turn back. Not now. MacDougall had, more than likely, discovered her absence by now. Wynn imagined the fit he was throwing and hoped neither Jamie nor George suffered the brunt of his wrath. At least the rain would extinguish the fire and, perhaps, soften MacDougall's callous heart a bit.

A burst of lightning blanched the darkness with

pale white light, exposing the sun-bleached planks of the line shack off to Wynn's right. An exultant yell escaped her throat and she turned Carmen toward the promise of shelter. Tears of joy streamed down her face, mixing with the cold rain.

"Come on, Carmen, we're almost there!" she called, but the wind seized her voice and tossed it hither and yon. Nevertheless, the mare responded as though she'd heard, bolting toward the shack with such force Wynn was jerked forward. In reaction, Wynn planted her weight on both feet. The abrupt pressure on her left leg threw her off balance. At the same instant, one of the cart's wheels rolled into a chuckhole. The cart dipped and swayed precariously. Wynn pulled on the reins, biting her lip until it bled, her tears no longer those of overwhelming joy, but of painful fear.

She felt herself falling, felt as though she watched her body sail off into nothingness, twist and then plunge, almost weightless, to the sodden ground. Her right side hit the earth hard; her hands still gripped the reins. The cart fell with her, landing on her left ankle, pinning it beneath its weight. She cried out as pain shot through her ankle and into her foot and calf.

The reins slipped from her hands as she opened her fists and clutched at clumps of grass, attempting to use their anchor to pull herself forward. When the grasses simply lost their mooring, Wynn gathered thicker sheaths in her hands, pulled again, and succeeded in uprooting more grass.

A splinter from the side of the cart caught on her skirt, tearing through the fabric and into the flesh of her calf, burning a searing path as the cart skidded across her lower leg. Wynn gasped, both from pain and bewilderment. Instead of hauling herself

355

out, the cart was being pulled off. Carmen! In her agony, she'd forgotten the mare. The cart bounced against her leg and tore at her ankle. And then she was free.

Folding her arms into a pillow to hold her head out of the muck, Wynn collapsed in relief. For a moment, she lay still, assembling her strength, attempting to ignore the scalding pain where the splinter had ripped into her calf. She pushed herself up on open palms and called to the horse, knowing in the depths of her soul that Carmen hadn't stopped running. Wynn tried to stand up and discovered she couldn't put any weight on her left foot.

Although she wanted nothing more than to collapse again, she knew she'd have to make it to the line shack somehow, even if she had to crawl. She had to get out of the rain, off the boggy prairie before the torrent turned it into a lake.

Michael lay on the narrow bunk, wrapped in a gritty blanket that chafed his naked flesh, but he was grateful for its warmth. He'd used the dry matches in the saddlebags to light the coal oil lantern he'd found hanging just inside the door, used the light to locate a brazier, then discovered the cabin boasted neither chimney nor flue.

Without heat, his clothes would never be dry by morning. And come morning, he was leaving the shack and heading for MacDougall's again, wet clothes and all. He was on the ranch already—had to be, he reasoned, judging from the age of the line shack.

Something was different. Michael listened carefully and didn't hear anything at all—no rain, no wind, nothing. An eerie calm had settled on the prairie.

Rusty whickered and pawed the dirt floor.

"It's all right, boy. We're safe enough here, I suppose. We got out of that howling wind throwing buckets of rain on us, and now it's all over. I think I'll open the door and build a fire in that brazier." But he didn't move off the bed.

The horse snorted.

"Don't go cynical on me, Rusty." Michael laughed at himself. "Listen to me—talking to a horse as though he were human!"

Rusty pawed the dirt floor again and neighed loudly.

"What is it, boy?" Michael asked, his words lost in a sudden roar of wind. For an instant, he was eight years old again, trapped in a cabin no bigger than the line shack, huddled up in a quilt on the floor, listening to the sad, lonely call of the wailing wind, praying for death.

The roar gained quickly in volume, sounding like a freight train barreling down the tracks at full speed.

"Oh, my God!" Michael moaned. "This time, I *am* going to die. Son-of-a-bitch!"

He threw off the blanket and slid out of the bed. His bare feet had barely touched the hard-packed earth before the line shack collapsed on top of him.

As she struggled to make her way inch by inch toward shelter, Wynn told herself over and over, *If I can just make it to the shack, I'll be safe.* She stood up again, thinking to accelerate her progress if she limped, but the slimy, slippery muck prevented proper traction. Fearing she would fall headlong again and perhaps twist her good ankle, she pulled her skirt and petticoat up out of the way and dropped back down on her knees.

The rain was petering out, the wind dying down. Wynn breathed a bit easier. The storm was over.

Then suddenly the wind picked up speed and squalled so loudly she thought her eardrums would surely burst.

Wynn fell to her stomach and pressed her body as hard as she could against the sodden ground and held onto the prairie grasses for dear life. The wind yanked at her hair until the last few strands came loose from the bun, then used its mighty force to beat her cheeks and neck with the wet tresses. The grasses, too, became her enemy, whipping her hands with their sharp edges, drawing blood.

If I can only hold on for a few more minutes, this will blow over, she thought, clinging to hope as tightly as she clung to the stems of the prairie grasses.

The roar grew louder, the sound and motion one and the same, sweeping over her and around her, flinging her hair straight up and dragging at it so hard she feared it would come out by the roots. The wind alternately beat at her and pulled at her, flogging, trouncing, tugging, and hauling at her hair, her clothes, her body until she screamed in terror. The tempest laughed at her, throwing her scream back into her pounding ears. A veil of water hit her hard in the face, slapping and burning her skin. She gasped and choked on a mouthful of water, felt it burn a dual path upwards into her nostrils and downwards into her lungs and thought she would surely drown.

Suddenly, it was quiet again, the gale over as abruptly as it had started.

Wynn coughed, gagged, and coughed again, trying to clear her lungs. Her eyes stung, her throat felt scalded, her arms ached, but she struggled forward once more. The mire sucked at her, slowing her progress, but the shrill whinny of a horse somewhere ahead lured her onward, gave her strength to continue.

Finally, she reached the clearing. Wynn lifted her head, sitting back on her haunches to rest for a moment, to soak up the beauty of a rundown line shack.

What she saw astounded her. A strange light burned from within one side of the shack, illuminating the scene; the wind had reduced the other side to a pile of rubble; and between her and the shack stood Rusty. It took her a moment to assimilate the fact that Rusty—not Carmen—stood before her.

"What are you doing here?" she asked, her heart soaring suddenly with the presumption that either Michael or Doc must be near. She called out to both of them, their names tearing raspily from her throat. When no one answered, she pulled herself forward again, her fingers digging into the damp earth, dragging her left leg, her right foot and knee pushing her ahead. After advancing another few feet, she called to them again.

Rusty snorted and nudged her arm with his nose. "Move out of the way, you big lummox!" she said, her voice lilting, teasing. He nudged her again, trailing his reins across her arm.

"Michael!" she cried, certain it was he who'd ridden Rusty. Doc would have removed the saddle and bridle. The horse whinnied and shook his head, tickling her hand with the reins then jerking them upward with a twist of his neck.

Was it possible? Was Rusty actually attempting to communicate with her? She supposed she'd soon find out. She reached up and grasped a stirrup. "All right, Rusty. I'm holding on now. Pull."

He did. He pulled her right up to the edge of the pile of mangled lumber. Suddenly, she understood everything. The strange light sifted through the fallen timbers, revealing Michael lying prone on the dirt floor beside the bed, a heavy timber resting on his head.

Where was the light coming from? She turned to look more closely at the opposite side of the shack, the side that remained intact. There, a fire burned slowly. The dampness of the timbers was the only deterrent to the flames; even now they were licking the wood dry.

"Michael! Michael, please! Wake up!" she cried, to no avail.

She had to get Michael out. How she was going to manage it with a broken ankle and her modest strength constituted the least of her worries. It was the prospect of entering the dark cavity and becoming trapped there herself that scared her witless. Her blood pounded in her head and she broke out in a cold sweat.

Michael was in a hole—a small, dark hole with the bed on one side, a broken straight chair on the other, and splintered boards balanced precariously over his head. The passage itself was barely large enough for her to squeeze through, and were she not very careful, she could bring the hanging timbers down on top of both of them. Then, if she managed to reach Michael, how was she going to get him out? A rope. She needed a rope.

"Be still, Rusty," she murmured, using the stirrup to pull herself up. His bulk blocked much of the light from the fire, but somewhere on his saddle should be a length of rope. "Lord," she breathed, "please let it be here."

With trembling hands, she searched blindly for the feel of rough hemp. Perhaps it was tied on Rusty's right side, she reasoned. "Don't move, Rusty," she ordered, hoping the horse had the good sense to obey. Slowly, painfully, she limped around him. The sight of the coiled rope hanging there fully compensated her pain.

Working as quickly as her trembling fingers would allow, she removed the rope and tied one end to the saddlehorn. The other end she tied around her waist.

Exercising extreme caution, she moved a piece of wood away from the opening and then another, enlarging the space enough to accommodate Michael's broad shoulders. For a moment, she stared into the dark space, seeing a puppy fall into a root cellar, seeing herself as a little girl going after him, seeing the close, dank darkness, feeling trapped. She closed her eyes and willed the memory away. Then she whispered a prayer, took a deep breath, and thrust her arms into the hole.

Little by little, she crawled forward on her belly, forcing herself to move ever deeper into the dark hole until she could grasp the timber propped against Michael's temple and move it out of the way. Wynn found one of his wrists, felt for a pulse, and wept with joy when it pumped weakly against the pads of her fingers. A low groan escaped his lips.

"Rusty's going to pull you out of here, love," she murmured assuringly. "Just lie still."

Wynn tied the rope around Michael's wrists, then circled them with her hands. "Pull, Rusty!" she called over her shoulder.

The horse obeyed without hesitation. She realized her mistake instantly. "Whoa!" she cried, her heart pounding in fear Rusty wouldn't stop before he'd pulled Michael on top of her—and disturbed the unstable broken lumber. With her ankle broken, she couldn't scramble backwards fast enough.

Again, though, Rusty obeyed her command.

She could hear the crackle of the fire, could smell it stronger now, could feel its heat. Wynn didn't want to leave Michael, but she could devise no other way to get him out. Backing out of the hole proved far more difficult than crawling in, but she managed it. When she was clear, she rolled to the side, away from the opening, away from the fire.

"All right, Rusty, pull!"

Golden yellow flames leaped high behind the horse, clearly illuminating his wild eyes and prancing forefeet. Rusty jiggled his head from side to side and whinnied nervously.

"Pull, Rusty!" she ordered, but the big horse jerked on the rope instead. Her heart sank. "No, Rusty. Still! Be still."

She knew she had to calm the horse before he shifted the teetering timbers. Her head raced with bits of memory, of Johnny telling her he'd calmed Rusty during the windstorm by singing to him. A folk song, he'd said. Which one? She closed her eyes, replayed the memory, heard herself laugh at the utter ridiculousness of Rusty's liking a song about a sow. She started to sing, heard her voice croak from the tightness in her throat, swallowed and started again.

" 'How do you think I started in life? I got me a sow and other such things. Pig or hog or any such thing. The sow got the measles and she died in the spring.' "

Slowly the horse backed up. With bated breath, she watched the rope slither through the opening inch by inch. Michael's hands appeared, then his forearms; finally his head. Her throat constricted as the seconds passed and she waited for his shoulders to come through. It was as though Michael Donovan were being reborn and Rusty was delivering him. She prayed she'd made the opening large enough.

Wynn gasped in horror as his right shoulder caught on one of the boards. The wood cracked loudly and the whole pile shuddered violently. "Pull, Rusty!" she hollered. "Pull hard!"

Michael's naked torso slipped by, then his hips and thighs. Wynn grabbed his ankles, cried out from the pain that shot through her twisted frame until Rusty's tow straightened her out. Farther and farther the horse pulled them, one behind the other, away from the burning line shack, away from certain death, and into the uncertain promise of their future.

Chapter Twenty-one

"Please tell me you're not going into town dressed like that!" Wynn teased from her perch on Rusty's back.

Michael's green eyes flickered over her. "You ought to see yourself, young lady. You have no room to talk. And, yes, I am—we are going into town like this. When you're as lucky to be alive as I am, what you're wearing makes little difference, but if it'll make you happy, I'll go in the buff. That would give Delaney something to talk about!"

Though Michael's tone brooked no argument, Wynn started one anyway. "But MacDougall's ranch is only an hour's ride or so to the west. We can bathe and borrow fresh clothes there."

"Oh, no! If I saw MacDougall right now, I'd break his neck. My plans for the future do not include going to jail." He pulled himself into the saddle behind her and reached for the reins. "You ought to file charges against him."

"For Jamie's sake, I'd rather just let it lie. We discussed this last night, Michael. Don't you remember?"

"My memory's a bit fuzzy. Did we resolve anything?"

Wynn laughed. "I think we resolved everything and you know it. Your memory's no fuzzier than mine."

"There's at least one thing we haven't resolved, but I intend to see to that item as soon as we get home."

She purposely misinterpreted his remark. "Surely we could find some homesteaders between here and town who would feed us. Aren't you hungry?"

Michael groaned in her ear. "Damned straight, I'm hungry, but not for food." He removed an apple from the saddlebags and handed it to her. "Here. This ought to hold you for awhile."

"But, Michael," she pleaded through a mouthful of juicy apple, trying another tack, "I don't want people to see me like this."

"Well, I do! You're a warrior, Wynn, a fine warrior. You fought the elements and won. Warriors return home wearing their battle scars, not hiding them. This is called making a memory. You'd better get used to it. I intend to make many a memory with you. And just to be on the safe side, I'm not taking any chances this time, Wynnifred Spencer."

"What does that mean?"

"It means I'm not letting you out of my sight." He urged Rusty into a gallop. "If we don't hurry, we'll miss the Wednesday train."

"Heaven forbid, Michael! I'm not getting on that train without a bath!"

"Not us, love." He chuckled and rubbed his chin against the top of her muddy head.

When he refused to explain, she hushed, snuggling back into his embrace, allowing the warmth of his love to envelop her. He was the one, after all, who would reap the most embarrassment. If this was the way he wanted it, so be it.

* * *

For years to come, people would reminisce about the October tornado of 1884, recounting their individual tales, recalling where they were and how scared they'd been the night the heavy rains and fierce winds blew through Jennings. But at the end of every story, those who'd witnessed it—and some who hadn't—tacked on their account of the pair who rode right through the middle of town late in the afternoon of the following day. No one who saw it ever forgot the sight of the two of them, riding double on the big red horse.

Wynn rode astride in front of Michael, her countenance so gilded with dark gray mud she was almost unrecognizable. Indeed, had the gaping townsfolk not known Michael had gone in search of her, they would probably not have been able to identify the bedraggled woman as the doctor they'd come to know and respect.

She sat with her skirt above her knees, her feet and legs bare of either stockings or shoes, though her left calf and ankle had been wrapped with strips of filthy, once-white cotton. A splint, fashioned from weathered, cracked boards and tied with more strips of the filthy cotton, covered the bandage. Her hair hung over her shoulders and down her back in thick, mud-coated strands, and virtually every exposed inch of her skin bore streaks of mud.

But never had she looked so beautiful. Her blue eyes glowed in her beaming face, and though she leaned back against Michael's chest with her torso nestled in the security of his thick-muscled arms, an inner strength radiated from her entire being.

As the two drew nearer, the sight became even more memorable. Only the spectators' deference to

Michael Donovan prevented ribald laughter, al though many concealed smiles and snickers behind open palms. The crowd tittered perilously close to losing their composure when a teen-aged boy hol lered, "Ride on, Godiva!"

The boy's reference came nigh to hitting the mark. While Michael certainly wasn't a woman, nor was he exactly naked, neither was he wearing appro priate garb for a man, much less a man of his age and social standing. Upon his shoulders rode what could only be a woman's petticoat, its waist string pulled up and tied around his collarbone, its length—what there was left of it—hanging off his shoulders and around his trunk like a cape. Two slits had been cut into the skirt to accommodate his arms. As the horse bounced along, the ragged edge of the petticoat floated up to reveal rows of delicate lace encircling his legs at mid-thigh.

"My stars!" Granny whispered to Doc. "He's wearing bloomers!"

Doc giggled. "Damn if he ain't! Reckon they're Wynn's?"

"Who else would they belong to? He'd best be careful about getting off that horse with 'em on."

As Doc considered Granny's remark, his bushy gray eyebrows flew to mid-forehead. "You think they're split?"

"Of course," Granny replied smugly. "All wom en's drawers are split."

"Where you reckon they're headed? They've done passed by Wynn's house. Wonder why they didn't stop there and save themselves this embarrassment?"

"Who's embarrassed?"

Doc conceded Granny that point. Still and all, he couldn't help wondering why Michael chose to pa rade himself through town wearing Wynn's under-

367

garments. He didn't have to wait long to find out.

Michael stopped Rusty in front of the depot and surveyed the crowd gathered around the horse. His gaze settled on Slim.

"Has the train come in yet?" Michael asked.

"Nope. Due in any minute, though."

"Somebody find Johnny and put him on that train."

"Here I am, Mr. Donovan." An arm bearing a dark blue garter on a pin-striped sleeve indicated the clerk's position in the dense group. "What do you want me to do, sir?"

"Get off in Opelousas and find a preacher who wants to earn himself a month's pay for a half-hour's work. And then get back here with him as fast as you can. Dr. Spencer and I intend to be married before the week is out."

A cheer went up from the crowd, a loud hurrah that followed Wynn and Michael most of the way home.

Home.

Wynn leaned against Michael in the front hall and stared, her mouth agape, at the home he had created for them.

"Do you like it?" he asked sheepishly.

"Like it? Oh, Michael, this is beautiful! When did you buy the furniture?"

"A couple of weeks ago when I went to New Orleans. I saved several rooms for you to decorate, and if there's anything you don't like, just say so. We'll pitch it all out and start over if you want to."

"Oh, no. I mean, I don't think so. Will you show me the rest of it?"

He bent down and scooped her into his arms,

grinning down at her. "Later."

She grinned back, her smile cracking the coating of dried mud on her cheeks. "Where are you taking me?"

"To the mudroom."

Wynn giggled. "You aren't serious."

"I've never been more serious in my life."

But he didn't sound serious. He sounded deliriously happy.

Wynn twisted her head around, trying to absorb everything at once. "Tiled fireplaces, oak floors and woodwork, stained glass, plants . . . Michael, where did you find all these plants?"

"In New Orleans, when I bought the furniture."

He walked through the kitchen, pushed open a door with his shoulder, and set Wynn down in a chair in a long, narrow room equipped with a counter, pump, and sink.

"This, my dear, is the mudroom," he murmured, his fingers moving to the fastenings on her dress, "where we remove our muddy clothes and shoes when we come in from working in the garden." His inclined head indicated another door opposite the counter, which Wynn assumed opened to the outside.

"Aren't you putting the cart before the horse?" Wynn asked, thinking that as much as she'd like to get out of the clothes she was wearing, they needed to prepare a bathtub first. The cliche, however, reminded her of her own cart and horse. "Oh, Michael!" she gasped. "What are we going to do about Carmen?"

His fingers paused in their labors. "Hope she comes home. But if it will make you feel better, I'll send someone out tomorrow to look for her."

"Thank you, Michael."

"And yes, you're right. I got a little ahead of myself. Come, sit in the kitchen while I fire up the stove and heat some water for our bath."

All the while he worked, Wynn sat in one oak pressed-back chair, her left foot propped on a pillow in another one, and marveled aloud at the efficiency of the large kitchen.

"Everything is so clean and neat, Michael, I'm—"

"Amazed?" He chuckled.

"No," she corrected him, feeling her cheeks stain pink beneath the mud at his implication, "though I can well understand why you'd think that. Michael, I'm sorry about calling you names and saying you lived in a pigsty."

He shrugged away her distress and saw that she was staring at the ugly splint. "You won't have to concern yourself with keeping house, Wynn. You're a doctor, and I expect you to continue with your practice—when you're not having our babies."

"But, Michael," she protested, "you don't have time to clean house."

"That's why I've hired a maid—and a cook and a gardener. And later"—he added, making goggle eyes at her—"I'll hire a nurse."

Wynn worried her lower lip. There was one problem they hadn't yet discussed. "What will become of Prairie?"

"She'll stay with Granny for the next couple of weeks, and when we come back from our wedding trip, we'll start adoption proceedings."

"Are you sure, Michael?"

"Of course, I'm sure. She's a delightful child."

"But she isn't yours."

"If you're referring to flesh and blood, Wynn, she isn't yours, either."

"Will it be difficult for you, Michael, raising an

370

orphan?"

A loud sigh escaped his lips and he ran his fingers through his hair. "Growing up in an orphanage was difficult. Letting myself love you was difficult. And I expect learning to be a father to both Prairie and our own children will present its difficult side from time to time. Life is a series of trials, Wynn, but I'll never allow what happened in the past to control my emotions again."

He removed a large, heavy kettle from the top of the cast iron stove and headed for a door set in the wall opposite the central hall. "I'll be right back."

Wynn watched him walk back and forth several more times, hauling another kettle of hot water, then several of cold before he seemed satisfied. When he had refilled one of the kettles and set it back on the stove to heat, he disappeared into the mudroom. She heard him work the pump, heard the water splash into the sink.

"What are you doing, Michael?" she called.

"You'll see!"

A moment later, he returned to the kitchen, carried her into the mudroom, and laid her down on the copper-clad counter with her head over the sink.

"Michael! This is c-c-co-old!" she gasped out as he hand-dipped water over her head.

He grinned down at her, wicked dimples appearing in his cheeks. "Would you rather wash all this dirt into our bath water? This won't take long."

She shivered, as much from the delightful prospect of his veiled promises as from the shock of the cool water and cold counter.

"Now, my darling, we can take your filthy clothes off both of us and have our bath."

Wynn plucked at the remnant of her petticoat hanging over his shoulders. Her laughter was warm, full-bodied.

"Don't say a word," he warned, his voice a low growl.

"I wasn't going to."

He went down on one knee and began to remove the rags tied around the makeshift splint. "What do we need to do for this?"

"Tonight? Hot fomentations and rest. Tomorrow, I'll get Doc to put a fracture box on it."

He frowned. "Will it interfere with—"

"No," she quickly interrupted.

"How long will it take it to heal?"

"A month or so, though it may be several months before I can walk properly again. Can you live with a crippled wife until then?"

He looked up at her, tears glistening in his green eyes. "I can live with a crippled wife forever, so long as it's you. Now, close your eyes and keep them closed until I tell you to open them."

She complied, her head spinning from myriad emotions, chief among them a deep, abiding love for this dear man who seemed bent on indulging her. Wynn felt his fingers slide inside the open bodice of her dress, heard the fabric give way as he ripped it through the waistline and down the front. Michael slipped the gown off her shoulders and over her arms. A moment passed before he took her in his arms and pressed her naked body against his.

"Where are you taking me?" she asked, the memory of the time he'd blindfolded her and sat her in the chaise replaying itself on the curtain of her eyelids.

"You'll see."

Their journey was short, a trip across the kitchen and into the room where Michael had carried the water.

"Now," he said, sounding inordinately pleased with himself.

Her breath came out in a whoosh of awe, the adoring look in her eyes and the smile on her lips speaking volumes. They stood in the middle of a hexagonal, brick-floored room filled with tall potted palms, huge baskets of ferns, and white wicker furniture piled with blue and green paisley print cushions. Soft light from a few strategically placed candles frolicked among the shadows and glistened in the steam emanating from a huge white ceramic tub, which was banked with palms and rubber trees.

He lowered her into the frothy bubbles and she leaned back against the sloping end of the tub, reveling in the scent of lilacs rising with the steam, in the silkiness of the warm water eddying around her, in the display of Michael's masculine torso beside the tub.

Her heavy-lidded gaze followed the course of dark, crisp curls from their origin just below his Adam's apple, to their spread across his broad chest, downward to the point they made just above his navel and to its twin peak just below, then downward again to the thick nest that surrounded his throbbing erection. Her pulse raced at the magnificence of him, at the knowledge that he could respond so completely to her when mud obscured any beauty she might possess. She felt herself go warm and liquid deep inside.

His own heavy-lidded gaze followed the track of her scrutiny, and he felt himself grow recklessly hot and light-headed. *Slow it down, Donovan,* he mentally cautioned. He took a deep breath, stepped over the side of the tub, and sat down gingerly, facing her.

"I've heard mud masks are supposed to be beneficial to the complexion," he teased, his eyes twinkling, "but I think you've worn yours long enough." He removed a washcloth from the stack of folded linens on a low wicker table nearby and doused it in the water. He washed her face, her neck, her arms and legs, his tender ministrations at once soothing and sensual; then he bathed the grime off his own body.

"Now it's time to wash your hair," he whispered, his voice husky and seductive.

He moved around behind her, lathered her head and drove his long fingers into her scalp. Wynn sighed in unabashed contentment, closed her eyes, then sighed again.

Wisps of sparkling, lilac-scented steam floated around them, caressing the pink blush of her cheeks, hovering on the fan of her dark lashes, providing an excuse for the sudden mistiness in Michael's green eyes.

"When you were sick, I promised myself that one day I'd bathe you as your lover," he murmured, his mouth close to her ear.

"Uhm-hum."

"I always make good my promises."

He slid his soapy hands down her neck, over her shoulders, and downward again, cupping and massaging her breasts. His lips nuzzled the curve of her shoulder and she mewed softly.

"God, Wynn! I can't believe I almost lost you," he groaned.

"Last night, I thought I'd lost you, Michael. I don't think I've ever been so terrified of anything."

"Not even close places?"

"Not even close places. I had to conquer that fear in order to get you out."

"We have each other now, Wynn. Together, we

His right hand moved lower, over her abdomen and down to the soft mound of her womanhood, his fingers dipping, caressing, probing. She shivered against him, let her head fall back into the pillow of his shoulder, succumbed to the wicked sensations his fondling initiated.

"Tell me you want me," she whispered, raising her hips, moving against the play of his fingers.

"No," he teased. His left hand squeezed her breast, the pad of his thumb massaging its nipple until it throbbed. His tongue trailed a hot path across her shoulder, up the side of her neck, and around the shell of her ear.

"Tell me you want me," she persisted.

"No," he mocked, even as he wreaked more delectable torment upon her. He lifted her buttocks and sat her on the hard length of his shaft. She felt its tip, velvety soft, against the lips of her womanhood. His fingers parted her and stroked her until she thought she would scream with impatience.

"Tell me you want me," she insisted.

"Yes! Oh, yes, Wynn. I want you."

He drove into her then, his finger continuing to work its own magic, his tongue dipping in and out of the cavity of her ear. She rode him hard and fast, her need as great as his. Water, warm and silky, whirled across her breasts, trickling in delicious runnels over her nipples and down her rib cage as he rose against her, pushing her up with him. Down they plunged into the scented, frothy bliss, back up then down again. Water splashed out of the tub, puddling on the brick floor, mirroring the shudders that racked their frames as they reached their individual heights of ecstasy.

Michael's arms encircled her waistline in the

aftermath, his long breaths flowing like warm breezes across her shoulder, his sprinting heartbeats pounding slower and slower against her back.

After awhile, he collected the kettle of water from the kitchen and rinsed her hair. When he had toweled both it and her body dry, he laid her on a wicker chaise and proceeded to comb out the tangles.

"You're going to spoil me rotten," Wynn teasingly accused.

"Ah, but this is just the beginning," he promised, leaning forward and planting a playful kiss on her mouth. "It's my way of getting back at you for calling me a yokel. Indulge me."

And she did.

Epilogue

Galena, Illinois
June 11, 1892

The long, gray shadow of a spire fell across three white marble tombstones in the churchyard, their polished surfaces shiny new despite the dates carved into them.

A man moved among the graves, bending and placing a single red rose on each of the three before straightening his tall frame and standing back to gaze for a moment upon the inscriptions: *Donovan, Baby Girl, February 4, 1860; Madeline Patrick Donovan, April 15, 1834—February 4, 1860; Jason Michael Donovan, August 31, 1829—June 30, 1859.*

He left the shadow of the spire and walked slowly toward a petite woman standing under the spreading arms of a black oak tree some distance away. The late afternoon sun glinted off white hair salted among the darker strands, lending him a distinguished-gentleman quality he hadn't possessed as a younger man. He drew up beside the woman and wrapped an arm around her shoulders.

"I never thought I'd want to come back here," she said, her husky voice low, her pale blue eyes awash with unshed tears.

"Me either."

She pulled her gaze from the pair of tombstones before her and looked up at the bluffs rising steeply behind the churchyard. "Galena is as beautiful as I remembered."

"Are you sorry you ever left?"

She turned her face into the crook of his open arm and smiled up at him. "No, Michael. Our Jennings has grown into a lovely town, but it wouldn't matter if it were still a wild prairie. I left here running away, planning to live out my father's dream, thinking I was in complete control of my life when all the time fate directed my every step."

Gently, he turned her toward the gate, directing his own steps and, therefore, hers as they walked out of the churchyard and onto the sidewalk. "It was fate—all the time," he agreed, "all my life, I suppose. The night you were born, the night our destinies entwined, I wanted to die because I'd let my mother and sister die. I would have frozen to death had your father not shoveled his way out to that cabin the next day. By that time, I'd allowed hatred to consume me. It would guide me yet, were it not for you."

He'd told her this story before, the night she'd pulled him from the burning line shack. It seemed appropriate that he repeat it as they walked the streets of the town they had shared as children.

They entered a small cafe and ordered a light supper. Midway through the meal, a blond-haired man in a three-piece suit strolled by their table, gave them a cursory glance, and sat down in a booth across the room. During dessert, Michael inclined his head ever so slightly toward the booth and asked, "Do you know that man?"

Wynn used the pretense of adjusting her napkin

to cut her eyes briefly at the man. Her heart skipped a beat. "Yes. Why?"

"He's done nothing but stare at us since he sat down. Who is he?"

"Do I detect a note of jealousy in your voice, Michael Donovan?" She smiled conspiratorially, pressed her napkin against her lips and pushed back her chair. "Come and meet him."

She took her husband's hand and half-pulled him across the room. The blond man stood up as they approached, then lowered his eyes and fingered his gold watch fob.

"Hello, Jonathan," she said, her voice masterfully smooth, devoid of emotion.

"I thought that was you, Wynn. You've . . . changed, but the years have been good to you."

They had not been good to him, she thought, noting the deep furrows in his forehead, the tracing of lines around his eyes and mouth, the receding hairline and red-veined nose. She couldn't believe a part of her actually felt sympathetic toward the cad.

Wynn made the introductions as brief as possible, then offered a lame excuse to get away. Once they were outside again, Michael chuckled and said, "You looked for a minute like you'd seen a ghost."

"I suppose I did, in a manner of speaking."

"That wasn't *the* Jonathan, was it?"

"Yes."

He laughed again, hugging her against him. "All these years I've been jealous of *him?*"

She laughed with him, feeling deliriously happy.

They walked hand-in-hand along the riverbank, pausing to watch the colors of sunset frolic upon the water, and then strolling away from the river, climbing steps connecting terrace-like streets and thus into a section of small, gingerbread-trimmed cottages, most of them deserted.

"The shallow lode had to play out eventually," Wynn observed. Michael stopped often to inspect first one and then another lead-miner's cottage in the fading light. Finally, he moved confidently to the sagging porch of one with peeling blue paint and sat down on the top step.

Wynn joined him there, took his hand into her lap, and held it between both of hers.

"I miss the children," Michael said after awhile. "I wish we had brought them."

"They're fine, Michael. Doc and Ruth will take good care of them."

He snorted. "Who would have thought the old man would ever remarry—and a school teacher, to boot!"

Wynn laughed. "Who would have thought the boy would marry a doctor and sire three sons?"

"They're fine boys, Wynn. And Prairie's turning into a lovely young lady. Have I told you recently how happy you've made me?"

"Not recently enough," she teased. "I don't think you've mentioned it since this morning."

"Look. The stars are coming out." He squeezed her hand. "I used to sit on my porch at the old house sometimes and gaze at the stars for hours. That's what I was doing the night you came to Jennings."

"Before you started playing cards with Doc?"

"In between games, actually. I remember that night like it was yesterday. It was the last time I saw a shooting star."

Wynn's heart fluttered wildly for a moment. "You saw it, too?" she breathed, a tear escaping and rolling down her cheek as he reiterated her thoughts from that night so long ago.

"I was like that shooting star, Wynn. Looking for something to hold on to, only I didn't know it at the time." He pulled his hand from her lap and held her face between his palms. "And then I found you, and I don't ever intend to let go. I love you, Wynnifred."

"And I love you, Michael."

His lips brushed hers lightly, plucking, teasing, tasting, savoring every nuance of feeling before he traced his tongue along her lips, requesting entrance. She moaned softly, opening her mouth, offering him its sweetness, taking her own pleasure from his kiss.

At long last, he groaned and pulled his mouth from hers. "Are you ready to go back to the hotel?" he whispered.

"Yes," she answered without hesitation, but he made no move for a moment, turning instead to gaze once more at the heavens. Wynn snuggled against his side and set her own gaze on the myriad twinkling stars, the narrow white slice of a waning moon.

Across the blackness streaked a blaze of golden fire, brilliant and shining and beautiful one instant, gone the next.

"I wonder who that one was for," Michael murmured, standing up and pulling Wynn with him.

"Well, for us, of course! As a commemoration of the beginning of our relationship."

"That sounds awfully close to a toast," he teased. "I say we hurry back to the hotel and order up a magnum of champagne. What say you?"

She tore loose from his grasp and dashed ahead, her limp barely noticeable. "I say what's keeping you?"

Author's Note

To the residents of Jennings, Louisiana, I apologize for tampering with your history. Although a general diphtheria epidemic swept this country in the 1880s, I have no record of its occurrence in Jennings. Nor do I have knowledge of either the February windstorm or the October tornado of 1884. I apologize, too, for ignoring many of the earliest residents of the area, among them several doctors, a number of black people, and the French farmers who taught the Midwesterners how to plant and cultivate rice.

Otherwise, I have attempted to follow your history as closely and accurately as this fictional tale allowed. The only historical figure in this story is S. L. Cary, who has been called "The Father of Jennings."

The next Elizabeth Leigh release from Zebra will continue the Jennings story with the tale of a wildcat and a wildcatter during the 1901 oil boom.